"A novel that com[   ]
carried out by the v[   ]
This historical fictio[   ]
training and experience as a Historian."

—Ph.D. Alma Montero
Doctor in Latin American Studies, Member of Conacyt (Mexico National System of Researchers), Historical Research Coordinator, National Museum of Viceroyalty, and author.

"The sensitivity of the author takes us with the magic of her words to reflect on our History; to think about our actions, confronted with the ways we address and treat those who are the least favored by life. The charm of her voice as an author transports us to look at what happened in our beloved Mexico. Seeing through her eyes, we get to feel their souls. That is the spell that this book casts"

—Dr. Yolanda Montoya
Registered Clinical Counselor and member of the BC Association of Clinical Counselors

"A story that includes the emotional growth of the author through her own experience. An account of ordinary people who prove how acceptance leads to liberation and how grace can not touch an individual until his mind has been prepared for it".

—Gerardo Flores Gil
Therapist

"The history of slavery in the United States is well-documented, with *Roots* at the front of the tide of cultural consciousness. Rosa Elena Rojas has written an affecting history of slavery in Mexico, detailing how much of that country's history is attributed to people stolen from their homelands and forced to relocate across an ocean. I was drawn into the humanity of her characters and learned reams of information without even realizing it."

—Gailyc Sonia Braunstein
Writer & Editor

"FOR THE WATERS ARE COME"

PERSONAL BATTLES WEAVE THE FABRIC OF A KINGDOM

ROSA ELENA ROJAS

AUTHOR ACADEMY elite

This is a work of fiction. All of the characters, organizations, and events portrayed in this novel are either products of the author's imagination or are used fictitiously.

Copyright © 2018 Rosa Elena Rojas
All rights reserved.

Printed in the United States of America

Published by Author Academy Elite
P.O. Box 43, Powell, OH 43035

www.AuthorAcademyElite.com

All rights reserved. No part of this publication may be reproduced, stored in a retrieval system, or transmitted in any form or by any means—for example, electronic, photocopy, recording—without the prior written permission of the publisher. The only exception is brief quotations in printed reviews.

Scripture quotation, Psalm 69, 1, is taken from The Authorized (King James) Version. Rights in the Authorized Version in the United Kingdom are vested in the Crown. Reproduced by permission of the Crown's patentee, Cambridge University Press. "THE HOLY BIBLE, Conteyning the Old Teftament, AND THE NEW: Newly Tranflated out of the Originall tongues" frontispiece, 1611 edition of the King James Bible, is a media file in the public domain in the United States. This applies to U.S. works where the copyright has expired, because its first publication occurred prior to January 1, 1923.

Poem by Hughes, L. B. (1921). *The Negro speaks of Rivers*. Text is available under the Creative Commons Attribution-ShareAlike License and additional permission to use it has been requested to the Estate of Langston Hughes

Map is a composition made by the author using information from Candiani, Vera, *Dreaming of Dry Land: Environmental Transformation in Colonial Mexico City*, Stanford University Press, 2014 and Filsinger, Tomás / Aguirre Botello, Manuel http://www.mexicomaxico.org, July 2018. Written permission extended by these authors has been previously obtained.

Paperback ISBN-13: 978-1-64085-388-1
Hardcover ISBN-13: 978-1-64085-389-8
Ebook: 978-1-64085-390-4

Library of Congress Control Number (LCCN): 2018953353

Save me, O God;
for the waters are come in unto my soul.

Psalm 69

My people, just like you, are made of water,
of ancient rivers, of lakes and oceans.

I dedicate this book to them.

To them and to everyone who has been invited or forced
into a journey
and finds a way to reach a sheltered harbor.

And for the one who is undertaking a new voyage,
may there be many a summer morning
with what pleasure, what joy
you come into ports seen for the first time.

May you defeat each of the choleric monsters
that cross your path.

Arriving is your destination.

Rosa Elena

CONTENTS

Map 1. "The Places, the Journeys. 1629-1634"........... x
Map 2. "Desagüe de Huehuetoca" xii

Preface xiii

PARTE I. THE JOURNEYS

Chapter 1.   The Conspiracy. 1612.................. 3
Chapter 2.   The Journey from Ghana. 1629 15
Chapter 3.   The Journey to Santa María. 1629 41
Chapter 4.   The Journey from the
             Kingdom of Spain. 1629............... 71
Chapter 5.   The Journey through the
             Islands of Mexico. 1629 105
Chapter 6.   The Journey from Macau. 1629 131

PARTE II. THE JEOPARDY

Chapter 7.   For the Waters are Come. 1629 165

PARTE III. THE JOY

Chapter 8.	The Kwara, the Tagus, and Acalan. 1634	215
Chapter 9.	The Niger and the Guadalquivir. 1634	227
Chapter 10.	The Tagarete and the River of Shrimps. 1634	239
Chapter 11.	The Freshwater Lake. 1634	251
Chapter 12.	The Pacific Ocean. 1634	257

Epilogue 265
Endnotes 271
About The Author 275
Derivation of Title 279

I've known rivers:
I've known rivers ancient as the world and older than the
flow of human blood in human veins.

My soul has grown deep like the rivers.

I bathed in the Euphrates when dawns were young.
I built my hut near the Congo and it lulled me to sleep.
I looked upon the Nile and raised the pyramids above it.
I heard the singing of the Mississippi when Abe Lincoln
went down to New Orleans, and I've seen its muddy
bosom turn all golden in the sunset.

I've known rivers:
Ancient, dusky rivers.

My soul has grown deep like the rivers.

The Negro Speaks of Rivers
Langston Hughes, (1901–1967)

Written at age 19, on a train traveling from Ohio to Mexico, where Hughes's father, the son of a slave, resided. Hughes visited Toluca, México in 1907, 1919, 1920 y 1921

THE PLACES, THE

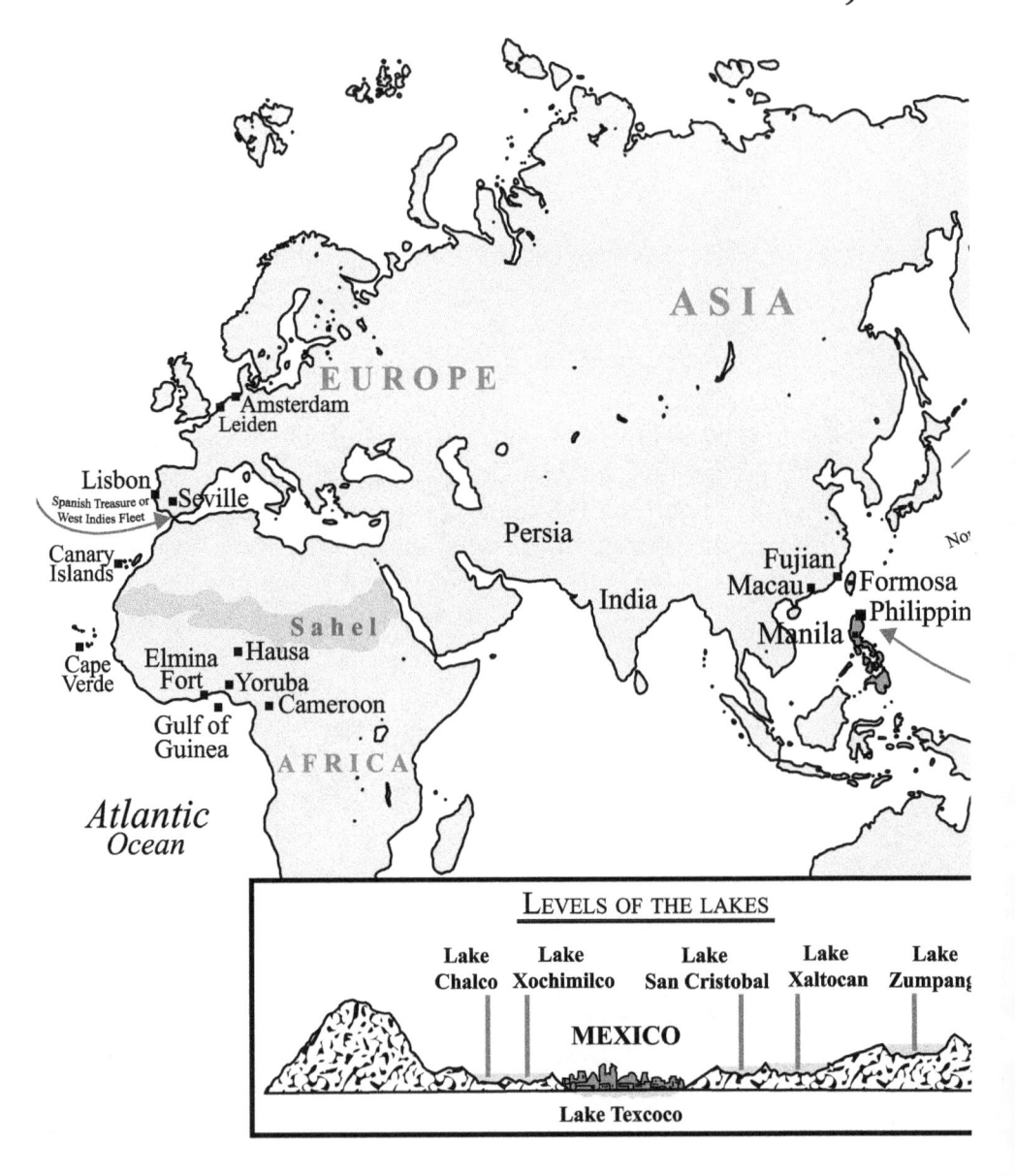

LEVELS OF THE LAKES

Lake Chalco   Lake Xochimilco   Lake San Cristobal   Lake Xaltocan   Lake Zumpang

MEXICO

Lake Texcoco

Map crafted by the author, based on information available to the public in open domain so More information, including an interactive map of Post-Conquest Mexico, available at A URL <http://mexicomaxico.org/introTenoch.htm>, [July 2018], Art: Paulina Rojas.

JOURNEYS 1629 - 1634

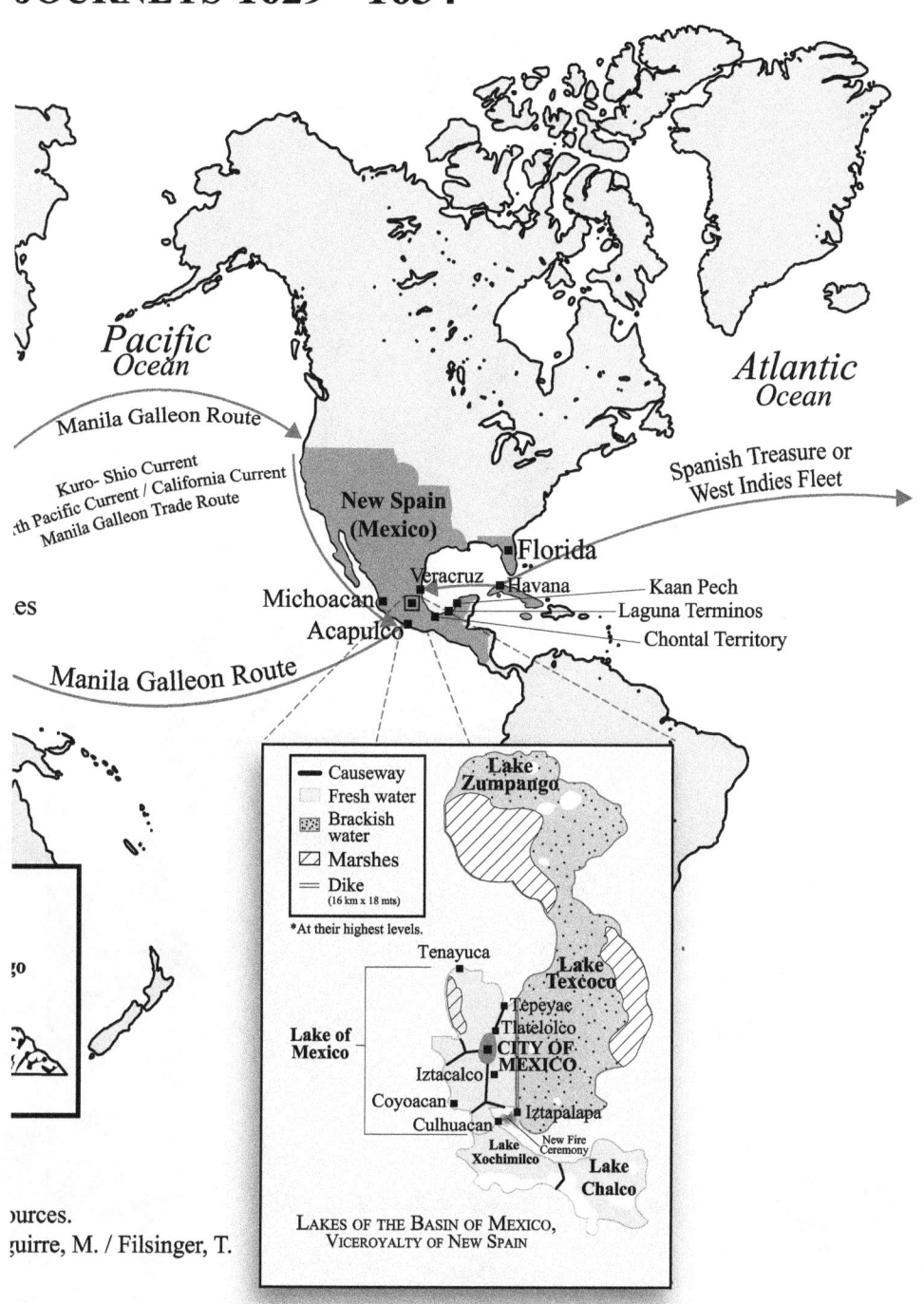

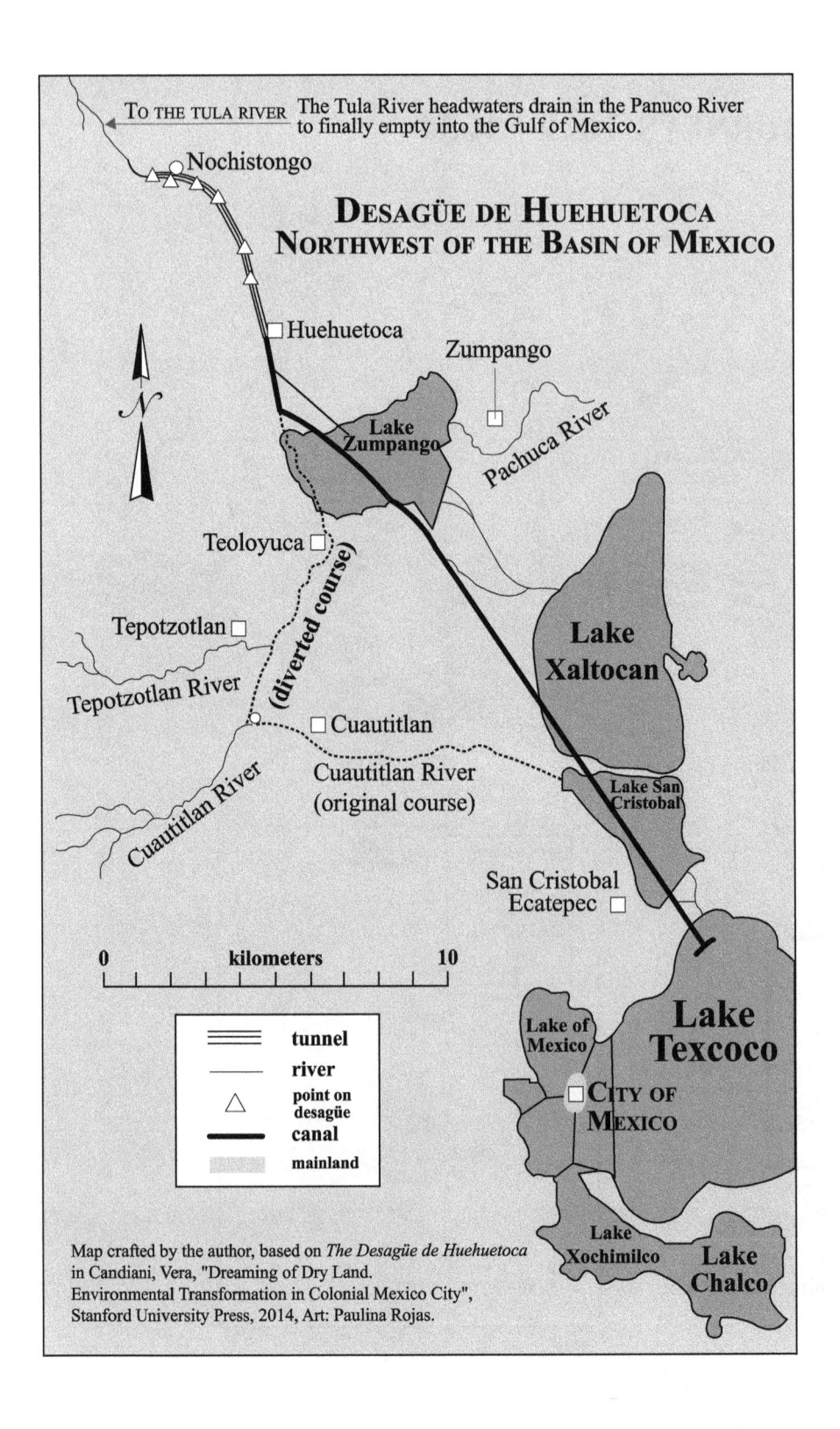

DESAGÜE DE HUEHUETOCA
NORTHWEST OF THE BASIN OF MEXICO

TO THE TULA RIVER — The Tula River headwaters drain in the Panuco River to finally empty into the Gulf of Mexico.

Nochistongo

Huehuetoca

Zumpango

Lake Zumpango

Pachuca River

Teoloyuca

Tepotzotlan

Tepotzotlan River

(diverted course)

Cuautitlan

Cuautitlan River (original course)

Cuautitlan River

Lake Xaltocan

Lake San Cristobal

San Cristobal Ecatepec

0 — kilometers — 10

Legend:
- tunnel
- river
- △ point on desagüe
- canal
- mainland

Lake of Mexico

Lake Texcoco

CITY OF MEXICO

Lake Xochimilco

Lake Chalco

Map crafted by the author, based on *The Desagüe de Huehuetoca* in Candiani, Vera, "Dreaming of Dry Land. Environmental Transformation in Colonial Mexico City", Stanford University Press, 2014, Art: Paulina Rojas.

PREFACE

This is a magical book. The yearning to write it was a beautiful eighteenth century painting by New Spain painter Manuel Arellano, "Diseño de Mulata", ordered by His Excellency Fernando de Alencastre, Duke of Linares, 35th Viceroy of Mexico.

Since my days as a senior university student, I knew I wanted to study blacks and their part in the building of Mexico and its culture. I explored a lot of fields, Franciscan archives, etc., until I landed in the national archives, the Archivo General de la Nación colonial repository, for information. There, I discovered the book of records for the Santa Cruz brotherhood, founded in 1638, a brotherhood authorized by the Dominican church of San Juan Bautista in Coyoacan, Mexico.

Brotherhoods (cofradías, in Spanish) are a type of church-based, civil authorized group, similar to guilds, providing confessional support and religious burials to those affiliated with them, in exchange for previously agreed alms. They provided series of supportive actions to members that were unique to each brotherhood, based on their location and the necessities of its members and the community. They had been previously studied, mainly for Spanish and Indigenous groups, but only until a 2006 study revealed that there were nearly sixty, exclusively for blacks throughout Mexico, it was generally believed that there was little representation of the black population forming these organizations. With still more to be discovered, brotherhoods of black people are only a sample of the long road to go regarding the study of black population in Mexico.

During the fifty-six years covered by the Santa Cruz book of records, this Coyoacan brotherhood had around two thousand members. Because the records relating to alms detailed the names and amounts paid, as well as the recipient of the monies, I was able to trace vast amounts of information.

So, it was that while observing Arellano's maiden for hours, a young girl portrayed in a beautiful brocade and lace dress, I realized that those devotees, black slaves, mulattoes, and mestizos who decided to establish a brotherhood in Coyoacan, Mexico one morning of March, 1638 were asking to give them a physical body, at least one in the shape of the characters of a book.

Their Book of Records was a memorable find in the repository. Only after several days I managed to pull it from the restoration vault where it had slept, misplaced by mistake for decades. I used this document to elaborate my Master's thesis in History of Mexico. It was by then that we had our first encounter. In my research, Arellano's mulatta appeared in one of my sources and since then, a reproduction of the painting now presides over the place where I write.

I finished my research in 2008, already living in Canada, and I returned to Mexico to defend it a year later. The Santa Cruz book of records arrived in a box, bare, to be studied in the Simon Fraser University Library, where I finished writing my dissertation, in the middle of one of the worst winters in the Province.

Dying of cold in a place that shone like a pearl in the snow, slaves and free were teaching me how much consolation devotion brought to them.

When I left Mexico, Doctor Alicia Bazarte, pioneer in the study of Brotherhoods in Mexico, had heard of my research and by her invitation I was able to present it at the International Congress of Americanists of 2009. She was preparing an investigation about a *Nazarene Jesus of the First Fall*, a masterpiece by mulatto sculptor and gilder Lorenzo de Palacios. De Palacios asked to be buried in the space of his brotherhood, in the Church of the Most Holy, a few blocks away from our National Palace, paying for his grave with his sculpture. Alicia took me to witness the restoration, being made on-site.

Tortured, bleeding, broken in pieces, laid on a surgery table, the Christ formed the closest metaphor to what slaves from Africa suffered in their own flesh.

A request made by Alicia in a soft whisper, full of respect the centuries old carving inspired, blessed my departure to Canada. That Nazarene comes to me often and the story of the mulatto, the sculptor, touched my heart, lost in the oblivion where it slept for decades and just as Alicia did, I decided to take the brotherhood out of the darkness and turn its members into characters.

I, like them, am an immigrant, with all that it entails. Remembering the process of adaptation, even today, ten years away, moves me to tears, an anguish that only those who have left know. When we chose Canada, we never contemplated how emotionally devastating the decision can be.

Besides the slaves in the brotherhood, how much had all those who left their homeland to pursue the illusion of the New World suffered, as well? Destiny -which is no other than what we forge ourselves- wanted me to work with immigrants in Canada, first in a volunteer service and now at Coquitlam, School District 43, British Columbia. I have felt for their battles with the language in a new country. I have felt their fear at leaving the place you are born. I have lived their joy on reaching a goal, getting a job, graduating, or receiving recognition, and that has all enriched my writing.

I do not feel fully authorized to talk about the facts that the color of black slaves, as an ethnic group, arised and made them went through, but I can say that the events I narrate, based on historical facts, transcend those borders. We mirror each other simply because uprooting, and the feelings around that fact, makes us human, without distinction.

All the beauty of the applied arts, silverware, painting, sculpture, figurines and porcelain that I included are the fruit of my work with the kind and wise Doctor Alma Montero, who heads the Research Department of the National Museum of the Viceroyalty. Her visit to this, my beloved adopted country, a few months ago, was a balm and our conversation on a highway facing the sea and the islands gave me the confidence I needed to continue.

There is a long list of works that I consulted with the same rigor that I used for my thesis work, sometimes transformed into a short paragraph or a line only. Without them, no scenario would exist.

I extensively read Vera Candiani, Salvador Guilliem, Eduardo Baez, Rebecca Horn, Martha Fernandez, Angel Muñoz Garcia, Lutgardo Garcia, Eulalia Ribera, Idalia Garcia, Josep Maria Estanyol, Maria Elena Ota Mishima, Edward Slack, Javier Villaflores, Richard Salvucci, Diana Magaloni, Edmundo O'Gorman, France Scholes, José Manuel Flores, Guillermina del Valle, Alberto Carrillo, Agustín Grajales, Mario Ruz, Marcela Montellano, Manuel de Toussaint, David Marley, Leonardo López Luján, Alfredo López Austin, Eduardo Matos, Pilar Gonzalbo and Rafael Castañeda, all researchers; all eminent in their fields of study.

Consequently, the facts I describe are part of the historical reality that they, and the authors on whom I supported my thesis, documented. The dramatization is all mine.

I went through the maps and recreations of Tomas Filsinger, Manuel Aguirre Botello, and Luis González Aparicio, and I re-visited the chroniclers of the religious orders, the work of Dr. Miguel León Portilla and countless Mexican and foreign historians. I toured the *Museum of Asian Civilizations*, in Singapore, and the collection of *The Getty*, to whom I owe as much as to the island of Java, the Convents of Culhuacán,

Coyoacán and del Carmen and the ports of Campeche, Veracruz and Acapulco.

I chose real people, from the farthest corners of the world, found in historical archives. They are the characters I honor, with the sole purpose of highlighting that our differences do not exist at all. Our phenotype has changed through thousands of years to adapt to the environment and these absurd classifications that we have invented are a construction that only divides and separates.

Under their skin that matters so much for some people, each of the characters is a remembrance of what we long for when we leave our country, and how human endurance let everyone, even those most unfortunate, to come forward once they find acceptance, make peace and start building over their new circumstances.

Our faith and willpower write the epic of our times and, as writers of the history of the Kingdom of Spain, we weave the continuous fabric that fills the pages of history. From the results, each of us takes charge.

I am grateful that my emotional support was lovingly provided by Yolanda Montoya and Gerardo Gil. Also, the support of *Cultura Santa Rosa* was decisive to complete the project; without its financing it would have been impossible.

This book would never have arisen without the conjectures I made with Dr. Bazarte regarding the brotherhood, one morning at Los Azulejos, where I wondered if the brothers from Coyoacán imitated or were, themselves, those who migrated to dry land in the aftermath of the great flood.

Sarita Murillo introduced me to Alicia one fine day, in a coincidence that feels like destiny. I faithfully follow Alicia's footsteps and her research on Chinese barbers in Mexico she has studied extensively, which even generated a character of his own.

My romance with History started at my University, Centro Universitario de Integracion Humanistica, that I carry deep within my soul. María del Pilar Galindo, founder and chancellor, has my admiration and respect for her work.

The celestial axis that gave order to this story comes from three stars that once were aligned with my life, Mary Moirón, Mary Piedras and Maribel Alemán. Their names start with an "m", as majesty there is in what they taught and shared with me.

The dear members of my Reading Club and my Advanced Spanish students group have been the support and encouragement I needed, and a powerful amulet of ivory tusk and an iridescent shells necklace.

Kary Oberbrunner deserves the finest gold and silk threads of this fabric. You blended the Historian in me, trying to bring stories out of an archive and the academic circles, with the immigrant I am, whose wound of leaving her country was healed by writing, just to find out, through your fine teachings, that serving those who are in the spot I used to be, might ignite their souls through my experience. I thank you, dearly, for that. *Author Academy Elite and The Tribe* sheltered and gave impulse to my project. Gailyc Sonia Braunstein, from *The Guild*, did a spectacular, invaluable job with the English version and they are all now the key that I treasure, the one that opened a door for me while in exile. I will be forever grateful.

My incredible family, the four of them, my beautiful girls, Rosy, Andrea, and Susana, followed every one of my steps, tucking my days of doubt, overwhelmed by translation into English or resolution of a thread. They tirelessly, lovingly, discussed, challenged, contradicted, and contributed to this book. Carlos was always breeze and support on each cliff; with him, waves are surfed better. They all know well, they are the strong richly embroidered fabric that surrounds everything I love, like a bundle of greatness that accompanies me everywhere I go.

This entire process, my beloved parents know well, has been a collective prayer I have whispered to their ears and it rises like mist before you as a prayer from my heart.

PART I
THE JOURNEYS

CHAPTER 1
THE CONSPIRACY
1612

A cobalt blue morning greeted the boy's footsteps. He almost lost his footing on the wet tiles moistened by the night dew. A soft breeze announced the new season. The song of birds confirmed it was a brand-new day, while the liquid streets, a few steps away, belied rumors of mellow water with waves crashing against the shore. The mist on the beach of the Great Lake was floating and ethereal, covering everything. It was a warm and humid morning, like the hope he harbored in his heart.

The boy shuddered. Because he was a slave, his ragged clothes covered only the intimate parts of his body to allow him to cope with the heat during his daily work at the weaving mill. That was the place he was born, the stained fiber mat unraveling on the dirty floor where his mother gave birth surrounded by pots of all sizes, boiling with the water used to mix dyes for the fabrics made there. It was home, the only one he had known. That was the place where, as a toddler, he had been forced to wade into the river up to his knees and challenge the flow, stumbling for hours, to soak, rinse, and fix the colors on every piece of clothing until sunset found him numb and shivering.

The boy joined the other slaves cleaning the fibers from the thorns and encysted branches, one by one until his eyes were drenched in tears from rummaging through the fibers. This was his life –every day, week, month the same. There was a feeling in his heart he could not name. A kind of emptiness had developed, risen from losing the freedom he had never known. He had been born a slave, but this particular morning his eyes were filled with hope. The day before he had given a thousand thoughts to the idea of release, but ultimately the thought vanished, evaporating in the boiling indigo and crimson dye pots.

The news about the uprising of black slaves in the city center had reached the Villa de Coyoacan in pieces, through the voices of merchants traveling to and from Don Tomas de Contreras's mill. It was not the first slave revolt, nor would it be the last. During the previous century, the Province of Silver had begun to work the mines of Taxco – the Real de Minas – importing slaves in such number that blacks outnumbered Europeans nearly ten to one, which only increased the probability of a revolt.

Two hundred Spanish miners exploited the silver seams. The miners lived in fear that at any given moment some of the thousands of blacks crawling through the tunnels reaching the heart of the mine would revolt against them. The Viceroy had passed another law against fugitive slaves, and the Bishop was considering his options on how to force the Crown to ban new slave and trader import licenses. The threat of life confined in a weaving mill, chained and locked, was ample deterrent to slaves seeking unauthorized freedom.

The mining town of Amaltepec had suffered the ravages of previous uprisings. In 1569 a gang of blacks and Indians paid for their boldness with jail and the fierce cracks of a hundred whips, but they were so great in number that when the rebellion was extinguished, many fled to the mountains, leaving the mines deserted. More brutal punishments were enacted, causing new inconveniences for both the Crown and the mine owners. Royal forces soon learned they would have to deal with runaways in the roads, assaulting and ravaging the endless flow of merchant caravans. Any fugitive found who could not legally prove his freedom was immediately made a prisoner without further investigation. Those caught and so convicted were castrated or hanged.

The new century had brought more rumors of conspiracies. Punishments of fugitive slaves became more creative. The public dismemberment of rebels and whippings on top of wounds, covered with salt afterwards, became a display in plazas and main squares. Stories of public executions in neighbouring towns were recounted in detail by workers and slaves traveling throughout the kingdom of New Spain. The stories were repeated again and again in low voices until they had reached the workshops of Coyoacan at the lakeshore. The stories were as numerous as the threads of the fabrics made there.

Cheap and rough blankets were worn by the Indians, mestizos and blacks, or used to cover the backs of mules and horses. The anecdotes left listeners in fear, their emotions hanging on the spinning wheels that worked ceaselessly in the mills. The workshop of Contreras stood on the banks of the Magdalena River, where the mill had been established to make the most of the hydraulic force. A dozen wooden blocks constantly struck and tightened fabric using the force of the water. Enslaved hands carded, spun and wove the wool until night fell. Only a few of the workers, the free ones, were permitted to leave the facility at the ring of the church bells announcing prayer for the souls spending the night in their huts in nearby San Jacinto, San Jeronimo, San Nicolas and Santa Rosa.

The slaves who belonged to the master fell exhausted on the wooden pallets and mats. The oil lamps flickered in the corners of the workshop. Along with the children that were born here into a lifetime of captivity, the adult slaves slept the night away crowded, whispering, sweating, with nightmares of the river flooding every space.

The slave boy was awake before dawn. He jumped up, side-stepping to avoid the still sleeping bodies scattered all over the floor. Some sensed the smidgen of space free up and stretched towards it to claim a little more freedom in sleep. The heaps of coarse wool cushioned the noise while the boy tiptoed out stealthily. The sunlight was about to burst in a carnival of pale yellow as he reached the dusty road just in time to see the dust cloud the approaching mules and horses were making. The muleteers always brought fresh news from downtown Mexico, and Coyoacan, linked as it was to the capital of New Spain, was the first place past the crossroads leading to firm land.

The autumn breeze prickled against his black skin. The danger of being flogged if the master discovered he was out of the mill facility was a minor worry. His curiosity to hear the news and learn was primal. He heard the muleteers making small talk. The Viceroy, his court, and the Audiencia, the government branch representing the King in his American possessions, were in the heart of the big island that indigens still called Tenochtitlan or the City of Mexico, as the Spaniards did. It was a grand plot of land divided into four main neighborhoods surrounded by crystalline waters. The men talked endlessly about the conspiracy that purportedly would set all slaves free and provide liberty for all. The child had been born in the Coyoacan village, a jewel in the long list of the Conquistador Cortes properties and had known no place else.

Of unknown father, he had learned from birth there are many kinds of shackles, more than those that tied you up to a weaving mill, but he was here for the news. All in the facility had heard something was going on in the capital of Mexico, that fantastic place full of palaces, churches, and wealth that sumptuously grew in the imagination of every worker and peasant in the village. If he got no details ultimately, he could easily fill in the gaps of what the muleteers and servants did not describe in full. Workers at the mill would cover his absence. The threat of punishment was worth it in exchange for the latest news, but he had to be fast.

A revolt of some slaves had occurred. Dozens of men had armed themselves with daggers hidden beneath their ragged clothes in order to bring the

> He had learned from birth there are many kinds of shackles.

condition of prisoners to an end and to release those who had been taken away from their tribes —princes and commoners alike— and forced to come to these lands. The prisoners pretended to worship the crucified one with pomp and devotion, that white man with bleeding sores hanging from a cross, whose body had known the punishment their skins understood so well.

The traders spoke of the courage of the revolt leaders, all black slaves, while grooming their beasts. Sleepy masters and patrons, lying in the bushes, were taking short naps while the sunbeams shone on the great mirror of water.

"Ya'all know it. They did it, cause the Church says ain't no' right to allow the maste' to abuse slaves. And there they went. Thousan' blacks of the hermandá 'de la Mercé,' tha' brotherhood who was buryin' the black siste', their queen they said, those fools. Made her funerals, all devotees, all lined up, cryin' and tearin' their blouses when suddenly, knives showed up", said one of the black helpers; the boy could guess it just by his accent.

"Tiernitos, those youngste', tender bones yet, but all conceited Congos brought the hidden metal from their pants. They knew they were more. Many more. More than the maste's", continued the voice.

"You saw how the mob turned all goods in the market upside down. Fruit rolled all over the square, and the crippled ones crawled to reach one, one at least, blackening the street in tattered clothes, all muddy. They tore open so many sacks of coal, they took bunches in their hands and cut bundles of firewood to run away with the sticks, whatever they could hold with both arms." This time the Spaniard, a servant, was loud.

Even the Baratillo market and its vending posts of cheap stuff suffered the destruction. Such was their greed that they even disputed for the trinkets, pulling and tearing all that second-hand clothing, breaking away till they reached the nauseating street of the Canoa, where the sewage drains". The Spaniard's voice was like a whip.

"Those must have been the ones who knocked the door of the Estanco de los Donceles down, the place where all the young male slaves are bought and sold. They freed them all, even the youngest, the children they call mulecones. A pack of miserables running away, terrified but drunk in freedom like dogs, sick with rabies." The muleteer, clearly a mestizo for the soft brown of his face, whispered his words.

"¡Sí! By the corner, as soon as they could see the house of the factor Cervantes, they turned around never to be seen again."- A sweaty and emboldened Indian said loud

Mulattos and Indians, poor Spanish assistants, ridiculously dressed as cavaliers, were all trying to give full account of the conspiracy, being generous on their opinions about the black slaves and the events.

"Those who did not fall for muskets slipped in that mud of blood, dirt, feces, and crushed vegetables that now smeared the street."- The Spaniard added, grinning.

"Others, with their legs broken by the mob that was passing over them, crawled looking for a corner, sobbing in their languages: Enyemaka, taimako, msaada, help me God, this humble servant, to you I pray." The black servant pronounced the words with such accuracy that he blushed and went away, lost in the bush.

"Oh, I swear to God it was like that. You, pardos, whenever you feel in danger, you always return to your languages! You never forget! Nzambi to Mpungu! Zambitupungo, how you love to cry out loud, like saying, Good Lord, we pray to you for us!". This time, the Portuguese finally spoke.

"The leaders of the revolt said they would kill all the males. They wanted to impregnate their women according to their whims; the most beautiful, they would forgive them, they said, because they would have the privilege of taking them as their wives. Bastards! They promised to annihilate all the men, both old and young, especially the male children of the masters to end their lineage once and forever. They did not want anyone

THE CONSPIRACY 9

to grow up, to remember and look for revenge. They would even kill the friars, everyone, except the Jesuits, who would become their teachers. But first, they would mark their mouths with fire to subdue them."- the Spaniard spitted when he ended his comment.

"And also 'sabemo' that when everything calmed, they were thirty and five souls executed. Nothing was left. They thought they could do as that black Nyanga, in Veracruz. The one who claimed being of royal blood and heir to some throne, in remote Africa. That night that crowd pretended to do as he did, ransacking the hacienda' and the finca', that black slave from Córdoba, they say? Or from Orizaba? That Yanga inspired those brave negritos there in downtown Mexico. But nothing was left."- sentenced one of the mulatto servants.

The murmurs and whispers ceased as soon as the masters returned from the bushes, cleaning their boot buckles on the grass.

For weeks, a series of rumors was heard all throughout the region. Authorities blamed those meetings of their brotherhoods. Blacks and mulattos of Our Lady of Mercy had made all the fuss, mourning the death of one of the members.

It was not clear whether the dead woman was the slave of Don Salvador Monroy, the one who had died at the hands of her master after a brutal beating. The slaves had claimed the cadaver to organize a funeral procession and had carefully embalmed each part of her black body, beaten and broken to pieces. They kept her at the chapel they were assigned and despite the stench had sheltered the coffin for days until they could bury her. The black slaves brotherhood had helped with the expenses with the scarce coins they made if their masters allowed them. They supplied each candle and flower and even paid the fee to have a priest heading the procession. They all went out in silence, a long line where all were black, black like the dead woman.

Rumor had it that the praying crowd became infuriated after the flutes gave a high note. The woman's death and her body released all the suffering, each wound bleeding out the suffering stuck in their souls for years: the capture, the jungle in shackles, the hell in the factory of San Pablo de Loanda, in Angola, waiting for months for the galleon to arrive, the burning mark of iron and fire crossing their chests that labeled them as property of the Portuguese. The loathsome journey lasted at least eight weeks, more if the weather was against them. The slaves were chained to wooden bunk beds without mats during the entire trip. Dozens were thrown away in the sea, dead bodies packed with dysentery or famine. They had endured everything, but nothing was worse than the humiliation of their sale and exhibition.

"Teens without stain, do you see?"; "Perfect genitals, somewhat weakened muscles. You know this is always only because of the trip, Sir! It is a guarantee that they will get better once they are filled with the good airs of these lands."

Anointed with coconut or cheap olive oil, they tightened their lips, powerless, as soon as they felt numerous hands that scrupulously checked each orifice. It was precisely the humiliation and the abuse what had triggered this rebellion, neither the first nor the last one.

Neither were the slaves protected by the authorities. Nobody advocated for them. There were no reforming friars who wrote Memorials of Remedies to the King of Spain as the naturals had, and the gospel said nothing about good treatment for bodies that shined bright like the moon on a dark night. The substitute Viceroy had lasted only a few months. The gentleman had unexpectedly died after a fall from his carriage, and the Provisional Audiencia was governing this minority of Spaniards and their slaves, ten thousand at the most, living in the Bishopric of Mexico, slaves who seemed to multiply like sheep.

For centuries, mestizos, afromestizos and pure black slaves lived and died alongside the indigenous people in these lands. The possibility of uprisings gave authorities shivers and caused them to pray every day. Even the shrieks of the herds of pigs that entered through the city gates were to their ears the howl of black rebels.

The morning of the funeral the revolt began with the sound of the flute. The embalmed body was taken out of a rough wooden box. Lifted by strong arms, she was paraded at the front of the row until they were right in front of the Palace of the Viceroy. The wild cries, the yelling, and the complaints were a mixture of broken Castilian, Hausa, Igbo, Congo, Angola, and a dozen other languages.

-"In her death, we all die," they hollered.

Her master's jealousy was to blame for the beating that killed her. She had been a gorgeous, black female, worth six hundred pieces of gold. Some said she had been accused of theft by her master. Nobody knew that she had been proclaimed queen in one of the sessions of the brotherhood to which she belonged.

Revolts were happening and increasing while hundreds of slaves were sent to the mines, haciendas, obrajes, weaving mills and construction sits all over this branch of the Spanish Kingdom. Slaves were the black shadow that lurked daily in their white consciences.

The revolt ended when harquebuses, swords, and crossbows meted out deadly thrusts, panic and resentment in equal measure. The mob was out of control almost every day and that morning desperation was drowned by the slaves' yearning for blood and revenge. The mist that covered the lake had already dissipated, and the beasts began to move slowly. Some of the masters headed towards Huitzilopochco while some others followed the path to get to Villa de Coyoacan. The child slave ran away from the group just in time to hear the last bits of the stories being told, but in his mind only one sentence dominated.

Nothing was left. Everything was just as before. For the umpteenth time, skilled blacks who mastered daggers hid their anger when the Army showed up, fearing the gallows and the pillory. After a few months, a new Viceroy with an iron fist assumed authority over the kingdom and legislated again on new ways to effectively control blacks, pardos, and mulattos.

In the black brotherhoods, prayers were still said for the souls of the massacred. The devotees kept tending to requests for help from the wounded ones whose masters had found in the event an opportunity of learning: Antonio, black of the Bran tribe, sick, would receive a visit from the brotherhood mother on Fridays; Julia, free mulatta, convalescent, was entitled to have two hens for her sustenance; and Matias, a mandinga slave of the brickworks, would provide his promised donation of a piece of brocade for the new canopy of the Virgin's altar.

Slowly and painfully, weeks after the revolt, the council meetings of each brotherhood received permission again to have their meals together. That was their only consolation. When the sun went down, their frugal table was cleaned of the wax they had rescued from the piece of the Paschal candle, and with new light, their dinner ended thanking the good Lord for their meal.

A soft whistle could be heard at one side of the table. They took care not to disturb the nap of the friar who presided vigilantly over the meeting. If everything went well, someone would turn the empty pot of soup upside down to make a drum and then with palms, wooden boxes and a tiny clay flute like those made by the locals their joy was unleashed. If allowed, women sang vigorously, joining five or six voices in praise of the Lord. The friars no longer objected to the volume or the bliss. Emotions were freed in everybody's hearts by the timbre and the beauty of the highest notes.

"Tumbucutu cutu cutu."

"Teque, leque-leque leque-leque, leque-leque."

"Antonya, Thomé, hagámole."

"Sansabé, sansabé."

Those wearing zapatones, rough wooden shoes, would beat the floor to make the wooden floor sing until each splinter released the memories everyone hid inside their songs. Childhoods came back with lullabies, Lucumí and Wolof tunes were improvised under the dancing light of the candles. They took turns intermingling sacred verses with well-known old lyrics until the Prior's glance repressed the rapture.

Words forbidden for their foreign origin were spoken at the table, some of them brave enough to voice a quick phrase or a joke. Those who understood celebrated the bold move with a wide smile. Memory organized a meeting of its own in their minds. They always found it hard to resist the call to dance, jump and hit their chests in joy, but in the middle of the noise they all wondered, when is the next time? How much will we accept again? Who would be the next brave slave to lead a plan, even at the cost of his life?

The heads, rocking to the beat, nodded. Nothing was left.

Thirty-five blacks, including seven women, were hanged in the Plaza Mayor that morning in May 1612 as the result of the conspiracy. The bodies of the sentenced were dismembered and their heads, nailed to the pillory, were on display in the square for days, a warning to whomever might plot to revolt again. Dozens more received new marks on their backs, already embroidered in scars from the whips and lashes. Nine gallows were erected in front of the Casas de Cabildo, the local ruling building, to receive the Royal Audiencia, a court established to administer royal justice, who would watch the executions, public as a lesson to anyone bold enough to even think of rebellion.

Nothing was left. The boy finally understood.

The group of merchants and helpers crossed the Altillo bridge, over the Magdalena river. Clouds of flies devoured the bodies of the insurgents for days, disturbing sellers and buyers of vegetables that crossed the busy Plaza Mayor, the main square. The bugs spread to the market of produce blocks away from the plaza. Weeks later, floating on the waters of the Royal ditch the remains of insects were removed in disgust by women who came to fill their clay pitchers.

Nothing was left.

Hope floated all over like the silk organza that wrapped the voluptuous body of the dead slave, their queen. They would have to wait, again. How long? Nobody ever knows how long.

> Nothing was left. The boy finally understood.

CHAPTER 2
THE JOURNEY FROM GHANA
1629

Twenty-three slaves, hungry and thirsty and led by Sa Loné, dragged themselves through the sand. The heat of the Kaan Pech jungle was rabid, as was the heat at the Portuguese fortress of São Jorge da Mina, or Elmina for short, the main slave trade post of the kingdom of Portugal. That hellhole in the Gulf of Guinea was burned into their memories now; the cells were dark dungeons that cooled down only at night when the roaring waves raised the breeze.

"Did you hear the hunt dogs up there? I swear I cannot stand their barking anymore! They are getting closer! Can you hear them?"

"Help, My Lord, mercy! They say those are starving hounds! They say the last time one even pulled a shred of skin from Bioka's side! And all the blood, oh Spirit of the Sea, so much blood all over!"

"Can you hear the howling of the wind? It is telling how many of them are coming. All those manhunters coming.

I tried to warn everybody in the village. I know the Great Punishment is near."

"Quiet, you all, or I will make sure a bunch of you fall from that bridge to become a shark's mouthful! Damn escravos, pretos cambujos!"

In the fortress in far, remote Africa, captives have heard those incomprehensible phrases for weeks, in so many different languages! Portuguese, Spanish, and other dialects. Now, here on the sand, an ocean in the middle, they were all light-headed, delirious from the many hours spent walking under the sun, drunk on saltwater, their thirst a blade cutting at their throats like daggers. They feared the calm of the turquoise sea and were suspicious of the shadows the trees projected on the sand. Any silhouette made them recall the lugubrious walls of the fortress they briefly saw, while crossing the bridge to get into its dark guts, a sight they would never forget.

Elmina was a castle blackened by mold, holding the echo of two centuries of laments within its walls. The profits of slave trade had filled a thousand Portuguese coffers, before any other European kingdom, and this trading post had opened its gates to send thousands of slaves, captured in the kingdoms of Kanem and Bornu, Benin, Ngabou, and Senegambia, to the New World.

Sa Loné and the others walked for hours, moving into the jungle at times, but fearful of straying too far from the shore. The boys had been trained by their tribal elders to understand the sounds of water and dangers hidden in the thickets, but down here, even the cries of birds and the wind were different. The trip had made them lose track of the lunar cycles, and the smell of rain was everywhere. They walked and walked, lost, without guessing that they had crossed a continent so far.

Hearing the noise of a flock of birds, they ran, crouching. They spoke in low voices, although their languages were as different as the sun and the moon. The shipwreck had mixed their ethnicities. Nevertheless, they found a way to communicate. When the sunset approached, they knew they needed to get into the unknown jungle. They feared the darkness coming, as it brought the torchlights that illuminated Elmina, and knew that the jungle might provide their only chance to run farther from the fortress and escape.

They saw their violent re-capture as a mirage playing out in the vapors that rose from the golden sand. Proof of hands and feet shackled were on their skin, but it was the fear, pressing on their chests as if a flat stone that was a much more painful, invisible wound. Perhaps that was exactly what the power of the Spirit wanted. This was what the stories of the elders were about. The emissaries of the world of the souls, spirits in charge of the lightning and the storm, had transformed themselves into men and had been sent to the villages to collect those at fault to bring them for a lesson in the Unknown Place. The string of conch shells around their necks had not helped at all. Such blessed protection had not saved them from the dungeons built by the muzungu, as they called the white men. In the dungeons they had learned everything about torture and crying and right outside, the Spirit demanded with voices made of wind to bring them to His presence as soon as possible.

They had reached this enclave from all corners of the world. There were still so many villages from which to capture men and women. The captors, of flesh and bone, selected each individual and led them to the trade post walking in a row, tied and shackled, for days. Stupor drowned their tears and lodged sobs in their throats. In the distance, the Elmina fortress, immense when compared with the huts in their villages, warned them of their possible fate. Little did they know that there, on the coast, the factory was at once a market, a warehouse, a trading post, and a customs office, and they were the goods to be dispatched to Europe and America.

They had been warned about the place of punishments so many times that these horrendous walls looked made for bitter lessons, just as the elders described. They had worshiped the gods from the beginning of times and had bargained and humbly accepted each and every reward granted and disgrace handed down. The gods' voices of thunder were interpreted by the elders, and it was they who had presided over the councils forever. Their wisdom kept possible transgressors at bay. Facing the fury of their judgment had been explained by the elders with each blow of their rod of justice.

The narratives of the old people around the fire were intended to be preventive. Any behavior that would endanger the stability of the tribe would be punished. Adultery, theft or homicide were the worst and therefore were more heavily penalized. The Spirit spoke through the elders and without doubt knew who was guilty. Envoys were sent to be told about transgressions, and the whereabouts of offenders were always revealed.

That was why everyone in the cell was busy making an examination of conscience and crying bitterly for their wrongdoing. Many of them remained bewildered, because they did not understand what they had done to deserve such punishment. The Spirit would know and be merciful. Or not. After weeks here, daring winds and unknown currents of the infinite ocean, inhabited by the Spirit, would devour those who deserved the ultimate penalty.

Sometimes the captors raided the villages at night. Some others remained waiting on the roadside for youngsters or maidens reaching the riverbank. Incursions were often previously agreed, and the chief of the tribe received a good payment in advance to let them know the right time. The raid was later attributed to the fury of the gods, and creepy details were given by the chief, filling their minds in full, picturing captives and torments with their fertile imagination.

Of those gone, none had ever returned to the hamlets. They were emptied, one by one, and soon each village was left without their best men and women, year after year, century after century. They all reached the same point: a trading post and a bridge they believed would lead them to the heart of the ocean, though the true purgatory was the ship itself. Once inside, they would be piled up on narrow, horizontal planks, breathing with difficulty the salty, hot air that barely moved through the opening to the ship cellars. Their bodies were disoriented by the swaying of the ocean, and their stomachs emptied every time the Spirit of the Water extended his arm to churn the waves. The hull creaked frightfully with each billow.

Sa Loné and the other four-hundred would lay stretched in the darkness for more than fifty days to reach the Spanish markets in America. By then, they would have lost almost half of their body weight, and many times they begged the Spirit to take them and bring their ordeal to a merciful end, but as much as they prayed and begged, their wishes were not granted. With barely enough space to turn to one side, women and children, separated from men, spent weeks covered by layers of a mixture of body waste that slipped through the wooden bunk beds and coated their bodies, until their precious curly hair was stiffened by the thick liquids that reached to the floor.

They had to fight to protect the only daily bowl of food. Once the meal was in their hands, they swallowed the disgusting contents at once. They knew they must eat it before it spilled. The ship's sway made the watery soup fall, adding yet another layer of filth to the skin of those below. The traders had captured and shipped the best ones, the strongest ones, the youth who would leave mother Africa without new children. The slave trade made no distinctions: princes and commoners were all spectres, dozing a thousand nightmares during the journey.

Yes, there was war among their tribes, and that fact had turned their own into slavers and traders. Africans also orchestrated ambushes against enemy towns, who exchanged their victims in the factory for salt, flour, horses and carpets. The wars became deadlier when trading in harquebuses and swords began.

The price set for each life began with the payment received for the capture and increased until the ships reached the American slave markets. The Indies began to fill up with slaves. The Treaty of Tordesillas split the sovereignty over the young New World into two. An unexplored continent was conveniently granted to the two most powerful colonial ruling empires at the time, united into one, Spain and Portugal, by Spanish-born Pope Alexander VI.

"A line must be traced from the Arctic Pole to the Antarctic, which is from north to south, at three hundred seventy leagues from the Cape Verde Islands, all over the ocean. And going from the said line through the Levant, these lands will belong to the King of Portugal and his successors forever and ever. And it is my commandment that everything else after this line, both islands, and mainland, found and to be found, be granted to the King and Queen of Castile and Aragon."

Cape Verde, in Africa, was an uninhabited and mysterious volcanic archipelago off the Senegalese coast, discovered by the Portuguese. It was the territory that Latinos called Afri, to the south of the Mediterranean, the Africa Proconsularis of the Romans. The continent, its dimensions unknown and lands barely explored, was the generic homeland shared by thousands of tribes with countless customs and unique ways of understanding life.

It was Afri or Afar, the "land of dust" of the Phoenicians, the "land of men who live in the caves," a Bantu word that explained the disdain Europeans felt towards those people they identified as savages, believing the farther into the Continent they went, the more they would find them living in a cave.

The Portuguese had attempted to circumnavigate the continent. It was larger than their most exaggerated estimates, and in 1494, the Portuguese Christian crown began to supply Europe with slaves from those lands.

The African trade was initially exclusive to the Portuguese because Africa was within the mark and extent of the possessions granted by Rodrigo Lanzol Borgia, Pope Alexander VI. The assent and enlisted papal support made it all possible. Portugal used their men as labor, in low scale, but the discovery of the New World skyrocketed the demand while the expansion of empires and their colonial enterprises grew exponentially.

The Portuguese kingdom had started profitable sugar and precious wood plantations in Brazil and from its possessions in Guinea, also known as Ghana, they received their slaves. The divine Providence and the Papal friendship with the

Borja family from Aragon set the line of demarcation for the Spanish possessions.

The Spanish had named their first continental possession as the Viceroyalty of New Spain. The name Mexico was only a dream at that point. It was a continent of unknown size and riches that proved over the years to be unequalled. The Spanish-Valencian house of Borgia (Borja, italianized) continued to dominate the politics and economy of the fifteenth and sixteenth centuries.

From then on, Spain, always faithful to the Papal Bull, advanced in all directions, and reached the known ends of land and sea, establishing posts and missions north and south of the Pacific coast, in places as remote as Nootka, 49 degrees latitude north, an island bathed by the Arctic and a century later claimed by Captain George Vancouver for the British empire.

"Itchmenutka, itchmenutka!" shouted the natives to the first Spanish explorers. "Turn around! Return to where you came from!"

Missions in California made the friars set their sights to the west, and their faith eventually reached the islands of Asia. The first archipelago they landed on was named as the Philippine Islands, to honor the Spanish emperor, Philip II. Such was the way New Spain became the bridge that would connect two continents and two oceans.

A route navigated by galleon to Manila twice a year was established. The Port of Acapulco received fleets of ships loaded with porcelains, ivories, silks, and gems that crossed all the way to the heart of New Spain and from there to Veracruz, to be shipped to Spain and Europe by the fleet of the Indies to an audience hungry for adornment and lavish exoticism.

Turn around! Return to where you came from!

All these efforts demanded strong hands to load and unload, to farm and feed, to supervise and discipline. They demanded labor. They demanded slaves.

Western Africa was depopulated by the Portuguese at the height of the slave trade and with an insatiable appetite, other empires set their sights on disputing Portugal's dominance in supplying slaves to the colonies in the New World. The mortality of Native Americans caused by European epidemics was draining fields and mines of workers, and slave traders plumbed further into the African heart to fill their quotas. With each decade, they devastated towns for hands to extract silver, spices, woods, grana cochineal, indigo, sugar, and tobacco in America.

The first slaves had landed in America with Columbus. "La Niña," was overseen by the mulatto Alonso Prieto, while Dieguillo, a slave of his trusts, administered the sale of merchandise and property of the discoverer in La Española.

Prietos, pardos, and morenos retained the nicknames that referred to their skin color: brown, black, as their surnames, and for some fortune was good enough to be allowed to work in menial jobs that allowed them to save and pay for their freedom. The master's generosity and nature could make a world of difference.

Once free, they chose to use their color as a surname. They could not avoid the name of their former owner, marked by iron and fire on their chests.

Slaves replaced the Indians, the "poor children of God." The indigenous population owned souls that needed salvation, but with scarce diets and forced labor, they were dying by the thousands, defenseless against diseases brought by conquistadors. Uprooted to remote congregations to farm Spanish plots, far from their places of origin and without their women, they reduced in number alarmingly beginning in the sixteenth century.

By sea and land, slaves were transported everywhere. Black people sold in the Canary Islands or purchased on the Spanish peninsula, auctioned in the markets of Cadiz or Coimbra, were shipped to America documented with a Letter of Property, just as it is done with merchandise, notations showing that taxes were duly paid. They were also introduced as contraband, to avoid paying for the alcabala, a tax required by the Crown.

They made up an anonymous list that grew with each century, whose number no census or file recorded.

Their owners took them to Europe, as well, to be used at the docks of the Netherlands, a Spanish possession by then. In Genoa, they served the bed and the residences of merchants, friars, and bishops, while others crossed the Atlantic to find an end to their days in some mining town in New Spain, an opulent house in the Viceroyalty of New Granada, or serving in workshops at the Rio de la Plata. The businesses and fortune of their masters decided their fate and after a lifetime of being exploited, they would end up in the suburbs wandering as beggars, called useless because of their advanced age or illness, thrown by their master into the streets, torn from their children, still enslaved and left behind to serve.

The oceans moved crowds back and forth.

But Sa Loné and the other survivors knew none of this. They had traveled under the main deck and had not even seen one another's faces. Any attempted contact was a disobedience that would result in a whipping.

A flock of macaws screaming and the cool shade of the jungle received the fugitives, still quiet, fearful of speaking.

"These are the last bags! The gold deposits of Ashanti have been prodigal this time. Now to the Indies, negroes! We will get some good spices there. Bragança and Porto are all yearning for them!"

"Barrels and bales, all in place! Now you, miserables, get used to the shackles! That piece of wood will be your only companion until we get there!"

Wood and iron held their ankles and made long steps impossible. The rubbing of their shackles produced suppurating sores that would later be cured by old sailors. Once land was in sight, the traders knew they had to hurry to prepare the slaves for the auctions. Elders in their bunk blames blamed the fury of the spirits, but the trip to slavery, from which there was no return was actual earthly agony lasting weeks.

This was a galleon for slaves only. Elmina was bid adieu by yellow sails leading the squadron. The Iberian Union had tied

Spain and Portugal together, since 1580, but only the Portuguese crown kept control of its factories and routes with zeal. They were two kingdoms, two separate crowns, only governed by the same king, the great Phillip II.

An unexpected storm had delayed the departure, and the endless ocean was the only thought in the minds of the captives. Other than praying, weeping and the gnashing of teeth was the only sound heard. The spirits inhabited the jungle, and the savanna and the ocean represented greatness. In confinement, they tried to decipher the noise of the storm that seemed the roar of *nkisi* and *bakisi*, the underworld bearers of the laments of the dead.

They had uselessly hidden carved wooden figurines of the bearers on their roofs or buried them in their doorsteps to save them from punishment or bad will and envy. Fortune-tellers locked in the dungeons of Elmina claimed to have understood the messages of the wind, before departing. The spells were the same as those announced by the voice of the iridescent conches they exchanged with foreign traders in the villages.

They cried in whispers at the revelation of torments that not even the healer could have conjured, no matter how many hundreds of powerful pearly shells were hanging from their skirts and altars. The *malungus*, the white people, were the incarnation of evil. Restlessness and fear grew by moment and the prisoners' laments caused the foreman come, whipping and hitting iron cannons while shouting.

"Gelofes, mandingas, all those from those tribes! Silent, you all. Forbidden it is to speak in Guineo, the language of prietos, the language of blacks! I am coming down to impose silence, I warn you!"

Back in the village, under the auspices of the wind, the hollow spiral of mollusks had predicted it all. The Spirit had expressed His wishes; he demanded as many offerings and rituals as possible. When pleased, captures stopped for a time. The witch doctor was the one to thank since his amulets had proved effective. Good hunts, abundant fruits, a large family, and a good life was all they needed and asked for.

So, why were they all here now, facing the oceans fury?

Three ships formed this fleet. They sailed the first days in calm; their only wish was to leave the Gulf of Guinea and navigate to the Canary Islands to leave the cloudy days behind. The constant trail of foam gave certainty to their enterprise and at ten knots an hour – twenty at the most – the stain of Sargasso weed disappearing announced the open sea. On deck, sailors exchanged glances. A full week of misty days was still to come. Soon, they would be at the point where the current was faster, and the roaring winds were sirens song announcing the assault.

They spotted the enemy ship and her two smaller skiffs on the sixth day, the cursed number. Her badge was a Star of David flapping on the flag, hung to the main mast, outlined by a familiar phrase, not entirely understandable. "Mazel Tov." Good augury. Carved into the wood of the bow, the name of the ship left no room for doubt. "Shield of Abraham." It was the carrack of a Jewish pirate, the Portuguese Moises Cohen Henriques. Escorted by another smaller flagship, it was the most feared sight for a merchant ship.

The attack happened in minutes. Although the Portuguese pointer was a veteran, the artillery of the Jewish pirate's ship had made the first shot, strategically wounding the fleet. Larger in size, the "Shield of Abraham" attacked with a vengeance. All the sailors had been recruited in Amsterdam, Henriques' adoptive homeland. Most of them were strong, young men crossing the ocean for the first time, desperately seeking the fortunes the New World promised. Some others were experienced sailors who knew the Baltic or the Mediterranean, but had lost everything in the arms of liquor. For them, the West African coast represented a strike of luck that could bring back their fortune.

They did not share the motivations of their Captain, the Jewish-Portuguese pirate Henriques, educated in the infantries of Lisbon and Seville, a youngster who had travelled against his will to Amsterdam, and who was filled with bittersweet tales about the Hebrew exile of the previous century, the main demand of the Edict of Expulsion originated in Spain. 1497 had been a deciding point in the fate of Jews in Portugal, and thousands were forced to leave Sepharad, the place they had chosen to be the biblical spot of uncertain location. Such was their name for Hispania, their land for centuries, the name for the whole Iberian Peninsula.

The Spanish alliance configured by House of Austria was trying to set the Spanish peninsula borders in order, and the Edict of Granada was forcing so-called infidels to convert to Christianity or leave the territory into exile. For many, their faith was first, and they chose to settle down in other lands. North Africa, the kingdoms of Italy, Eastern Europe and the Netherlands all accepted Jews from Sefarad into their communities: civil servants, farmers, artisans and merchants with a legendary sense of community, rich and poor endured exile together.

Henriques the pirate belonged to this lineage. In Sepharad he had heard stories of peace, zithers and lyres in the aljamas of his neighborhood. These were the self-governed communities of Moors and Jews living under Christian rule in the Iberian Peninsula, where poetry was made in the language of the Torah. In Sepharad the converts who decided to stay, new Christians, secretly kept in their hearts the pride of belonging to the ancestral lineage of Christ. The due date for converting and being baptized or leaving Spanish territory came along with riots and destruction, in which Christian fanaticism reigned. On the decreed date, the doors to the Jewish fortified neighbourhood were forced open, their archives burned down, and the tower left empty with no one to raise a voice to alert of danger.

"The Jewish quarters are down, ransacked to misery!"

Christian peasants and low people attacked Jewish possessions with holy fury, taking everything away. Many of those who had chosen to stay, opted for death that night, throwing themselves from the top of the walls, their souls to remain forever in Sepharad. Those who left formed an endless caravan, accompanied by the sad cry of their lutes. Flutes were broken, a sign of the desperate battle between conscience and a burning heart, sighing for the land they were leaving and where they were born.

All throughout the kingdom of Spain, the lament of exile was heard. The Jews went on mules pulling carts loaded with their dreams and their belongings. On the roads, Christians yelled and threw stones at them shouting, "Choose baptism!" staining the sacrament with the furious foam from their mouths. Those who chose the more liberal Netherlands tried to forget with each verse the accusations that made them responsible for all calamities. They left the dusty roads and the persecution behind, and under public scrutiny they commenced their long journey just as Abraham the Patriarch did. The glorious leader of so many feats, who like them had also left Mesopotamia to reach "that land that I, your God, will indicate."

> Those who left formed an endless caravan, accompanied by the sad cry of their lutes.

Wandering was in Henriques' blood. He, as all his family, knew about the changelings, those who could not stand exile and returned to the Peninsula for conversion. They called them anusim, new Christians, converted Jewish. Leaving Sepharad and enduring the future was both an act of heroism and a wound they would carry for years, the loss being transmitted to their children, and to the children of their children.

When Henriques started his maritime career, he set eyes on the Levant. He had inherited the iron key that would one day open the main door of the house in Sepharad that his family had been forced to abandon. He had sworn he would not rest until he used the key in that lock again. Two previous generations of Henriqueses had already made their fortunes in Amsterdam. Their freedom was to them a precious diamond, and in the Netherlands they decided to add to their family name the noun that identified them as descendants of the lineage of the conahim, the Hebrew high priests in charge of the rituality of the Temple. After their arrival in Amsterdam, they chose to be named Cohen Henriques to proudly show they were part of the covenant they had established with their Almighty God.

In this first decade of the seventeenth century, no city was as powerful as Amsterdam. Full of uprooted Jewish, comedies written by famed Spanish writers were translated to Dutch for an enthusiastic and nostalgic audience that found the words Hispanic writers, Calderon de la Barca and Quevedo resonant.

Henriques' first sailing excursions were to Lisbon. His child's eyes had seen Portugal from afar, scrubbing pots in the ship kitchens. The scent of the sea had permeated his spirit, calling him to adventure. He would always remember the day he set foot on Portuguese docks. He wandered for a couple of days while the goods were organized and he managed to get into a ship to steal from a drawer an animal skin, wrapped with care. He did not immediately understand the size and importance of his robbery, but his soul had heard the call and he responded.

What he stole was a navigation chart!

When at last he understood the importance of his theft, he knew he would dedicate his life to deciphering the chart's coordinates, lines, and edges. His hands felt a thrill at tracing coastal contours drawn on the portulan chart and slowly he developed a nose for quick rewards. He easily learned assault ships were the way to glory. Avenging the expulsion of his own by snatching the fortunes of Christians, both Spaniards and Portuguese, became his life's ambition.

Investors in an Amsterdam orthodox community presided over by a Rabbi of great virtue liked to discuss plans that would finance pirate fleets. Mocking the authorities was a diversion and avoiding their tax obligations while getting a hefty percentage of profit on the booty was a delight. They supervised their legitimate businesses during the day and in the afternoons, as a hobby, they went to the shipyards in groups to supervise assembly of the ships they financed. A fee to assign construction of the ship was part of their profit. They never interfered with the planning of a voyage, and when a ship or an entire fleet set sail, there was a long wait to endure, buoyed only by faith, before any return on their investment was possibly realized. In piracy, luck, not effort, decided destiny. Along with a great assault, pirates could gather royal perks and titles. Death under the arms of a wave or a disastrous shipwreck was also a price they could pay, being at the mercy of the vast ocean.

Henriques was ready for his clandestine journey. He knew his future as an assailant and smuggler of fame would be tested. A group of wealthy Jews had financed the "Shield of Abraham" based only on the guarantee of the Portuguese chart he held tight. The map detailed the ocean currents, the position of the main factories on the African shore, and beyond in to unknown lands, pointed out in small and elegant letters the locations of food and water supplies, the dangers, the tides, and the winds. Stars were the guide that guaranteed the information described by the chart, the key to the New World markets that neither he nor his Jewish funders had ever touched before.

The vast Guinea Sea, leagues away from Elmina, witnessed the shot that announced to the Portuguese crew the pirate's intentions. The Portuguese had displaced part of the defense artillery to the ends of the ship, increasing the weight excessively, and making maneuverability difficult. The Portuguese were superior in number, an advantage in a possible hand-to-hand fight, but they decided nevertheless to wait. The "Shield of Abraham" traveled light, half empty. Henriques preferred one of the ships escorting over the main ship. He was an expert in onboarding via ladders and bridges, so he had planned a sudden attack of warning, followed by a quick negotiation.

The "São Pantaleão Martyr" shivered, large pieces of wood on one side broken. The ship was suffering as the Saint did, a rich pagan converted to Christianity who triumphantly defeated death six times, the last one fighting the sea and the fury of the waters. Unharmed, with the help of the Lord, the III century martyr was the patron of the slave fleet.

The Portuguese decided instead to protect the two smaller frigates. Everyone knew the smaller ships carried food and minor supplies, so despite themselves they decided to give up the contents of the larger, wounded ship, including the slaves. Smoked meat and oil barrels hid the gold and the gems they had brought from Ashanti and through the merchants of the Sahel. The slaves were only an excuse. However, for Henriques, slaves earned their price in gold. Ignoring the smaller ships, his crew found slaves enough to return the investment and make an even higher income. His fame would also be rewarded. Doors to major operations would open for him and his most faithful sailors, and the zithers would sing his glory on every European dock.

The two sides negotiated a full load of slaves, cattle, and spices in the Portuguese jargon of Henriques, the language he had used to love, sing, and navigate. Both crews knew that a battle could be fatal. Four masts, twenty-six guns pointing at them and their main galleon damaged persuaded the slave traders to surrender. The agreement produced a fuss of goats, pigs, and greyhounds. Cursing their luck in their language, the crew gave them away. Henriques' men diligently inventoried each piece, mentally noting their own individual profit. Then they received the slaves, who stayed on deck, trying to ignore the seduction of a quick death by throwing themselves into the ocean.

When the sacks of spices were loaded, the breeze filled with aromas of pepper, cinnamon, clove, and anise. The perfume overwhelmed the smell of latrine for a few moments. A bag of turmeric powder from India was broken, and their yellow footprints fading on the wood made the marching slaves smile for a moment.

At dusk, satisfaction illuminated Henriques' face. He verified their position on his precious astrolabe. Shining stars would cover the dome of the sky. He was convinced the success of this mission would open gates to fabulous enterprises. He verified his coordinates to reach the equatorial current. He had a year to get back and give an account of the revenues, and the New World would transform human flesh into gold to fill his coffre. The Captaincy General of Cuba, an administrative district of the Spanish Empire, would be the place to negotiate the sale of the smuggled captives. Without intermediaries, everyone's profits would increase.

Henriques slowly opened the chest of precious wood and silver fittings in which he kept his most treasured belongings: a curl of hair, a letter, and the key to the home he longed for, wrapped in turquoise silk with golden threaded edges. Into each fiber the wishes of his soul were woven, and he was sure now, more than ever, that the day he would stand in front of that door was nearer. It was the house of his childhood in Sepharad.

The Portuguese malungu, the white men, enduring tears of rage at the insult, fell on their knees to pray in thankfulness to the Saint for saving their lives. The time and opportunity would come to have a new reliquary made to adorn an altar in appreciation to the Saint. Now, however, the "São Pantaleão" had to be repaired, sealing its wounds with revenge in the resins used to caulk it. The Junta de Negros, the council that regulated black slaves trade, had received one hundred forty thousand ducats for the license granted to Joao Coutinho to introduce slaves. The assault was thirty thousand ducats worth, three and a half grams of gold per ducat, that is one hundred five kilograms worth in gold for the slaves, spices and cattle apart.

The voyage of Henriques continued across the Atlantic. They would try to approach Matanzas, in Cuba, to anchor there. After the assault, the pirates had endured the laments of the slaves for five weeks. The slaves kept silent only to rest from throwing up, tossed about by the waves. In the island, Canimar River and the bay temporarily lodged smugglers who settled there to wait for smuggled slave cargo. Fraud was punishable by the Spanish crown, but the smugglers feared no Royal Mayor of the Crime. Canimar was a stop not recorded in any logbook, in Cuban lands, deserted after a couple of unsuccessful attempts to plant yucca and sugar cane. The north of the island, semi-deserted, had been abandoned by Spanish conquistadors tired of fighting the scorpions and the stubborn weeds in the muddy land that not even the native Arawak Indians had tried to farm. It was indeed a safe route for black slaves to be introduced into glowing Havana.

The "Shield of Abraham" did not even manage to see the shores of the bay. The strait was thick with Spanish ships. They would have to change the place for anchoring, against their will. A few days away, the General Captaincy of Yucatan was known to also receive smuggled slaves at various points, but the staples would have to be stretched to the maximum to withstand these extra days. Back in Guinea waters, it had been a wise judgement to accept the cattle. Henriques, the highest priest of his ship, decided they would continue to Campeche to bring the slave cargo as close as possible to the markets of Veracruz, which paid the highest prices in the New World. He was aware that delay would concern his creditors, but when the sale was over, they would get to the port of San Francisco de Campeche and fill the ship with merchandise and that would more than compensate for the delay.

The ship turned towards the endless Gulf of Mexico. The chart and the tables showed the proximity of Isla Bermeja. Stained by sweat and humidity, the vellum chart showed the mysterious island that many other maps depicted, too, but that none had viewed. Neither would they see it, not even as confirmation of their coordinates. The jaws of a sea serpent pointed in the direction of La Bermeja and seamen took turns scrutinizing the horizon with their Dutch lens telescope to be the first to discover a non-existent island, fruit of seamen legends only. In the afternoon, murmurs of uneasiness and superstition swept through the crew, and they decided to release all sails to cross the area as fast as possible. They ignored the iridescent vapors of the distant rain.

Fainting slaves below, out of breath, sensed the speed increasing but were too weak for further complaints. On deck, goats screamed, disoriented, and two of them, loose, jumped over the railing, disappearing into the waves. Henriques, indifferent to the omen, was too busy, verifying his calculations, and new instructions were cheered by the crew.

"Hurry up, people. Let's reach the shore! Coastal navigation will prove to be better for our hopes! Full swing! Winds will get the message, and in two days we will be reaching mainland. Go, set the fire, that my bed is ready for those lamb skins after the banquet. I will regale a celebratory roast for my brave crew tonight!"

The steward checked the scarce contents of the grocery compartments. They deserved a banquet, indeed. They had fresh water, and their spirits desperately needed a break. Pots and fires were glowing by sunset. Eighty souls would have a feast of lamb, and a boiling cauldron would receive the bones that would make the soup of roots and scraps for the slaves. The crew chose to ignore the gray clouds when they set up their mats for the night. A fine drizzle cooled their appetite, and they slept, satisfied.

Henriques calculated the landline would show up at noon. He redefined the course once again, in the hour that precedes dawn, when darkness is still all ink. The "Shield of Abraham" had made the long journey in relative calm, but he and the crew knew in their hearts that calamity can be found just around any corner. Torches were extinguished and were substituted with their five senses. Henriques' eyes narrowed to see better what seemed to be a Spanish company, floating in a majesty of red and gold, guarding the Gulf of Mexico, more than a million square kilometers of surface and a possession of King Phillip IV. The Spanish deemed any ship without a flag an intruder.

Upon sighting the "Shield of Abraham," the companionship immediately notified her sister ships with the sound of a trumpet. The "Shield of Abraham" was positioned in defense and the Spaniards fired their cannons without mercy. The Royal Coast Guard of New Spain, heavily armed to fight filibusters, attacked with devastating precision. It seemed the very possession of New Spain was at stake. The Spanish aimed to first hurt the main ship, whatever its cargo, than to suffer the landing of pirates. Failure to stop the intruders would lead to the ransacking of San Francisco de Campeche, still not fortified by the Crown against invaders as it should be.

The "Shield of Abraham" had turned right a few degrees, exhibiting her vulnerable quarters and its Spanish counterpart attacked there several times. The misty darkness hid the move of the smaller caravel. Cohen Henriques was leaving with only a few fortunate sailors on board, while the shouts of four hundred miserables roared below deck. The brunt of the Spanish artillery attack provided the perfect cover for the coward's departure. Henriques' crew knew they had no chance to organize a counterattack, but the "Shield of Abraham" honored her name, protecting them. The ship was now leaning towards the seabed and death. The four hundred tons of the "Shield of Abraham" were burning. Young, inexperienced sailors and four hundred slaves left behind, formed a macabre dance of bodies, all black in the darkness, bathed in a fine cloud of powdered cinnamon. Sailors and tied captives were now sinking slowly in the opal waters.

A crew of victorious Spaniards only perceived what they believed were brief, agonized shrieks in Angola, the African language of familiar-sounding idioms, as those spoken in the daily bustle of the ports. As soon as the Spanish realized the mass of wood was crunching, and the sinking would only take a bit more, they backed off their attack. All the cargo was lost, the ship would soon be gone. No one noticed that a few managed to keep afloat, quiet, grabbing a piece of the skiff to kick for their lives, invisible in this black hour of the night.

Sweaty and feverish, Henriques spent days aboard the surviving "Esther," rubbing his coffer in anger, his wrapped key inside, crying as a child does for the loss of the "Shield of Abraham." He swore to avenge the disaster, even at the price of his life.

• • •

By the grace of God, Our Lord and Saviour, back in the factory Sa Loné was hurriedly baptized Anton. Faith was first. The day before the departure of the ship, each slave received a new name and was forced to repeat it out loud in the new, incomprehensible language.

"Em nome de Jesus Christ, receibe batismo no Espírito Santo"; "in the name of Jesus Christ, receive the Holy Spirit".

Every journey to the New World took victims. Passengers to the Indies tried to follow the advice of receiving the sacrament of reconciliation, taking Communion, trying to make peace with their souls and their enemies. If they died during the trip, corpses of both rich and poor were thrown to the sea after brief prayers. The anointing of the sick was administered when in death from illness was nigh. Such were the ways to be prepared for a place in Heaven.

Baptism was an occasion to verify the inventory of slaves all over again, and accountants appointed by the Crown were responsible for giving full account of expenses and taxes owed to the Royal Treasure.

> Ytem: *Rosario, as of age twenty-three to twenty-four years, with no blemishes or diseases known to date, valued in the amount of three hundred pesos or seventy ducats.*
>
> Ytem: *Jusepe, who is almost fourteen years old, big swelling of the upper lip and with only the sight of one eye, healthy and strong, valued in the amount of two hundred pesos gold, common currency.*
>
> Ytem: *Nicolás, man with a pustule on his right shoulder produced by the carimba, the branding iron. Promised for sale to the Portuguese merchant Gonzalo Váez in the Port of Veracruz.*
>
> *Salvador, twenty years old, of regular height, full and sharp teeth; Andres, forty years old, no gray hair, with marks all over his body because of ways of the religion of his land; Lucia, almost eleven ...*

Christian names, price estimates, calculations and the payment made to the Crown of a fifth of the price were meticulously recorded while the last red of the sun covered the books and the skin of slaves and traders, making them all look equal and the same. Their new names were like the crack of thunder, announcing the end of something. Neither prayers nor promises nor amulets saved them from feeling their lives torn in pieces. A violet sky fading away announced a new storm in the distance and the power of the Spirit of the Waters. The castaways grabbed the barrels of Malvasia grapes wine that floated in the foam with their last flicker of strength. Yellowish tarps, treated with elderberry resin, were floating all over. The juices of the tree could protect the fibers from moisture and salt, but not from the swirl of a sinking ship.

The loss was recorded in the Royal Registers:

> A foreign ship daringly approached the shores of the possessions of the Kingdom in the Gulf of Mexico, and a quick response of the Spanish Armada defeated the enemy, who found their ship collapsing entirely. Contents were unknown, but tarps treated with resin on the beach lead us to affirm it was a ship loaded with goods and groceries."
> The ship never displayed an insignia that proved her origin. Events reported occurred on the margins of the Intendancy of Yucatan, on lands that the natives call Kaan Pech, 18 degrees north latitude and 91 degrees west longitude. Such an account is recorded for the royal archives and the purposes to which it may take place.

The chronicle mentioned that the events had occurred by the Island of Tris, the Island de Terminos as abbreviated in Spanish cartographies, and it omitted their suspicions of carrying black slaves.

Sa Loné was Anton, because of his baptism at the factory, and along with twenty-three survivors of the shipwreck, they laid down scattered on the sand, vomiting seawater near the mangroves, tired of kicking and dragging to reach this blessed beach. When they awoke, they recognized one another under the moonlight, certain the first half of their lives had been taken away by the sea currents.

They came from distant and different places. Their languages were as varied as the nuances of their faces. Rosario was Hausa, Domingo was Fula, Hernando and Felipe were Mandingas, Jusepe was Congo, and there were also those from the Kingdom of Akan. Their skin crossed all the known shades of black and mahogany. Hair, curls, lips and the wings of their noses were the only features that announced they all belonged to the same land. Their baptismal names were the first ritual each one had mutually witnessed, and in this new reality of jungle and wetlands, they began calling each other with those same names. It was easier. Lucia kept her eyes fixed, walking but lost in a hermetic silence and staying well behind the group. Rosario had to come back and pull her small hand to urge her to continue. No more Sa Loné, but Anton. No more Kon Fata, Sekondi or Lawalo, but Nicolas, Rosario, Lucia or Jusepe. Saying their names out loud sealed their fate as survivors of the shipwreck.

They tore into the jungle with bare hands. Their lacerated feet ran now with no direction. They were running away from the beach. They ran like the Mandinga hero Sundiata, who had pacified and united a thousand towns and villages in a single territory of red soil where some of them belonged to. They had to move on, drag the sick ones, looking back with the fear in their bones, while the wind blew the hours past. Some places resembled their hometowns, and for one confusing moment, they believed they were back there.

> ... tired of kicking and dragging to reach this blessed beach.

The noises were different here, even if the same seductive green surrounded them. The position of the stars was different, and their fractured memory made it all like a dream. Once safe, they might get together to join the broken pieces of their memories. The wounds on their arms and legs were aching. They knew it would be better to stop and cleanse in the water stream. They knew they should try to heal their bodies, but more than anything, they wanted to give peace to their souls. They could establish in this place, fortify their enclave, but who knew how much more was still ahead?

They chose a clearing where the generous stream brought shrimps and fish. They were exhausted and could not forget the capture, the dungeons, the weeks of desperate hunger, the saltwater filling their lungs, pulling their bodies to the bottom. The girl they called Lucia bled from in between the legs and Rosario was gripped by fever. What seemed to be the Gallic disease, the evil sequel to the rape she had suffered in the factory, was taking over her limbs. As in all the African ports, the trade of bodies and the mixture of sperm in the wombs of public women had extended syphilis all over, for those who took them for one or several nights, the Gallic evil. With each contact, the disease spread in the villages and beautiful but infected bodies were the perfect bait for lechery. Pustules and small tumors alerted those infected, when the malady was already too advanced. Liquor and the urgencies of manhood made them forget all caution and right after the first sores, the fevers began.

Rosario was engaged to the heir of a chief at the neighboring village. But here, her head was on fire. An invisible rash whipped her limbs with more ferocity than the attack of the mosquitoes. The morsels of fruit in her empty stomach were expelled from her twitching body, all swollen inside, as soon as she swallowed. They entered the jungle where a man-made platform showed on the beach. Pieces of ancient, broken walls, made with millions of seashells, were ruins now. The construction proved that ancestral human hands had been here, and continued far into the jungle. The dozens of mounds all around, covered with grasses and sand, gave the idea that for hundreds of years they had been like this, abandoned.

The fugitives agreed to gather mangrove branches, logs and some of the rocks that were once buildings to form a primitive fence tied with grass, just as they did in their villages. Five of them took care of a small fire. When the fence was done, and they felt fictitiously safe, they got into the water, one by one, to get rid of the salt, the sweat, the pain and the tears. Not being a child anymore, Anton hunted a deer. Women broke the animal into small pieces and wrapped them in leaves. They tried to make their fear and fragility go away with the smoke until their weeping and sobs were indistinguishable from the crackling fire.

They spent a couple of days recovering in their temporary beds of sand and leaves. Rosario, burning with fever, her belly spinning, lay down, dozing, ignorant of the vigilant guards that took turns to kept their surroundings safe. On the third day, voices destroyed their calm. Canoes descended in a roar, tilting with the weight of their loads, forcing the fugitives to run and hide in the jungle. Their improvised fort was no more than a couple of yards high. With the tide and the network of rivers mapped in their memory, a dozen indigenous people warned each other with their eyes when they noticed the palisade and the fugitives. The slaves knew they were lost when a circle of strong men surrounded them. Their canoes, loaded with mahogany, guayacan logs and palo tinte formed a blockade to stop them from escaping.

Rosario, moaning on the sand, led the interlopers to the spot where the fugitives had been hiding. One of the Indians who looked like the chief of the group closed the circle with the final turn of his canoe. A metal weapon was shining under his clothes, hardly visible under the canopy. Twenty-three shaking bodies, terrified, were forced, one after the other, into the canoes. The Indians captured them all without saying a word. Their black, naked bodies were covered in pieces of cheap blankets, and the group of Indians continued their way crossing the green of the lagoon, rowing at full speed.

> They tried to make their fear and fragility go away with the smoke.

The capture had been their salvation. Without knowing the secrets of the marks on the trees, a stranger could lose his footsteps in the marsh for weeks, wandering at the mercy of jaguars and wild boars. Although the prodigal jungle might feed them for a while, tropical diseases would eventually devour them.

Pablo Paxbolon kept his eyes wide open. The labyrinth of waterways led to the place where his people cultivated palotinte. They used the sticks of wood to dye fibers and clothing, and upstream, lost in miles of water, they were the only ones who knew the water roads to get there, in the heart of the Peten. Palo tinte for the Indians, called bloodwood or logwood in Europe, the logs were the most important commodity that Indians like Pablo traded with the pirates in hiding, who infested the Island of Terminos.

The group reached the pirate campsite at dawn. The smell of fresh cut wood filled the air. The calculations that Pablo made for the profit he would get from the sale of the captured black people made the journey light and fast. The Heart-Soul god in the boat filled his mind with prayers and petitions for a smooth negotiation. They crossed the last lagoon and tied the boats behind the thicket. All the Indians whistled towards the campsite, and a man with red hair waved in the distance, trying to hide a smile of black teeth and satisfaction on his freckled face. A small fire behind the men was ready to cook pieces of deer meat.

Pablo and the tall red-haired man understood each other. The bitter taste of the bulbous roots the black slaves had been chewing before the capture filled their mouths. Their fate was about to change, once again.

CHAPTER 3
THE JOURNEY TO SANTA MARÍA
1629

Black as ink, bloodwood hides under its bark a plentiful pallette. It renders deep purple when left alone in boiling water or yields a vibrant shade of red when it is mixed with iron sulphate. The colors of empires and kingdoms. Chunks of wood offer up a dark red liquid, as thick as wine, that humanity has used for centuries to dye rich mantles of princes and capes for bishops in dazzling European courts. When mixed with alumina, bloodwood creates the indigo shade viceroys wear to preside over ceremonies, and royal blue is obtained by adding chrome to the mixture. When copper is added, a rich dark green dye is used in velvets for tapestries to cover the bare walls of colonial palaces.

English pirates stopped to repair their ships here, on the beaches of Campeche, and while preparing for the next attack, they diversified their pillage activities. At the end of the last century they started buying bundles of bloodwood directly from the Chontal Indians to trade back in their gray Europe, a continent always in need of color. The pirates had a permanent shelter in the Terminos lagoon that connected fresh waters with the sea of Campeche and the Gulf. They were content with such a lucrative type of commerce and had abandoned their effort to get the Indians reveal the secret of bloodwood extraction.

Coming from an unknown place in the remote south, Chontal Indians crossed the wetlands all the way to Atasta, rowing a hundred rivers with Christian names –Candelaria, Palizada or Grijalva– where water avenues hid the secrets of the Mayan lowlands. Chontales knew all about botanical remedies to heal almost every disease and had also used juices of plants and roots to get natural dyes to decorate caves and grottos, and to embellish their garments made with the precious tassels offered by cotton flowers.

Pablo Paxbolon of Acalan had guided the boats of his Indians since dawn. Proud of all the lines of his lineage, maya, putun, and nahua, and heir of the wisdom of his ancestors, his group had been seen intermittently in the Villa of Santa Maria de la Victoria, crossing the swamps to pile up bundles of wood they would later sell to the English. They were experts in finding places on the scarce dry land to protect the merchandise from moisture until it was time to sell.

Pablo had learned to trade with the pirates using no words, but only the language of his hands, always alert to possible betrayals and with countless numbers of his people in hiding behind the solid green of the jungle.

The English had traded with them for over a decade in this small inland quarter, despite the persecution of Spanish authorities. Here, on the fine sand, frigates arrived looking for fresh water and food. The pirates organized raids to pillage neighboring cities while the storm season passed over, and they were able to get back to the sea after the god Hurakan, the god of hurricanes, had granted permission.

They fished and hunted while fighting unbearable clouds of mosquitoes that crept into their mouths as they spoke. Famous for their cruelty, a century of Spanish viceroys had fought them until they gave up. Conquistadors had penetrated the endless mangrove patches Pablo carried in his memory, one by one, and had given up, too. Some Spanish cartographer still believed the lagoon of Terminos marked the end of Yucatan, an island in their minds, and after briefly using sisal fiber for ropes and ship moorings, they found their trade in swampy waters and infernal heat, to be poor and difficult.

The English rediscovered the abandoned zone and made it their lair, mocking the Spaniards in their own possessions, but try to leave the labyrinths in peace. Buying the wood from the Indians was enough for their ambition. Here, they could use the guayacan tree for masts, mahogany to carve ratchets, and bloodwood to trade. Assault and siege of coastal towns, of warehouses and ports, was the true objective of these English pirates. They filled their coffers over and over and satisfied their pleasures. The destruction wrought at each surrounding town made everyone think the number of English was larger than it was. The terror inflicted produced numerous petitions to the Spanish Crown to fortify the ports, but a century was gone without walls and bastions.

Back in Europe, fervent Protestant countries saw the wealth their pirates and corsairs got as heaven's mandate and enjoyed what the alliance with these delinquents offered.

When they learned that Pablo's canoes were there, some of the bandits, wounded or sick, felt a great relief. They had been waiting desperately for the Indians' herbs, ointments and remedies, so Pablo was received with genuine joy. The spyglass had warned them this time that the canoes had more people than before and they cautiously began to search each corner of the jungle from afar to determine their precise number. A handful of what seemed from a distance to be miserable black Africans were behind the regular group.

The English knew fugitive slaves were claimed by masters offering fortunes. Advertisements described the slaves' features in detail, but it could nevertheless be years before a negro returned to his owners. Often, the reward was collected by free blacks, too, since it was easy for them to get information in their languages about the whereabouts of fugitive slaves. Only the strongest and the best fed made it, and their value in gold was the best incentive to find them.

Wallace spat the piece of wood his black teeth were chewing and waved to accept the bundles of logwood as they were unloaded. Black slaves were an unexpected commodity, and he acted indifferent while he mentally multiplied their value and his profit. There were three women among them! The sturdy black woman could stay. Her abundant bosom let him know she was a possible mother to procreate good captives for labour. If Pablo was selling, he was ready to negotiate. The brand of fire in their skin would decrease their price, but a red-hot iron could always be applied again to try to eliminate it. Indians had good herbal powders for healing. Wallace was predicting all kinds of uncomfortable questions in auctions, because of the brand. He would better pretend not to be interested. He knew that Indians loved bargaining.

For the castaways, it was all drowsiness and hunger. Tied in bundles of five human beings and rowing the placid waters of the lagoon for hours had made them sick. It was only when they crossed the delta of Atasta that the dozing came to an end and left them wondering how long this new torment would be. Suddenly, the lagoon opened to virgin lands by the sea. Pushed by the Indians, a total of twenty-one tied captives remained on the scalding hot sand, bare and naked except for Rosario and Lucia. Wallace and his people came to inspect the quality of the wood and agreed on a price. No explanation was needed. The pirate had negotiated the pay for this, the last load of wood of the season, and since he knew that the Indians would disappear as soon as the transaction was completed, he pointed towards the miserable slaves shaking in fear.

They knew well that the inspection would be repeated, fingers and hands would go into every orifice, just as it had been for them so many times before they had lost count. Their legs clenched, their gums fought the reflex of closing, and gripping grimy fingers reaching their throats. For the umpteenth time, they were scrutinized, examined, raped.

Wallace put them all apart. None of them had the carimba –the iron mark– he was fearing anywhere on their bodies, and without a brand, there would be very little room for bargaining.

He took out the pieces in gold he considered enough, and Pablo approached in silence. He opened a small cotton bag he wore tied to his waist and accepted the gold in silence. Without looking back, he returned to the boats, followed by his people, who quickly finished distributing dry herbs and powders to calm the unbearable pain of rotten teeth and infected wounds.

Wallace smiled, anticipating how that night be. A soft carpet of bare skin would receive his desires at his whim. When the English pirate ship departed, the destiny of each slave would be uncertain. Perhaps they would storm the General Captaincy of Guatemala and the captives would be sent to collaborate in the attack. Pirates might contact a local smuggler afterwards, and the cargo would almost double their price there. The Consulate of Merchants was always in need of stevedores. Some other slaves would be sold halfway through the journey to new masters in Havana or Santiago. There, they would weave a new story along with brothers and sisters of their same skin. If the islands were their destination, they could reach a sugar plantation in La Española, as workers in the harvest, or they would be made the delegantly dressed servants and company of some devout Spanish lady who would make them carry a delicate laced cushion for her knees, holding in their hands the book of prayers for Sunday Mass.

> For the umpteenth time, they were scrutinized, examined, raped.

Those unsold or unwanted would pay with their sweat for their bread and rationed water on the terrible journey back, crossing the Atlantic, to reach the Canaries or the Thames docks. Just maybe, one might seize the opportunity, and a strike of luck would let him flee. That's how it was, and that's how it would always be.

• • •

Pablo Paxbolon and his people were called "indios del monte", wild Indians. Baptized in Christianity, they had been a lineage of importance since Conquistador Cortes founded the Villa de Santa Maria de la Victoria, the first Spanish city in New Spain. But that was all forgotten now.

Like Pablo, many Chontal Mayans had been regrouped and taken by force to populate the Villa. Proverbially brave, they belonged to the Province of Tabasco, one that had seen its brilliance when the chiefs helped in the advance to defeat the Mexica empire. After that glorious moment, they had witnessed the gradual depopulation that had left this site half empty, while Spaniards, tired of the pirate attacks, were leaving Santa Maria. The town was founded in front of the largest river in this part of the kingdom. Spanish masters forced Indians to farm the scarce lands bordering the swamps, but nothing could keep these proud and brave indigenous people quiet and submissive. There were not enough muskets to stop them and just as it happened in all the possessed territories, many had rebelled. By the seventeenth century, this wild and inhospitable village was almost forgotten by the Viceroy.

The decree for Indians to provide personal service without pay, established in the first years, had been abolished, but here, Spaniards still fought to extend it to perpetuity. The Mayor exercised power at his discretion and complaints were not heard in any proceedings, as there was no judge willing to arbitrate. The Village was left to its fate, and indigenous uprisings took place almost with every change of season.

Pablo led an elusive group that traded with palo tinte, bloodwood. They had learned to speak essentials of the Castile language, as well as Maya Chontal and Nahuatl languages. His ancestors were the Lords of Acalan, who guarded the entrance to the kingdom of Yucatan, the portal that connected the Mexica with the Mayab, the center with the South, as far as Nican Anahuac, Nicaragua. Pablo's people called themselves "true men" and had inherited the wisdom and knowledge of both worlds. When the Spanish began organizing the territory in their method, alcohol had made indians slaves, and drinking was enough reason to get to La Victoria. After some weeks of drunkenness, they got back to the jungle, fugitives again, to worship their gods.

Persecution of their rites by authorities had forced Indians to disavow and destroy their idols, but how would they ever abandon a stone than symbolized the Soul, the Heart, the Spirit that inhabited their flesh bodies? It was only in the secrecy of the jungle where they could worship freely. Idols were carried on boats, under forced tribute to Spanish masters. Once in the swamps, Indians covered their stone figurines with honey and flowers. While in the village, they accepted the charity of friars who would forgive their sins in exchange for alms and they even participated in services in the main church, worshiping Christ along with the local brothers and sisters in charge of ornamentation of the chapels.

Before the storm season, Santa María received in its docks up to forty ships per month, full of merchandise from Castile. Indians made good use of the ships' arrival to get lost in the crowds. If love crossed their path, they would stop for more than a few weeks, impregnating Indian women and filling the villages with children born out of wedlock, who would go on to live the same story. But the call of the water made unsubmissive Indians climb on their boats and once there, Spanish shirts were taken off, thrown into the boats, to barenaked follow the streams and currents again.

With the sale of the slaves completed, Pablo rowed opposite the lagoon to get lost. The English would not follow his footprints and heading west into the river for an hour was a longer detour, but it would keep them safe. Once in the village, his people would go unnoticed, submissive, silent, barely smiling. That is why, in the eyes of the Spaniards, Indians all looked the same.

Santa Maria de la Victoria was no more than an elevated embankment protected by rusted cannons that had remained on the plaza for a century. The town was so fed up by pirate attacks that there was discussion whether or not to change the city's location. Struggling with nature, plagues and epidemics, as well as the constant flood of the rivers resembled a biblical fight; further, when clouds of locusts devoured the fields, everything turned scarce, even life.

In the boats, Pablo tried to interrogate the young black woman he had decided not to sell. Her answer to each and every question he posed was only, "Rosario". He had decided to keep both the child and the girl for himself. Totally aware of her fevers, he gave up questioning her and as soon as he noticed her brilliant eyes, he found a container of medicine at the bottom of his boat. He motioned for her to put her hands together so that she could have a sip of the healing drink.

In these lands and marshes of Campeche and Yucatan, water decided the destiny of people. Water was an endless ocean, a fresh river or a green swamp full of mosquitoes and disease. A few hours later, the potion took effect, and Rosario's fever subsided. Rosario understood that this man, who commanded the line of boats, dominated every corner, a firm voice giving brief instructions, full of authority. Her destiny was now in his hands, but Pablo had abandoned any attempt to establish a conversation with her. At nightfall, Pablo made a sign to force everyone to keep quiet. Rosario knew they had arrived somewhere. They were all ravenous. Miles and miles of marshes and the noise of wild beasts accompanied the course of the rivers, and therefore she knew she would have to postpone the idea of running away. Her tied feet would have made it impossible to float in the waters, although the idea of ending her life just by bending her body a few degrees to fall down had been difficult to resist. It also seemed quite absurd to cry out to death after having defeated it in the wreck. She and the child were two of the twenty-three survivors.

In these new moments of acute consciousness, free from fever, Rosario was able to hear the whispers and moaning of a small voice. It was Lucia, the girl who was bleeding between her legs. Unconsciousness had prevented her from noticing it was only the two of them remaining with the group. All the others were gone. She did not even remember the sale of the rest of the group.

"Gidan, gidan," the child said. "Home, home".

Time and space were still confusing in her mind, and the tender, little voice cried out for that place where her people were, while looking at her legs, horrified. Rosario had already known the nature of this bleeding and, without thinking, she repeated the same words in the girl's ear with an undertone of consolation.

"Gidan, gidan."

The words were like a spell. They spoke the same language, Hausa! In their complicity, Rosario looked the child in the eye, and both fell silent, Pablo was shouting instructions to the group, and they were exchanging words that were as loud as her hopes. Rosario and the girl's shared language was a possibility to conjure loneliness with only a single word. At least they would have the possibility of comforting each other in Hausa. Rosario went further, asking the girl which name she was given in the fortress.

"Lucia," the girl replied.

Rosario embraced the girl like a puppy and, taking her onto her lap, she softly whispered, "Kwanta, kwanta"; "Lay down, lay down".

Then, she dipped her hand into the water several times and rinsed the blood scabs on the child's thighs. Pablo looked at them with a perplexed expression.

• • •

"Bana ya nzambi," "mutanen allah," "ndi nke chineke." In almost all languages there are phrases that people repeat in rite and liturgy. The meaning is just the same: "we are the people of God". Everyone assumes they are the chosen ones. Nzambi means god in Bakongo; it is Allah in the Islamized Hausa, and Chineke in the Igbo of Niger. The people of God. The ones He chose.

The black neighborhood of Santa María de la Victoria had existed for more than a hundred years, since explorers brought black slaves with them. The village had received bozales, black individuals who had recently arrived from Africa, or ladinos, those who had been bought as servants in Europe, who have learned some Spanish already. They had made the move to

America along with their masters. They came from everywhere. The neighborhood occupied a few streets in the lower area, bordering with the seashore. They participated in and contributed to the slow prosperity and arduous defense against the attacks that plagued the town. Workforce and weapon for Spanish authorities, they actively collaborated in the persecution of rebellious Indians, who in their opinion were mental infants who did not fully understand that the Spanish Crown had been given a celestial mandate to help them achieve the salvation of their souls.

> We are the "people of God". Everyone assumes they are the chosen ones.

Epidemics decimated the number of inhabitants alarmingly, but to baptize them, teach them, and save them from themselves was a decades-long task that black foremen supervised. They collected their tribute and guarded and portered the doors of every authority, institution, palace or hacienda. An endless exodus of indigenous families relocated in distant regions produced runaways from the Spanish control, too. The runaways remained hidden in the intricate mountain ranges, the jungles, and the most remote corners, giving rise to the legend of the pariah, he who worshiped demons and gods made of stone in desert places where evil creatures had always dwelled.

Governed by local caciques, indigenous nobility was now appointed by the Spaniards, and new nobles claimed dynastic rights that were recognized in the confusion of the first years of the Conquest. Feeling superior, Indian nobility mediated between those of their own and their masters and, with that little power given, soon they turned from victims into victimizers.

Pablo Paxbolon liked to say he belonged to the true Chontal nobility. His title was handwritten in an old document he carried in his chest. As a fugitive, he had made the most of knowing the royal lineage of merchants he belonged to and used it to make alliances, buy and sell merchandise, and exchange messages. Indians recognized his nobility with that gesture of their heads only they knew. When the zeal of the guards searching for fugitive Indians worsened, Pablo would squat down beside market merchants, pretending to be closing a business, or getting the flock together as shepherds do, whistling along as soldiers approached.

Since part of his family had been forced to live in Santa María, they received his visits on the outskirts of the riverbank, admiring his condition of relative freedom. When drunk, he proudly brandished those papers that nobody understood but that were extremely effective. He found his cousin Damiana boiling corn with the turbid water of the river while her husband, Cosme, the son of a black slave and a free Indian, struggled on the dock, stowing and sweating the loads with his one eye. Their four children, mestizos of even a darker color given by the sun of the Gulf, spent hours jumping on the stones, playing with the sail boat they had built with rods of mangle. As soon as they saw Tio Pablo walking down the only cobbled street, they ran to hide under Damiana's waist loom, to avoid reprimands for their pranks.

Pablo pretended to be angry, chasing them, reed in hand, until someone stumbled, and the "punishment" ended with the children rolling on the ground and laughing loudly. Of twisted vines and covered with a mud and grass mixture, the neighborhood huts were inhabited by old and sick blacks and mulattoes who preferred to stay there until death. Their masters had chosen to move their residences to the interior after yet another pirate raid, and knowing their black servants were old and useless, some sudden Christian sentiment made them free the useless slaves.

As soon as the slaves completed the loading of mules and carts with their belongings, the masters left them in La Victoria with a notarized letter certifying their freedom, a diamond to their eyes. The benevolent gesture came at a high price: the masters took with them the children these blacks had fathered and raised. They departed in search of better fortune in milder and safer climates. The alcabala, the sales tax that would grant them true freedom was still pending to be paid to the Crown. When the master had left, it became an obligation in charge of the abandoned slave. It would take months of working for half the wage freemen received to get the small fortune together, pay and be considered totally free. By the time the debt was settled they had found an Indian woman to live their final years with, raising children of all colors in the confines of the black neighborhood, doing some manual work that would help them survive.

Those who had managed to work a few hours to purchase their freedom because they had been lucky to be owned by a merciful master, paid twice or three times their price and left the town younger, chasing luck in Merida, or on their way to Veracruz, or perhaps risking to reach Puebla de Los Angeles. Masters had no choice but to release a slave who had duly paid for his price.

But these were exceptions. The freed were only a few. Their freedom letter was with them in every stop, stuck to their bodies day and night, while they listened to tales of fortunes made in the north they liked to believe. The mining enclaves, people said, were full of houses with a hundred rooms in carved quarry that were owned by black masters, gentlemen whose servants were all black, as well. It was that or accepting to live in Santa Maria, raising ragged mulatillos born of their Indian wives, who served Spanish families, struggling between the shanty town and the main square, the most elevated part of the village, the one that never flooded, where the Spaniards had their houses built.

The freed slaves might also work on the docks, dragging their feet, full of mud, after the torrential rains covered their legs with filth brought from the heights. The port was full of sailors, merchants, and opportunity. Nights spent in the embrace of their women was the only chance of freedom from work, from farming communal lands along with those of the masters. But Spanish families were leaving. They left for Nueva Vizcaya, the Kingdom of Nueva Galicia or the Villa de Antequera. The centennial wooden cross erected by the Spanish founders was always waiting for their good-bye prayers in the square, facing the course of the river the Indians called Tabscob.

The powerful current had transported merchandise from the Chontal zone for centuries. Traders came from Petén, in Guatemala, or further south, from the Mayan kingdoms of Quetzaltenango, Usulután or Nic Anahuac, Nicaragua. Fluvial roads, shaded by canopy fronds, housed flocks of red and green macaws; the birds' twittering accompanied sacks of salt, cotton, jade, shells, gold, coral and cocoa for the markets, along with the uproar of Indian dealers who came to sell their vegetables. The endless chatter of sailors, soldiers and merchants completed the noisy days that went on until sunset.

Ships and brigantines increased the town's population, especially during celebrations. 1629 was the year they would commemorate the centenary of the Battle of March when the armies of Cortes faced thousands of Indians in nearby Centla. Spanish victory had given this town its name, setting it under the auspices of Mary, Virgin, and Mother. A re-enactment of the bloody struggle was improvised, and the rain of Indian arrows fell again, as brave Spaniards pretended to fight with real sabers, leaving the plaza full of fake fallen bodies. Performers then went on to receive coffers full of gifts, cocoa, and flowers the same way the defeated cacique Tabscob offered, recognizing the conquistadors' bravery and victory.

The performance ended when indulged winners pretended to receive a group of Indian slaves, just as had happened a hundred years ago when Malinche was given to Hernan Cortes. She was exactly a Chontal and bilingual as Pablo was. The luster of the armor, the damask hanging from the trees and the golden harnessed horses used for the annual re-enactment called people from the vicinities and the celebration preceded a bonfire that heralded the heat coming with the spring. And there, in the celebration, black slaves were side by side with the colonizers, theatrically representing the battle all over again.

Juan Garrido, a free Christianized black born in Africa, was the first slave to arrive with Cortes. As his faithful soldier, he advanced with the Spanish armies until the fall of the Mexica empire, and he told about these moments in his letter to the

King of Spain, claiming favours, land, titles, and justice for his participation.

> I, Juan Garrido, of black color, neighbor of this city, appear before His Majesty to present the proof in perpetuity for my services in the conquest and pacification of this New Spain in the times of Hernan Cortes, Marquis of the Valley, services I made at my own expense, without salary or assignment of Indians, none of those granted in exchange, neither for my services in the discovery of the islands of Puerto Rico, nor for the Californias in the ocean, in the Pacific, or for my participation in the discovery and conquest of the island of Cuba and Florida. Thirty years of my service have been rendered to His Majesty, and I will continue to serve my King, but after these reasons, I appeal to his kindness...

In the probative document, Garrido affirms that by his initiative, the first grains of wheat were planted by him in the New World. He used his black hands, he says, to remove the soil that nourished this crop before anyone in Coyoacan. The wonder of bread came to New Spain from the hands of a black slave, and Juan follows his allegations telling how, as hundreds of Africans did with their masters, he traveled all over the territory, up to the last corner to support the Conquest.

Three hundred more blacks would arrive as reinforcement to join Cortes in his expeditions, following the story of Esplandian, a fantasy of cavaliers, hidalgos, and explorers so popular in Spanish literature. Coming from wild Africa, their skills were extraordinarily useful, although ignored by the chroniclers of the time, who only briefly write about them. Slaves knew how to find fresh water, they endured the rigors of the climate, spent days starving, defended their masters with their own bodies, and deftly extinguished the fires Indians started in attempts to chase them away from their lands.

The anonymous bravery of slaves accompanied expeditions that reached the Andes, where they died of hunger, fever, and cold. They crossed the equator, the Salt Desert of Uyuni, and the Pampas, en route to Argentina. In some places, fugitives remained so isolated that they even invented their own languages. In New Granada, Palenquero was the language that interweaved ancient Portuguese with African words and phrases. Benkos Biohó from Guinea, escaping his master in Cartagena, led the Palenque de la Matuna, and after years of banditry, the Spanish Crown recognized the town giving it the title of Villa of Saint Basil, its Christianized name.

On no trip did conquerors go alone. Black and mulatto slaves went with the troops, started their fires and warmed their beds, both men and women, all using the surnames of their masters. Some others used their skin denominations to put in front of the name of a martyr or saint. According to their color, America became full of Damian Pardo (brown), Gaspar Moreno (brunette) or Vicente Prieto (dark). These names substituted Ewondo (beautiful men), Eyola (one who beats the ground), or Budé (the one who opens the way), their names in African languages.

Roads and crossings carried their voices, ways, and diseases. Smallpox arrived with Francisco de Eguia, a black slave of the Spanish militia, who spread death from Veracruz to Cempoala, Tepeaca, and Tlaxcala up to the very heart of New Spain. European and African strains infected millions of Indians without immunity and killed more people than Spanish swords. Unwittingly, newcomers brought measles and typhus. Cocoliztli and matlazahuatl were the names to identify the pustules that covered millions of indigenous bodies. Then rats multiplied mortality rates, doing more harm than the Holy Cross and the harquebus.

Processions of palms and the ornament of the Cross invoked the protection of the Divine Providence. During epidemics, nobody ventured more than two leagues from village boundaries, fearing contagion and escaped rebels lurking everywhere. Also, the plains out there were believed to be inhabited by the spirits. Near Lake Atasta, in the Chontal territory, escaped blacks had established a mocambo, a tiny community of maroons, hidden in the jungle and protected by surrounding lagoons and swamps.

The Ensenada de Negros, an inland bight, faced the sea, and indigineous slave hunters were afraid of venturing in to bring back the fugitives, despite the rewards, for fear that negroes were turned into those mythical spirits, haunting labyrinths of water.

Pablo was a teenager when his community was torn apart and forced to group according to the needs of the Captaincy. The encomiendas, or assignments of Indian workers, had been banned by royal decree of the Viceroyalty, but along the Gulf coasts, it was still valid. They used Indians to enforce the fighting against pirate raids. Young Pablo and his people were forced on a painful march towards Yucatan, while Spanish led his group throughght the jungle, fearing what they considered local savages of painted bodies and infernal cries.

People were made to leave their sacred gods, preserved in cotton shrouds, tutelary deities that looked after them, wrapped along with their most precious magical objects. Old women risked their lives to hide the figurines under their garments, fervently believing faith and prayers would one day set them free. Clay and stone housed the symbols of all the things they believed. They crossed rivers and waterfalls, crying as they left the wetlands that held the ashes of their beloved ancestors.

They were clever, but they were desperate, too. Four families with no tie other than language, mocked the escort that was taking them to San Francisco. They grabbed a couple of canoes during the night and ran like jaguars for the plains. Pablo's father, a member of the group of royal messengers, had taught him the network of white, cobbled roads built by the Mayans of these lands. They were family for them. He had memorized the map of all the sacbes, the roads, despite the jungle having already swallowed hundreds of them.

Pablo and the others ran all night furiously until they were out of sight and breath. Sun started to rise making the jungle a suffocating embrace. At daylight a girl noticed a tiny piece of the white road, invisible to inexpert eyes. Millions of slabs had been carefully arranged for hundreds of years to receive caravans and processions. Voices of pilgrims and traders, of women changing their residence to fulfill a matrimonial alliance, and captives of war, had used these roads for more than a millennium.

"Pateni, naach kuntabá ten!"; "Get away from me!", Pablo shouted.

He was in Mayan lands and respect for ancestors demanded he use that language. An ape shrieked from up the treetops, throwing fruits at the group, indifferent to his guilt, grief, and the uncertainty, stirring up in his heart. His young mother had fallen during the escape, and a soldier hurried to hold her while the rest managed to flee. He would never forgive himself for hesitating. The soldier's musket burst the orbit of the woman's right eye while Pablo, attending the respect he owed to his elders, chose to help the old ones, leaving his mother to her fate. In confusion, a black-skinned hand slid a handful of papers into Pablo's young hands. He would never forget those eyes.

The sacbe was now stained with his mother's blood, and although rainfall would wash away evidence of the incident, Pablo would never forget the place. This was also the spot where the heavens changed his surname through that bundle of documents the dark-skinned hand had given to him and linked his fate to a dubious nobility whose only privilege was to hold him free to row from the village to his hiding place without disturbance. The god in the sacred bundle told them they were approaching a safe place to settle. Or maybe it was only their wise, inner voice.

Surrounded by tall mounds of grass, unusual in the flat Mayan lands, these were all ruins of temples long gone. The kingdom of Acalan had been abandoned for years, devoured by the jungle, and now the remains of lost splendor would give them shelter.

They dedicated the site, burying the figurine gently. The beautiful and intricate carving was made on the same polished white stone that peeked through the dense roots of the Jabin tree. The god had talked to them through that inner voice they always heard and had shown them this was the best place. The perfume and the weight of the tree's crimson flowers had given the branches the shape of a perfect arch, a natural framing that hid the corner of a huge platform with plants crawling all over. Before the sky cried tears of pain and grief for these children of God, before any Spanish victory, there was the Lordship of Acalan Tixchel, one of the greatest cities north and south of the wetlands from Kaan Pech to Tabscoob, successors of the great Mayan cities of Palenque, Tikal, Uxmal and Bonampak.

Long ago these groups had made a pilgrimage to reach these flat lands of underground water and deep caves fed by the sea. They brought with them the tradition of black and red ink, metaphors that represented wisdom locked in their sacred writing, blessed icons painted in amate books, of sheets made with the bark of amate trees, that recorded the path stars follow and the rules for painting and ornamenting temples. Once in the flatlands they made alliances with the itzaes, the water sorcerers, who had built Chichen Itza until the mandate of the Gods, bad crops, and a widespread revolt made the founders return to Petén in Guatemala.

That is how great kingdoms fall. Subjugated peoples rise against the rulers, overpopulation leads to scarcity, and periodical droughts contribute to make it worse. But after the fall of the kingdom, survivors remain. Pablo, like the four fugitive families, spoke the language of the Putun, the language of the Chontalpa and the Nahuatl, the lingua franca that hides in its voices the spirit of the warrior nomads from the north.

> That is how great kingdoms fall. Subjugated peoples rise against the rulers, overpopulation leads to scarcity.

The last transparent drop of resin was burned to consecrate the site. They knew they would have to double their offerings to show how grateful they were for this opportunity to start again. They were the God's chosen ones, and from here on, they would repeat embellished sagas, full of metaphors, about the hardships they suffered, just as their ancestors had, leaving a land of abundance, cotton, and colored corn, to come to fight in the swampy marshes of the south. Stories were to ensure that they never forgot the courage of those who had guided them and broken their enemies into pieces like clay pots dropped on the ground. History is written but also verbal. Memory was preserved in the genealogies carved in walls or painted in codex. Those they left behind in their escape would tell their tale time and again.

They would never know about the thousands of bonfires that burned the books of their memories, of friars wisely serving the Lord, contemplating victorious flames burning those books of heresy. Everything they had learned from observing the universe and recorded in their books of knowledge, everything was gone.

Once settled, Pablo knew that he would risk his life to feed and protect his new family. He was the strongest, the leader. As soon as he could, he organized everyone. They built boats and those documents the black woman had slipped in his hands would be the key to bring all the staples the sacred gods and his people deserved: honey for rituals to bathe the consecrated place and the altar, jade for votive ornaments, and resins to burn and elevate prayers. Food was the least of their worries. They knew how to take care of themselves.

Transhumance ruled Pablo's life. Now that they were getting to Santa Maria de la Victoria, his instinct had told him of the profits he could get by reselling the feverish black woman as soon as she was healed. There was also the child. Someone would appreciate the curve of her hips, but that did not arouse any interest in him. He knew he had to separate them. He had noticed they seemed to understand one another. They spoke the same language. He tightened the small cotton bag with gold, his part from the sale of the twenty-three fugitives, around his waist, looking to those other brothers, Indians like him, who had joined the group on the way. Their bodies were all anointed in propitiatory colors, purified by the rites they celebrated in the jungle, those that demands red, white, black and yellow covering up the last patch of bare skin.

Rosario calculated that the four shades the Indians spread over their bodies would stand out even more in her own dark skin and she wondered if those in Pablo's group would ask the child and herself to paint their bodies too. In her village, only the fortune teller wore colors on his body; women were only allowed to use white. A chill anticipated the fever coming back. She confused the silhouette of Pablo with the young men of her tribe, dancing in shiny red around the fire to impress maidens. That was the last image she kept of her people the night slavers scorched her town.

Pablo, dancing in her delirious mind, was now puncturing his left ear with the spine of a stingray and his blood was dripping onto a piece of amate paper. The paper was burning, and the prayers gone up in smoke would please the protective spirit of the swamps. They wanted to finish the business of selling these last slaves so they could return. In their hidden village, hunger was imminent; harvest had been scarce. Fishing and hunting would do, but the barn was empty. A decade away from the night the four families had run away, their community had grown, receiving others, fugitives like them, and shortage was now a problem to deal with.

Across the lagoons, Santa María de la Victoria was preparing to face the hurricanes. They were tired of fighting storms and destruction, and their thousand inhabitants began to look at San Juan Bautista de la Villa Hermosa as an alternative residence. If the Spanish had had the knowledge Pablo had, perhaps they would have fantasized about moving the village to the healthy temperate climate of Santiago de los Caballeros in the Province of Guatemala, belonging to the Audiencia de los Confines.

With an overcast sky, natives and black servitude at Santa María were all equal to fight adversity. By decree, blacks and mulattoes were forbidden to meet in groups when the sun set. The Spaniards feared their number, greater than their own, and revolts and conspiracies had intensified the always insufficient surveillance. But under the cover of darkness, anything could happen.

Alcohol gave the elders courage to break the rules and congregate in the cool of the night. They told stories in front of a small fire they extinguished intermittently to scare mosquitoes away. They had nothing left to lose. Those from Africa had tales of wreckages and storms during their journeys to America, coming from different factories. Those from Spain, forced to be

Christianized, had ended up embracing faith and, in imitation of the Spaniards, performed all the rites religion dictated. They were granted permission to organize themselves into a brotherhood, under the name of Saint Mary the Virgin, as they did in the Peninsula, and they loved to compare and describe how great and lustrous was the procession of the Brotherhood of Negros of the Christ of Foundation in Seville.

By the light of the fire, their perfectly white teeth gleamed when describing the unparalleled finery they had seen in churches and cathedrals beyond the sea. Only black slaves could head the procession, competing in the number of lashes their backs could resist in mortification, in imitation of the suffering of Christ.

Flagellants displayed the trickles of blood that ran through the wounds of their naked torsos in proud penance and musicians chanted funeral marches that encouraged respect and silence. Their bodies enjoyed the cadence of the instruments and fought to suppress the jumps and pirouettes that naturally electrified their arms and thighs. Their feet had walked the monumental central nave of the Cathedral of Seville right before being brought to America. They had seen the world. Their chopped Spanish described all these marvels, and they looked at the locals with disdain, brutes coming directly from Afri, they said, the wildland. They felt superior and tried to spice up their stories up with details while the rest listened enraptured. They talked about altars embroidered in gold and jewels, built for the glory of God Our Lord while the Spanish Court accompanied all religious celebrations with black choirs who sang with voices of angels in the choir loft.

Here, at miles of distance, fortifications and buildings at the Peninsula grew in splendor. These were truly organized ports, they said, and not this imitation of a dock of Santa María, that despite its activity, was incomparable to the effervescence of true Spanish commerce, the first power to discover and own this New World.

The Guadalquivir River was a delight to see, the shores packed with thousands of merchants doing business in all languages. Hundreds of strong blacks, as powerful as they had been themselves in their youth, sweated and whistled to the distant beat of the music from the gypsy neighbourhood of Triana while loading and unloading a thousand ships. Their melody was one the authorities tolerated until the merriment seemed to get out of control and their swords silenced the uproar.

The Almighty God of these black brotherhoods may not have been the God everyone worshipped. Some of the empires of mother Africa that surrounded the Portuguese possessions of Guinea had been converted to Islam, six centuries before the arrival of Portuguese Christian navigators. Allah had come with the caravans of Berbers, the merchants of the north, who occupied Morocco, Algeria, and Tunisia, and through the groups that crossed the Sahel belt, from Sudan to Senegal. Islam had expanded all over, and when Moors were expelled from the Spanish Peninsula with the Reconquista, they advanced steadily, splendidly, towards the extreme east of Europe, along with the armies of the Ottoman Turks.

With exalted spirits, old blacks competed in fabulous stories about the places their eyes had seen. They highlighted the qualities of gold and textiles wrapping the bodies of abundant women and wives of the boss in turn. They pondered the splendor of the bell tower of Seville, a former Moor mosque minaret, and compared the luxury of tapestries, of flowers and woven foliage and incomprehensible signs, which extolled the glory of Allah in the curves of Arabic calligraphy.

Djenné, beyond the plains of the Bani River, was the temple chief Kuburu had built, prostrated before Allah revelation. He chose to demolish his palace to build a mosque and dedicated his life and his kingdom to Allah-u-Akbar. Muezzins in charge of calling to prayer from their towers of solid gold were imitated by these old blacks at Santa María, while alcohol turned their tales more and more unbelievable. Then some in the circle expressed their audacious hope of making the mythical journey to Mecca, according to the mandate of their faith, disdaining the ocean as an obstacle in the middle of their wishes.

Allah was still inflaming their hearts, they carried his mercy in the most distant corners of their minds and here they could not help but pretend to adore the images of the God of the Spaniards. When someone tried to pronounce a couple of suras, those passages of the Koran, their Holy Book, the meeting by the fire ended, with some of them crossing themselves, bringing the flames to ashes immediately. Words burned away, and no one would even mention the conversation of the night before.

Pablo was crossing the last lagoon, his eyes fixed on the shining of a distant fire. They stopped to get into the water and rub their bodies with grass to erase the paintings of their bodies. He advanced, cautiously, just to make sure it was safe to go ashore. There, in the first shacks, he saw Adouma's black face and white smile, presiding over the small bonfire. There had been many nights when Pablo had listened to Adouma's stories, until he dragged the old man inside the hut, while the vapors of liquor brought incomprehensible words to his mouth.

There on the mat, Adouma had found a restless sleep and Pablo had wondered how many spirits were crossing the mind of this immense body. Adouma dreamed of forgotten battles, Islamic warfare, faith, and piety. So many battles had his sword known against the Tuareg, the Toubou of the north and the Bulala of the east. At the command of his army, he was convinced that it was his duty to purify and convince infidels and his valiant soldiers to accept Allah. Trained by the Turks, he had already set the Hausa region, under their command. Only the Sahara had stopped the advance of their troops, and people were embracing Allah but not leaving the offerings they owed to the gods of the forest and the savanna.

This night, in the darkness, Pablo quietly slipped down until he sat next to Adouma, Miguel for his practical, christianized life in the Villa. As soon as Miguel saw him, his mouth drew a huge smile, showing a row of bright pearls that neither the lack of hygiene nor the privations had tarnished. They hugged each other and Pablo knew Miguel would feed and shelter the group a couple of days there while he ended his business.

Rosario and the child, Lucia, remained a few steps behind the bonfire, waiting along with the group. Rosario had received a dose of medicine in the boat and rumors of voices in a foreign language were heard when they reached the river banks. If in Hausa, she thought in her fever, she would have told about the horror of invasions, when Mohammed was a strange name, difficult to pronounce. The neighbouring Yoruba already talked about the prophet, while the elders in her town struggled to preserve old beliefs and teachings, fearing that betrayal of their ancestral cults stopped the rain or took the borders of the rivers out of control, flooding the village. Before she was named Rosario, her native village resisted the onslaught of new beliefs and dust at the crossroads was raised by the feet of pilgrims towards Mecca.

She had heard of the softness of silky prayer mats and perfumes behind walls and with these religions embraced by all, everywhere, she even doubted of the effectiveness of the daily water offering to the spirits her village worshipped. For her family, the name of the prophet symbolized clashes, plundering, and doubts, deities witnessing mass conversions in rage that gained these children of God for Allah, the protector, the Almighty.

Miguel looked up to see more and more Indians coming out of the shadows. Everyone would spend the night here. He burned cloves of garlic they anointed on their arms and legs to protect themselves from mosquitoes, and Rosario felt Pablo's gaze on her firm thighs when she raised the shred of cloth she had wrapped around her body with African mastery. She put the garlic past on Lucia too and they were all told where to sleep. Briefly, no more human noise was heard in the world. Fever and lack of food had left Rosario without strength. They slept for hours, despite the fuss of the jungle. When she opened her eyes, the near smell of the sea made her realize the day before had not been a dream. By now, hers and the child's were the only dry lips and sweaty bodies left. The rest of the group was gone. During the night, Lucia had rolled next to her, and now she was crying, her arms swollen by the attack of mosquitoes the garlic paste had not reached to cover.

She now clearly remembered the boats and the Indians, painted, but they had all disappeared. Miguel seemed to sense they were waking up and brought two clay jugs of a sweetened infusion, mumbling curses in Castilian, none of them understood. Lucia, the child, drank with her eyes closed, scratching her arms with fury, while tears ran down her lips. At the call of Miguel, a skinny black teenager appeared and guided them to the river bank, where the delta met the sea in swirls. The water stream took the shred of cloth away, while a pair of rough blouses awaited on the stones. Lucia's was too big, and Rosario looked for a fibrous branch to tie it like a belt around her waist. She spread the juice of its leaves on the mosquito bites and both sat on the stones to wait.

They knew Miguel was watching over them, fanning himself up inside the hut. The ruined skin of the chair threatened to break under his weight, and they heard him calling to come in. Women of the neighborhood would come for water as every morning, and he wanted to save unnecessary explanations. Inside, the sun filtered through the palm roof, revealing the rough wood of the building. Two smoldering wrappings, cooked, filled the room with their aroma. Rosario ceremoniously unwrapped the food and devoured it slowly. Lucia pricked the contents with her fingers and ate too, tearing huge pieces.

With each bite, Rosario felt she could not hold the tears anymore. The slits of the hut showed all the green of the surroundings and hanging branches, like festoons, and it all took her back to her village for a moment. Uncontrollable tears rolled down her cheeks and uncertainty mixed with the food, rendered a taste of sorghum. The food of the village! Women singing, and cooking returned to her mind and Lucia should have recognized the taste too. Not knowing what else to do, she and Lucia smiled and repeated in a single voice, "Dadi!"; "Delicious!".

Miguel opened his eyes wide when he heard that word. It was true, the food had an incomparable flavor, but all the accents and music of his language were encompassed in that adjective. *Dadi* was a Hausa word. They shared the same language under this blazing sun!

Water and birds announced that the group of Indians was back. Pablo got in first and exchanged some hasty phrases with Miguel in Spanish. They would leave the child until the shapes of her body got a better price. Meanwhile, she would be like the orphans in the village, a swarm of mulattos and blacks, running around the neighborhood. If he accepted to look after her, his authority as an elder would keep questions at bay and the girl could serve him in many tasks while he raised her.

Miguel nodded, and Pablo made Rosario follow him, while promising he would be back at night, and there Rosario went, without understanding why the child was not joining. He would try to sell the black woman and half of the Spanish money would feed little Lucia for some months. Miguel's frown showed it would be way too expensive to raise this child. At nightfall, Pablo would take his people back to the water labyrinths. Rosario followed Pablo through the streets. They went to the inn, the winery, and the dock, in vain. Nobody would buy Rosario. The Spanish Crown had reinforced the prohibition to sell slaves individually, to combat tax evasion. The sheriff would enforce the law for a few weeks only to relax it a bit afterwards. Pablo urgently wanted to sell Rosario, as he feared that the rash on her palms and the ulcer on her thigh were symptoms of the disease that had taken his wife. The Gallic disease. Filibusters included the virtue of Indian women as their loot, and the venereal evil had taken her body in a few months.

Rosario was a few steps behind and this was Pablo's last attempt to sell. The scandal of placing a black woman with syphillis was not worth exchanging for the stealth of years he had enjoyed moving free, along the routes. Perhaps the elders in Acalan would know of the right herbs to cure her. The pustule would produce a scar that would make any buyer cry foul. He judged it better to leave and come back, after the rains, to try to complete the transaction again.

A Spaniard, in a ragged cloak, absurd in the tropical heat, would be his last attempt. The tone of their voices had Rosario in awe. Words are almighty, and she was now aware of the power of language. If she had stayed in the hut for the day, she would have shared Miguel's amazement with Lucia, the child, and her words in Hausa; the bliss a single familiar phrase might unleash is like a spell. Silence had followed Rosario since her capture. In Elmina, no one else understood her language and the dark well of being isolated was deeper with each throng of threats the slavers uttered in Portuguese, which was to her the language of fear.

The man in the cloak spat and walked away, while the sun of Santa Maria dyed the defeated spirit of Pablo in red. He pulled the black woman by the arm, hurting her. Rosario, without understanding anything, gave him the same look as had the black woman who had handed him the papers, the night he and his people ran away. The contact with her skin unleashed in his heart all the colors of the sky.

In the meantime, the shore of the Grijalva sheltered a bunch of kids. Watching Lucia from the height of his hut, Miguel had his head full of questions. In all these years he had never heard his language. Knowing they could understand each other was bringing back his childhood from a buried oblivion.

The survival instinct forced him to shut up. Slaves, even freedmen, were forbidden to speak their languages. He knew of negroes who had seen their tongues cut to avoid complicity. But nostalgia was making him bold. He was a huge man with a couple of syllables in his heart looking for the right moment to shout, like the mothers in his village did, "Lucia, gani!"; "Lucia, come!"

> **The contact with her skin unleashed in his heart all the colors of the sky.**

He wanted to scream out remembrance, too.

"Lucia, come! Look at me! Kill this pain in my soul and convince me that you are not the daughter that I lost, the one they took from my arms on the bridge to the slave ship. Your words, Lucia, had released the shackle from my memories, and now all that love I had sent to the bottom of grief, stranded, is here, back. And for Allah, how painful it is and how hurting!"

In the hut, bundles of grass waited. Dried in the sun and piled up, the fiber was ready to stretch and be woven. Lucia was not the daughter the captors had pulled out of his arms, but only a couple of extra hands for rope making to pay for her meals. Markets demanded all lengths and thickness the black neighborhood might produce and even Pablo took several bundles with him to use as currency.

When Lucia finally got to the shack, Miguel observed her as if she was a precious gift. A couple of words more and there would be no doubt. If the girl was older, he could even question her about his tribe and his people, but he had to be careful. Language sneaks through the cracks of wooden walls and goes flying to the House of Council. The Mayor needed little provocation to order floggings in the square for bored audiences. He and Lucia would weave until their hands reddened, until the girl dominated the craft. He would try to forget the thirst, the longing for that liquor that burns throats and memories more than the sun of Santa Maria, more than the bonfire of remembrance.

That word in Hausa had brought the smell of the red soil in Africa and the satisfaction of the battles he had fought. But what we remember cannot be selected. That is the price of bringing back the past. Hausa language unlocked the bleeding wounds and the steel blades, the dungeons, the loss, the capture, and the misery. He tried to kill the thoughts of years in servitude, up to the moment when he learned of the wish of his master:

"It is my will that my slave, baptized Miguel, recovers his freedom and from now on he is able to do as he pleases."

When that happened, the dream of all slaves, he was old, way too old. He had nowhere to go, so he did as all do. He stayed in Santa María.

Strings of fiber twisted by his old fingers, worked tirelessly to avoid the moment when darkness covers the guilt of drowning the last years of a life of distress and suffering in alcohol.

Lucia received brief instructions in Hausa that she understood without showing surprise and even answered questions briefly. That night, he knew he would be sober. The sound of the village and the scent of love would intoxicate him more than any liquor.

Pablo's rafts were nearby, and Indians had loaded them with farming implements and knives all throughout the day. She was not allowed to even say good bye to the child. Well hidden by the reeds, Rosario and the Indians waited. An effigy of basalt, covered with flowers, presided with majesty the prow, while the moon, in a smile, reflected approval. Instructions in Spanish were completed. Pablo left a bottle of alcohol on the table along with the money and did not even turn to see little Lucia, who was now sleeping, exhausted. They carried the rope to the boats and the candle that Miguel lit shed a few small teardrops of wax. Pablo crossed the threshold and went down the four steps in silence. They headed for the marshes that Rosario was now seeing with new eyes. After two days of potions, she was free of fever.

The dark water of this stream was like that of the Kwara river, in her hometown, where the spirits float in whirlpools and springs, hiding in the shape of a frog or a lizard. The journey had made her understand that there were much more terrifying spirits. The worst demons the river had brought were the slavers, who were said to devour people, separating them from their families. She now knew this was the place for all of those taken. She deemed absurd to have feared the subtle vapors of the Kwara. She had already defeated the greatest waters she had ever imagined. She had escaped from the embrace of death and had bathed her body in peaceful shores, far from the dungeon, the whips, and the curses in incomprehensible Portuguese, an ocean in between.

They sailed the night away, and at dawn they saw the outlines of polished white stone poking through the underbrush. The hillside offered a multitude of ghostly buildings, buried under the bush of the jungle, preserving fabulous interior walls of paintings and carved masks. Only the Indians knew these places. They docked by the reeds and carried the cargo down the white road. They had delayed their return for days, and the elders would surely have consulted the omens, alarmed, looking for reasons to explain. Rosario opened her eyes, walking gracefully in the darkness, eyes trained to be alert, without losing detail.

When the cloud disappeared, the huge masses of stone that flanked the settlement shone in the moonlight. She remembered the stories of the giants, who had inhabited her village in the past. She could almost touch the colossal femur found in the sands, which received the offerings of her people. They entered the first shady hut, barely lit by a tiny beeswax candle. It was by then that Pablo's grandmother could see her up close. A scream of fear took the old woman's strength away. Pablo was here with a dark spectrum. Was she the woman of the documents? Rosario was black like the fringe that bordered the eyes of the god of the occult, the smoky mirror that turns things visible to men. Such was the god who presided their destiny.

Like a presage, a flock of toucans as black as Rosario crossed the treetops announcing the dawn on the white sand of the Gulf, among the ruins of everything that has ever existed there.

CHAPTER 4
THE JOURNEY FROM THE KINGDOM OF SPAIN 1629

"Open my door once again. Come and rebuild what is broken. Tired of waiting for your letters, my eyes are fixed on the sea, beyond its western end to where you are.

Here, the buds that bloomed after your departure are gone, giving way to autumn. No news from you at all. March is here again, and waters are warming up, after a year. A whole year. And here I am, writing to you one more time, from this silver reflection on waters that keep me from following your tracks, your footprints gone where the sand took away your beloved shadow.

Father says that in a few weeks we will receive your letter. We are all ready to head for the House of the Ocean. The Rojas and Burgos families will leave next year, as you might know now, and together, with them as my companions, we will get license to cross to the Indies. Their favor will take care of me and my belongings, and I am sure you will find their friendship of assistance, even if you do not know them yet.

Father has set aside the amount he discussed with you to pay for my trip, and he has partially paid for the services of Don Emilio Rojas. The funds have stimulated his kindness greatly, and you know that as soon as we receive your instructions, he will take me to Don Leonel de Cervantes, merchant agent of great fame in Seville, and to take care of the rest, as needed.

Father insists I must be patient, that soon we will hear about you, of the goodness of your contacts and advances in the business, and that it is very possible there will be a place for me on the "Immaculate Heart of Mary," the passenger vessel to the Indies next year. He is confident you will be generous and that there will even be an amount waiting for me upon my arrival at the Royal Customs Office in the port of Veracruz. Father is writing about all this, in a separate letter, as always to accompany mine.

Don Emilio has agreed to receive the other half of his payment in gold when I get there, and both have signed the commitment before a Notary. It is a great responsibility to protect my virtue and possessions during the voyage and we have agreed to reward him generously. I can tell this agreement weighs heavily in Father's pocket, but I trust that when we meet, the fortune the Indies have reserved for us will bless his personal estate to reimburse those debts in full, since it is for our own good, yours and mine, that he is contracting them.

Weeks gone are taking your face away from my memories, Alonso, and at the time of Lauds, to start the day, I pray Our Lady, Mary the Virgin, that you are healthy and in the best shape. I pray also that our God, Almighty Father, great and sovereign, who has summits and mountains in His hands, keep your forehead high to receive my kiss and blessing as soon as I see you again.

May God keep you for long years for my consolation. My heart melts in torments, wishing for the day when I will finally set foot on those kingdoms to begin the pleasant and happy life that we promised ourselves.

Loving you dearly, Mariana.

• • •

We committed your interest and my honor one morning of March when it finally seemed that my destiny would change. When I was born in the year of 1605 of Our Lord, lady fortune seemed to turn her back on Father's commercial businesses, and with the shadow of their firstborn, a boy, deceased at an early age, melancholy occupied every corner of the old house where I took my first steps. Inherited by Mother, the house was the dowry Father had received, a dozen streets away from the blue river, the Guadalquivir, in the main port of Seville, the only one authorized to send goods through the Mediterranean that were shipped to the American colonies by Spain.

Philip III, King of Castile and Aragon, Portugal, Naples, Sicily, Sardinia, the East and the West Indies and Flanders, was a monarch who preferred hunting to governing.

> Open my door once again. Come and rebuild what is broken.

The indebted Royal Treasury issued titles of public debt to finance the Court's splendor, along with the exploitation of nearly each existent industry. Licenses to export agricultural products to the Americas were the most common source of income, since the Royal Tax Remittances that arrived with the Indian Fleet were not enough for a Royal Treasury always in a precarious situation. Evasion was an everyday affair.

Father's business had always been to place the bonanza of the Sevillian harvesters in the Fleet. He was an expert at negotiating with the owners of olive groves in Aljarafe and Alcala, who sent half their wine and liquor production, and almost all their olive oil, to the Americas. A third of each vessel was reserved for Sevillian products.

Reaching the river to witness how the vessels sailed on their way to the sea was Father's pride. From our region barrels of oil and wine had left the docks since the Roman Empire dominated Hispania and when the Moors were expelled from the Peninsula and the collection of their taxes, paid to Rome or the Arabs, ceased, the guild of oil and olives was even more exclusive, since their fields and agriculture passed again into the hands of Spanish families. Olive oil of four qualities, to garnish luxurious banquet tables, to burn and light residences, or to make soap, arrived at the ports of Veracruz, Havana and Cartagena twice each year. The oils carried the soul of southern Spain and the funds from its sale relieved the expenses from the endless wars the Empire fought against France or England, to subdue Flanders or to stop the advance of Protestant Lutherans.

Since he ascended the throne, Philip III had left the government to the whims of the Duke of Lerma, a gentleman heavily in debt. The government was *de facto* ruled by the Duke, who moved the seat of the court to Valladolid, where complaints and requests for trade were even slower to be heard and attended to. The taxes on the shipped goods had increased exponentially and adding the cost of a transatlantic trip resulted in absurd prices for the American colonies.

Oil production had been prohibited outside the Peninsula, and the government was more occupied speculating with land, granting titles and preferences for a sum in gold, than with enforcing the laws. So it was for twenty years, until the Duke, before falling into disgrace, paid for the crimson cardinal's hat, which allowed him to withdraw from public life. To avoid hanging, the biggest thief in Spain dressed in pontiff red.

Father had foreseen that with the expected death of Philip III and with no one in charge, business would only worsen. In New Spain, the Jesuit Order was beginning to plant olive trees, and American merchants were already buying from them not only the finest oil, but also the lower quality one they used to light the lamps that illuminated Viceroyalties all over the

European continent. For Sevillian harvesters, it was impossible to compete with American prices, yet they had to maintain the appearance of a solvent life. There were years in which orders were so scarce and the Crown took months to endorse necessary certificates and permits, that Father's back bent more and more with the weight of uncertainty.

The grief that began with the death of his beloved firstborn was aggravated by the threat of bankruptcy. He spent entire days absent, in meetings presided over by the guild representing the interests of the oil and olives business, formulating lawsuits, and writing long letters to His Majesty with bitter complaints against the traitorous Jesuit harvests that flourished in American lands despite prohibition. The letters dealt tactfully with everything related to customs and local taxes, but the guild's fury went beyond, detailing how the Jesuit Order had taken over even the grinding of the olives, building mills for a business that belonged only to Andalusia.

In adoration of the Blessed Sacrament, every tabernacle should be illuminated day and night. Six arrobas of oil a year, multiplied by the growing number of temples and convents that continued to open like fires to the glory of God, had been all the fortune of the guild for the previous century. Father continued to negotiate local transactions in the brand-new Lonja de Mercaderes de Sevilla building, the Council of Merchants, but those amounts were nothing compared to overseas demand. Conversations ended up cursing intermediaries who shipped cargoes to the Indies and how they pocketed the profits.

Olive bushes had been sent to the New World in an attempt to adapt them to the different climate, but there was no intention to supplant the Peninsula production; the blessed, fertile Antilles lands began bearing fruit abundantly and from there they had reached New Spain, going south to Río de la Plata, and locals looked positively at the self-sufficiency. The exchanges among the Viceroyalties was very successful and from Callao, in Peru, goods were being sent back and forth from Acapulco to Huatulco. Hundreds of blacks, paid with silver from the Potosi mines, were busy loading and unloading dozens of ships, much to the chagrin of the Spanish monopoly.

All this news took years for the King to receive and decide. The Jesuits were favourites of God, being blessed with the lands they owned. Precise calculations backed their wise administration, and many letters had been sent, asking the court to avoid imposing such burdensome charges on their faithful vassals of the Viceroyalties. Production, as planned and managed by them, was easily supplying American demands. Oil was a dressing but was also used for the consecration of the King, to anoint the sick and for their Extreme Unction, as chrism for baptism and for the three ministerial orders of bishop, priest and deacon. Oil from the olive's fruit produced the light that shone at the feet of saints and virgins, was a blessed remedy for wounds after it had burned in the temple, infused with the power of Jesus and preserved in copper lamps to be healed by His Intervention.

Back from the shed that the guild had on the docks, Father directed his prayers to the heavens. When crossing the shipyards, the scent of orange blossom and the stone wall that protected the city were left behind with his hopes, until one day, sent by Providence, the blond countenance of Alonso García de Santamaria appeared on his way. Alonso's ancestors had been converted to Christianity a century before, and the shadow of Jewish blood sometimes weighed on him. Four generations prior, Selemoh-Ha Levi, Pablo de Santamaria after conversion, was ordained a priest, forging a distinguished career in the ecclesial hierarchy, until he was named His Excellency Bishop of Burgos. Biblical commentator and adviser of nobility, historian and scholar, he was a Santamaria, like Alonso, his ancestor, in fact, with blessed Mary in the surname, but bearing the accusation of being born from those who had stuck Jesus on the cross.

The Santamaria family had seen, as had Father, days of better fortune. The funds trading in the Jewish quarter had taken them to a high position, but because they had embraced Christianity in order that they needn't leave the Spanish lands with the Edict of Expulsion, they rejected luxury for a reward in heaven. Asceticism separated them from earthly riches and his ancestors' testaments left all their worldly goods to a Christian chaplaincy for the benefit of the poor. With empty pockets but infected with the fever of making a home across the ocean, Alonso surrendered to the frenzy of looking for a way to travel to the New World.

The galleons back from the Indies and the letters read aloud by the neighbors, detailing the good star of their emigrant relatives, moved Alonso's adventurous spirit. He tried by all means to make the journey. He had obtained the letters of recommendation that the University of Mareantes of Seville, the school for sailors, required to accommodate orphans who wished to make a career in the merchant navy. With pain, Alonso learned that places were assigned, but not to any orphan. Alonso was not the bastard son of any rich merchant, authority or friar of any order. Any letter that would have given an account of his virtues, without a verbal endorsement in his favor, or a noble lineage that was not supported by an economic arrangement, would be unsuccessful.

University protected navigation to the Indies and regulated the actions of pilots and masters, but enrolled relatives and friends only, and also illustrious orphans, by an arranged pious exception. But that did not defeat Alonso. He had his mind fixed on the trip and after months of wandering on the docks, of whole evenings spent in conversation with the river outside the walls, he finally accepted that he could only aspire to travel without shields and honors.

Alonso gathered the cost of his passage while daily crossing in front the Tower of Gold to work the docks and he devoted his cause and devotion to San Ferdinand, Knight of Jesus Christ to protect his savings. Had San Ferdinand not he defeated the Moors with an emerald and ruby sword? He would then grant Alonso territories beyond Al-Andalus, beyond Spain, someday.

As sent by the Saint, fortune showed up in the figure of Don Bernardo de Salazar y Couto, father of Mariana de Salazar y Miranda. This daughter of his had been rejected as a postulant to profess with the Poor Clarisses of Santa Inés. He had planned to offer his daughter in marriage with Our Lord and profess in a convent for a life of prayers that would return the family's fortune. Don Bernardo was sure that dedicating his daughter's life to the cloister that had hidden the martyr Doña María Coronel was his best chance for the Lord to hear his humble requests.

A century ago, Doña María, fleeing the harassment of King Pedro I of Castile, The Cruel, burned her beautiful face and much desired breast in boiling oil so as not to be unfaithful to her beloved husband. She wanted the sores to make her look like a leper. The legend claims that years after her death, the almost forgotten intact remains of Dona Maria were discovered in the convent. Her uncorrupted body, exposed, touched the faith of Sevillian society. Twisted and deformed, she was found wrapped in the humble dark Franciscan habit, smelling of holiness. The vision of the nun, her grimace haunting Don Bernardo's nightmares, proved to him that any required sacrifice by his daughter was worth it.

When problems in the oil industry worsened and Father, desperate, had exhausted his prayers to all possible invocations, he remembered the story of the boiling oil that saved Doña María from opprobrium. The oil had granted her purification, and by her intermediation, it would restore luck to him. He would give his daughter Mariana to the Poor Clarisses. It had to be her, since Concepción, his eldest, had already married a skipper from the north. But entering the convent requires a dowry, which he did not have. Don Bernardo prostrated himself and begged. A servant for the convent she would be! A cook to feed the poor and those in confinement and contemplation. Let others became abbesses, administrators or teachers. Mariana would be the humblest servant.

Rejection was the last failure Don Bernardo could bear. He could not tell society Mariana had been denied the heavenly favor because his apparent fortune was none. Noble friends and acquaintancies would not have Sister Mariana in her prayers to gain glory for them. This event turned his faith into bitterness. Who would pray as close to the Lord as a nun for his luck to return? His harsh heart blamed Mariana for everything. Her presence in the house was one more sign that her father's days were marked by misfortune and, now that even the sky had turned its back on him, he could only expect misery.

By then, walking through the shipyards, leaving the storage of oil behind, Don Bernardo met Alonso and saw the gallantry that his steps radiated, despite the labor of loading and stowing all day long. The brightness of Alonso's eyes gave him security to plot a plan. Alonso was beautiful, indeed, leaning on a worm-eaten wood fence, resting after his tasks, sweaty and dirty. Alonso looked out at the horizon, making plans for America now that he had the money ready, with his bundle of letters of recommendation still stuck to his chest.

Bureaucracy turned a deaf ear to the demands of the oil guild, and the outpouring of blessings the man had hoped to receive with his daughter in the convent had dissipated. Since then, he had mentally planned how to smuggle oil barrels to America as contraband. The threat of imprisonment was a strong deterrent, but so many did exactly the same. Wine was the most dangerous cargo to smuggle... All he needed was a man who had his complete trust.

In his musings, Don Bernardo concluded that only an emissary could explore the possibility of placing illegal oil there in the Indies, eliminating intermediaries and bribing authorities. He would be responsible for arranging the shipments from Sanlucar de Barrameda and with a safe route he could even diversify the contents of the shipments. Commercial agents made fortunes with smugglery, money that cared for their children and their children's children. Families with only women had their sons-in-law to continue the enterprise, and the circle of alliances crossed the ocean.

Perhaps the good looks of a good groom for Mariana would make it possible. Alonso's blue eyes and his determination to travel to the Indies gave Don Bernardo hope when he had almost lost it. Opportunity was available for both, he realized, unfolding like the petals of a rose. They spoke briefly, and Alonso assured Don Bernardo that he was the one who could help him. With a renewed spark in his eyes, the old man calculated that Alonso's eloquence and charm could make it in any enterprise beyond the sea.

The men shared secrets while smoking tobacco and it was discovered that Alonso's satchel with his little treasure would not be enough for the transatlantic trip. In addition to the money, there was another main impediment that Alonso was finding it difficult to overcome. Old and without any interest in undertaking further adventures, Don Bernardo had almost forgotten the Edict, which Alonso had memorized, spinning around it every day, looking for ways to avoid it. Specifically, the Crown did not permit any person to pass to the Indies, without being married according to the order of the Holy Mother Church. Not without a wife.

Don Bernardo's eldest was already married, but of course, Mariana was available. Under the full moon, the oil trader assured Alonso there was no other candidate interested, and of course, they could talk about marriage.

Having a daughter rejected by the convent for lack of dowry had already called into question the Salazar's fortune. A wedding with a dazzling stranger and a hasty exit to the Indies would bring suspicion of a hidden pregnancy. They had to fight the opprobrium, especially with the creditors and distinguished friends, a possible source of financing. Don Bernardo hatched the whole plan in his mind and invited the young man to dinner a few days later. Alonso would travel in the fleet and Mariana would wait for the following year's ship to join her fiancé in the Port of Veracruz. That would provide Alonso a year to start a buoyant commercial career and to make the most of the family's name.

A year later, Mariana would go to America at the call of her fiancé. Twelve months would be enough to confirm the chasteness of their union, freeing her from any suspicion on her virtue. As for Alonso, once he had a place and the first shipment was arranged, he would receive advanced payments and along with them his first salary. He could get a thousand clients for the finest oil, the one coveted by clerics and counts, which Don Bernardo knew how to supply.

The first cold press of the olives would distill the best oil from the fields of Spain that Alonso would sell. They would arrange loans for the voyages as needed. The Villa Rica de la Verdadera Cruz, the village of the True Cross, would be the setting for a modest wedding. Once Don Bernardo and young Alonso arranged the deal, the young man began to frequent the house almost daily. A few weeks later, the family sealed the engagement in the presence of Friar Antonio Carrascal, vicar prelate of Seville, in the living room facing the stars over Triana.

That night, Mariana wore her only lace outfit, worthy of an event of such magnitude, perfumed by the box of orange wood. The only words of approval her Mother pronounced were to praise the dress that fitted her fine figure so well. The pink velvet ribbon of the neckline discreetly encircled her beautiful bust while yards of lace gauze came down to her thighs, in hundreds of folds that veiled her skin. There was nothing like the lace of Bruges to disguise the gifts a groom would receive on their wedding night. There was nothing like business relations to exchange some vessels of oil for such a beautiful dress to adorn dazzling Mariana, the consort. She spent only a few minutes in front of Alonso, feeling his breath when her father introduced him, to be forever under his spell. He had the profile of an angel, distant and indifferent, and the glare of blue water in his eyes would be engraved in her adolescent memories for a lifetime. There was nothing more that any maid would ask for than to look into his eyes of blue, saying yes to becoming his wife before God. That was how the simple thread of an instant weaved infinite imaginary moments at his side, for months, sighing for his hands on her shoulders, while marking the calendar with a piece of coal to count the days until they met again.

Alonso had attended to the formalities; however, he was full of curiosity and thankful for this fortuitous promise, coming from the will of Saint Ferdinand for sure. Once in the Indies, he would figure out how to fulfill it. Friar Antonio Carrascal, without a single gray hair despite his age, controlled some mercantile wills in Seville, and in his position as confessor of the Marquise of Guadalcazar, he was a magnificent contact to unlock any obstacle blocking the oil business. His great figure used to walk on the other side of the river, without wearing the religious habit, and rumor had it that more than one black woman from the outskirts had received forgiveness from his lips. While presentations were made and deadlines and promises were fixed, Alonso's mind was already in the Indies, knocking on the doors of some Count's mansion, received with honors by liveried servants, who barely blinked under the lights of chandeliers, their gold buttoning and ponytail peeking out from a peak of their hat.

Now a year has gone, already.

> [...] come, open my door, reconstruct the collapse of my mind, gift and good of my eyes, that look for yours, that I have only seen a few times. I am all tears and sighs and do not dream of anything else but a life at your side."

> [...] "Let me know of your plans, of your whereabouts, a letter or a word given to those who return to Spain would be enough. That ship took the scent of your clothes away in the salt of the ocean, leaving my soul restless. More than a year without any news! Father reeled his patience next to mine and returned from the guild headquarters late and in a bad shape, hiding the questions nobody in this house dared to ask: Did you get there safe and sound, Alonso? Will you ever write? Will you ever fulfill your promises?

> I long for your answers your news, in the noble and loyal city of Seville ..."

• • •

Letters had flowed incessantly since the fleet left Sanlucar at the end of June, with Alonso and one thousand more souls on board. Thirty-six ships had sailed and were joined by seven more from Cádiz. The month of July found the fleet gathering fresh water in the Canaries and heading west, some to Cartagena and others to Cuba. The Fleet of the Indies proudly displayed its red, white and yellow flags with an eagle in the center.

Alonso landed on the island of San Juan de Ulua in Veracruz by mid-September. Crew and passengers arrived, hoping to avoid death after such a hard trip. His ship was third in tying itself to the rings of the wall to begin the descent. A half-a-mile canal that separated the island of Ulua from the docks was full of dinghies to transport passengers to the mainland, while exhausted sailors shouted instructions for anchoring, folding sails, and securing the ships with heavy ropes of American henequen.

When the cargo began to be unloaded, flat-bottom barges would be filled to continue towards the Huitzilapan River to render accounts in La Antigua. The slave ships, which were also part of the fleet, would arrive the next day. The merchandise was delayed on purpose to give a break to the dock, which would be filled with officers recording arrivals and amounts according to the licenses of the slavers. Like the rest, the "San Francisco de Natividad" turned its thirty-two guns facing north. The threat of piracy was ever-present along the coasts, despite the escorts. The fleet had reached Santiago, Cuba and there, a third of the fleet diverted their course towards Cartagena.

Alonso, curled on his bunk bed, refused to leave the ship, so weak was he from vomiting and dizziness. The soup of boiled bones that disguised the rotten taste of the last legumes had not revived him at all. On leaving the Captaincy, his spirit improved, and fresh supplies helped his health. The fabulous stories about America were heard for days, and on the clear horizon, the dark line of *terra firma* came to life, stirring the spirits and rejuvenating the patience of everyone. Settlers descended, while black and Indian paddlers transported them to the new Contracting House. Merchandise had been destined for La Antigua and the shallow sandy bed of the Huitzilapan separated that post from new Veracruz. Since its brand-new appointment as a city, Veracruz officials came from the royal headquarters in central Mexico to spend weeks scrutinizing the two annual fleets.

In the afternoons the cool breeze dissipated impatience while the sailors waited for a turn in the boats. More than ninety days of sailing, enduring the rationing imposed by storm threats that could lengthen the journey, they emptied the ship´s warehouse out of salted meat and fish. Rows of starving passengers were lying on the floors waiting for customs and entrance clearance, trodden and dirty, in sturdy clothes better suited for cold weather than for tropical heat. On the mainland, officers registered on scrolls the generals of each ship, its origin and master captain.

Although in Seville they had claimed they were old Christians and therefore the only ones able to obtain a license to enter New Spain, revisions and meticulousness were now demanded. Entrance to the continent was delayed even more when passengers traveled with servants. Property deeds and purchase origins of slaves covered complex routes from Cabinda, in Angola, to Canarias or from Cádiz to Riohacha in New Granada, and Santo Domingo. Each letter of property had to be checked with care.

In the queue, a couple of milkmaids, two black slaves, responsible for the upbringing of two babies, doubtless future counts or marquises, made two dark-skinned hungry children wait for their breasts. The hungry mouths belonged to twins of a female slave who had died on board. Without their mother, they had to be nursed, sharing the milkmaids, too valuable not to be included in the American adventure. One child was already crying without tears, a sign of certain dehydration.

Under their heavy Spanish clothes, the slaves' breasts were bursting with milk, but, they had to wait to satiate the rosy mouth, plump-lipped children and wait for questions posed by the clerks to be answered by their masters. Demonstrating ownership of slaves became a strenuous series of explanations: documents seemed to leave officers unconvinced. Beautiful handwriting recorded names, places, exemptions, and any other information that would account for the whereabouts of each passenger. They were trying to avoid colonizers passing without authorization. Charges were set starting at this desk, as was the order to apprehend Bartolomé Guillen, accused of transporting foreign and European sailors to bring them to the Indies without a license.

With two filthy bales containing his belongings, crumpled papers, rotten breath and an endless dizziness, the procedure for him ran smoothly.

> Alonso Garcia de Santamaria, ship "San Francisco de Natividad", a native of Seville, of old Christian parents, grandparents and great-grandparents, all deceased, as documents credit it. Promised in marriage with Mariana de Salazar y Miranda, who will travel in the fleet of the Indies next year.
>
> A deposit before the most illustrious Don Fabián Manrique, Notary-Accountant in Seville, has been issued, as guarantee of the arrangement, and their wedding will be celebrated in a near date upon arrival of Mariana de Salazar. A letter or promise is shown, endorsed by an official letter signed by Friar Antonio Carrascal of the Holy Major Church of Seville, who dispenses him of immediate nuptials, therefore arriving at the Indies as a bachelor. It is his destination the city of Mexico, capital of the Viceroyalty of New Spain, and the following letters confirm his identity for whatever the purpose it may take place ..."

With a beautiful beard grown over the weeks on shipboard, Alonso went on giving account of his trade: merchant, future son-in-law of Don Bernardo de Salazar y Couto, from the Oil and Olive guild, coming to complete and sign contracts and agreements with the Consulate of Merchants of Mexico.

The buzz of conversations among newcomers, who knew how to recognize the lineage of those who preceded them in the queue, rose in pitch. Letters of presentation made them forget for a moment how weak, sick, and fed up they were after the long journey, and a woman dared to whisper to her daughter that this good-looking young man was the one they had had a conversation with on deck. The mother regretted her lack of discretion on noticing Alonso, such a good match, according to his statements.

The scrutiny each passenger patiently endured would be the beginning of their American dream, which already seemed a nightmare. They had crossed the ocean with the intention of establishing and pursuing fortunes. Despite the hardships, they would not look back. Whatever they were asked for, they would give, spending days detained in the port, until every administrative hurdle was cleared courtesy of the opportune bribes that always softened the officials' wills.

Silver bars were concealed in the "San Francisco" cellars, small fortunes in double-bottom trunks.

Fleeing inmates, running away from their countries' justice systems, were hidden behind the jars that the Court of Wine pretended not to see, along with insubordinate sailors who arrived as prisoners accused of mutiny or sabotage. Gallant women, of exorbitant beauty and price, lovers who had been granted a travel license, promised in marriage like Alonso to a rich merchant already settled in New Spain, were also there.

Legal passengers of proverbial ancestry and their families, along with the friars committed to the administration of Nahua, Huastec and Totonac doctrines, where they would learn the languages, came on board first, followed by men of science, so demanded in these wildlands. They had brought the light of knowledge and civilization to the Indies and to handle the destiny of the new continent. All, looking for a new life, following the Huitzilapan, the river of hummingbirds, that seemed to shelter in its bed all the colors of a promised future.

The sun warmed the customs building, a century of receiving all kinds of travelers and fighting pirates and hurricanes contained in its walls. It was scorching hot by noon. Alonso made a mental comparison between his Seville –an older, bigger, and statelier lady– and Veracruz, which seemed like a wild and dirty girl, with toasted skin, to be tamed. Almojarifazgo was the tax to be paid for those bringing merchandise and collection would begin the next day. Many would have to stay until their goods were downloaded and danger would increase by then.

The most important port of the Crown was unprotected and the wall where ships were tied could not provide more shelter. The docks had been moderately fortified but were still decades away from a substantial defense or a wall surrounding the city. Viceroy after viceroy had written to the Crown, detailing the costs to finish a proper fort and the royal answer was always delayed, lost in the mist. Reefs were a natural protection against invaders, and only the secret Spanish cartographers knew of the exact place where they were, under the sea. But the barrier turned against them in the storms, tearing hulls and bottoms of Spanish ships.

Alonso's name was finally in the colonists' entry books, in between the name of the precentor, born in Córdoba, who came for a position in the Cathedral of Michoacán and the Jesuit friar who would teach the Christian classics among the Creole youth. It had rained all week long, and a brief shower was rinsing the docks now, every authority with a desk in the open running away, trying to protect royal records. Alonso remained there, enjoying the scent of the clean coast.

Without any fortune to record, Alonso emerged into the clean light of the day. He had observed the movement of the port with curiosity and decided that he would spend some time in this port to learn its ways. People proved to be enthusiastic for the mining enclaves and the Royal Treasury office, presided over by the portrait of Don Diego Fernández de Córdoba, Viceroy in charge, that seemed to approve Alonso's glee.

He was ignoring the weak laments of the ship of slaves, who were still a day away from descending into the burning dungeons of Ulua. Moldy velvet chairs were right on top of the labyrinth of cells, and once inside, a roar of insults would only be silenced when food was thrown through the holes, bowls banging the floor, giving the shivers to rowers, stevedores and marauders in the port. Beyond the huts of Veracruz, the jungle cut the view with its green belt. Alonso was walking in doubt, stately Seville coming to his mind, surrounded by magnificent walls centuries old.

As Alonso looked towards a small church, a group seemed to advance in parade. The small chapel, without a tabernacle or baptismal font, swept and ornamented on this day by the faithful fellows of the Brotherhood of the Holy Cross, opened its floor of fine sand for Indians and blacks who lived in the outskirs of the Village of Veracruz. Alonso deemed the solitude of this humble temple better to thankfully pray for his good arrival, kneeling before our Lord. The cross with a tortured, bleeding figure was leaving the altar to be carried on a litter, surrounded by faithful devotees praying and sighing under a sunset of fire. The procession honored His suffering on the cross, which gave its name to the Villa, and with this new symbolism the cross had redeemed the wood of the tree, that of the forbidden fruit, in the story of Eden. The poorest Spaniards who had established in the Villa, those for whom the adventure had ended, found hope marching along with Indians and freed slaves on this celebration of the Exaltation of the Cross. The brotherhood had decorated the hermitage with cracked and damp boards and coarse iron nails, like those used for the crucifixion, and the procession was now stepping on the sand dunes of the river, fermenting fallen fruit at their feet.

Palm thatched huts remained exactly as Conquistador Cortes had left them a hundred years before, and Alonso, discouraged by all this rusticity, thought of the Oil Gate of his childhood memories, one of the minor gates of Seville wall, with battlements and a masterly carved frontispiece. The door had overseen his infancy wanderings among the barracks of the market while he listened to stories about the New World. The tales stopped only when the alamin, the authority checking weights and measures of the market posts, broke through. In exchange, nothing here reflected those fortunes they talked about, a dream of wealth echoing in the water of Seville fountains.

At the end of the procession, Alonso's eyes viewed the town with pity. Brothers of three bloods marched together. Indians, blacks and Spaniards had decorated the street in an indigenous way, with threads of amate paper piece hanging and rocking with their prayers and the breeze. Alonso crossed himself. He gave a long sigh to the lavish processions of his memories in Seville, turned around the corner to leave the chapel behind and went to the inn. The streets were filled with multitudes by the second week. The fleet had brought awaited passengers and small goods to be sold in the street, lace and tanned goat hides from either bucks or does, shoes, socks and pieces of fabric. Merchants had signed and even prepaid for larger and better quantities of all these goods.

Alonso discovered that ships bringing quicksilver from the mines of Almaden, in the Spanish Province of Castile-La Mancha, hid smuggled slaves they have brought from the stop at the Antilles. Their landing would be arranged with a gracious gift for the inland authorities. And there were women, as well! A good milkmaid would now be resold as a servant, leaving the negrito who had made her a mother growing in the islands. The pair of good, strong blacks would be purchased to be sent to Orizaba, and the adolescent would warm the house of some clergyman, coming to the Indies to teach how to live a holy life. Slaves from the islands had the catchy intonation of the musical Antillean Castilian language, dotted with Taino and Caribe words.

Those with a pre-arranged buyer looked strong and well fed and Alonso did nothing but giggle when noticing how easily they could slip away with smuggled negroes, after the long queues of colonizers arriving legally he had witnessed. He wondered at the meanings of their language, that seems to be a broken mixture of Spanish with African languages as Igbo, Fula, Lobangi and Kimbundu. With all these influences, the language of the islands composed a song in perpetual change.

Daily amenities arrived on the ships. New Spain was full of nobles and militia with diverse habits to please. On these ships supplies that were not manufactured in the colonies arrived: small instruments to fill and gild the books authorized by the Inquisition, the iron types and dyes for printers that would reproduce the content of oral treatises that were copied by hand and in a small number. Print shops would enable European ideas in Latin to share their wisdom with America, if authorities permitted it.

European paper was brought on these vessels, as well. Reams from Valencian and Catalan mills for printing the history of young New Spain were here, along with some of the Italian descendants of Juan de Pablos, the famed printer. His enterprise was bringing some books too, carefully packed, along with two brand new printing presses, in iron and Mediterranean wood, that had left Andalusia to print news sheets and enacted royal laws to be advertised in towns and city squares.

Over the next few days, waves rocked ships carrying fabrics, spices, wines, gunpowder and weapons. Boxes labeled "arts" had copies of books to be sold in the Plaza Mayor, the Main square stores and there were long wait lists for one of the three hundred Nebrija Grammars (a Latin primer), the nineteen Ciceros, or the forty Virgils. Their content would rule court decisions, ecclesiastical thoughts, and knowledge. Books of prayers and florilegios, compendiums and essential anthologies for spiritual support were wrapped together with copies of pastoral novels and a multitude of Italian and French texts without author.

The "Index Librorum Prohibitorum," the Church's list of forbidden books, marked the reading pattern for all Latin Christianity, keeping Protestant authors away. The list included the Pole Copernicus, the Italian Galileo, and even some pious works. But there they were, arriving from Europe, even if the Index prohibited them. Titles that omitted authors or languages that the authorities of New Spain did not dominate were hidden in boxes labeled "Bruges Lace," or surrounded by fine threads, buttons and taffetas; clandestine, preceding the ideas of Illustration to America.

In those days the city did not sleep. The arrival of ships was cause for joy and night was the best cover for contraband, barrels and boxes and even some passengers of dirty blood and bad note, that slipped in the shadows to go north for the mines, to Zacatecas, where they would erase their past and rewrite their destiny. This was the commercial flow Alonso had to master and well he thought his contacts must begin in the taverns. For weeks, every food stand had accumulated groceries, women and wine in abundance, to offer to the crews in simple dining rooms or outdoors. Meager bushes sheltered latecomers and sandbanks accepted the repressed affections of new couples after the trip.

Gambling and playing cards, with printed medieval costume kings, decided the fate of a cargo that had not yet touched land. The cup of Bacchus, the sword of Mars and the rod of Saturn decided who would be the owner of Jose, seventeen years old, who would descend the ramp of the ship shaking, thinking the rumors of his village about the taste of Europeans for human flesh would finally become true. His rag, full of vomit and feces, would come off before he disembarked, his body, shiny in olive oil.

Landowners of the surroundings had arrived a few days before, waiting for the first loads, emptying barrels of sugarcane alcohol they had brought for sale. Their black foremen, whip masters supervising their lands, came from Punta Delgada or Alto Lucero, from Almolonga, Jalapa, and Actopan. Singers would make the wait lighter. Foremen were here for tools and instruments for farming, and the sailors, farmers themselves when not in the sea, brought fine iron tools that could easily be sold. Foremen had learned to forge, and they would replicate the new tools in their shops. Drunk, they would all dispute the favors of black fandangueras, dancers who took advantage of these days of fortune, multiplying their bodies to reach bunks and improvised beds on the sand, after spinning and moving their feet on shaking stages. Their hours of company at night were much more entertaining than the click of their castanets. The heat and the mating songs of the thousands of birds bordering the jungle infected everyone.

After some days, Alonso began to better understand the broken Castilian of blacks and mulattos of all shades, brown as honey or dark as the remains of boiled sugarcane juice. Blonde Alonso had fun with the bragging of blacksmiths, boasting about how good they were for forging and copying, fooling around with their imitations and spitting on the ground when they found something disturbing. He was learning about the pieces that articulated the New World. He was trying to follow their ways of drinking, catching some air while insects prowled the cuts of meat that were boiling in the backyard, hiding the rotten green hue the heat quickly produced. Outside the taverns, there were also the Indians, silent, treating the legs of wounded mules with their ointments and minding the bundles of tobacco their masters, muleteers, have brought to sell.

The Indians sated their hunger, excited by the smells of the kitchens, chewing cane, while distrustfully answering Alonso's questions with a rehearsed smile, the one he had learned to distinguish. Trees were full of fruit, free food for the Indians, and only the most damaged was left to the birds. Waiting outside for their masters, they gathered dry branches to start a small fire to boil a handful of beans or corn. Their foreheads pearled by the sweat of the coast, they kept their eyes down giving brief answers to Alonso's questions. Their weeping eyes were tired of waiting for the master and only after a drink would they tell stories from the fields, about the cane being cut, slicing the skin of their arms and legs, scars of whip hiding, of mutilated limbs and phalanges lost. Unlike the blacks, the Indians' silence hid the ways of harvesting, cutting, boiling, and pouring the syrup until they got the brownish powder and chunks to pack. A stolen piece of the sweet treat would make its way under their loose clothing to sweeten the infusion of herbs they boiled while waiting.

With so many Maestros de Oficio, trade masters, and peasants temporarily crowding the town, Alonso García reflected that the sole lineage of his ancestors and his condition of pure Spanish of the Peninsula would not be of much use here. These people knew how to earn their bread working the hardest jobs. He could come and go on the barge that crossed the stretch of sea as he pleased because he had made friends with Sebastian, the black oarsman. While the tide of people lasted, he could win a few coins the way he had in Seville's shipyards. When the last ship of the fleet departed again, the village would return to the usual tedium. Fortune in the Indies was not done with recommendations or a huge smile.

The black rower, of long and filthy nails, mocked Alonso every time they crossed from the island of Ulua, and then Alonso pretended dizziness. He would run to hold the rusty chains and pretend to vomit the entire content of his gut while the black man laughed. That big and thick mouth laughed easily at the simplest amusements. All his life he had been the slave of a usurer, a vessel commander, who dragged a useless leg all over the place. Prematurely old because of his bitterness, dysentery came to keep him away from his whole day long cursing. Sebastian nursed his master's fevers until, in a moment of lucidity, and feeling death close, he sent for the notary, freeing the slave. He buried his master and, set free, he spent a couple of years, wandering in the port, not daring to go beyond the only place he knew.

The oarsman was not an old man, but he had nowhere to go. An elderly rower taught him the trade, and when the rower died, Sebastian took his place and there was no one to dispute it. That year, right in October, the last group of muleteers would leave for the capital and the black knew that would be a good chance to pursue the business Alonso had half discussed with him. At the beginning, he was not comfortable following Alonso to the inn. He knew he had to be cautious to trust a white Spanish. There was a job downloading the last ship and they agreed to see each other at dawn.

They worked all day long. Alonso, weighing the possibility of leaving with the muleteers had to decide where to start. There was wealth in many places in this New Spain, down here he had seen wine and firewater abundantly, but the only oil was the one that made the skin of black slaves shine. He was assailed by doubts and questions. Would the wealth of the Viceroy's Palace be true? Where were the oil merchants here in Mexico? Where would the mansions of the most illustrious merchants be, in Puebla or Mexico? Where were his chances better? A whole ship of quicksilver for the consumption of one single mine was proof of fortune in the north! How cold is the road that crosses the mountain range, how many days would it take to leave their white skirts of snow behind? Did he know the snow himself?

Sebastian always tried to respond. He was used to the stories in the port, and since he was a child he had known about all the roads to get to Mexico, but he had never left the village. He ended up scratching his ear when he ran out of answers. The longed-for connections for the oil business would have to wait. The land was valuable in and of itself, Alonso concluded.

The friars were learning this lesson indeed. The intellectual strength of the Counter Reformation made the Society of Jesus a paragon of virtues. Indian workers and slaves supported their colleges and novitiates' businesses; oil, along with other products and goods, was already being locally supplied and they were being known for the abundance of their harvests. They would do everything in their power so that the Crown would not stop production. Thousands of olive bushes were thriving in this climate. Like sugarcane, local olive harvests were on their way to being a success and Jesuits headed this slow-paced agricultural bounty; they had the most prosperous and organized haciendas and were even requesting a license to charter a ship to provide themselves with slaves from Guinea.

At the inn, a Portuguese man boasted of how soon they would totally leave Spanish goods aside. New Spain was consuming less Canarias sugar alarmingly, preferring the sugar from the cane fields of Veracruz and the torrid Cuernavaca. Now that the kingdoms of Portugal and Spain were united, Brazil was doing the same. Sugar plantations, tobacco, and ultimately, olives seemed to be a better business. Alonso had to decide what direction to take. The silver mines were the frequent mirage in the story of the Indies, but the few coins in his pockets and so many leagues away brought him to a more immediate reality.

The merchant's company would soon leave the town, with dozens of mules loaded, fleeing the infernal heat and the clouds of mosquitoes. Joining them seemed to be Alonso's first choice. The memory of Mariana de Salazar y Miranda and her family, enthralled with stories about Alonso's deceased grandparents and their industrious spirit, told during their dinners, made him smile. It was amazing how a few well-spoken words astonished people. He only confirmed with his words what people in their hearts craved to believe.

Countless nights his ancestors and his lost fortune still tortured him. He had lived a life of shortages based on the promise that the riches of heaven were much more precious and eternal. They were Christians inside the walls of the Sevillian Cathedral, but in private, his grandmother continued to scrupulously wash leafy vegetables, totally avoided pork and seafood and never used a container that had stored cheese or milk to store other foods. They had lost the rites, but dietary habits were essential and made them special. Alonso breathed in these small practices a confused pride, but he ignored their origin. No one had ever dared mention the religion of Abraham in their house. He did not belong to any place, though he had unknowingly been raised in the practices of the tribes of Israel. Grandmother liked to say all others have passed, but the spirit of those of their kin would remain. She never mentioned who were those whom she called "their own."

Alonso learned to fade into the landscape until he discovered that conversation was one of his talents. They had rejected him in the seafaring school and a marriage alliance crystallized with his words and the spell of his hands, describing storms, surviving shipwrecks on trips he had never embarked on. The agreement had set aside bags of perfumed cinnamon and ginger powder. Alonso had gotten a fiancée, while Mariana's father only wanted to ensure Alonso was the intermediary he desperately needed. After being a guest for several nights, his manners exerted such fascination that Mariana was convinced that her father really wanted the best for her. On the night that indolent and sick King Phillip III passed away, Don Bernardo knew their world would soon end up falling right after the betrothal was agreed upon. Burning oil in a carved silver lamp from the Indies embedded with bezoar stone and pearls lighted the room splendidly when Alonso said goodbye to his fiancée. Blushing and love-struck, Mariana's low voice said only a few words. The farewell was very brief.

Sebastian, the rower, was getting closer to Alonso and just to test him he had tried to convince him to travel in the "Santa Maria de las Ánimas" towards Cartagena, with the silks and martabanes, those jars from the Philippines, that came from Acapulco, but Alonso refused. He did not want to know anything about seasickness ever again. Flying fish had been part of the wonders that kept him cheerful on the way to the Indies during the first weeks, but nausea had locked him up for the rest of the trip. Spanish settlers were not descriptive about the hazards of the journey, but every fortune cost blood, tears, and sickness. A huge fortitude and all the possible faith in heavens were a must to survive in this unhealthy land.

Alonso and Sebastian worked in the unloading of "Our Lady of Almudena" for a nice wage. Francisco de la Cueva would leave the Port of Veracruz to deliver "one hundred and eighteen quicksilver boxes of His Majesty, that arrived in the Fleet." The company had to reach Mexico with all diligence. Departure had been delayed a week; a dozen of his workers had fevers and vomit, and a couple of Indians had died already, victims of the unhealthy climate. Quicksilver, extracted from the millenary mines of Almaden, north of Toledo in Spain, was already late on its route. Mules and tumbrils were loaded. This would be Alonso's opportunity

Sebastian had spent weeks with Alonso and never had he laughed as much as in those brief days. His fifty years had been dulling and somber, and the contagious enthusiasm of Alonso had brought him back to life.

"What do you say, Sebastian? Quicksilver for His Majesty!"

With nothing to lose, Sebastian squinted, staring at his shadow on the ground, until he finally said with a determined voice.

"What if I carry the doublet for ya'? Would ya' really take me with ya'?"

They agreed Sebastian could join the group. The load was ready, and on the oarsman's advice, they went to thank Saint Sebastian, the martyr who offered his torso to the arrows of the enemy, for their shared fortune. Kneeling in the hermitage, ornamented at the expense of an old Havana mulatto, they said their prayer.

The pay was good; they would remain watching the cargo at night during the whole journey. Alonso declared his next destination at the port office and received approval to enter the kingdom, offering the address of Don Francisco de la Cueva as a reference for his whereabouts. He made his way out through the darkness of the inn´s kitchens. The bundle with his belongings brushed the skirt of one of the cooks, a female Indian who had tried to engage him in private conversation. In the doorway, struggling with a box of vegetables, she widely smiled, hiding her disappointment at his departure. Sebastian sold his old nacelle to the mulatto who organized the rowers. He did not even count the coins and put them along with the rest of his modest wealth, into the bag hanging from his waist.

The sound of golden waves found them joining the caravan. They would stop in Cotaxtla in the afternoon before heading towards the valley of Orizaba. Freshwater from the Atoyac would refresh everyone from the heat of the port they were leaving and the mules, the most precious possession on the roads, would rest there. They would suffer the unspeakable in the ascent to the great mountains. Sixty beasts and the carter, a strong Indian in command of the tumbrils, along with the owner of the company, would head the journey, as they knew every route, crossing, and shortcut.

They had delivered cotton clothes, flour, bacon and other foods they traded for the ships supply on route to Spain. Stocking up in Puebla and Cordoba was cheaper than in Mexico, and it was better for the mules. Now with His Majesty's quicksilver, they carried dozens of packed pistols bought from the sailors. They left with the first rays of sun.

Don Francisco de la Cueva had hired several northern Chichimec Indians, and some were still ill, but they nevertheless were ready to move on. They knew the roads, the rivers and their dangers. They traveled with their women, who procured them in everything. Female Indians were practical, and on their way to the port, as soon as the hot breeze from the tropics was felt, they stripped off the heavy clothes they had worn in the mountains, as they did in the dry northern heat of their lands. Sebastian's eyes were used to half-naked Indians in the harbor, and as soon as they headed down the Camino Real, the women paid no attention to those who watched them with prurient interest. Short cotton tunics, fastened with beautifully embroidered girdles, barely covered their private parts. Those with a husband rode stuck to their men, moistening the mounts with their sweat and bodily fluids.

Three strong logs, cross-linked, were attached to the pack of animals and wheels were firmly hooked to the tumbrils bed. Indians were fast, tireless, and indispensable. When night fell, they lost themselves with their women in the bush to cook the occasional prey they had hunted, and they could not forget their grain, corn, beans and chili peppers, for a nocturnal fire and a banquet.

Sebastian and Alonso had the hard task of spending the night watching out for robbers and raiders on the road. They were armed and had been warned to alert the group at the slightest noise. Although the merchant rarely used strangers, the haste of the delivery caused him to succumb to the charm of Alonso. In Cotaxtla, they filled wineskins and guajes, those hollow gourds nature offered, with all the freshwater they could. When starting the ascent to the peaks, there would be a long wait before they came across new streams to replenish.

The first night, the sounds of the forest and the silence brought some memories to Sebastian. From the Bamileke nation, he had meekly embraced the customs of the Vessel Commander, who had bought him as a child. The Spaniard had been Sebastian's only master and he had made a small fortune by lending money. Other than that, he spent his days on the veranda, limping and rubbing his useless leg with ointments, apathetic, using the negro for all collections and errands. The master had started Sebastian up in all aspects of his life. In all of them. He had grown up fond of this way of life, the only one he knew, despite the ruthless scolding. He had forgotten the jungle surrounding his village, the rivers full of shrimps and now here in Veracruz, this was all jungle he knew. He was used to being invisible. The zappy child he had been, running on the banks of the river, naked, and counting the missing moons to prove his bravery, had become a silent and obedient slave.

Upon the death of the commander, it took him several days to accept that he was free to leave until he realized the remote family the Spanish master always talked about might cross the sea and claim the house and him, as their property. With his letter of freedom, conditioned to care for the master to his grave, the black man then ran away as fast as he could, breathless, his skin bristling with fear until he ended up sleeping on the docks of the harbor.

> The master had started Sebastian up in all aspects of his life. In all of them.

Free at last, he had hidden for months until his instinct told him that only among those of his own he could go unnoticed. He would not risk giving the Notary an excuse to claim his freedom was void. The Spanish family he feared the most would never cross the seas, for it did not exist.

Now, Alonso and the caravan had made him leave the salt of the sea behind, along with the fear and the memories. He would not look back and at dusk, when he finally understood the distance in between would make him unreachable, his sweat ran down his cheeks, mixed with tears of joy. Sebastian began to whistle a couplet to conceal his emotions. With a bright smile, he pulled at the tip of Alonso's brocade vest. Here in the fiery jungle, with muleteers and porters, there was no need to pretend to be a gentleman of presumed ancestry.

The humidity and heat decreased after a few days when coffee plantations opened like a flower. There were seven lodges before arriving at Orizaba, but the haste of Don Francisco had required sleeping by turns, while riding, and only for a few hours, without stopping, to make up for the lost time.

The view of the fertile valley clearly showed the village where Indians had settled, brought from many places. They would take rest at the Spanish side. Alonso, a bit weak, had been using Sebastian's back as a pillow and waking up like a prince, his eyes admiring the extension of all this cultivated land. For Sebastian, this was the first time he could count fruit trees, and coffee and sugar cane plantations until his fingers ran out. He had heard people extolling the wealth of New Spain for years and believed he would die before witnessing it.

San Miguel de Orizaba of the Spaniards was completely separated from the Indian plots, and the torrent of so many water streams seemed to wash everything away. The travelers stopped, wet soaked, the rain falling like a cascade to spend the night at the hostel. They would leave the leading Indians at the entrance of their town, and Don Francisco would pay for one night only. Indians would manage alone, with those of their kin, as always. San Juan Bautista, a thriving sugar plantation since the previous century, belonged to the heirs of Viceroy Mendoza. His successors had continued his work and transformed the valley, their mill making the most of the Oztoticpac River and its waters, granted all to his family by royal decree. It irrigated the rest of the industries of Spaniards around in exchange for favors and parcels of land that were extending their possessions.

The rusticity of Veracruz contrasted with this green valley, a true city indeed, with a building for archives, a Public Notary and a Franciscan church under the patronage of Our Lord of Calvary. All legal plots of land were assigned using the temple as the point to start any measurement, counting the number of varas, a unit of length, from here onwards, in a straight line. The layout of roads and houses in all directions started with the church. As everywhere, industries were managed by the descendants of the Viceroy: the mill, the bread ovens, the paddocks, and the extensive agricultural lands.

The first Count of the Valley of Orizaba and a dozen Spaniards had obtained noble prebends, and hundreds of cattle dominated the view. Blacks, covered in mud, shepherded herds on both sides of the road and the wet soil had briefly taken the whiff of the tannery away, its waste poured into the river. Other hosts at the lodge told them how these peaceful fields concealed a fierce fight for the rights of water. Don Rodrigo de Vivero had purchased large plots in the outskirts he immediately dismounted and, in less than a year, they were already producing. Even land whose property was defended by Indians, proving ownership with maps, letters, and primordial titles. Legal allegations would only be resolved in the next generation, while his domains now reached the Metlac ravine, and with such an extension of land, he had decided to rent part of his plots to the Indian caciques, who were beginning to grow tobacco successfully.

All the crop was bought by the Count, and at least they had a piece of land to cultivate their food, too. Forced work in the hacienda and the extra payment for dismantling and sowing the new lands made them privileged when compared with neighboring towns. The olive harvest, a new venture of Don Rodrigo, had taken seven years to get the first fruits, though he had been told of coffee berries by those slavers that visited Orizaba, selling blacks from Cuba. While the smells of baked bread perfumed the valley, he was trying to decide what his next crop would be.

Orizaba of the Indians had its own hall and community lands. There were rumors that olives and oil were having such a large market and that the fertile valley would benefit from this business. Orizaba would soon receive the status of Villa, belated since its importance was great, as the passage of all travelers to central Mexico. They would spend a couple of days here, long enough for the mules to recover their strength on the way to the summits. Twelve slaves bought in Veracruz had joined the convoy before leaving and now they were all shivering. They would spend the night in the barn of San Juan Bautista, and without proper clothing, they begged their masters to return to the port. They vowed to serve them better in the benign tropics, swearing and calling the Blessed Virgin for help on the cold of these lands.

They were bozales, blacks coming straight from warm Africa, who were about to go up the rough mountain ranges of pines and cold. Alonso dismounted, feeling the icy rain in his Andalusian lungs, while the red-cheeked Dutchman who joined them, with the City of Puebla as his destination, laughed about their complaints against the temperature. Sebastian took his master's, the old captain's threadbare jacket out of his luggage. It was the only larceny he had dared before leaving his deceased master's house and he sighed with nostalgia at the smell of strong tobacco permeating the garment. They fell asleep right away.

At dawn, Alonso shivered and coughed. Sebastián went out to get that bitter brew from the Indians and forced him to drink, throwing sacks on his body to warm him. The day, grey and cloudy, had Alonso staying on his hay bed while Sebastian explored the region on foot. He was free. He returned at noon only to confirm that Alonso's cold had become disturbing. He coughed, and, in his dreams, he was imagining that Saint Ferdinand was stumbling down from the stone shield that adorned the Oil Gate, back in Seville. Saint Ferdinand was implacable, bitterly reproaching him for not having brought young Mariana. With every stroke of the fever waves, he could see her, sighing in her balcony, facing the Guadalquivir.

On the third day, a superb sun emerged on the clear morning, letting the travelers know they should prepare to continue. Sebastián dressed Alonso, placing rags of the sacks under his clothes to keep him warm. He had agreed with the Dutch to leave one mule for Alonso so he could lie down on its back during the day trip. Now, he knew all about olives, tobacco, and coffee berries. He would let Alonso know as soon as he was better. Together, they could figure out a plan to change their fortunes. He was proud that Alonso had asked him to accompany him on his adventure route.

Tied to the saddle to avoid falling, Alonso had a private argument with himself about his rights and legitimacy. His grandparents had always criticized all those hidalgos, those noblemen of secondary rank, who got lost in endless discussions. Were the Mier a family of gentlemen? Had the Ribera, all male, inherited a title? Nobility was about keeping horses and weapons ready for the call of war of His Majesty, The King. But who was Alonso? At times he woke up, asking Sebastian if the university had finally admitted him. Frost was on the leaves, and chill was getting to the bones.

"Cover me, Sebastian, I'm cold."

Then he fell asleep again, a barrel of oil dripping and flooding the road, making the mule slide and falling down the slope, came repeatedly. Quicksilver would continue its inexorable march to cross the peaks, until descending in the Pass of Cortes, the passage of the Conqueror. The Royal Treasury awaited the load to process the silver for the Spanish Crown, and the speed of the mules would not concede the health or welfare of anyone.

Only Christian charity prevented the merchants from leaving Alonso and his black servant halfway. Thick forests ended, and the road was too much for sick Alonso. Closer to Mexico, the weather was better, and they agreed to be left at dawn. Alonso would never know that the following summer, Cadiz would continue its efforts to move all the Indies trade to this port, a much more strategic and better positioned spot on the map, than Seville. A door to the sea that did not require navigating any river.

The Crown would also reinforce the formal prohibition to plant vines and olive trees in New Spain, under severe penalties, and the few olive mills would start an endless fight against importing wine and oil produced by the Peninsula, making the economy of it uncertain.

Precious olive oil to burn the lamp of Alonso's heart would have to wait a while before anointing his forehead and fortune.

CHAPTER 5
THE JOURNEY THROUGH THE ISLANDS OF MEXICO
1629

Here in the island of Iztacalco, in the House of Salt, the house of the ancestors, I am a song. In this small chapel, devoted to Our Lady of immemorial antiquity, my people have swept the floors, just as they do every twenty days, and have adorned with reverence the simple niches housing virgins and saints, calling upon the Heart of the Earth.

From up in her spotless niche, Saint Anne of Bethlehem, mother of Mary, the Immaculate, watches with sweet eyes the stool where I find myself. Her slender and elegant figure is molded in cane paste, and her eyes of glass, seem to read my thoughts. My mind is not here, it is flying away just like the precious birds I can see over the lake in the distance. My prayers are whispered to a different lady, a dear and beloved one, with a skirt of corn ears, abundant breasts, and precious jade earrings. She presides the births of our children and bless them, since we established our people here.

This chapel is presided over by Franciscan friars, a humble temple that looks towards the shore that received the footsteps of the precursors, our grandparents who came from the north, following the path that goes beyond the volcanoes, our guardians there in the land of the Culhuas, where our domain used to be.

Our island is a sister islet to Zacatlamanco, coastal mangroves are rocked by the wind, bending towards the neighboring islands, the peninsula of Iztapalapa and the causeway that goes to Coyoacan. From here, mule carts can be seen, silent in the fog, in a slow, merry movement. Here, on my island, midway the great Tenochtitlan, now the Capital of New Spain, that is Mexico, the founding fathers stopped long ago. They were called many names, especially Tenochcas, led by the legendary hero Tenoch, who came from Aztlan, the reason why they call us Aztecs, as well.

Here, in Iztacalco, in twin Zacatlamanco, the fathers hid, running away from the attack of the real owners of these lands. It is true they had arrived before and they were only defending their territory, but it was written in the prophecy that a day would come when they would be defeated by newcomers. Us. A rain of arrows accompanied their prayers for victory. We were brothers, that, we knew, but who can challenge the dictate of the gods? They fought fiercely, protecting what they owned. No shields stopped our advance. Their resistance was useless.

The portent told that we had been chosen for this place. We had the approval of the heavens, the mandate to settle here, where the eagle cries, on top of the cactus, displaying its majestic wings pointing to the sun, there in the heart of the lake, where the best fish swim.

We came here on a pilgrimage, seeking to fulfill our destiny, to find our land, Tenochtitlan. Out of all the tribes that had come from the north, only ours would make it here. We were the chosen ones, the heirs of the gods. Of the twelve tribes, we were the last. We arrived and stayed here in the place on the lake that is the navel of the moon, which in our language is called Mexico. Since then, we have called ourselves Mexica.

Long after, with the arrival of beasts and steel weapons, of the friars and their religion, the victory we had achieved, was vanquished. We were forced to learn Castilian, while Nahuatl, the language of our founders, was used only to speak among ourselves, to bolster the claims we presented to the Crown to prove our land boundaries, and to lament the loss of our heroes and our dead.

That is how we became all these: Tenochcas, Mexicas, Nahuas, Mexicans. They also simply called us Indians.

Our temple here is ruled by the Franciscan order and two of their friars permanently live in the Convent of Saint Matthew, on the neighboring island. I am the female chief of Iztacalco and Zacatlamanco. The friars celebrate mass on Sundays and once a year they baptize. It is then when our twin islands are all embellished, with thousands of flowers covering the walls and the entrance to the church, which is made of the same stone that once built our temples and gave shelter and adoration to the holy spirit that brought us to this land.

It is in the walls of this church that we hid the stone-carved spiral of water and the serpent that shapes the furrows from which we take our harvests. In the building foundations, we placed our symbols, to make them everlasting, just as we are. We know they will always be there, honoring the spirit to whom we dedicated the temple, just as we did with the ruins that remain underneath. The spirit we own and keep in each of us. Our ancient constructions were made of rocks rising to the sky in imitation of the sacred mountains, to take us higher, closer to Heaven, so our gods could better hear our prayers.

> **We became all these: Tenochcas, Mexicas, Nahuas, Mexicans.**

We built hundreds of them in these lands, four-sided platforms and our offerings are under their foundations, bundles of fifty-two reeds, like the cycle when we renovate everything, tied according to the number of years of our century. There are also carved flat stones with the names of our families and the main events that had marked our history. All of this and much more is under this floor.

We are the creators of the strong fortresses and lookouts rising on the river banks, well above the lake. We look after the four directions; we care for our people, sentinels for whom the favor of heaven was granted. From what was once a position of privilege, now only some piles of stones remain, all rubble after the two of our centuries, after two cycles of fifty-two years, when the Spanish conquerors got here. Those who came here, crossing the mountains did only the same we did. Mounted in beasts that spit blood and fire, they arrived and conquered. Just exactly as we did before.

I was born on one of the islands next to the wall that separates the fresh water in the Lake of Mexico, from the brackish water in the Lake of Texcoco. The land is fertile because of the silt in the lake and we have created artificial islands, too, interweaving reeds with stakes beneath the lake's surface, creating underwater fences. A buildup of soil and aquatic vegetation we pile into these fences, until the top layer of soil is visible on the water's surface. We fill them with our hands, of stakes and reeds we wove, four-sided, always four-sided. Their stability relies on the roots of a tree we place in the center, reproducing with this grid the universe as we know it. So, we are the ones from the islands, guardians of the swamps, lookouts deeply rooted in the millennial depth of these waters.

Today, the brotherhood of stewards made sure that the entrance to the church is fully decorated with garlands and arches of flowers, seeds and fruits to invoke abundance and fertility and ensure the favor of nature, our Mother. I presided over it all.

Doña Eugenia de Olmedo, female cacique, that's what they call me. Necklaces of precious jade beads adorn my neck. They commemorate events, alliances and victories made by divine mandate, but they also represent our tears and my personal grief over not having my fine husband with me. My lineage will die with us and that is another reason for my sorrow.

Here, watching Jesus nailed to the cross, bleeding and suffering, I am a sad song, pale as the salt my people mine, mourning for those who have passed, already gone to the place of no return, the place of nowhere. If only our gods allowed us to take our flowers and songs to that distant house!

I am Eugenia, wife of Miguel Mauricio, a principal Indian of the Tepanecan stonemasons lineage of Coyoacan. Our union was decreed by the elders, who enjoyed the favor of the Franciscan friars of Tlatelolco. In their college, they once prepared caciques in the art of politics to govern our people, just the way it was in Coyoacan, the place from where Hernando Cortés planned the conquest.

The son of a cacique himself, Miguel Mauricio had entered the Imperial College of Santa Cruz de Tlatelolco as a child, until he mastered rhetoric, grammar, logic, and Latin. His neighborhood, like mine, had been broken in pieces by the last epidemic and to the friars there could be only one explanation for the horror of rafts and carts full of deformed bodies: God's punishment for sinners.

Classmates were locked behind the walls of the College of the Holy Cross every time death arrived in the Kingdom, and the best of Miguel's adolescence was spent there, while outside, those who did not die remained waiting for the next strike of disease. A hundred years of forced relocations of our people to distant haciendas and mines, where we were needed, had taken its toll and some towns were so empty that only women and children remained. Ultimately, they fled, as well.

There in confinement, in Tlatelolco, Miguel Mauricio became a man. When the storm of disease was gone, and those who came from distant villages got permission to leave the College, immediate alliances for marriages were made. We needed our children to repopulate, to re-establish our numbers and make ourselves countless as the stars.

There in Tlatelolco, they would become caciques, learn how to illustrate new books of paintings, or to be educated in the arts, with the hope of continuing what was best for our people, who had fought to their last breath. This is what we did, nobles of Mexico. Those of our ancestors here, ruling, belonged to Tenochtitlan, belonged to Tlatelolco and from those larger twin islands, they were guardians, warriors and wise men that extended the ruling of our people to the horizon, to the four corners.

Miguel Mauricio, an Indian like me, had been educated in the best European tradition. There, at the Imperial College, friars and teachers discovered what our people knew from the day of his birth when they read his future. His trade was encrypted in the auguries. The evangelical message would come from the artistic hands of my husband, who earned the title of being the best craftsman of his time. But after endless disputes, some of a theological nature, the Imperial College of Tlatelolco abandoned the initial dream of ordaining indigenous priests prepared by the Franciscan order.

> Miguel Mauricio, an Indian like me, had been educated in the best European tradition.

In a twist of fate, the College restricted the priestly order only to Spaniards, leaving the mastery of the arts to indigenes. Of those converts to Christianity who wrote dazzling treatises of medicine and botany, both in their local languages and in Castilian, there were only a few who continued to reconcile that new Spanish world with ours. In the cloister they tried to use our knowledge, to reconcile it with their teachings, and soon they discovered the fine skills of our people that supported their divine endeavors.

This is how Miguel Mauricio grew up, in a family of stonemasons who transferred the secrets of quarry sculpture to the soft contours of wood, rejoicing in his mastery while reliefs, carvings and figurines contributed to consolidate the advance of our young and new Christian faith. By then, the friars had already put aside conversations. They had learned enough, despite the air of idolatry that permeated their judgment. That brief, unprecedented and controversial exchange of knowledge in the first decades of the Conquest had to be halted with each epidemic. Disease continued with the seventeenth century, and that would bring about the decline of the College.

Our artists had demonstrated their cartographic skills there in Tlatelolco, painting delicate maps that had been sent to His Majesty to give him an idea of the magnitude of his possessions. Lakes, roads, mountains, and rivers were reproduced with care and detail, reaching the Court on the ships returning from the Indies, along with scientific treatises annotated in Nahuatl, Latin and Castilian. Our wise men had tried to explain what friars considered our mysterious and magic practices, as well as the lists of lineages that confirmed our pre-eminence.

Our elders tried to impart our knowledge about the stars that supported the cycles of our calendars, the rituals and the attributions of each of our gods, the properties of medicinal plants and the ways of governing. A series of volumes, written by friars but profusely illustrated by our artists, with thousands of small drawings, had awakened scholars' interest, and long manuscripts and compilations they made continued for years, their writing being the work of a lifetime, even when they were moved to remote places by the demands of evangelization.

The content of their chronicles was enriched as they moved from one doctrine to another. Every book in process was the glory of an order –Franciscan, Dominican, or Augustinian– and they carried their writings from town to town, from village to village, and treated their findings with almost the same reverence we devoted to our sacred bundles, where our sacred stone guardian god, carefully wrapped, accompanied us on our pilgrimages, a sacred consolation that still gave meaning to our families.

It was common that all those Indians with an education be called Latinos. Miguel Mauricio was one of them. He dressed in the Spanish way and spoke his language along with Castilian and Latin. That is how they knew. Through interpreters. We knew the friars struggled to hide their amazement at each colloquy, each discourse with our people. It all stirred up endless conversation that continued in the solitude of their cells, questions they had never considered previously, realities they could not have imagined before coming here.

The friars had crossed the ocean to educate, and the city they came from was attached to their names: Ciudad Real, Valencia, Sahagun, Benavente or Ghent, in the Kingdom of Flanders. The fraternal dream of understanding our cultures and exchanging knowledge with the guardians of our memory was brief; when it was deemed contradictory to Christian faith, such interactions slowed and eventually halted.

Soon, just as disease took over our bodies, so they considered everything of ours to be infected. Our houses of paintings and knowledge were destroyed. Without the guardians of our memory, the wisdom of our ancestors, everything was lost. New artists without refinement altered the use of mineral and plant pigments. Cochineal dyes were used to paint flowers and burned corn was used to draw the contours of birds. It was all a bad omen. Our ways were inverted or reversed, and everything was lost, the style, the tradition, the right way of thinking.

Successors were working on canvas and sculptures in only the themes that rendered the best service to the Christian God and His Majesty. Conversed Indian devotees were imbued with a faith that became fanaticism and whoever became a teacher or a friar was not permitted to be of our ethnic groups, neither black nor mulatto. Being Spanish, old Christian, and white, became the only requirement.

Everything was forgotten, and darkness was all over. The urgency of the evangelical work, based on the mastery of our people, made obsolete. Religious themes were the only ones addressed. Indigenous carvers, gilders, and scribes whose skill and ingenuity exceeded those who instructed them made polychrome sculptures to inspire reverence for the saints, to move the will, and to awaken devotion. Saints, Christ, and virgins were honoured, so the walls of refectories or open chapels were filled with works so perfect, so proportioned and expressive that there were none better.

Ships, gunpowder and disease were the manners of destruction in the first century. For the royal and noble Mexico City, the most demanding need was food. People depended almost entirely on crops planted mainland and on what we, in the islands surrounding, could supply. Fruits and vegetables from the islands had reached the city for years, and thousands of canoes, transporting, had saved inhabitants from hunger since its founding.

After the last epidemic, when disease was gone, our nobles arranged marriages everywhere. It was urgent to establish alliances between families from the islands and those on the mainland to secure all supplies. That was how my union was arranged. The only heir of the houses of Iztacalco and Zacatlamanco, the islets that produced grass to feed cattle, salt and a thousand types of flowers, would marry Miguel Mauricio, the youngest son of the Teopan's cacique, an artist who was born right in the place where the mythic eagle on the cactus was seen.

The Spanish city had superimposed the names of the four evangelists to the four main districts that formed Mexico Tenochtitlan. The neighborhoods, Cuepopan, Teopan, Atzacoalco and Moyotlan, were arranged following the model of the four corners of the Universe. Saint Paul Teopan, the site of the foundation of Tenochtitlan, facing my islands, would keep merchandise flowing freely with our marriage.

Nobody opposed our wedding. We were the last members of the nobility that helped the conquerors govern indigenous partialities according to Spanish law a hundred years after they set foot here.

At our wedding, our grandparents' toothless mouths smiled with satisfaction. Meek after so many losses, only one was a witness of how our original world was torn down in pieces, but they congratulated themselves for the union of our houses. Those who had fallen into the night of eternity did so with the hope of once again witnessing the celestial axis that gave an order to the construction of our cities. Our valley, they used to say, would be one day the same, just as it was when the ancestors arrived.

In its design and construction, our cities had followed a straight line in the sky, a path of stars from north to south, from one river bank to the opposite, that we used as the guide to build up here on earth. The celestial axis began with a star pinpointing to the mountain that was the place for the ceremony held every fifty-two years, our century, the New Fire. The axis went on in the direction to my islands, Zacatlamanco and Iztacalco, to continue crossing Teopan, where Miguel Mauricio was born, following to the great Temple of Tenochtitlan, and to her twin city, Tlatelolco, until it reached the temple of Tenayocan, on the mainland.

The axis joins the South with the North. We all came from the North. Stars connected with the places, and we devotedly followed them to build towns to shelter those who came later. A long pilgrimage dictated by our god brought us here and here we settled only after demonstrating that we were warriors and a thousand death clay whistles confirmed that our brothers here –the Otomi, the Tecpanec, the Culhuas and the Matlazincas– would grant their permission.

It was our courage that made us worthy of these lands. We founded two mirror cities that would be the heart of the earth, the center of the celestial axis. There was Tenochtitlan, dedicated to war, championed by the eagle, and Tlatelolco, the city of commerce, under the protection of the jaguar.

The stellar event that gave us a beginning is carved in the ridge of our eternal Sun Stone. Its alignment corresponded to the intersection with the zenith of the Pleiades. The complicated calculations of sky watchers considered the North Star, and the Morning Star, for a precise blessed date to begin our history here. But now, after so many New Fires, no one knew how to explain for certain the calculations that explained our foundation. Everyone was dying and how confused we all were! The Houses of Paintings, our books and the ones who write by painting were all gone.

The Sun Stone is a polychromed recount of the eras that preceded us. It has frozen time within. It tells about the past, the separation of stillness from movement, carved in basalt from the Xitle volcano. A large stone of solemnity and honor with the animals that have presided over each cycle so that no one forgets what we have gone through, what we have done. When the Great Temple was destroyed, the Stone was thrown away in the aftermath of the Conquest battles. It was by the royal acequia, an open canal that connected the city with my islands.

There, gangs of blacks made it their hiding spot and when together, they danced and got drunk on top of it, profaning it. They were so noisy, their dance so provocative and condemned by the friars that no one dared to get near. Our people visited authorities so often to beg for our Stone to be protected until the heart of the Viceroy was moved, and it was buried. No one cried for it ever again, until it started to be forgotten.

To mitigate the pain of living in this new world, now a century old, the elders blessed our union twice because two lineages, two principal families were coming together. The axis was on its way to rightness again. Do you remember, Miguel Mauricio, how the bells tolled? There was a wedding being celebrated in my domains where I was the legitimate heiress!

People from other towns and islands came to rejoice, and father Francisco came to Zacatlamanco from the neighboring convent of Iztacalco to celebrate the liturgy. A group of our people played music with their flutes and drums, and a large procession formed by our families marched from one corner to the other, honoring our gods with the sound of the conches, the primordial sound that elevated our prayers to the ears of the gods.

Living here, on one of the thirty islands that surround Mexico Tenochtitlan, allowed my people to celebrate without censorship. They prayed for numerous offspring, like the sands of the sea. A century later, friars still condemned the times of gentility when, they say, we procreated like herds of sheep. Our men had to be satisfied with one single woman only now, not like we used to do before, three or four wives, raising all our children together. It took a long time for us to get used to it. Those caught with more than one wife had their hair smeared with resin and burned to the scalp to set them as an example.

My island heard the melody of our instruments in my wedding, so different from those church organs, and the elders led the procession along with Miguel Mauricio. We all ate and drank and then dozed, closing our eyes, feeling the music of the earth, coming back to the first dawn when we lit the first fire here. With the first New Fire ceremony at Iztapalapan, light had been distributed everywhere then until simultaneous bonfires made the Valley shine like the Sun.

With the times of weeping and crunching of bones, in 1556 the Spanish monarch prohibited torches descending from the sacred mountain and ten plagues punished our land right afterwards. Smallpox, measles, hunger, war, and forced slavery were whipping our people. Friars and priests blamed idolatries for all these calamities. You must stop, they said. Your world is gone; it will never come back. No other sumptuous ceremony will ever be repeated. The new cycle to honor the giver of life, of majesty greater than that of the Spanish monarch himself, was prohibited and slowly forgotten.

When Father Francisco officiated at our religious wedding, the following day, Indian singers raised their voices during mass. His eyes, blue as water, shone in sanctity and satisfaction. After a long sermon, the ceremony culminated with the baptism of a crowd of new Christians in the atrium. How many lives, purified of all sin, were rescued that day! Our people just watched and accepted in silence, bowing their heads and squinting just as they did when facing the sun. Because we were of the principal families, we could dance our way.

The tlatoani of San Pablo Teopan, the Lord himself, danced, and the Otomíes of Tenayocan came, and ours, from Iztacalco, also danced along with them. The elders asked for permission to put us on an elevated altar, sitting on a mat to receive congratulations of people. We were gifted lavish garments and trappings, and wine made our hearts happy.

To commemorate this glimpse of hope, we were painted on an amate paper book, face to face. Miguel, sitting on the chair as a junior chief, an icpalli without a backrest, as befits junior leaders. I, Eugenia, was painted sitting on the floor, my wedding dress all over the mat, simple cotton fabric beautifully embroidered all over the front in threads of a thousand colors, my arms and ankles in red feathers and bells, a living music instrument, my whole body, that celebrated our holy union.

Daughter of the defunct Lord who carried the rod of justice, I enjoyed the privilege of appearing in the folded paper book that our people kept, an honor reserved to main women only. With our union, the passage of goods through our canals was resolved. Our people would not disturb it anymore, as they used to. The supply of vegetables and flowers from mainland, would continue.

These were the unions that friars and priests blessed with most devotion. The city was being filled with residences and palaces, built with the stone of our temples, and with a growing population, food was the main concern. We knotted the hem of our wedding garments and Miguel Mauricio returned to the College of Tlatelolco at age seventeen to continue working in the manufacture of wooden sculptures, in the year of 1595 of God, Our Lord.

Most Indians graduating returned to their places of origin. Those who studied politics went back to head the government in the Spanish way. But Miguel Mauricio, dedicated to arts, remained suspended between both the Spanish world and ours. He could come periodically, using the boats that communicated Zacatlamanco and Tlatelolco.

With his mastery, he was soon appointed the head of the sculpture workshop. He knew all the secrets of stonework and wood was more noble and easier to carve. His family of basalt artists made lace out of the stone and had been forced to move to Tenochtitlan from Coyoacan, as soon as after pacification, the Marquis of the Valley decided the layout of the new Spanish city. His ancestors collaborated in the rebuilding, with the materials they handled so well.

Cortes, the conquistador, was also inflaming the hearts of the new Christians with his devotion to the holy cross. It had blessed his routes and facilitated his wanderings to gain lands for his King and, belonging to Brotherhood of the Knights of Santa Veracruz, he chose a couple of plots in the north on which to build a temple for the Spanish nobility, which would house a hospital that would alleviate ailments of the body and soul of only the increasing Spanish population.

Indigenous stonemasons of Coyoacan, the headquarters of the Marquisate, worked friezes full of angels and cherubs. Their work was preferred to teach the faith and thus facades were books of lessons. Miguel's family showed such skill in carving basalt stone that his fame spread throughout the kingdom. They worked all over the territory on the many churches that silver mining and faith were financing.

Those whose actual nobility had been taken away stubbornly fought for rights to get land in courts, sometimes for years, wielding their noble lineages and painted documents, maps in color called primordial titles, as we did before, as evidence. There were many hurdles to clear, but his family was perseverant. Supported by the work they had rendered to conquistador Cortes, they were granted lands and titles in Teopan. Sealed and signed paper from Europe confirmed their perks, and that is how they were given a rank and the privilege of education at the College in disciplines that were forbidden to unnoble indigenous peoples. His family could now abandon the hard work of stone and explore other materials.

The Christ of the Seven Veils was their first foray into wood carving. It was infinitely easier than basalt and opened the way for Miguel's ancestors to crating dozens of effigies of saints, the hundreds of exemplary lives that clerics wished to represent, with their attributes extolled from the pulpit.

After our wedding, Miguel Mauricio returned to my bed only once a month, such a brief time in which we tried unsuccessfully to prolong our lineage. His visits were short and spaced from the beginning, pretending the rigors and the discipline of the College were overwhelming. I knew Miguel Mauricio belonged to that generation educated in the lights of European knowledge and when he was here, he constantly criticized the doings of the island. Hispanic ways had exercised their powers over him.

His classmate, Hernando de Alva, a mestizo, never ceased to praise the lineage of his grandparents and the courageous role of defense of his noble Texcocan family, but he also exhibited the pride of carrying three-quarters of Spanish blood, more than anyone else among the students. Of clear and eloquent speech, as soon as de Alva completed his training, he left the College to become Governor of Texcoco using the art of politics he had learned so well.

After hours of class, the workshop and all his woodwork, Miguel Mauricio liked to tour the convent plots, adjacent to the school. The orchard was prodigious, the precious water that blessed the trees reproduced the biblically promised paradise, a space of inspiration to reflect on the true creator of nature and earth. He also enjoyed the Tlatelolco market. Known for abundance, it was filled with the bustle of sales and disputes, as well as the aromatic scents of flowers and fruits.

Our merchants were true ambassadors. Those who knew the roads well had permission to work as traders. All kinds of goods were permitted to them, except Spanish weapons and silks, and the Crown authorized them to keep up to six horses for their business. They were received in towns with music and dances because they brought merchandise and news from remote places.

The church of Santiago de Tlatelolco continually welcomed pilgrims and merchants who came to the altars to thank for their profits and arrival, safe from road rustlers. They made two stops: one here, for their business, and another in the Tepeyac mountain chapel, to thank the Mother.

An aqueduct brought the water from all the springs in the north to irrigate the convent's orchards and supply people of the nineteen neighborhoods that made up the populated Republic of Indians of Tlatelolco. It was the place of the final siege, where the last chief fell, and where the Spanish were victorious, just as we were when we first came to this valley, long ago.

We had a hundred temples dedicated to the earth, the wind, the rain, the sun and the commerce, and after the defeat they were all buried under tons of debris. The best stones were used to build the convent and the builders, natives like me, made it the way we had built our main temple. There too, as in the islands, as everywhere, we hid our own offerings in walls and foundations: arrows and hammer symbols were carved in the facade, and the stone figurine of our goddess of the earth was buried in the left main corner of the temple, to preside over the magnificent building. Our feet knew that they walked on top of our lost splendor and parents always told the children about all this, in whispers.

The sacred bones of our divine rulers were hidden under the four evangelists who looked towards the altar in the transept, covered with stucco. Nobody would ever know what else the foundations and cornerstones supporting the building were hiding. We just did the way it had been done in almost all the constructions. To evoke, to remember, so those born later, new Indians, christianized, would never forget.

The cistern and its walls were completed a decade after the fall of our world. The first need was water and cutting off its supply had accelerated defeat. Water, crystalline and falling in a small waterfall, quenched the thirst of the republic.

The outer walls of the magnificent open-air cistern were embellished by strikingly-colorful murals that reproduced the Creation, the biblical garden was like this valley we inhabited, surrounded by mountains and five lakes and that is what our artists exactly painted. As much life as there was here, conches, herons and turtles were depicted facing a blue water mirror. We knew what colors to apply so the structure would not be damaged by moisture, and presiding over the scene, right at the center, artists painted the Son, crucified.

Miguel Mauricio spent days there, seeking to avoid coming to the island, his new home. Since our marriage, he was no longer a son of Teopan, but of Iztacalco and Zacatlamanco, higher in rank than his lineage. But we were too rustic, simple peasants who worked the land and extracted salt. He preferred Tlatelolco, its hectic daily life at the workshop, perfumed with his logs and planks of wood and his pigments. The world order that he liked was there, in the stillness of the orchards, watered by the springs coming through the aqueduct, and the College.

Women carried their pitchers to fill them up at the open-air cistern, stepping four steps down, always four, forced to bend when filling them, an act of reverence to the Crucified. But on second thoughts, it might also have been in reverence to the jaguar, painted on the same front wall, perched on the stream of a spring, almost lost in the other animal figures depicted, sneaking up to the east. Or to the eagle, resting on a curly-leafed cactus, looking majestically to the west. Both were symbols of our twin cities we resisted to give up.

Upon entering the walled cistern, everyone was amazed by its spectacular colors. The sound of the water softened the hardships of the day to start, and you could spend some time watching butterflies and hummingbirds depicted in a transparent lake, in which an infinity of fish swam, with childish expressions of joy. Fishermen, of indigenous and European features, linked both worlds, while worshiping the Savior with their efforts. With a bit of imagination, echoes of songs we had learned resonated on the walls.

"We are like sand minnows in jade waters. On to the dry land they threw us, they took the water away from us, fish tiddlers, Mexicas, jumping on the grass, all over, suffocated, asphyxiating. Still shining like pearls, but looking for our waters, a stream gone that will never come back."

This was a sacred place, a center for ceremonies that mirrored Tenochtitlan since before they came to conquer. And Miguel was happy here, like nowhere else, a master of his own kingdom. In Tlatelolco, he was Miguel Mauricio, the artist of great and admired mastery, the carver of wood.

> On to the dry land they threw us, they took the water away from us, fish tiddlers, Mexicas, jumping on the grass, all over.

As for myself, I continued to look after my people, keeping good account of tribute and the number of canoes filled with flowers, fruit, grass, and salt that were sent to the court, waiting in despair for our monthly appointment. Miguel Mauricio's arrival was always announced by children running all over the place, and my heart jumped in joy, despite his concealed shame at being married to me. My lineage was ruling with wisdom while farming the sacred land, working the salines, so necessary in the kingdom, just as before, but not something of which to be proud, under the new order.

The young child with Mary his mother were carved in Miguel Mauricio's workshop in a dozen positions while I prayed to welcome the next under covered ceremony devoted to the New Fire surrounded by children of our own, crying in silence for my sterile womb. The baptismal font of the convent of Saint Matthew, ornamented with angels whose wings resembled those of the sacred eagle, those of the ears of corn, our sustenance, waited in vain for our son. The built-in ring of the sacred ball game we have hiden in one of the walls under the stucco remained empty, awaiting a warrior of ours to represent us in one of the ceremonies. There in Tlatelolco, wood and pigments obliterated the unfruitful wife, and more and more he found it increasingly difficult to visit. In other times, he could have taken a wife again, but friars preached abstinence when he was away.

Works to have the new church dedicated to Santiago, James the Apostle, had had Miguel Mauricio busy for more than a year. Sometime during 1610, the church would be inaugurated in gratitude for the disciple's support. Spanish conquerors had forged a legend that told how the saint appeared in the worst part of the battle against our people, flying over the war field to support and encourage those brave Spanish armies. Victory was granted to Christianity and to commemorate how they had defeated the savages, the scene was recreated annually.

Burning torches and a liturgical drama culminated with the appearance of Santiago, who had fought the Moors, and now the Indians of these lands, were made to represent the Saint, descending and cutting infidels in pieces with his powerful sword, liberating the captive hosts of Cortes.

With all the bustle the construction and ornamentation of the temple was causing, the demands imposed on the gilders were disturbing the slow pace of the workshop. Miguel Mauricio spent more days in his meditations. The walled cistern received the salt of his guilty tears, torn apart, divided between two worlds. He was losing himself.

Friar Juan de Torquemada, Guardian of the Convent, had not yet decided what the motif of the main altarpiece would be, and the monumental work was also unsettling him, quarreling as he was over the perfection of the frontal relief of the church that would carry the cross, Christ's arm and Saint Francis's arm, the emblem of the Order.

He had beaten to death an Indian of ours, whom he judged insolent, for refusing to gild on a Sunday a piece that was destined for Xochimilco. Indian builders had witnessed this second scourge in silence, squinting their eyes and feeling on their own backs each blow of the whip. Hiding behind a column, a mulatto child was weeping, snuffling and repeating in his incomprehensible language how sure he was the Indian artist had never uttered any insolence to the friar.

Miguel Mauricio got in the convent garden right when the lifeless body of the Indian was being dragged out of the cloister. In that red hour of the evening, when water pitchers are resting in kitchens and fire has been extinguished, the sight of the dead Indian, a perfect beater of gold leaf, being dragged, his inert skull striking the slabs, set Miguel's heart on fire. The Indian's hands were hanging from his bleeding back, like those of Christ. He was the Indian with the finest fingers, made to caress every fiber of the wood with fine gold leaves to reflect the light of faith in the thousand beams of oil lamps.

After a sleepless night spent sobbing, his eyes swollen, Miguel received instructions from Torquemada, the murderous friar. He was sending a printed picture with a messenger that would be the model Miguel Mauricio had to use as the central motif for the altarpiece. He had decided what he wanted, at last!

A combatant Santiago, James the Apostle, brother of John, the evangelist of the Apocalypse, son of the thunder, was to be carved brandishing his sword against infidels and insolent Indian pagans. The workers accepted the order with submission, hiding their rage at the homicide of the previous night. Miguel found a way out for his fury in the energetic strokes he outlined for the carving on a sheet of paper from Europe. The saint, riding on horseback, crushed the idolatrous Indians with justice, sowing the road with pieces of their corpses.

After giving the instructions, guardian Torquemada took good care to let it be known that he would retire to solitude for a few days, in recollection of penance, while the storm over the murder passed. During those days Miguel traced a monumental image, with the cloak of the disciple of Christ waving triumphantly, waiting defiantly for the friar's approval. The apostle looked as the friar.

When fasting and flogging were over, friar Torquemada took a quick look at the finished drawing, approving it without objection, feigning greater attention to the veins of the select plank of wood that awaited the tools of the master artist. When the friar left the workshop, tears flowed down Miguel Mauricio, the master of carver's cheeks, threatening to stain the lines on the immaculate paper.

Now, Miguel was ready to work endlessly and face the scene that his eyes had so much avoided. Our people had been broken into pieces, limbs rolling under the legs of the horse the saint was riding, according to his rendered drawing. It was an important moment, and he would spend the next months debating and reconciling his emotions.

With the drawing approved, my good, beloved husband, returned to the island. The sound of the waves could not extinguish the rattle of his soul. Water had accompanied his struggle, crashing against the boat. Every wave was judging the years he spent to be educated in the trivium and the quadrivium, the division of the seven liberal arts comprised of grammar, logic, and rhetoric along with arithmetic, geometry, music, and astronomy.

On landing, I noticed how he observed the rough fingers of the rower, docking, diverting his gaze to his own hands, noble and with long, dark artist fingers. The boat had brought Miguel, an Indian in Spanish garments, to the islands, who descended to the shore with an elegant demeanor, avoiding staining his stockings with the island's mud. I knew by Miguel's expression that my last hope to be impregnated by him had passed away.

He decided to extend his stay in Iztacalco and Zacatlamanco a few more nights than usual, confronting the elders claims and pleas. He lowered his eyes every time, as we always do before them, out of respect, without saying any word in his defense. Not understanding his absence, they asked him repeatedly why he always took so long to come back.

In our house at night, when the candle went out and the room was all dark, I heard his sighs, I watched over his insomnia, our bodies together, back to back, but separated by a thousand miles, each one ruminating the other's desires in that painful gloom.

On the last afternoon Miguel roamed the riverbanks, indifferent to the works in the House of Salt, his sight lost on the horizon, watching towards the volcanoes, looking for answers beyond Iztacalco, beyond Zacatlamanco.

I knew Miguel should now throw himself into the fire, imitating the legend of our gods, to be purified. He had to enter the bonfire of his grief to be consumed by it to then transform it into a luminous star, just like the old god did, to let the wind gently blow the last ash of fiery pain. He had to die to be reborn.

Back in the workshop, the fine brocade that wrapped the now-dry pine board that Miguel had cut in the waning moon of January revealed the surface that would finally receive the commanded work. It would be a testimony for the suffering of our people. Miguel Mauricio, the artist, would bring life from those dried streaks for a central altarpiece, giving each character a face and a heart.

There, by the shore, waving his boat good bye, I knew he would never again come back to the islands.

After Miguel left, disease, always hovering, reached Iztacalco. Hardly did I have time to attend to my own collapse. Nine out of ten of our people died. Nine out of ten, there. Water surrounding had saved us for so long, but this time there was no escape. Never had there been more death. So, we also became extinct, finished. A hundred years after all that had happened, two bundles of fifty-two reeds, two centuries of ours, only a few of us remained, from that fateful day.

The smoke from the pyres took away the great stench of mangy bodies and fog covered everything. Hairs floating in the mist, unroofed houses no one took care of anymore, of fallen reddened walls. No tribute, work or service would be enough to pay the debt we had not incurred. Disease took its toll and the heavens decided that at least for now that was more than enough.

Bundles of grass, salt blocks, hens, and flowers were the payment my islands made to the Crown. With our people dying, the cattle belonging to the Franciscan friars wandered now in the shores, herded by their black servants, helped by long rods. Friars, busy with the things of God, also received their part of the tribute to support themselves.

Engaged in religious instruction, printing religious books in our languages, grammars and catechisms, the friars went on with their sacred work to convert our people after each epidemic outbreak, but now there was almost no one left. Some just accepted the faith on their deathbeds.

Horses that had crossed the sea with conquistadors had multiplied, devouring the countryside, invading and destroying the fields. When they needed salt, insufficient in the grass they consumed, they made their way towards the House of Salt, breaking everything, devouring everything, chewing the white crusts on the shore for hours, until satisfied.

All kinds of lawsuits, based on primordial titles, painted exquisitely by our people, were presented to the Spanish mayors, denouncing the invasions, but soon there was no one to follow the course of the trials. When the arrow of the measles hurt a house, everything was left to its fate. Sick people were forbidden to seek consolation in the temples to avoid transmitting disease and in every house, lizards, swallows, corn shells and grass were the only staples.

Black slaves, immune most of the times, pretended to call the beasts back from invading but were attentive to the death of the last member of a family, so that they could ransack the miserable huts. Case files died slowly at the desks of justice.

Salt had been our fortune. It was the seasoning of our food; we used it in tannery, ceramic glazing, textile dyeing and in the preservation of meats and sausages. Here in Iztacalco, here in Zacatlamanco, salt became the main product, and became even more important when the Sevillian miner Bartolomé de Medina brought to Real del Monte in Pachuca his method for obtaining the last flicker of silver from a mine.

He had learned how to efficiently extract silver from its ore, using a mix of "charged brine," that used large amounts of salt, quicksilver and copper sulphate stirred for several weeks, along with the mineral. By substituting the smelting process that consumed entire forests, salt was used from the Province of Silver in the south and all the way up to the north, through the 1,600-mile long trade route between Mexico City and Pueblo, New Mexico.

Quicksilver, salt, and sulphate were crushed by driving mules over it in circles on large patios. After days, they managed to separate all the impurities, and the process was repeated infinitely in the mines of Zacatecas, Guanajuato, Taxco and Temascaltepec where silver sparkled in the mud, bright and twinkling.

Traders carried bags of salt and quicksilver tied on mules, their contents emptied in haste to be refilled in exchange with the precious metal that would alleviate the financial burdens of the Peninsula. The hunger for salt had our people working in the saline for months, except for the rain season, until the epidemic filled our faces with holes. Rats and rodents, consuming the waste of the sick, unknowingly carry typhus, yellow fever, smallpox and measles away with them. Rats were also destroying the corn in our warehouses for the year, and thus, after each episode of illness, hunger arrived.

But the scourge was never as great for our people as it was when Miguel Mauricio left. We had been more fortunate than those on the mainland, who had been relocated to the mines, paled with sadness, longing for their neighborhoods.

Women left without their companions and found consolation in devotion. In the temples, they could express their pain freely, pray in voices, rend their hair and clothes in the processions.

Towns were emptied of their best men, night fell over them forever. They were taken to the north or the tropics, to climates they had never imagined. To say a man was taken away was to say he was in Huitzillan, the remote south, Ehecatitlan, the far west, Tecpantzinco, in the distant north, or Yyacapan, the unseen east.

That was when black slaves, those with the burnt skin, the tlitic, began to arrive. With curly hair and wide noses, they were well able to cope with the heat of the tropics and the dry, scorching wind of the north. They began to occupy the places that our people were leaving. They were forbidden to live among us Indians. They dressed the Spanish way, wool shirts and stockings, and suede boots. Blacks were workers and foremen in mines, and, as property of adventurous Spaniards, there were more of them in the ports to help with the shipping work.

Their fear and their ire was redirected at us when they commanded us. Those who came from the island of Cuba were not even on the lists to get into New Spain, and soon their strength and stature made them the masters. Robust blacks were used in haciendas or to breed and bear more slave children; afromestizos created by the lust of the master, children who remained slaves from birth.

These children were used to crawling in tunnels and galleries, draining rainwater and digging, mixing minerals with their bare feet, soles cracked by corrosion, but the rigors for us, working at the mines were unbearable. Our people, leagues away from our families, preferred to let themselves die. They spent days without tasting their miserable meal, cooked corn and herbs, and asked for death as a mercy granted by one of their neighbors, or they killed themselves. Everyone knew that one had reached his hour when they broke their vessels, turned off the hearth and spread ashes on their faces, defeated. They stuck an arrow in their necks, threw themselves into the ravine, or tied ropes around their heads to die as the sun dies each night before indignity took their last strength to dispose of their life on their own terms.

We had always invited a representation of death to dance in our celebrations, and that terrified the friars. Death is the opposite of life and defeating it in our celebrations, was our victory; the victory of life. Emaciated skulls and bones were an abomination to the friars, and that was their first reason to label our people lost and in need of God's salvation.

That's how Miguel Mauricio got lost, too. Today, so many lunations away, I remember that afternoon, when he left, and I knew well that it was forever. That night I took my boat and paddled to the furious swirl of water of Pantitlan, beyond the flags that alerted of its dangers. There, where the great stone with the ancient gods carved was, I turned my back to the islands and cried out for death. I only had to let myself be carried away by the circles of water that swallowed everything. In there, there were boats with fishermen and animals already. There in the whirlpool hope had no place. And no coat of arms granted to my lineage was of any value, neither the position as head of Iztacalco and Zacatlamanco. I could not keep my husband with me. I was not able and worthy of being their chief again.

All this death in the islands about to start and I just wanted to cover the riverbed with my flesh and bones. I prayed to Saint Anne, Our Lady; I prayed to Tonantzin to protect and save me. She told me this was no time for penance and prayer, for fasting and lashing, but I rinsed the salt of my tears and offered it to the Lady of Sorrows. I prayed the Lady would not stop my boat.

> That's how Miguel Mauricio got lost, too.

There will be another time when Miguel Mauricio and I will be together again, somewhere, and while this happens, may the light of faith shine for me, Eugenia de Olmedo, chief of the islands, where music and songs were once heard.

So be it.

CHAPTER 6
THE JOURNEY FROM MACAU
1629

Winds of war lashed the Ming Dynasty relentlessly. The armies of the new, young Emperor Tian Qi, who was only fifteen years old, were at the mercy of the eunuchs, led by the powerful Wei Zhongxian, favourite of his mother. Of humble condition, the caste of the eunuchs was voluntarily subjected to the mutilation of their genitals to service the Court inside the Forbidden City, seeking to escape from their conditions of misery.

Officially, they oversaw all possible libertine behaviors among the concubines of the Emperor, locked behind the walls of the Palace, and they also served as messengers between the imperial dependencies.

Six silver ingots were paid to the surgeons in charge of making them sexually useless, keeping the sharpness of their adolescent voices forever. They wore long robes and gray trousers, bowed to everyone, as servants do, and were forbidden to learn to write. However, some of them managed to master the art of reading and writing, until on and on they became involved in the decisions of the palace.

In a twist of fate, young Tian Qi was appointed Emperor. His father, a brief emperor, had fallen gravely ill and died just a month after taking office. Young Tian Qi, in charge unexpectedly, had not even completed his education; he did not know how to properly write the thousands-year-old writing that his great civilization had produced: five thousand different characters, which transmitted ideas combining sounds and intonation.

This young, brand new Emperor made it simpler for the Empress' beloved, preferred servant, Wei Zhongxian, to take control of the imperial workshops. He was slowly entrusted with the armies and his voice and vote were decisive for the appointment of royal officials.

With the cleverness of his fifty-two years, the eunuch Wei Zhongxian played officially as the Secretary of the Office of Rites and head of the Imperial Secret Police, but he went on taking up positions in the Court for those faithful to him until all was under his iron fist. In other dynasties, eunuchs had already supervised merchant fleets or the legions that had fought the Mongols and had even developed their own bureaucracy, in parallel. Wei Zhongxian, ruling *de facto*, was no different.

Tian Qi, of brilliant ancestors and beautiful and delicate hands, had preferred to lock himself in the Forbidden City, immersed in works of wood and carpentry, forgetting in his workshop cold and heat, hunger, and thirst, and his duty to fulfill the mandate of heaven to which he was bound: to be a righteous and virtuous ruler.

Controlling an empire that stretched from the ancient steppes to the pine forests of the north, to the jungles and rice fields of the south, and included the ports, deserts and snowy peaks, was not easy. The royal treasury was struggling. All previous attempts to stop the Japanese invasion during the Imjin War had left it empty, and the fight to extinguish all kinds of fires throughout the empire was ultimately in the hands of Wei Zhongxian, the Royal Counselor.

The army was now ravaging even the smallest towns to recruit men by force, to replace the casualties. They ravaged entire villages to assemble battalions and threw them to the front, immediately. The Mongol threat, invasions from Siberia, and quelling riots in the interior were causing hunger and epidemics in the south, which continued to be the main headache. Artisans, farmers and academics were dragged against their will to join the army, leaving villages deserted. The splendor of the Ming Dynasty, of the Han, seemed to be heading towards extinction.

By omission, Tian Qi allowed the wind to turn into a tornado. In its fury, it struck the most needy and the valuable system of roads that united the remote corners of the celestial empire, serving the caravans that traded by land through the Silk Road. The assaulters were causing death and heavy losses along the road, moreover on shipments of porcelain, silk, and pearls which were transported on their way to the courts of Europe in the west, through Isfahan.

The Ming Dynasty had produced the best of the arts, literature, and government, and with liberal ideas, China had opened to the New World as never before. Portuguese, Spanish and Dutch were rambling around the gates of the empire through its endless coastline, seeking authorization to establish trade posts in Chinese ports.

To dominate the commerce of the Far East was the dream of Europe.

With the void of power left by the Emperor's death, a regime of persecution and terror was established. Enduring three hundred years of Ming power at once was staggering, and foreign greed was suspended over the kingdom like a black cloud, covering the continent, the islands, its coasts, and ports. Europe was waiting for only an opportunity to attack.

The great ancient capital of China, imposed by the Ming Dynasty, ruled diverse territory of countless dialects. Tibet had not finished prostrating before the Ming, and a new pact with the Mongols, which the Dalai Lama used as his army, stoked the fire of rebellion. Europeans were also fighting their own battles. Spain had yielded the Moluccas, the coveted islands of the spices, to the Portuguese, experts in navigation and pioneers in establishing in this corner of the world.

The Portuguese were granted Macau since 1557 on lease to serve China as a shield of defense against the expansionist attacks of the Dutch. People were starving in the cantons. Women and children begged in the Imperial Barns for rice, and a long-lasting, unusual cold wave had extended the winters, greatly reducing rice production. Subjects were dying, while the dynasty decided to reinforce the fortification of Chang Cheng, the long wall of ten thousand li long, of brick and stone, which prevented harassment by the Manchus in the north. So much was invested in the wall that there was no wealth enough to pay for the deficit.

That blue morning, Huá Tuó was filling a porcelain pouring vessel in the village spring. Some cracks in its body, whiter than snow, made trickles of water drip down, soaking the cobalt blue and the gold of the prayers, inscribed as tears on its body. The beautiful container was the perfect metaphor to represent the situation of the Empire. Its handle and lid, gold plated, were so opaque and with so many cracks all over, that soon it would be worthy only because of the metal. At its creation, the piece had been baked at high temperatures to make it stronger, and its elegance had served three generations of his family, used in all ceremonies that demanded pure water from the spring, as an offering to the gods.

Cobblestones in the street, soaked now by the liquid that dripped from its cracks, announced that the vessel's end was inevitable. The spring started in the mountain range that protected Fujian from forced recruitment and ended in Huá Tuó´s hamlet, on the slopes of a gentle hill, the last one facing the coast. An emerald forest also kept this coastal town isolated and was a natural barrier against diseases and rebellions. Facing the archipelago, it looked towards the sea and its promise of distant lands. Through the front window, Huá Tuó admired the endless diamond of water and guessed when the arrival of foreign ships coming to the port would start. The army could barely control the landings in the north while Huá Tuó, his eyes full of the blue sea, only stopped his watching for his training in the backyard, facing the mountains and the lands of the Ming, so alien to this corner of his world.

Water flooded a multitude of terraces in which peasants, bending their backs by the load of work, had harvested half of the ears of rice this year. Huá Tuó, kneeling in the family's chapel, bent his back too, his forehead touching the ground, begging the eight immortal deities for better times. Frost had prevented all the grain from germinating, burning the stems before gleaning, and clouds of incense, the last luxury they could afford, wrapped his songs and prayers, his heart imprisoned by uncertainty.

The power of the Lady of the Sea would soon reach the river delta this season. She cared for the welfare of her faithful devotees, but she could also turn her back on her people to show her contempt for such an indolent emperor, who had given up his virtue, thus betraying the mandate of heaven. These days, citrus fruits for offerings were scarce, and famine was casting a shadow. People claimed that this emperor had lost heaven's favor and the patronage of all their gods.

Young Huá Tuó did not know how to calm the despair of the villagers. The art of healing the body had always been the trade of his family. He had learned all the points he had to press with his healing hands or to puncture with his needles to bring relief to a sick person, but there was no medicine to cure hunger and scarcity. He knew how to return bones to the right place and balance excess or lack of body humours. His grandfather, the eldest of his clan, had already allowed him to participate in some surgeries, and he was able to stitch a wound with silk seams to make a scar imperceptible.

He used wine plasters made with *mafeisan* powder, the herb that brings dreams of colour to smokers, that he used to alleviate arthritis, and rheumatism and pain were sent away with an opium-induced dream. His soft words made a sick peasant become a brave warrior, without pain or torment, abandoned to the chase of the dragon to give families a chance to say goodbye before passing away.

Herbs and plants were used to treat a wide range of conditions ranging from burns, to ulcers, laryngitis, insomnia, and psoriasis. His young and magnificent hands could perform bloodlettings that gave hope. All that and more he knew, about healing the body, but he has not figured out how to encourage a defeated spirit when reality is a slap in the face, and everything seems to be lost. Trade had brought a robust root from America, a tuber that gave better consistency to their daily rice ration and satiated appetite. Contact with the world had brought new foods they had adopted in their diet and Huá Tuó wondered how much more in those mysterious and remote territories could be.

The first point on the journey from Asia to the New World, sailors said, was Macau. A gateway to the world and perhaps, Huá Tuó wondered, finding a remedy for despair, which seemed not to touch the hearts of the robust sailors who arrived in Qianhu, his village, in the Province of Fujian.

In these times of need, Huá Tuó attended births in exchange for a small basket of vegetables. He massaged legs and arms that hunger and anemia had twisted, and tightened bandages under perfumed trees. In other years, disease had been treated by his family, granting them honor and fortune. Today, the languid light of a lamp occasionally came to their window, at dawn, begging for the extraction of an infected molar or the remedy for fever, all services paid with fruit and rice.

A magnificent chest of gilded wood and cast silver locks, inlaid with mother-of-pearl, housed the family's last coins, a treasure too hard to eat and so useless to buy food in this simple land of farmers and fishermen. Like his grandfather, Huá Tuó became skilled in the handling of knives and scalpels that released stagnant blood and restored circulation. He drained abscesses and pustules that healed with tinctures and infusions. He was the heir of the secrets of healing, but the sound of the waves that kissed the garden of his imagination was a stronger call.

In high season, captains and crew stopped here and climbed the hill to reach his family home. They came from the north and would continue to Macau, along the Silk Sea Route, a water road for porcelain, packed along with fine garments, nutmeg, tobacco leaves and betel, leaving for remote destinations. Macau was a lavish pearl, and the British East India Company was trying to get a jewel of its own. Chinese diplomats had rejected the British, who remained in open seas for weeks, waiting patiently for a peaceful dialogue with the emissaries of the Empire. The Chinese refusal was categorical. The British were not allowed to disembark and they returned home, humiliated, without a single Chinese leaf tea.

Huá Tuó, an adolescent, prepared the family's infusion contemplating the line of the horizon, daydreaming of the marvels that could be found beyond. He mechanically arranged the utensils to serve the drink made from cured camellia leaves. The beverage comforted sick bodies, and the steam of boiling water made him fly away to fabulous places. He pronounced verses of veneration to the bodhisattva of a thousand eyes and arms, the spirit of compassion and mercy, looking for clarity before the storm that cried out in his heart. Wrapped in white linen, sitting on an old rice straw mat, he had received the anointing of grace that named him the youngest healer of his family.

He was now the master of his destiny and could choose to move to a canton, a province in the interior, beyond the mountains, or like others of less adventurous spirit, take a wife there, settle down and serve the increasing population. With some patience, calamities would come to an end and, if the arrival of the British was ever allowed, there would be newcomers looking for his services. He received the anointing oil with eyes closed, meditating. He invoked the protection of the benevolent-eyed goddess, who knows of all our dreams as she well knows of everything that floats on the waters.

Bringing his forehead to the ground, he remembered the ephemeral flower of perfect geometry that inhabited the town's fountains and pictured its

The steam of boiling water made him fly away to fabulous places.

petals on the stream, drawing away, out of sight and reaching the delta of the river. When he opened his eyes, his family was all hugs and smiles and their frugal celebration feast, he noticed, was based on the seeds and fruits of lotus, his flower.

Don Gabriel de Hogueira, the same age as his father, appeared on the doorstep of this medicine house a few weeks later, when the rainy morning had soaked the earth all over. His right hand was wounded, and he excreted the liquid that all sailors know shows up before the worm that rots the flesh and requires having limbs painfully cut off. The foreigner was requesting help with elegant courtesy and in perfect Cantonese, and with all the respect a person who heals deserves.

It was no coincidence that once the representatives of the British Company of the Indies had been dismissed, the port was receiving a Portuguese delegation. The unusual was that a foreigner mastered their language. The family had attended many, but this was the first time they had had a conversation with a foreigner. The pain made the visitor more eloquent. Hua Tuo's father listened in silence to how popular Chinese porcelain wares were and how they adorned the tables of the courts of Burma and Siam. Fortunes were blooming with special orders for banquets, placed by the Persian caliphates. Families waited for months for custom made tableware, displaying their monogram and a verse of the Quran, in appreciation for Allah's magnificence and their fortune. They were fond of offering lavish feasts served in delicate, exquisite Chinese floral-themed dinnerware sets and he was their supplier. Salons and court ballrooms in Baghdad brimmed with a dozen different dishes, platters filled with fruit, nuts and dates in a rainbow of hues.

Don Gabriel had news about the Dutch in Batavia, who walked through damp streets, unbearably hot, clad in opulent embroidered silk suits, followed closely by short wives of reduced feet and a retinue of black and Chinese slaves. When the wound was clean, the father invited Huá Tuó to the table, with the foreigner, and both enjoyed his conversation until late at night. Grateful to Huá Tuó for saving his limb from gangrene, Don Gabriel was now relaxed, and they offered him some *mafeisan* leaves to smoke. He was generous in his payment and, wishing to extend the effect of drowsiness, he paid very well for the privilege of spending the night there, too.

He knew of the warm hospitality of these lands, although this lean dinner revealed the extreme conditions of those times. De Hogueira had arrived in a small fleet as a merchant, but with other diplomatic duties to perform. He had traveled the world and knew that, if not for this effective medicine, the wound inflicted would have had the worst consequences. Grain and preserves of his property were in his ship, a gift for the healers, so grateful he was, and he knew that with such a present he would feed this family for weeks. They agreed to go down to the dock, and the father insisted on handing over his last coins in payment for the staples, which de Hogueira kindly rejected. He would always be thankful for the cure.

A morning cup of tea sealed their friendship, ephemeral as flowers. An overcast sky and the sound of heavy rain made Huá Tuó hesitant about the turns of their conversation. They needed a good doctor aboard the "Santo Nome de Deus," to serve the crew of the fleet. The foreigner made insinuations about this in his Cantonese, full of accent. Confused, Huá Tuó did not understand if mentioning a doctor alluded to his father or himself.

He had followed the travel accounts of de Hogueira without missing a word, and he only fully understood that it was himself the man referred to when his father stood up with a sad smile. He carefully brought some dried, shelled lotus nuts, his flower of traveling petals, to carefully grind them in the mortar and supply the Portuguese with more powders for his further treatment.

Huá Tuó's father knew his son was a navigating flower: he had always known. They had spent hours together, watching the horizon, in silence, each one immersed in their own, individual dreams and thoughts and this was the first offer, sincere and safe, to permit his beloved son to finally go out and explore the world.

There had been no travelers in his family, even though the father had always wanted to embark on a trip. There were so many stories he had heard and even memorized! Pearl fishermen had ventured to explore offshore and knew that those lands beyond the ocean held infinite mysteries, challenging diseases, so difficult to heal that all the powders in his apothecary would not be enough. Beyond the sea, there must be new medicines and remedies. There were languages as well, so many, and other laws and rights, and customs and ways. Different skin colors, as those of black men unloading ships they observed in the distance, as that of the slave fleeing like a shadow towards the jungle, hiding in the bush of their backyard, there were, too. This and much more that the Father, his back hunched and rheumatic, had dreamed of knowing and never would.

Huá Tuó had been blessed with the art of healing, and besides the promised good pay, his curiosity would be satiated. An adventure far from this sandy harbor decide him to leave. In their house, there was no mother to warn him of the pains of the soul he might suffer, of the longing he would feel for sharing a frugal table with his family. There was no one to remind him of the little things he would lose, those that piece to piece are part of the fondest memories: the cooking together and tasting, the fraternal embraces and the smiles before sleeping, talking about the events of the day. There was no one to warn him of the melancholy that would invade each of his days abroad, wondering about the whereabouts of his family, and it might take years for him to see them again. The ship would depart in a couple of days. Unknown to them was the danger looming from secret diplomatic meetings to stop the British.

The wound inflicted by a rope to the hand of a merchant had changed the life of Huá Tuó forever. He would make his father's unfulfilled longing to travel a reality. On board the "Santo Nome de Deus" the young man who had only lived seventeen summers departed that September, in the year of 4,323, towards Aomén, the Portuguese Macau, in his imagination the most remote place on earth. A calm sea of six hundred kilometers would satisfy his curiosity gently on the way to the territory granted by the Ming Dynasty in exchange for defense against pirates. It had been a win-win transaction.

Don Gabriel de Hogueira was a merchant who liked adventure and his ease for languages had earned him commissions from the government that he combined with business. He loved Macau, and his contacts made each trip an episode that gave meaning to his life. He had interests in a couple of the ships of the fleet, and with all the shipment of custom-made porcelain, he would have to make his first important stop in Mughal, India in a few weeks.

Mohammad Salim Khan would celebrate one more of his victories against invaders that threatened the continuity of his dynasty of Persian origin and Muslim religion. The stability that the court of Mughal emperors had brought to India was starting a golden age in every respect, and their victories had extended the khanate, celebrated with feasts and banquets that lasted for weeks.

An entire life in the maritime trade had allowed Don Gabriel to contemplate all kinds of wealth, in countless cities and kingdoms. Long days on the seas allowed him time to practice the rudiments he knew in several languages while perfecting a couple he had mastered already. He loved to question the crews for their customs and traditions, babbling phrases and searching for their exact translation, while sea foam and algae witnessed each conversation.

Silk, exotic spices, paper, lacquers, and perfumes were his beginnings, but he had preferred to supply the porcelain tableware market, manufactured in secret places of the empire, a series of millennial furnaces located in the north to which no foreigner had access. De Hogueira was the only supplier of royal porcelain. He had been allowed to sail the Chang River, in the Jingdezhen Prefecture. The secrets of jade green and cobalt pigments were there, and he had been warned never to disembark there.

He waited by the shore for shipments coming from rural family ovens, the secrets of porcelain transmitted only among their own. They made for him precious, translucent vessels, as thin as paper and as bright as a mirror. He ordered and supervised the decorations and emblems or chose traditional motifs that would be a novelty in the courts. The touch of spoons and utensils on dishes and saucers had the music of tiny bells, the specialty of the Portuguese merchant. The Chinese Bureau of Porcelain, which governed its production, allowed the buyer to go inland only on special occasions, to supervise a load.

The administrators of the Indian emperor, the Conqueror of the World in Mughal court always had a birthday, or a wedding, or a title granted they wanted to celebrate in the most beautiful way. These monarchs loved art. They beautified mosques, palaces, and gardens were proof that beauty was the central element of their reign.

For porcelain, clay, feldspar, and silica were first crushed using hammer mills. After cleaning to remove improperly sized materials, the mixture was moistened, subjected to forming processes: plates, saucers, amphoras, vessels and jugs, depending on the type of ware. The ware then underwent a preliminary firing step, bisque-firing, in an oven or kiln and after cooling, it was ready for decoration.

All colors were arranged in this shipment of hundreds of pieces, decorated with the classical salutation to Allah, the Just, the Clement, the Creator. A frame of flowers and bright foliage on a background as white as snow would present the banquet of the Khan. When meals were finished, a jade green circle surrounded the Mughal emperor's monogram in gold with a phrase of appreciation and homage to Him, The One with No Name.

That was why this trip was so special. Thousands of dishes and another simpler, utilitarian ware would be delivered in seven different stops, before reaching their final destination. Cinnamon and nutmeg would come to Puri, in the Bay of Bengal, before the year ended, hiding in its perfume the straw that surrounded the delicate pieces. Macau would be the first stop. Fortified to be defended from attacks, Portuguese seafarers had occupied the south seas since 1511, and the Papacy had granted them these lands, against the ambition of the Spaniards, marking an imaginary line of 180 degrees west that both Crowns observed.

Expert navigators, the Portuguese had preceded the Spaniards in these territories, and Hernan Cortes was not yet born when they already traded with the Sultanate of Malacca in Malay, the lingua franca for trade in these islands. The House of Austria presided over the Spanish Empire, the most powerful on earth, but here in Nan Hai, the South China sea, the Portuguese were at command. They charged port taxes, administered customs and controlled the flow of merchandise and people. The constant struggle between Spain and Portugal found a battlefield in this corner of the world. Spaniards came here after Portuguese and the same they were doing in Macau; they also settled in Asia as everyone was doing. In Manila, in the Philippines, Spaniards established their own maritime routes, to reach and supply America.

De Hogueira, a Portuguese himself, had promised Huá Tuó that when docking at Macau, the port his country ruled, they would look for supplies to replenish his traveling pharmacy. On the way from Fujian, the healer had served almost all the sailors, and their cure had emptied his porcelain jars.

He would be entering Macau as a protege of de Hogueira, the merchant. His business was diverse and he would let Huá Tuó do as he pleased while he spent the afternoon checking his cargoes at the harbor to continue on their way to the India. The skiff that took Huá Tuó to mainland had a pleasant surprise for him. Beginning with the rower, everybody there spoke Cantonese, his language. Macau was Chinese, after all. And here he was, finally.

He hurried first thing to thank the Goddess of the Seas and Medicine for this fortunate beginning. He had begun the journey of his life that would reach the Bay of Bengal, a remote jewel in the portulans, and he was now considered a man of honour and preference in the fleet. He would make an offering in the temple, begging for the health and long life of the Portuguese merchant, his benefactor, and the smoke of incense would elevate all his wishes to heaven.

The emotion of sailing the sea vibrated in his soul and made him feel more alive. A fine rain was soaking his hair, carefully combed and his embroidered shoes, of wooden soles, clacked on the tiles on his way up, to the temple, following the crowd. Attached to the continent by a ribbon of narrow land, the place was dedicated to his goddess, Ma-Tsu. Macau was the place dedicated to Ma, A Ma Gao, and such was the name Portuguese ears had heard when they first arrived. They decided to call the place like that, as a good omen.

Huá Tuó made his way between the fruit vendors and the handcarts. The din of languages, Portuguese, Cantonese, Malay, and the broken and strong Castilian of the servants, remained behind, in the lintel of its magnificent doors. A rod of sandalwood purified his body in turns of smoke, to make it clean and worthy of entering the Mother's Pavilion. Next to him, a rich landowner was barefoot by his slave, and in his carriage, two elegant blacks of absurd livery in silk and lace waited still for their master. He immediately remembered the runaway, that black slave crossing the fields like a wounded animal, back in Fujian.

He let his eyes adjust to the light of the candles and the opulence of red and gold in the temple. He crossed to the front of the prayer room barefoot. With humility, he knelt in front of his goddess, Ma-Tsu, the one with the headdress of fine crystals that tinkled with the sea breeze. He kissed the ground with his forehead, surrendered before the Lady of the Flowing Waters, and thanked this responsibility for the health of the crew he would honor. Intoxicated by the feeling of joy and satisfaction and the perfume of the resins burning, he asked for wisdom to heal his patients and a good eye to choose the best plants for cures.

He wiped a tear from his cheek and went out to enjoy the sun after the rain showers. People leaving the temple walked in waves to different points. The colossal church of San Pablo, of the Portuguese Jesuit missionaries, dominated one of the hills, and beyond the orchard everything was the green of the field.

Thinking of collecting plants and roots there, he followed the crowd, who went up the stairs. The church was different from all the temples he had been at, and when he was in front of it, he hesitated to enter. He spent a long time admiring the facade, decorated with all kinds of symbols, and then fixed his eyes on one of the dozen carvings: a lady, stepping on a monster with several heads, with a legend in Chinese characters, though this was not a Chinese goddess at all, but one of those the Jesuits adored: "The Holy Mother destroying the dragon's head."

In the back of the temple, some artisans were hauling materials, still working on the construction of the side portals of the church. There were so many details all over the walls and arches, but Huá Tuó could not stop looking at this woman whom someone had allowed to subdue the dragon. The sacred beast for Chinese was being represented defeated, prostrated under her tiny feet. Who would have allowed the emblem of the dignitaries, the dragon that dominated storms, typhoons, and floods to bend this way?

His people, who prowled around, did not even look up at what he considered a sacrilege. The temple had brought Europeans like Don Gabriel, Christian devotees, to come and worship and pray inside this temple. They also remained indifferent to his restlessness. His amazement gave way, his attention called by the sounds of a strange instrument, a clavichord, and a chorus composed entirely of blacks, who raised notes in their voices he had never heard before. It was a strange world, indeed. Nothing was like back home, at the harbours of Fujian.

He watched for minutes the winged, round-eyed babies carved on the stone, floating around the Lady, playing trumpets to her, surrounded by chrysanthemums, sailboats, ships and a Chinese vessel. Crosses and skeletons completed the scene, crowned by a copper dove displaying her majesty above the sun, the moon, and the stars. The almighty lions of his culture were relegated to the corners, instead of presiding the entrance, flanking the main doors as it should be, as the imponent guardians for his people.

He knew that this church was dedicated to the Mother of God, another mother that he did not know. Inside, there was a special chapel for her devotion, and the same as Ma-Tsu, his Great Lady did, she started her life as a human. Ma-Tsu was a silent girl from a fishing family who became a goddess and now some port lighthouses had one of her statues, dressed in bright red to guide brave sailors to port.

Confused, he turned around the church, on his way to the Jesuit College of St. Paul, of missionaries dressed in black who had the language of de Hogueira, mixed with words that he understood. Behind the building were a thousand acres of land for local peasants and Chinese authorities had prohibited the Portuguese from acceding.

Behind the wall that fortified the Jesuit College, the green started and a hundred creeks and springs sheltered healing plants in their humidity, and Huá Tuó decided to collect as many as possible. He estimated he still had a few hours before returning to the Portuguese vessel. He marveled at the bustle of the city, but he feared to provoke the merchant, who until now had proven to be kind and magnificent.

On the dock, merchants reinforced their crews, hiring local sailors. De Hogueira was coming from the north, from Quanzhou, the city of ten creeds and cultures. There, he had picked up all of his porcelain orders, watching the shore Marco Polo had contemplated four centuries before. There, too, he had employed youngsters who were fleeing from the armies. They would join him for the smallest fee just to get out of the torn heart of the Empire. Paid in advance, the stop in Macau was their opportunity for a new beginning. They were still in their territory, but fear of going farther paralyzed them. It would mean abandoning their roots maybe forever. Macau was at peace. And they needed some weeks to calm down and get their thoughts in order.

From there, Canton was a couple of days inland, up the Pearl River, past a hundred fishing villages. On their way in, perhaps these youngsters would find one last reason to stop, to take hold on the coast and forget the song of the sea, which sooner or later would call for them as a siren did. De Hogueira and those of his guild readjusted the cargo and loaded some bundles and vessels bought here, before continuing to the southern seas. The waves smoothly shook the pier, and they had to take advantage of the room they gained by unloading part of their cargo. Everything exquisite and admirable came from the East Indies, hence the success of all companies and they had so load as much as they could.

The adventurers who had just joined them in the journey had chances of finding what they were looking for in Siam, Ceylon, Kerala or Persia. The same scene was repeated in all the eastern ports, where hundreds of men and women of value, art, and great skills followed the merchant routes of the companies.

Jakarta was now the Batavia of the Dutch, who established the East India Company in this part of the islands at the beginning of the century. They fought for a place against Portuguese pioneers and latecomer Spanish, and there were plenty of cities to establish in the immense archipelagos. They got the Jewel of Asia, while the Portuguese hemisphere and its delimitation remained in dispute with the Spaniards.

The Dutch had already taken Formosa for themselves, even though according to the meridian the beautiful island belonged to the Portuguese. Two thousand men already protected their city; they had called it Zeelandia and from there they were causing the terror of the ships that crossed the Strait of Tayouan. Stories of Dutch cruelty had reached the port of Fujian for years. Once the healers had cured the crew of an assaulted Chinese vessel. The Dutch has severed the ears of all of them by the short time they held them captives. They were famous for that. Occupying Formosa had emboldened their ambitions, and now they were setting eyes on Portuguese Macau, their new obsession.

The first cannon shot flushed the heart of Huá Tuó. Busy digging roots with great care and still reflecting on the symbols of the Jesuit temple, nothing prepared him for the outbreak of fighting. He pressed the blanket in which he kept his collection against his body and remained crouched, not knowing what to do. Lightning flashes across the sky announced more showers and right after the thunder, the second shot burst, opening a new wound of light in the sky that magnified his daze.

Hesitating, he crawled to get protection against the wall, approaching the point from where he could see the pier. Smoke was making everything blur. This was the first time he would be facing the reality of destruction, and it left him paralyzed. A third rumble seized his ears, deaf to the rumors of the countryside and the copious rain. He pressed his head between his hands, waiting for the vibration of the floor and the wall with the next discharge and counted each jolt until he lost count of the number of shots. When he had the courage to lean out again, the fleet of seven ships, his fleet, was reaching for the horizon.

Up from the hill, his eyes saw with despair a sky of orange. The rain was hiding the shipwrecks, who were using the rest of shrapnel of their cannons against the invaders. The main flagship of the Dutch fleet was sinking, and one vessel intended a slow retreat. The ocean was a canvas of red and silver, like those marinas the artists of Flanders painted in their workshops. Curled up, not knowing what to do, he lost consciousness with the last shot, the one that hit the wall with precision. The early mist found him lying on the grass the morning after, facing terror and silence. He was alone. The crowd that was wandering the streets had disappeared. He would never know that the most deafening noise came from the Jesuit battery of the fortress, a few meters away from him, and that they had also responded to the attack.

The sunrise filled the deserted beach with gold smoke all over the docks. Huá Tuó understood that de Hogueira and his ships had vanished. The population, accustomed to these threats, had collected in silence and thus continued, confused until the sun came out in full. He got up like a drunk, walking aimlessly, whistling a slow tune of his childhood his ears could not hear. He forgot everything, how he got there and where he was going.

When he finally descended from the heights of the Fortaleza do Monte, the pier was still deserted. Locals had repelled the attack along with the anchored ships, and de Hogueira's "Santo Nome de Deus" made its escape with the valuable merchandise of millions, losing the moorings, flanked by one of the ships that resisted the skirmishes until, as a martyr, was shot on the starboard side.

The damage had seemed minor from up in the fortress. Down here, he walked by the skiffs, one by one, looking indifferently at the shattered bodies the sea was throwing on the beach. None of them had the Holy Name, nothing that would make him remember. His heart beat hastily when he witnessed fraternal meetings; he heard cries of surprise and the weeping of people who began to seek news of the survivors.

Nobody was looking for him.

He walked through the docks observing lips that seemed to describe stories of terror. Everywhere, in Portuguese and Cantonese, the attack and its casualties were repeated over and again. Their Lady's mercy had protected them, and each one looked up at the hill and bowed their head in reverence and appreciation.

When there was no more sand, and the wall that separated the Portuguese concession from Chinese territory ended, he turned around to continue walking aimlessly, up to the village.

At dusk, he reached the Temple of Saint Lazarus, dirty and hungry. On the cobbled path, a couple of old men were struggling to move the last trunks that contained the archives they were hired to move to the new headquarters of the Diocese. Ecclesiastical authorization had been received to elevate the Igreja da Sé to the category of cathedral, and since the Christian evangelizing work radiated from Macau to all the Far East, it was necessary that the Diocese counted on more suitable facilities that would benefit the work of God to christianize China and Japan.

Nobody was looking for him.

Neither rain, the sun's rays, nor the Dutch attack had stopped the moving of documents and records that accounted for the decades of Christian religious conquest. At each rest, the pair of old porters argued about the reasons for safeguarding all these documents that proved the advance of evangelization, threatened by the heat and humidity of this tropic.

In such a task, Huá Tuó, a young man with a lost look, approached to offer in silence his strong arms to move the bundles of books and documents, a blessing sent by heavens that would give respite to their job. He moved lumps and trunks, diligently, as used as he was to serving the elders. He waited patiently for the next instruction while drawing silhouettes with his hands.

Life went on. The same day, with the sunset, all the population pretended to have forgotten the attack. They buried their dead loved ones and organized brigades to remove the rubble and rebuild the main road. The old men had removed only half of the room, full of documents, and with an extra pair of hands, they sat down to rest, admiring the blue sea in the shade of a fragrant acacia, so prized by perfumers since the east had offered this tree to Europe as a curiosity.

They unwrapped the food they had brought and offered to share it with their unexpected assistant under a shower of golden flowers. They were sure that he was one of their own, that he understood their language, his eyes the same and his dress, but they could not get him to utter a single word. Soon they gave up, handing out rice and fish dumplings while their simple souls stopped asking him about his inexplicable silence.

People of so many qualities went and arrived at the port with the tide, men with rough bodies and calloused hands, strong-speaking women, cured in the struggle for survival. This kind young man, who traced figures in the air, had been deprived of the ability to speak, deaf and stunned by the shock of the Dutch attack and the shots. They noticed his delicate fingers, still busy in a monologue written in the air, and returned to enjoy the food, sharing a small part with him he devoured. He finished before they did and went on, reasoning that the old porters had to fill the cart with packages, to complete the task before the sun went down.

They braved the seven long streets that separated both temples and the night found them about to close the door of the whitewashed room that would be the new archive. Encouraged, the old men joked about the possible origins of this strong, deaf, speechless Chinese, without voice and a name. He followed them silently, down the sidewalk, and something told them soon he would be pleading for shelter with his tender eyes, without saying a word.

The elders were devout Buddhists, but their weak legs had only found jobs as payloads and cleaners for the Catholic church of Saint Lazarus. They used them in the relocation of the Diocese and now carrying the multitude of bundles, in a hustle and bustle of maps, dictionaries and religious books, everything that could support the congregations in Hirado, Yamaguchi and Bungo.

Missionaries distributed in Asia were only a few if compared with the titanic labour of convincing and defeating the strength of millenary existing creeds. The Treaty of Zaragoza had decreed possessions to precisely continue the work of extending Christendom throughout the Celestial Empire, of Confucian morality and politics.

Half-asleep, lying on the mat the old men shared with him that night, Huá Tuó had forgotten everything, even his goddess, whose mercy was only a few steps away, in the small homemade altar, hidden in the gloom of incense smoke that permeated this house with a family aroma. Smelling the scent, the young man felt protected again. The next day, he got up, ready to follow his hosts. They had had the morning tea together, and Huá Tuó had not realized that for poor, old people, his stay should be reduced to one night only. They had no idea the recent attack had sunk his voice and his sense of hearing into a deep hollow and that he was a healer, his only belongings, a few garments, and his medicine jars, had vanished with the fleeing ships.

Sandalwood and the night with the old porters had restored his calm, although his words were still lost in the roar of violence, struggling to find a way to come back. They went back to complete the job at dawn. For them, the trunks full of books, accounts, records, and acts in Portuguese were only reams of paper written in incomprehensible characters; bales to accommodate under the directions of the deacon.

A voice with a strong accent, in Cantonese of very limited vocabulary, was heard on the threshold. His initial tone of authority changed in a second, with a wince of pain. His pearly forehead demanded an explanation for the presence of Huá Tuó. The men gave all kind of details on how helpful and handy the young man had been. Maybe the mercy of the deacon would authorize one more worker, at least for that day, as they were quite old and weak, they claimed.

The deacon, limping and holding his immense humanity on one of the trunks, considered the proposal, trembling. Pain made him clumsy, and while gritting his teeth, he figured out he would offer to cut their pay to afford it. He accepted the extra help unwillingly but he would pay only starting that day; the stranger would only receive breakfast, like them and then he started, all sweat, underlining the urgency of having it all set.

The excess of uric acid was killing him. The thumb of his right foot was useless, and his swollen leg made him walk, dragging the limb. Only alcohol mitigated the thrust that made his body walk with fury through the rooms. The day ended while explaining Huá Tuó how fortunate the conditions of his new job were. The deacon returned with their daily payment, and the young man managed to observe this man of santity's feet.

Pain was coming back to grip him again, and he was about to kick the healer when he felt his insistent gaze. The young man left the room without flinching, and everyone thought he had considered the pay so low that he had abandoned the deal. The two old men sighed, resigned to finish accommodating without his strong arms. If they had been younger, they would have left, too.

An hour later, Huá Tuó returned with a dark green liquid he had filtered on his shirt. A large brown spot left by the potion stained it, making him look even more untidy. He went inside to get the small vessel of wine for consecration and, ignoring the sacrilege, he emptied half of the content to mix it with the distillate in a wooden bowl. The deacon could not react on witnessing such a violation. He received the bowl from the young man, who was making him drink, pointing to the diseased foot. So much had Portugal learned from the Far East! The Chinese herbalist had chosen his best ailments and mixed them with wine and the deacon, while skeptical, decided to give it a try. He had such a candid and sweaty dumb face and liquor was lately not being enough. He mentally recalled he had promised the Lord to remove all strong liquor from his table in the mortification and prayer, but could well offer this exemption to God, Our Lord.

The pain was unbearable. He drank the contents of the bowl in one gulp. The heat numbed his body, and for a moment he stopped feeling his limbs. A surge took the torture and pain away. Still, he expected the torment to return, refusing to recognize a medicine man underneath the sweaty rags. Huá Tuó just humbly smiled when he calculated the effects of the remedy. That's how he got to sleep on the floor of the archives room. The deacon had to take the potion several times a day, he had to be here to prepare it, and he could continue accommodating the salons, cleaning the rooms for the priests, bringing water or getting the liturgical objects ready to celebrate the Holy Mass.

The deacon knew that the remains of martyr André de Phû Yên would soon arrive from KeCham, Cochin China, and there would be a shortage of hands to prepare the church to receive the honorable relic. The clergy would establish a vicariate in the place of martyrdom, and a group of priests would arrive in a few weeks. With them, several French missionaries would require accommodation.

It was Huá Tuó who ended up getting everything ready. The secular clergy was not as rich as the Society of Jesus. Its two rustic churches in the lower part of Macao contrasted with the brick and mortar Fortaleza do Monte and the Convent. The Society returned the favor of the Chinese fortunes, and educated some of their children in the church university, the first of western style in the east.

Missionaries arrived the following month, burning with fever. The hottest time had begun, and some of them had survived dysentery. Several members of the crew had been thrown overboard, including the bodies of ten slaves of Joao de Abrantes, who had come to Macau to give a beautiful Christ made of ivory, on its appointment as a cathedral. His devotion was making very good money trading crucifixes and other sacred figures made of ivory, and in his holy cargoes he also carried some gems he used to sell to Spanish brotherhoods to adorn the robes of saints or the skirt of Mary Immaculate.

They all received shelter along with the vegetable soup Huá Tuó cooked to serve his powdered medicine and stop the flow of their bellies. De Abrantes was the only one who had not fallen ill, but he appreciated the remedy he considered preventative. That was how the healer earned the esteem of them all. He served in silence, closing his eyes while pressing on bodies to feel infirmity better and administer the precise remedy.

A year went by. The Dutch threat had been put on hold with the arrival of reinforcement, as Portugal could not afford to lose control of its only gate to China. The Mings had found in the Portuguese lease an important source of money, and from time to time a Chinese retinue visited to get an extra bribe. Other than that, Macau was autonomous and safe.

Nobody in the church had thought of baptizing Huá Tuó. He slipped like a shadow between the main nave and the corrals outside, always attentive to have everything ready and tidy for the Holy Celebration. He received instructions in Portuguese, blinking dozens of times until he understood, and then continued his hard work in silence, slipping away from the Liturgy of the Hours prayer in Latin. No one had insisted on his presence. His gaze looked beyond the garments and jewels of the rich Chinese and Malays, married to Portuguese merchants who attended the celebration as a social occasion to be seen, while murmuring in the atrium about the Cantonese servant's good looks.

He was still lost and did not dare to go beyond the path that connected the cathedral with its old headquarters, and his only content was looking for herbs and roots, soaked by the monsoon water. His dreams of adventure and knowledge had become liquid and ran through the cobblestones, in fine threads, to reach the sea. Oblivion had anaesthetized his aspirations, without remembering family or name. Here, he could live forever, without fear of war and hunger as in the north.

Macao, the city of the Holy Name of God, was a journey around the globe across the Pacific, a peaceful sea, free of storms, if compared to the furious Atlantic. Manila had announced a group of emissaries would be sent to Macau if they granted permission. The dispute over the limits continued, and the imaginary line moved according to each one's interests, clouding all kinds of deals. The Diocese would allow the Spanish Consulate of Merchants the use of their dormitories and there they went, the illustrious captains Juan Morales and José Nebra, natives of New Spain.

Their small fleet had requested permission from the Portuguese authorities for their vessel to moor in the port. Coming from New Spain, they had stopped in Manila for some rest. They had crossed the world! Seville was always in their yearnings, and although they had not been born in the peninsula, they knew that Santa María de la Sede was the model to follow to build the Cathedral of Mexico. If the Sevillian builders and sponsors had set out to make a church so beautiful and so magnificent that those who saw it thought they were mad, they would do exactly the same. Despite the delay and rejections of its imposition, the tithe of the Spaniards, coming from the indigenous tribute, was financing the construction works. The spiritual health of the faithful was first.

For the cathedral's procurator, it was being a headache to raise sufficient funds. Spanish masters exchanged with the Indians their tribute in money for personal services and thus avoided delivering cash for the financing of the construction. But there were also groups, brothers, and brotherhoods that had proposed to contribute with donations in kind to the church to avoid any more delays that took away the luster of the Spanish city of their dreams they wished to reproduce in Mexico.

Captains Morales and Nebra had paid towards the trip to the only place they deemed would be able to build the most exquisite wrought iron chancel rood screen for their cathedral's choir: China. Their smiths were famous for their works, and in America there would be no other viceroyalty that had an ornament of such manufacture.

In "metal of the prince," tumbaga and calaín, an alloy of copper, tin and zinc, the rood screen symbolizes the door that opens the holy site where angels sing the glory of God in heaven. Here on earth, it is the right spot that unites paradise and earth, the gate to where prayers and songs to the Almighty and Eternal God are elevated. In every major nave, the choir is right at the heart of the construction to sing the divine glory, to praise God Almighty and Eternal.

Plans to finally finish the majestic residence of God, in Mexico, were quite advanced. The decoration of chapels, the placement of a monumental organ and the design of the altarpiece were drawn on paper, years behind the original date of conclusion. New Spaniards agreed it was necessary to dazzle the faithful with the best manufactures, like no other in the world.

In a sort of competition for the most select materials, the rood screen Nebra and Morales had come to order would replace the simple wooden structure that was currently in use. No one in the Spanish kingdom could reproduce the beauty in the work of metals foreign Chinese sangleyes, their artists, had. Portuguese authorities had already exhausted all questions regarding the nature of this extravagant request, wondering why the hands of New Spain artisans, so perfect in all areas of sacred art, were not able to accomplish a work like this.

Nebra and Morales had crossed the world, and in the end, they were convinced that those who financed their manufacture wanted the richest and most unique wrought iron choir rood screen ever seen. They had brought with them seventeen thousand pesos in silver to place the order. That money was enough to provide the entry payment for the work, it was the equivalent to buy a hundred of the best slaves from Africa.

Encouraged by the earthly and celestial favors the Church would render by accepting this undertaking, they had arrived in Macau. In spite of the danger, the east had the whims of the greatest luxury and possessing them was the measure of every noble position. Had the Dutch not sought commercial positions in Batavia and Zeelandia precisely to fulfill this need? Eliminating intermediaries as possible would keep the price low, and that was what had made them come.

And this is precisely how it all started. From the spices for lavish dishes to the blue and white porcelain to serve them, everything was to fulfill the demand for luxury.

The Dutch were dazzled for the sound and color of Chinese porcelains, for instance, and they had even secretly sent craftsmen with the mission of trying to copy plates and saucers. Kraak porcelain, snowy white, evoked in its name the Portuguese carracks that had brought it to Europe for the first time. Decorated in cobalt blue, the color the Ming Dynasty had chosen to brand the empire, porcelain had a perfect glaze and beauty the artisans of Delft were struggling to copy. They never succeeded in achieving Chinese perfection, but their wares in white and blue were within reach of people with modest fortunes.

Copies posed on beautiful Dutch tables in a central place, like a treasure, full of fruits and flowers, pretending to pass as an original of those admired objects of Imperial China, and were immortalized in still-life by the Flemish painters of the Provinces.

From the Igreja da Sé, Huá Tuó observed in the distance the Portuguese ships that left the port of Macau, full. The blue line of the horizon hinted at distances the Spanish vessels had given up to sail, using Manila as their headquarters, their only domain. Morales and Nebra, staying in Macau, were an exception. They had obtained permission to negotiate directly with Qiau-Lo, the representative of the Chinese sangleyes guild. The captains were here, well prepared with detailed plans and drawings the Master Painter of the Cathedral of Mexico had carefully elaborated. The Portuguese agreed that, provided the deacon served as the interpreter for the purchase, the negotiation could be made here. They would not be allowed to get into Portuguese Macau and terms and conditions to give an advance payment would have to be agreed here.

After praying Vespers, the captains would spend the night, hosted by the deacon. Huá Tuó guided the guests to their room with a single candle, to spend this moonlit night. Negotiations would take place the next day. They walked through the corridors, ignoring the dangers of the tropics in the gloom.

An imperceptible bright trace of carbolin, staining the wall with a perfect fluorescent line should have warned the noblemen of its dangers. The sting that wounded the sweaty arm of Captain Nebra, following a silent Huá Tuó, made every one scream, shaking the candlelight. A jet of wax fell on the stone tiles, plunging the corridor into blackness. The beam of the insect disappeared in a crack, and Huá Tuó knew that he had to run and fan the embers of his stove to boil water to clean the wound at once.

Hua Tuo learned it was a scorpion sting to blame. The captain's arm was all swollen, and a desperate Nebra was crying out for a remedy. Huá Tuó was stirring as fast as he could in the mortar. He knew the poultice of herbs and olive oil would manage to attenuate the burning and tingling, but only after a few hours they would know how bad the venom would affect Nebra.

When the sun rose again on the liquid horizon, the Captain knew he owed his life to the young man. He had spent the night awake, delivered to his care, fearing the waves of deadly fever would come any time. Since the attack at the port, Huá Tuó had slept badly, and now he was thankful for this busy night. Only until he was sure the Captain slept soundly, out of danger, did he leave to go out and breathe the salty breeze. The sangley's visit would have to be postponed for noon.

After a meal of rice and meat with spices of these lands, Nebra felt better and stubbornly wanted to end the negotiations once and for all. The temperate and safe climate of the capital of New Spain was a blessing, and crawling insects were not as deadly there. With a grimace of annoyance, the captains, along with the deacon, who was acting as interpreter, received the retinue of artisans. In contrast to their own eloquence, the one who seemed to represent the Chinese artisans barely opened his mouth to offer understanding on the technical details the captains were offering abundantly, regarding size, length, pedestals, moldings, grooves, and flutes, the New Spanish requested.

The choir, they said, provides seating for the higher clergy, who sing the magnificence of the Creator along with the choir, and houses the church tabernacle and a lectern for scripture readings. The access door was the rood screen in question, the gate that leads to organ and clavicords music and human voices. Chapiters would carry metal flowers festooned with clusters of a precise number of vines and grapes, and the door must be topped with cornices, crests, reliefs, and medallions depicting a list of saints they had prepared. Bulk figures representing the thieves crucified beside Jesus Christ, and bells to play the hallelujahs completed the profusion of details.

They spent the afternoon explaining and translating the drawings with the help of the deacon, and by the evening the advance payment was agreed. Exhausted, the captains were satisfied and ready, wishing to leave Macau as soon as possible. Nothing else would be keeping them from departing for Manila at dawn before the port had awakened.

The next day, dawn sent shimmering rays over the ocean, bestowing a golden path from the shore. Lying on the grass, listening to the sounds of the nascent day, Huá Tuó got up at once when the Spaniards struggled out the door. He dragged Nebra's trunk and made sure that the luggage was properly tied to the roof of the carriage, as a good servant. They had offered in sacrifice to God Our Lord and the Blessed Virgin all the dangers of the trip in this infected, inhospitable land of arrogant Portuguese and sangleyes of simple speech. They would leave as soon as possible, satisfied that the order had come to a good end.

They commented how rejoiced the Cabildo, the assembly of councillors, would be upon hearing the request would be masterfully met in time and order and how they all wished the following year would come soon to receive the screen of precious angels and seraphims in Acapulco. The Assumption of Our Lady raised on a throne of clouds, and a crucifix would crown this work and grant a place in Heavens for the devote emissaries.

Huá Tuó jumped up on the seat of the carriage to check the bandage on Nebra's arm. Both captains smiled, and Nebra reached into his pocket for the coins that would express his gratitude. The cart was taking the healer and the foreigners to places he had not set foot on since the attack, running fast through the deserted streets. The heat was rising slowly, and fishermen began their hustle and bustle on the beach. The sea waves engulfed the clean, plebbled beach.

When he was satisfied with the firmness of the bandages, Huá Tuó sighed, sleepless and exhausted, facing the Spaniards, dozing for a minute or two. Once at the dock, he untied the two suitcases that had hidden the treasure in silver of the captains, now empty, and placed them carefully on the sand while Morales offered his arm to Nebra to board the carrack.

Huá Tuó followed them over the bridge, naturally, going all the way into the ship and arranging the luggage in their cabin, without difficulty or complaint. Nebra hurried to reach the fluffy bed, and Huá Tuó arranged the pillows, like a faithful nurse, looking after the patient in his chamber. That's how he had been taught. He went back to check the swelling and touched Nebra's forehead, while the breeze slightly inflated the sails and the rising sun broke in colors, like a choir song over the waters. The ship had lifted the bridge and was now advancing, kissing the waves gently. The aroma of the kitchen, where the cook had a stew of potatoes and fish almost ready spread across the deck. Observing the line of the coast, the light of

> **The light of dawn in full bathed the young doctor in a halo that seemed to raise him to the skies.**

dawn in full bathed the young doctor in a halo that seemed to raise him to the skies, where his beloved goddess lived. When the stew was ready, he came forward, just as everyone, with a bowl of cheap, defective pottery in his hands, waiting for the last turn.

The fleet said goodbye to Macau, leaving behind the last curl of the continent, death and war, hunger and the intrigues of the eunuchs, the temples of different faiths and the noise. Cranes and swans in cobalt blue, flying through the sky on a white background, were ready to be painted on pouring vessels by artisans, as every morning. Coffers for fine clothing and jewels for courtesans were being carved and crusted with mother of pearl, and bowls for banquets, decorated with slender ladies of flowing robes like the sails of this ship were being baked at the workshops, admiring the undulating rivers as fluff as their hair. Export pieces in kraak, blue and white porcelain of the Dynasty, were inventoried without fail, while the officers registered port and exit taxes.

Huá Tuó left as he had come, without a fixed route to follow, his back turned against the rocks, captain of his fate, free.

PART II
THE JEOPARDY

CHAPTER 7
FOR THE WATERS ARE COME
1629

They called me the "Saint Matthew's Gale." People said that following the mandate of heaven I had unleashed all my fury at once at punishment for their sins, but it was not like that, never. I did nothing but to follow my nature and gather all the rain of the century into one. The rest of it, they did it on their own.

For millennia, water had dragged logs, rocks and all the usual natural waste down from the surrounding mountains to the bed of my lakes. Seventy rivers flowed into the majestic Lake of México, all born in the mountain range that surrounds the valley. When indigenes arrived, they found ways to live by the shore, settling their dwellings on the banks and even on the islets. They designed canals that bordered floating plots they figured out as they grew in number to gain space for their crops.

From my free passage their entire existence depended, thus

> I did nothing but to follow my nature; the rest of it, they did it on their own.

we made peace to live together for hundreds of seasons. When they settled, after a number of bonfires burning on the mountains, the traffic of increasing thousands of canoes moved my waters in the central lake. With the dyke and levee of numerous gates the poet Emperor built, they regulated the excess of water when levels were deemed dangerously high. Five lakes of fresh water, separated from saltwater, were controlled with the dyke.

One day, augurs and omens did not tell of anything else but of an invasion. With the arrival of those coming across the ocean, with their unknown ships of great draft, destruction began. Dams and docks stopped being maintained because they were fighting one another. Waterways were filled with filth and debris and the diseases that came with them spread, leaving canals broken and neglected. Hygiene was forgotten. New palaces, residences, and temples were built on top of the ruins, struggling to find stability in an artificial land of swampy bottom. They forgot to repair sluice gates and I ended up flooding the avenues of water where I had reigned.

Thereafter, solutions had been tried to get rid of the torrent while I stubbornly returned, defiant, flowing through constructions that had forgotten my memory of centuries. Some engineering works tried to get rid of me, to take me away, until in 1629 I decided to raise my voice, with a loud cry of days, to say that this was my place, that it was here where I wanted to stay, alive, to witness all these events here, transforming the face of the earth, little by little up to the last corner.

September had always brought the last rainfall of the season, so I knew I must hurry to be heard. I started as a shy drizzle that intensified with the passing of hours and had everyone running for shelter. One hour, ten days, nonstop. Gallons of water covered the cobblestoned streets, buried under the roar of the storm. Then they figured out that the story told in the pulpits was true and so they all whispered, frightened in the darkness of their homes. A flood had once covered the face of the earth, gone astray and sinful, why should it not happen again?

Those stories of the indigenous servants at the Archbishopric palace also tried to explain the disaster. They said that the prediction had finally been fulfilled. There was a hidden sacred cave under the lake whirlpool of Pantitlan, east of the Lake of Mexico, and prophecies told a column of water would rise to the skies one day, in a spell of clouds, that would gather all the waters stored in the heart of the mountains. They would all get together to fall at once, one day, flooding everything, covering everything.

Beyond the stories of both sides, for me, it was a joy to recover the land I had lost with all the new constructions. With the first drops, I filled the valley with fragrances to shake everyone's memory. Pestilence of the canals, once clean and now open-air sewers, was forgotten for a few hours with the rain and the wet earth evoked the melancholy of those who had known me before, reigning without limit, worshipped. Longing is made of the smell of the rain, of its sound, of its freshness and the sight of lightning sparkles, flashing bolts of pure energy that announce howling storms.

On those days of September, my waters covered everything and, from there, I could romp at ease, stretch to reach the walls of every building, forcing people to upload their belongings on the rooftops. The rich and the poor were accommodating metal pots, fine porcelain, silk clothes, or simple cotton garments in piles. They covered their treasures and memories with wood planks to try to protect them, but it was useless because I managed to get in everywhere.

At the height of the roofs, canoes offered vegetables under the drizzle at twice their price, now that hunger roamed the streets or offered trip to shelters inland to those who could pay to reach the shore. But how to decide what to pack hastily from all beloved belongings, not knowing when or if you would return?

After weeks in resignation, they would leave their homes, having only servant in charge to look after their belongings, while others would secure with knockers and padlocks their palaces and residences, fearing vandals and looters. They paid fortunes for a passenger and a small cargo, and there were so many leaving the city that canoes began to circulate even at night. Carvings and ivories from the Far East, Namban lacquer chests, lecterns, boxes and caissons, inlaid with mother-of-pearl, keepers of old inheritances, linens and embroidered garments in gems and pearls, were piled up in the looters' canoes.

A month later, people prayed loudly, asking for the clemency of heaven. The lessons of the book they worshipped had been ignored. The construction of arks, they said, built in advance, could have rescued sick people, children and elderly, but nobody imagined by then the situation would reach these limits. Hours and hours of rain were exhausting the patience of inhabitants, while in the courtroom the vice regal authority blamed hydraulics for the disaster.

In the palace, the Dutch engineer, Adrian Boot, former director of the drainage works ten years ago and called for the emergency, tried to moderate his temperament, expressing disagreement with respect to the plans that the German cosmographer Heinrich Martin had implemented. In a struggle of nationalities, Enrico Martinez, his name in Spanish, was now in charge of the drainage architecture and neither the work of one nor the other had prevented this disaster from occurring.

The Consulate of the noble city had dismissed Boot's ambitious project of a wall surrounding the entire city with a series of dykes, sluice doors and water causeways to control excess waters and powering windmills, as in Holland, to use their energy for flour production and weaving mills. Canals would also serve for navigation, and he had presented actual solutions to the Viceroy, he argued, based on his experience at home; definitive measures that were not accepted due to their cost, relieving him of the position in favor of the cosmographer Martinez, who seemed to have acquired greater rights by castellanizing his name.

The Crown got rid of the Dutch and his windmills, sending him to fortify the two most important ports of the kingdom, Acapulco, and Veracruz, and preferred to remain struggling with budgets, complaints, recriminations, intrigues, and suspicions.

For years hydraulic works had been discussed, and without a permanent solution, plans were forgotten until each rainy season came back, powerful, transforming prevention into hasty emergency and provisional measures. That's why the Saint Matthew's Gale had destroyed everything. The poorest neighborhoods, on the outskirts of the city, saw their adobe houses crumble, an event that repeated in each of the four suburbs that made this city and even on the islands. Buildings of stone and mortar creaked, damaged, everywhere.

Faith then resurfaced in waves. With churches flooded, the cult was suspended, and clergy was dispatched in boats to officiate mass from the rooftops. Neighbors gathered around to atone for their sins under this punishment of water, crying loudly and forgetting in the open the respectful silence they all kept in churches.

The bells tolled, and repentance rose in volutes, then evaporated like dew under the sunrise. With the first bodies floating, confidence and tranquility disappeared in the flow of water causeways to the shock and fright of parishioners. Everything was chaos and a few weeks later the city, a daughter of the swamps, was rotting. Water reached the balconies and in front of the windows, remains of carriages with their beasts still tied up, drifted slowly, their bellies all swollen to near bursting and floating among junk and rags, furniture and dead birds, in a macabre parade of disease that began to claim dead bodies in the hundreds.

When fresh water coming from Chapultepec and Cuajimalpan stopped running, the aqueduct broken, the exodus began, to the alarm of Viceroy Pacheco y Osorio. Without water, nobility clamored to relocate the capital on the mainland, far from this unfortunate lake that regularly exceeded all level estimates. Months before, taxes imposed on wine had been used to pay for reinforcement of the arcs of the aqueducts, but funds disappeared or were not enough, and the repair was never completed.

Before the flood, ditches had been boarded up, looking to extend portions of land that water hindered. Others remained full of trash and debris, without repairs or maintenance. Some water causeways were kept clean by the voluntary work of indigenes, but without pay there was no continuity. It was ironic that despite their efforts to maintain them as they could, taking hours off their working days for waterworks, they had been the ones who suffered the most. Eucharist was transported in solid gold chalices, taken to the sick and dying in boats, while the custodian priest covered his nose with lace handkerchiefs from Bruges to avoid contagion, struggling on waterways, sheltered under a silk parasol to protect his face from the sun.

The archbishop had the idea of bringing the effigy of the Blessed Virgin of Guadalupe, down from her sanctuary on the hills of Tepeyac, one league from Mexico, to obtain her intercession. The rainy season passed, and the city continued to sink into the waters, fearing the dry months would not be enough to evaporate it before the following season.

Tiny shapes of arms, legs, heads, and eyes, all cast in gold and silver, precious metals, were pinned to the skirts of virgins and saints in prayer for the relief of sufferings derived from the great flood. Church coffers grew in number of solid silver figures, silk tablecloths and brocades, offered as alms in exchange for celestial favors.

From her shrine, the Venerated Virgin of the Rosary was also taken out in procession. People sang antiphons out loud for weeks while she was carried in a boat, sailing the waters, until her rich clothes, profaned with mud and dirt, had to be returned. With new clothes, her dirty robe was sold as a relic among devotees. Her Precious Son was punishing the sinners and the disaster could only get worse, if possible. A few threads of her consecrated garment were an amulet to gain protection by her intervention.

Indians, formerly reluctant, began to wear rosaries around their necks, praying the one hundred fifty Hail Marys in full, with veneration. Secretly they knew that neglect and oblivion in the altars had unleashed the devastating power of their ancestral gods. An image of Saint Dominic of Guzman, founder of the order of preachers also came from Spain. His effigy, they said, had been painted in the workshops of heaven and backed by numerous miracles, as soon as he stepped on New Spain -or sailed its waters, to be more precise- the silhouette of the saint was reproduced in hundreds of expensive prints.

Such was the consolation all throughout the next year, and faithful believers had already promised to pay for fireworks and music to celebrate the Saint at his Main Convent when the flood was gone, one of the few places free from water because of the height of its land. The friars prayed to Saint Dominic and asked what they had done to deserve the punishing flood. Only then did miracles began to occur. Isabel, Don Vicente de Monroy's favorite black slave, had drunk the oil from the lamp that lit the niche of Saint Dominic and was cured from dysentery. Pedro, accountant Tomás de Chandiano's servant, had slipped on the roof, had fallen and was left for dead. Through the saint's intercession he got up and was saved without any injury. Luis, babyson of silversmith Don Luis de Azuara, ill of fever, weak without strength to suckle, had his father pay for a mass in the convent and the patron saint granted him abundant health immediately, right at the end of the Eucharistic celebration. In their mystical outbursts, cloistered nuns began to hear celestial messages that promised divine mercy, and in their visions, they received answer to their requests.

"Have Mercy on us and do not forget your children, Virgin and Mother! Listen to the prayer of your servants. Work a miracle before the rains come again."

When it seemed the water level was giving way, and the Dominican Order of Preachers was awarded appreciation for the achievement, Saint Dominic was appointed Patron of the City but eleven months after, what all that the city feared, did happen for real. The following year I arrived almighty and on time for our appointment.

This time, Indians heated stones in the fire to throw them in the pools and purify water to drink. With songs and bundles of herbs, their poor offering, they wanted to call me to surrender. As many gods as they had, they praised them in hiding, asking for their help, one more auspicious than the other, and each one devoted to a special need.

Mixtecs and Zapotecs had a chapel in the Convent of Saint Dominic, and there they went to pray for the tribulation, from any corner of the city they inhabited. Their devotion had grown, for the preachers taught them in their languages. They used their languages for catechisms and to administer the sacraments to their nations. A lot of seriously ill people used to come to the atrium, their children on their backs. Jesus Christ's Burial Hall allowed them to stay there for a day, on the floor. Besides the prayers, they were coming only to check the level of my waters, seen from a lookout on top of the Chapel of Negros.

Sometimes in harmony and sometimes in dispute, faithful African nations spent the night there and prayed in the afternoons, while they flogged their backs, making promises in front of the altar. Night found them lying on the atrium, listening to the rumors of water in the distance, trying to sleep, while disease ascended and spread like the spirits of their beliefs. Indians and free blacks, old and sick, assembled improvised pumps with wheels tied to the backs of a mule to pump stagnant water and keep this place dry. They had nowhere to go. The request of the viceroyalty to move the capital had reached the Court of Phillip IV. It was now considered impossible to rescue her, and they proposed the nearby Tacubayan or Coyoacan as a new site, but the inhabitants had so much invested here. Twenty-six convents closed definitively, only after putting to good protection the jewels of virgins and saints.

Courts had not resumed their jobs, as busy as they were, rescuing bundles of documents floating like lilies on the water. Workshops, without production and struggling, began to dismiss their apprentices. Archbishop Manzo de Zuñiga had written to His Majesty that more than thirty thousand people had already perished, drowned or crushed under the ruins of their falling houses. More than twenty thousand families had emigrated. Only the most elevated parts of the city, Tlatelolco, and Tenochtitlan, were safe from the water.

Market stalls had lost their goods, and houses, abandoned, were slowly crumbling. Those who could pay gave a Christian burial to their dead in common pits by the hills, for sanitary control and holy piety. All the grain stored in the royal warehouses was wet and germinated, and then it began to rot, yet it was consumed until the polished stone floor gleamed empty.

After more than a year, water that used to be deemed blessed for harvests, the one that was used to clean children's faces, continued to wreak havoc. The city was already worth millions of gold pesos, and despite all the damage it was preferable to wait for water to recede, complete the works of diverting water away and move on. The day of Saint Matthew the great capital of New Spain suffered a flood that reached two yards high now, more than the height of a man, and the saint, a publican and tax collector in Capernaum, had had no mercy since that afternoon of September 21.

Change is the constant. My patience before the merciless detour of my rivers and springs was over and I would change the course of history and the face of New Spain, forever.

• • •

Sea songs were transformed into river songs in the voice of the black woman who traveled with Pablo Paxbolon. He opened his eyes wide when the endless mirror of lakes they mentioned in every conversation at Santa Maria de la Victoria was in their sight. From that height, the lakes looked like an ocean, merged into one.

The pair was coming from Puebla de Los Angeles, hardly noticing towns and places, as busy as they were trying to ignore the freezing cold weather and rescuing mules from the mud. In silence, when only the hooves on the stones of the road were heard, Rosario sang with all the strength of her voice, tempered by the sea and the mountains. They had left the warm shores of the Chontal wetlands in Santa Maria and her song got a brisk and tireless timbre that tried to recover the sounds of water, the music of the Bani, the river of her childhood. Along with this man, Pablo, joy was filling her throat in tessituras of bliss.

Rosario sang for Pablo, for both were born nearby a river. They had joined their lives, and gratitude unlocked a greater affection that increased day by day, magnified as the harmonies of her songs, black tunes of unknown lyrics. At the enclave, Rosario had confessed to Pablo's grandmother that two of her lunations had already been omitted. The herbalist arsenal of the Chontals had taken her disease away, the Gallic disease, and since then, Rosario was grateful for every new day.

The elder said all she had done with her was to make her recover her balance. Her soul was lost, stray, after so many tragedies: the rape, the capture, and the shipwreck. Herb potions, care and rest would be enough to heal her. The old lady understood this whole mystery only half-heartedly, just as the people of the hideaway had barely understood where Rosario had come from and how much her mind and body had suffered. Language would always separate them, but gestures spoke on behalf of words.

She knew that her executioners, who had taken women in tumult, had brought her the fevers, the ulcers, and a sore heart. When she felt her health coming back, she decided that the spirit of waters had shaped her destiny and that all these hardships were needed only to get her here. She determined she had received enough and that the iridescent shell that now hung from her neck would protect her, because it represented all the good and bad there is in the ocean that had taken her here. She closed her eyes, feeling the sun under the canopy of the forest and thanked the spirit. Her river and her village seemed now so far away, as from another life.

When Pablo could finally hear the song of the birds in her singing again, while traveling this road, he knew that the day he took her, a new account of his days had started.

When grandmother learned Pablo's seed had taken root inside Rosario in sufficiency and that two moons had already passed, she savored her triumph. Conceiving was proof that her arts had truly defeated the disease. It was then that Pablo decided to seek his fortune somewhere else. Santa Maria de la Victoria was coming to an end, and the merchant in his blood knew he could take advantage of the routes to establish contacts with the Mixtec colony and the center. There were at least two enclaves of Mixtec merchants in the capital of New Spain he could contact.

With Rosario's letter of freedom, a tumbril, and young mules they had taken the road. They got used to giving explanations in the markets of some towns they went through. Rosario waited for Pablo looking after their merchandises, sometimes shivering with cold, while some Spaniard waited for the owner of the mules to ask about the price of the black slave. There was someone who even dared to try to put his fingers in her mouth to check her teeth and refine his price position. The scene had infuriated Pablo, coming back with the goods he had purchased, shouting from the distance in broken Castilian that the black woman had an owner and that she was not for sale. The purported buyer fled away, turning his eyes and pretending to examine the blankets the Indians worked at the foot of their stalls. Weavers bit their tongues, amused at the string of bravado Pablo proffered in their language, questioning the Spanish man's virility, mocking his stale smell, his clothes worn for weeks and the soup he would make with his bones.

Skinny and pale, the Spaniard of rotten teeth, did not have the security that a bag of silver coins gives and went away, increasing the rancor of his soul one ounce more, explaining to himself that a dirty Indian was worth only his disdain, not words.

Pablo and Rosario started the trip when the heat of the coast waned. In Santa Maria de la Victoria, Pablo had disbursed a large amount to notarize the letter of freedom that put in writing the new reality of Rosario, a black without the mark of the iron, reserved only for him.

"I, Pablo Paxbolon, had purchased this slave's freedom in cash, paying for her three hundred and twenty-four pesos, for her own good and benefit, redeeming the aforementioned Rosario her freedom."

With her Christian name and the surname of the Chontal Indians of Acalan Tixchel, Sekondi sent all her past life to oblivion, although she kept waking up in the early hours of the night feeling saltwater drowning a thousand screams in her throat, sweaty and disheveled. As the sowing and reclamation of land of the Spaniards grew, the hiding place of Pablo's people, there in the dense jungle and the wetlands, would not last any longer. Many Spaniards were moving to the new capital, in Villa Hermosa and he realized that with his small fortune, he could travel with the black woman throughout the kingdom, between both worlds.

Some of his people refused to leave the place. Expeditions were known for capturing runaway Indians, as well as slaves, taking them to the nearest cane fields and plots. Every noise in the swamps, every footstep on the sand, was a warning. They should not be there any longer, so grandparents called their authority and buried the navels they kept for some members of the family on the side of a white road, as a sign. They forced everyone to leave, making them swear that they would return only if the conditions changed, if danger was gone, as if that was ever possible. They all departed, moving in different directions. Only the elders would stay. They knew that as old as they were, they would not be forced to do anything.

Now, before the fabulous view from the heights, Pablo stopped the mules to contemplate the lakes. From this point the road descended, leaving the pinetree forest behind along with the fog. The frozen glass the lake was, stretched without end, dotted with small islands and islets, surrounding what seemed to be a city of buildings and tall bell towers. They had never seen anything like that before.

Rosario was dizzy with the sight and the altitude and returned to the tumbril to lie down, looking at the sun and missing the red and dry soil of her childhood more than ever. They had walked together on the fine white beach sand, feeling the turquoise waters on their feet and her skin already loved this sun and this soil, stretching out in a carpet of endless water. With his eyes lost in the sight, Pablo wondered if the canoes he had brought, mounted sideways on the tumbril, would serve to approach the central part of the city, dry and shining as seen from above. That, they would know the next day. They decided to camp here, with the sun exploding in orange, tinting the lakes, the salt of the beaches on the shore shimmering.

Pablo rummaged among the blankets and reverently rescued the bundle of embroidered cotton cloth, dried flowers, cocoa seeds and precious feathers that protected the sacred effigy of stone, the God of the black mask. They had managed to overcome all the obstacles on their way under the god's divine favor. He would bathe the image in honey and pray in appreciation before the last ray of the sun was gone.

They would start a different life here, under his auspice, and they owed Him. All the stories and tales were right. This city looked great, magnificent. The future opened before them like a rose and before closing his eyes, Pablo reviewed once more the message he would recite to the elders, there in the chapel, where the Dominicans ruled.

Mixtecs would help to find accommodation and establish contact with the millenary colonies of merchants. Soon he would know if bloodwood was in demand here or what other merchandise he could supply to start over. Down below, curtains, fragments of bone, buckles, medals, small crosses, gold pins, a complete library and remains of porcelain vessels floated on the stinky waters.

Preachers were tolling the last bells of the night, calling devotees to complete the liturgy of the hours in their homes.

• • •

I write under the rule of emotion. I conjugate your name and actions in different tenses and in my mind, I shape your face with words. You command my imagination to make you alive in my mind.

"I looked for you. Did you notice? I miss you! Where are you?"

"My name is Diego."

"I am Lucia."

The branch in my hands repeated that magic of pronouncing words in a new language, those I had learned through the tenacity of Negro Miguel, Adouma. By now, I was struggling to transform sounds into signs learned from the friar at the village. Some of them had stayed with me, after rehearsing their writing on the ground, tracing on a slate of damp soil each word repeatedly. Proper nouns gave way to more complex words: soul, punishment, heaven, and hell. Now I knew that phrases formed on the ground came from a mysterious, hidden place.

"What are you doing with my soul, Diego? Have you noticed me? I am Lucia. I really missed not seeing you in the mill, by the river, today! Your hands, working on that fence, left a trace of fire, imagining your touch, in my heart."

> I conjugate your name and actions in different tenses and in my mind, I shape your face with words.

While I tried to capture all these feelings in writing, the same emotion I felt with my discovery, up in the mountains, on the way to the Lake of Mexico made my heart jump in joy. Up there, I realized my thoughts could take shape in my breath. I could make words that came out of my mouth to form signs, with the icy wind. It was then that all those lessons I learned at the coast from old Adouma came back to me. Words saved me when the nightmares of surviving the shipwreck threatened to be an every-day sorrow.

Repetitions, pronounced by the black old man with his strong voice, while his fingers twisted knots and turns that made ropes, and his determination to make me recite them, came back to life in the fog. From his lips, new voices figured out their way down to me, a thousand voices, silencing the music of our shared and hidden language. Hausa was only used when his hoarse, unforgettable voice tried to explain a term my eyes did not fully understand and was limited to one lullaby only, reserved for the night. His voice held the rumors of the jungle, the face of mothers cooking and teaching stories to children by the fire, naked children dancing in the smoke of burning dung, under another sun, just as hot. Black Miguel had insisted on banishing all accents from my voice. And he had almost made it.

"So, they do not make fun of you, Negra, bold and burned face. So that you speak well, as people of respect. Say like that! See? Like this! Come on, repeat!"

Months later, on the next trip of master Pablo Paxbolon to the village, my sale was settled. Frigates still arrived in Santa Maria de la Victoria, and some preferred to buy slaves that had already acclimated to the humors of these lands than to risk their investment.

Master Pablo took advantage of smugglers and newcomers and incidentally offered a female slave of good manners, trained in the domestic arts, ready for the upbringing of negritos, doubly serving as a milkmaid insofar as soon as she got pregnant. Master Pablo's pockets were full of the monies he got from the price he set on me and his canoes were loaded with iron goods. Once sold, traveling without knowing the extension and scope of the kingdom is usually not surprising, after having known the width and depth of the sea. My new master arranged for us to leave the unhealthy coast at once on the hacienda he had just bought at auction from the Holy Mother Church, on the shores of a lake in the heart of New Spain.

There, he said, he would plant wheat, and with so many acres of land, his cattle would run at ease and the olive grove of his childhood, back in Alcala, would take life in the noble New Spain, the place to replicate his memories by the shore of the lake. So much was yet to come! Obeying his father's mandate, as soon as the part of his inheritance was located there in Santa Maria de la Victoria, my master fulfilled the advice his late father had given so earnestly.

"That the first funds in which you spend be used in the purchase of a slave to serve you on the roads and may you later get as many as you need, trained to your please and used to your ways. Such is the task of a master to gain obedience from workers to take possession of your property as befits your fortune from now on."

I, was his first slave purchase and it was such good luck that I spoke the language of Castile. God had given me an unlimited curiosity and I had memorized all the places I had heard from sailors and officials back in Santa Maria, without losing detail. In only one season of fleet arrivals, I had learned of mosques in the Sahel and cathedrals in the Spain of the King, where black kids accompanied their masters in services at fabulous cathedrals.

I only showed disgust at the stories of the oceans, plagued by pirates. Those tales closed my throat with the brackish taste that had never left me since the shipwreck. I spoke without respite, and my name since master Pablo sold me was Lucía. I had learned Spanish language from a black Hausa soldier, a peasant of cane, pineapples and rope maker, who had taught all the words I knew. That was me.

The spell of writing, learned at the hem of the Dominican friar's tunic, had transferred its magic to the reed that gave life to the damp soil of the atrium and then continued all throughout the hacienda. House chores were done under repeating the phrase the friar had put in my mind, without understanding it very well.

"Write as we pronounce and pronounce as we write, write as we pronounce and pronounce as we write."

Sweating by the coast and going up the mountains range on our way to the capital of New Spain, I realized that every word could be represented with traces on the dust, locking its meaning on them. Only intonation and nuances would escape, flying away, just as it happens to everything you feel when you pronounce a word: capture, factory, shipwreck, lunation, Lucia, sale, and ports. Emotions related to these words surely go to the same place where memories float. The house in Santa Maria de la Victoria, the river and its suburbs, the water roads, the servitude, the manners I learned there and the lace tablecloths, hanging to dry under the sun preceded my sale. A new owner was now giving another full turn to my life.

The road guides, the brocade rooms with tapestries, the polished pronunciation to keep up with the language spoken in the house, the inn, and the square, waited for weeks for news about Don Pablo Paxbolon, lord of the river trade. I started serving in the big house of whitewashed walls after the hurricanes, and I had become a clean and friendly black servant, of good conversation, who had almost lost the accent and beast manners of the suburbs. When Master Pablo started to lease me as a servant, old Miguel stayed there in the hut, forgotten, dragging his varicose and swollen legs, oozing, unable to move.

"Lucía, yo' so bad, so bad, yo' goes away yo'."

As a black maid and servant, my departure under master Pablo's commence started the slow death of Adouma-Miguel. It was not until the end of the year when the whitewashing mortar waited for the end of the waters to whiten its walls again, that a mule arrived at the big house with news. Old Miguel had died and his body, full of grief, was thrown into the river by the souls of charity that had found him. They said that in the roar of the waters meeting the sea, the wooden pier had howled when his body was thrown on the muddy shore. Water had said his name, Adouma, the one his Portuguese captors had heard, the one given by his clan, where canoes are made of okume wood, bathed by the Ogowe, the Sebe, the Loula, and the Libiri rivers.

With the news of his death, I drowned in the storm the cries of longing that contained all the losses and sufferings of the last year, my village, the child games, the kidnapping and the flies devouring our waste, there in the dungeon at Elmina. The pier seemed to wobble with my sobs, and I am sure my tears increased the flow that began to flood the near streets. Disaster and that year's storms sent away, once and for all, the last Spaniards of Santa Maria de la Victoria. Before turning my back against the waves, I said a prayer in his memory, and I tried and promised to pronounce better than anyone the words in Spanish he had tried so hard to teach me.

My efforts would honor his memory, and there he would be, always, when my lips imitated the accent of the owner of the house or that of his old maid from Cuenca; the lisp of the messenger, the bastard of a lieutenant who had put him in servitude, even if his tare murmured obscenities, captivated by the sight of my breast, while he spilled the flour that would cook the bread of the afternoon.

It was in Spanish that master Pablo finally agreed to my sale, as a slave of Don Luis de Dueñas, that newcomer from Spain. His Spanish housekeeper had buried another black woman on their journey here, the victim of a recent miscarriage, and her recently acquired hacienda had to be organized immediately upon arrival. Don Pablo sold me, and Master Dueñas matched the price in gold he demanded. This is how I left Santa María de la Victoria one August morning.

Master Dueñas' family was making some wealth in the found veins at the Province of Silver that had re-opened the ancestral road to Taxco. Indigenous roads, which for hundreds of years had been used between the ports of the Gulf towards the south of the continent were now transporting quicksilver, tools, and equipment for mining exploitation.

Don Luis de Dueñas, flanked by Indian servants, drove mules and cargo in the river passes, on the way to his new property in Mexico, while I, a house slave with selected manners, tumbled between cocoa sacks, farming tools, and spare parts. I was capable of marrying a slave and giving Don Luis descendants to work the orchard, the cornfields and his lands on the banks of the Magdalena River, a property of this Spanish owner to the service of his Majesty.

From Puebla de Los Angeles we took the road to Atlixco to reach Don Bernardino de Dueñas in Cuautla, Don Luis' cousin and owner of a couple of small mines in Sultepec, west of the Taxco road. There, they would exchange miner's bars, sledgehammers, wedges, picks, bellows, and scales, so useful in the mining sites, for twelve slaves that would complete the crew that Don Luis would use in his hacienda.

Don Bernardino was making a medium fortune at the Province of Silver. He had been blessed by the Christ of Forgiveness and the production of the Real de Arriba, his property, would cover his family with wealth until the end of their days. Silver mining was just beginning down here. He would come with us all the way to Cuautla where he would also try to fulfill the oath he had made to pay for a painting of the Our Lady of Light for his town's parish, and he was sure her favor would illuminate his next mineral search.

Master Luis had offered this valuable tools and utensils, so scarce in these lands, to bring them to his relative, of such great esteem. We would spend a few days in Cuautla and emptied, the tumbrils would transport the slaves Don Bernardino had given to Master Luis in exchange for the tools.

They had eliminated intermediaries, and this would be the only occasion to stock up at better prices. Don Bernardino had brought a dozen bambara, lunda, and mandinga slaves in exchange, highly appreciated for being the most expert in tools. The superficial veins of the Real de Arriba had been exhausted, and he had temporarily withdrawn from mining activity, seeking to obtain the capital of several chaplaincies, administered by the Carmelite Order, to finance deeper excavations. That's how mining was. A series of chapters of boom and decline where fortunes were a fickle river, as unsteady as the strong Bantu slaves that would join our entourage.

It was such an annoyance to travel like cargo, next to trunks and bales, but it was worse to be seating surrounded by a herd of blacks, dirty and disheveled. United in brotherhood, at each stop they made fun of my efforts to trace signs on the damp soil from afar. They were just a bunch of black devils who did not understand that the rattle of the wheels was an occasion for a rhythmic review of what I had learned with old Miguel. Their cracked and callused hands made them proud of their strength and ability to domesticate the wilder beasts.

The fortuitous visit of Don Luis to the only covered cart of our caravan happened when we left the rivers that flowed into the coast. Cold of the mountains started, and it was no surprise for me. I was already accustomed to quelling the masters' anxieties, those that the friars so condemned in the pulpit, at any time and any place. Taking me and deceiving nature, withdrawing from my inner, happened almost daily, even while the wagon was running. Those meetings lasted only a few minutes, with white snow melting on the highest peaks in the background, silent witnesses of the event in the distance.

When the master was done, he had a small talk for a few minutes, telling how profitable the hacienda transaction had been or the convenience of increasing the workers for his farmland or how long was the journey still to go. I got used to pretend to pay attention to his small talk, while the yearning for writing words disappeared under the dirt and the sweat of days, mingling with the stink of rusted iron and tools settled between sacks and trunks.

My mind started to think if it would be possible for me to decipher the ink signs on that crumpled paper that Masters Pablo and Don Luis called my Deed of Trust. My impatience longed to have it in my hands, to master its reading, to understand how its content held me and was able to specify terms, duration, custody, and property. This trip had lit a light in me, back in the mountains, when Lucia, and everything that I am, began to draw words my breath expelled in the cold. Slave, mountain, maid, black and withdrawal were exhalations roaring louder as Mexico City got near.

The more temperate climate had unleashed stories of lavish residences that fortunes were building. Those brute black slaves coming with us defiantly talked to each other in their languages, just as they did in their mining enclave, despite being forbidden to speak them. They also whispered to one another without fear of being reprimanded, stories of Mexico, even if they had never been in the city before. Brazen, whenever they could they talked to each other. Don Bernardino had allowed them to do their way on his property.

Don Luis' housekeeper, who had followed him from Spain, censored such behavior daily because blacks never forget. Being in a group made them bold, braver, and stronger. She would have to warn the foreman at the hacienda about prohibiting this behavior, she said over and over. None of their languages was mine, and I knew that they would be punished as soon as we reached our destination.

We arrived in Coyoacan before sunset. Kumuhameka Nzambi! Praise God! Only after we spotted the bell tower of Saint John the Baptist and set foot on the property, we knew that we would be safe from the waters. In Cuautla, Don Luis' cousin had informed us about the news. The lagoon of Mexico had overflowed, and the city, formerly an island, was completely flooded. On getting closer to Coyoacan, the news became more and more alarming, and Don Bernardino quit his intention to pay for the painting and have it made in Mexico. His faith was great, but his need was not. He forgot his commissioned painting, happy to have an excuse for his conscience and his pocket and decided to return to his mine. His Spanish fragility fled from any source of disease, and well he knew that after the flood, disease comes.

He said goodbye to his faithful black miners and reassured his cousin these slaves had already beaten malaria previously. At Cuautla we learned that palaces and gardens the Spaniards had built there in Mexico were now underwater, submerged for weeks. With the view of the lake shore, its beaches hidden under water and rubble, everything turned out to be true. The stain of aquatic plants and debris was visible from the road, larger while descending, leaving the immense lake with only a few crystal reflections shining under the setting sun. The remains were cornered on the banks of the road that came from Mexicalzingo.

And now, right at the main gate that opened to welcome us to the "Hacienda del Apantle," highlighted by his huge smile, the young night illuminated with silver burst the face of Diego, the foreman of the hacienda, who had patiently waited for the arrival of the new owner.

My body immediately knew when I saw you, Diego. A bonfire started inside, devastating everything.

On the sight of his new property, master Luis forgot the fatigue and listened to all the details about the state of this place, enthralled by the magnificency of his treasure.

You knew everything going on here at the hacienda, Diego, up to the last corner It was in the Apantle that you became a man and the master was so excited to see the extent and abundance of his new lands. The attorney who had completed the sale for him was right. The weaving mill, the plots, were the most productive and he was ready to discuss with Diego the figures on the accounting books the following day. The housekeeper certified that the old grocery room in the kitchen was habitable and the angel carved in the lintel smiled at the creaking of the door that received black Lucia in this room.

Lawalo, my name in Hausa, would never have dreamed of turning a reed into a pen tip. Life changed more than twice for me, and here, my long fingers would be in charge of sweeping floors, oiling the clavichord, polishing the pots, the silver vessels and cutlery, repeating the litany of the Blessed Virgin in front of the lintel angel, making a new prayer out of it.

"Diego in health and illness, the most admirable, singular vessel of devotion, house of gold, ark of my covenant, door of heavens. Diego."

• • •

Eight Augustinian monks prayed before their meals in the refectory, when they called the huge wooden gate of reliefs that represented the Passion of Christ. The water wheel that operated the mill was already still, after a long day of work and the sluice door that fed the cisterns was shut. There, behind huge walls of whitewash, the current flowed crystalline, until it reached the lake. The Saint Nicholas of Tolentino fountain supplied Mexico with the best water in the kingdom, and it also provided the Augustinian's enterprises and endeavors.

The mercy shown by the family they had met in Orizaba had left Alonso and black Sebastian at the gates of the Convent of Culhuacan, refusing to take them along the road to Mexico. They did not want to attract attention. They agreed to leave them at the gates of the convent as soon as the lake was in sight. They convinced the anguished black that he and his master could spend a few days here. The family would pay for their stay so his master could fully recover. From there, the

Spaniard and his slave could get to neighboring Coyoacan or Huitzilopochco to look for the destination the sick young man had insistently pronounced in his dreams.

They had left Orizaba when Alonso's bleeding sputum and fever had subsided. The quicksilver caravan that had employed Alonso and Sebastian was gone, and their employer did not bother to ask about the health of the Spaniard. Both had hardly served the caravan. His black got all in charge when Alonso got sick, and the muletter had no difficulty in finding other servants to protect his precious load of quicksilver from assaulters.

Preparations to get on the road again were made though Alonso's fits of violent cough left him without strength. It took him a month to feel a bit better and, encouraged by Sebastian, both men had asked for the charity of a family of four, spending the night in Orizaba, to get them back to the roads. Mexico was waiting for them; Alonso needed to fulfill some orders there, and the family estimated that the pale Spanish and the black could contribute to take care of the family, two more men who would also support their alibi.

Sebastian was always alert, always faithful to Alonso, and he got the family's permission to let him spend the night on the tombril, along with their luggage. He was an expert at attending the mules, he promised, and on rubbing and cleaning their paws, using his ointment of herbs and oil to cure them. He was also a good hunter, and he proved so with the deer he got, one that fed them all for days. In short, he knew how to be useful. They were running fast, almost without stopping, reaching for the last mountain range and resting for only a few hours, enough to have the animals recover. In the last stretch, when they climbed the endless pine forests, the glorious sun advised the weather was finally getting warmer.

Cold had been left behind, and only now they could camp a full night before heading to the city. The only two children in the family, a boy and a girl, were fed up. Only the composure of their manners and the nearness of their mother quieted them, barely poking their noses out through the curtains of the covered wagon.

The proximity to Mexico gave them all relief, and when they stopped, the father left as usual, far from their sight, as he always did in each stop. Standing erect and facing the road, no one could guess that every time he closed his eyes, touching his left forearm with his right hand. His thumb and index finger made a ring that started on his elbow, sliding slowly, seven times, until reaching his wrist and then his middle finger. Whispered words no one could hear went along with the movement of his hand.

When they stopped and the father went away to the front, nobody dared interrupt him. Sebastian wondered what disease the man would be suffering, rubbing only one of his limbs to later come back and take the reins with determination, no expression of pain at all. It was also easy for him to tie the bales or carry water without any expression of suffering.

This would be their first full night sleeping under the stars. Everyone got a blanket while Sebastian wrapped Alonso with the only ragged one he could get with the pay of a month's work, fallowing, back in Orizaba. The two children ran out of the covered wagon as soon as the mother allowed them; the boy began to jump between the fallen trunks, and everyone was grateful to be able to stretch out at ease. The girl cleaned and flattened a space on the ground and began spinning a wooden toy. The spinning peg top spun, while each lap hid the engravings, inked, on each of its four faces. The girl's curls shone under the light of the bonfire while the small piece of wood turned around in perfect balance.

Alonso remembered a toy like hers in his hands, spinning on a street in distant Seville, like a dream. Soon, stars were gone, and the song of the birds brought a new day. They would arrive at the convent a bit past noon. "Our Lady of the Forsaken" had left Cádiz at the beginning of the summer, and a couple of Augustinian friars on their way to Tlayacapan had talked extensively with the father, explaining diligently the efforts their congregation were making to bring the faith to these lands. The eloquent friars regretted that the family was heading north, a place of many dangers and dedicated an afternoon to warn them of the difficulties they would find inland.

The caravan stopped before the extraordinary wooden gates of the convent. The family would leave Alonso and his negro without even knocking, nor would they seek the hospitality of the friars in the hostelry. The family showed an unusual hurry to leave and the father was grateful. The history of his people was full of exodus and captivity, and it was his duty and his appreciation to pay for the shelter of these strangers and share a bit of the fortune the God of Israel had granted his family.

The money would pay for a few days there, and his soul could leave quietly to take his family to a good destination. It was Friday, and they wanted to be settled with their relatives before the night closed. The blonde girl poked her head through the curtains when the father urged the mules and offered Alonso the carved wooden figure that had so entertained him. The top in his hands snatched a smile from Alonso and memories came back to visit him.

"Nun, Gimmel, Hey, Shin." His grandmother used to spin a piece of wood just the same, engraved with the same peculiar signs that formed an acronym for an expression, "a great miracle has happened here," and the toy going around always started a story grandmother would start saying, touching the symbols with care and putting her finger on her lips, the warning of silence Alonso so well knew.

They hit the thick iron knocker on the convent door when the caravan was out of sight. Sebastian would take care of the payment and the arrangements, as befits the servants, while fables of wonderful kingdoms, of hanging gardens that had surrendered to the One returned to Alonso's memory. Those were stories to put someone to sleep, only for that they were, his Grandmother used to say.

When they were installed in the Augustinian bedroom, he spun the small piece of wood on the austere table once again. His grandmother appeared, humming and asking Alonso what his luck would be, on what face the peg-top would end up.

Would he get everything, nothing, a new bet to be placed or taken? Bets by then were all paid for with the dry peas from her garden.

Those were his choices: to leave everything to random fate or to decide his future, against luck, against destiny. To find ways out of the only four given choices and place all his bets, settle them for winning.

Alonso put the toy in his pocket, with a bright smile, his beauty shimmering under the moonlight coming through the window. He covered himself with the blanket up to his eyes, as when he was just a child, looking at the masterly carved wooden ceiling and listening to the slow breathing of his sleeping black nurse.

For that night, the cough gave way, and both slept soundly, to the cooing of the water spring that shone in that silver light that so many generations had observed, while Alonso fervently said the prayer of his childhood till he closed his beautiful blue eyes.

• • •

To you, the owner and master of everything, I call you. My offering is here for you, now that nothing blooms on our plots anymore, now that everything is bathed in tears. The omen was fulfilled, and us, the naturals, the nahuas, we knew the water cave of the ancestors raised a storm column indeed that furiously fell into the lake, driving everything crazy.

In other times, a flood of this caliber would have been attended by the elders. We would have made a meeting and elders would know how to solve it, what to settle, what were the measures to solve the disaster in full. Our gods would talk to us through them and then we would do what needs to be done. We would have called the men of wisdom for construction, those who had planned our water causeways, our roadways, the dams and the dikes. The small and humble house of Iztacalco, the house of Zacatlamanco, were no longer.

We were just ash in this account of the days, a silk of corn flying in the wind. Some of us had survived the epidemics, but there was nothing could we do against water, that was now everywhere, covering everything. A few weeks later, we understood that we should leave our houses down here. The thirty islands around the lake, of different sizes and industries, of hermitages and convents superimposed on our old temples, began to empty themselves in its four directions and all were escaping to the mainland.

Most of the islands produced salt or flowers or vegetables or served as the foundation of the roads and were now emptied. The causeways that connected Tepeyac and Tenayucan, Tlacopan and Iztapalapan with Mexico-Tenochtitlan were now flooded, blocked. The dyke that ran from Tepeyac to Iztapalapan had not been completely repaired, some parts of it were filled with improvised planks of wood, stone, and mortar. That had not been enough to keep the saltwater of the Texcoco Lake in its place. Our hearts were afflicted with their usual sorrows, but it was more unfortunate to see the fury of our ancient gods taking the shape of water to remind us that these were their dwellings.

Before leaving the islands, we all passed our hands over the arches of the Convent of Saint Matthew. The gale had been named after the Saint. We carefully touched the arches and floors of the Church of Iztacalco before leaving, the main one of these islands, because right underneath what was ours was there, hidden.

Our building artists had left on top of its walls evidence of what we had been. Serpents, swirls, spirals, and some other shapes, carved in stone, their meaning only we knew. The east wall, now covered with water, remained as a custodian of the site and those angels on top of the four columns, inside the church, were wearing the copilli, the headdress of precious feathers, and their faces were those of our young heroes, our people. The seven hermitages the friars had built suffered more damage, but their foundations kept bundles of reeds and amaranth effigies, kneaded with honey. Our gods were still there, looking after them, but water had risen almost to cover the arches of the Convent in the first weeks of the storm. Friar Francisco, the head priest and his aides, could have been left to spend the nights on the second floor, but who would feed them? Those rooms were dry but everything else was gone, not even the grass to feed the few animals that were not drowned by the flood.

Nobody ever imagined that disaster and hardship would last so long. Water and land were often one since the conquerors had the main dyke destroyed to allow their thirteen brigantines to come to attack the sieged city of Tlatelolco. The dike, fractured, was also a roadway, the bridge was eight varas wide, the size of three men lined up, and more than three leagues in length. It linked the thirty colhua neighborhoods of Iztapalapan with the Sanctuary of Tepeyac and was also a wall to contain the lower waters of the Texcoco lake. The repairs and landfilling had been made intermittently by our people, but their labour was defective.

All who knew about hydraulics had died and without their knowledge, how else would we rebuild it? With death and disease, who else would come to work on it? Now, every building was covered by water. Only the higher grounds of the main islands, only Mexico-Tenochtitlan, only Tlatelolco, were dry. Our people sought shelter with relatives on the mainland and despite our separation, Miguel Mauricio was my most immediate family, the only one I could ask for mercy.

That was how water took me back to him. My needy heart accepted his shelter for a few days in the neighborhood populated by the Tlatelolcas, the place of the piles of sand, the place of those who now looked at my people with hatred because they had been the bravest, they had resisted under the siege the conquistadors had set a hundred years ago and they were the last ones to fall. They would only forget when the last one was gone.

Miguel Mauricio was already an adopted son of that neighbourhood, and although for years I did not know anything about him, rumors about of the splendor of the dedication ceremonies of the Church of Santiago reached my islands. With so many years gone, I had even forgotten the altarpiece we discussed only once. The wooden piece presided the altar, shining triumphantly on its main wall. Only once had I had brief news from Father Manjarrez, from the Order of Preachers, who so well spoke the language of our people.

"Did you know, Eugenia, that Miguel Mauricio completed a grandiose masterpiece when he was back in Tlatelolco?"

You, Miguel Mauricio, had left in haste and there was no time for us to untie the knot of our dresses, to break the vessels we had been given, to express our wish to break our matrimonial engagement. My hope -or my arrogance- had always believed that one day you would return to my body, that the offerings to the goddess would have some effect. But the time of herbal offerings and incantations was gone. No more dancing with bells in the bracelets and burning incense for Saint Anne, who was Toci, our Lady. No more plucking my hair or tearing my garments down, weeping and lamenting this hollow belly of mine, empty like a pitcher for water, broken and tearing its content.

I had to move on and I returned to the labours of ours, to the saline and the boiling of our waters, to the pots we used to fill with salt water that we then broke to get the white powdered condiment sedimented, after stirring in fires fed with hundreds of burning logs that had desolated the islands.

Here in Iztacalco, Iztatleros, salt artisans, were the best to separate white seasoning salt from the dark, cheaper one we used for pottery, mining and witch spells. Salt blocks of different qualities were kept in sacks for the royal miners, while black slaves, servants on the mainland, came here, sent by their mistresses to buy salt to preserve meats or as a component for their superstitions.

Ointments with medicinal herbs to make a lover come back, wax candles with names written on paper, and salt crosses to damn someone's future were heresies that had come from the lands of the slaves. Priests knew their color was malignant and they feared and condemned their powers for magic, black just like their skins. They knew how to poison a Christian soul, prepared talismans to send enemies to exile, and potions and filters to obtain revenges and punishments. They adulterated prayers, whose words would satisfy scorned lovers or attract prohibited and impossible relations.

So well I knew that the tyranny of unrequited love was the main reason to believe in the effectiveness of these tricksters. Spite had always been the bleeding wound that opened impossible paths for solutions, and the pain it produces is like the sound of a howling hound that seeks ways to heal. Salt also worked to wish the worst of luck, scattered with dissimulation in the corners of a house, while visiting. Sprinkled on the table, it told the whereabouts of lost beloved ones and mixed with mud to shape the tiny figure of a lover would ensure fidelity forever.

The skirts of marquises hid precious prints of saints and virgins, wrapped in salt bags and gadgets, to which they prayed, grinding their teeth, looking for revenge after infidelity, as per the advice of an old black wet nurse, a faithful and toothless mulatta who knew everything about love. Yielding to the suffering of her mistress, whom she had raised with her own milk, black servants came here, looking for the purest salt to rub their bodies along with herbs bundles, to calm and ease the fire of passion or jealousy.

In the traffic of boats crossing the lakes, healers of souls came to our shores. There were also the regular visitors, who came here to beg for the favor of Saint Anne, lady of pregnancies and births. Their number multiplied with the moon when they spent the whole night in our church, the only one allowed to remain open, with dozens of women whispering, supplicating, promising.

For fertility, we prayed equally, Spaniards, mulattas and mestizas. In our minds, in each of our hearts we sang in silence, in our own languages, heads bowing reverently with our eyes closed. We were all together in the same effort. Our men, we said, were the cause of our empty bellies, but we were the ones who came here to supplicate.

Those who had already felt a child in their womb that had not come to fruition howled in pain during the night and each scream, birth, story, remained trapped in the church walls. And yet, on all of our islands, there was no filter, prayer, or spell to cure our spirits, Miguel Mauricio, to heal and get together what we never had.

With my feet sunk in the swamps, I loaded the boat, fighting the floating debris. Petals of carnations and poppies framed the waters in red, like blood, and

> For fertility, we prayed equally, Spaniards, mulattas and mestizas.

when we reached the island of Tlatelolco, I hardly found a space on the shore. A few of us arriving were received by family on the pier. I went down dragging my saddlebag, my own bundle of greatness that kept the objects of my faith, guarantors of who I am, of my authentic genealogy. The Community Funds box kept the history of my people inside and I was its guardian, too. It contained primordial titles and deeds that proved the property of our communal lands or the ancestral possession of a Title of Nobility, vain and empty now amid the disaster, just like my womb had always been.

In this tragedy, Miguel Mauricio received me in silence, indifferent. He did not have anything to give me. The dormitories of the College were forbidden to house women and only for the charity of the friars, and because almost nobody had thought to take refuge in the heart of the disaster, they agreed to receive me for a few days.

I went there to close a circle and at each step I accepted that as soon as the church celebrated the Nativity of the Lord, I would renounce Miguel Mauricio forever.

Before the flood, these days were days of rejoicing everywhere. Naturals donated fruits and flowers and friars and priests offered a good meal, in return. But nowadays, the church could not spiritually serve and feed thirty neighborhoods. Water in the cistern was almost gone, and its walls were seriously damaged. Population was decimated just as everywhere and only the elevation of this island, the result of building on the remains of everything that was ours, had saved the convent.

I offered my help in the kitchen that attended the hospital, now full. The frugal food of the interns was prepared simply, and the orchard was still a good resource. The shortage greatly complicated the work in the kitchens. I asked for the help of interpreters to obtain permission to pray Vespers inside the church, afterwards. The deference to Miguel Mauricio from guardian Torquemada, who saw him grow in art and expertise along with Domingo Francisco, the one who returned to govern Texcoco, granted the interpreter his favor. Father Torquemada had returned from Spain to live his last days in his beloved College, devoted to study and reflect. Miguel Mauricio was grateful that as cold as the reception had been, exchanging glances in the tables, I conveniently disappeared in the corridors, to avoid explanations.

This would be the only occasion to see the fruit of his mastery, the last work Miguel Mauricio had barely discussed with me. As soon as I opened the wooden gate of forged ironwork, light illuminated the altar, all gold leaf sparkles. I walked, listening to the echo of my steps in the solitude. The hustle and bustle would begin with the impoverished party, the next day. And there was the altarpiece, in all its grandeur. Monumental Saint James, right at the center of the entire composition, riding victorious, intervening in favor of the conquistadors who stepped over severed limbs and calling on their legions to continue the offensive. A dazzling warrior passing over infidels, broken and torn, as we already were, Saint James was framed by a beautiful indigenous leg, severed and superimposed, forming a macabre angle in the right corner. Our people, wounded, fainting, defeated ressembled those souls burning in the flames of purgatory depicted in other churches.

I knew right away that the motive was key to solve Miguel Mauricio's dilemma and his anguish. The triumph of the Saint was the victory of this world of art and letters that Miguel Mauricio loved so much, one I did not understand, distanced by Spanish, this language of his that he mastered so well and that he could use only here, in the workshop and the College. It was a world that had lit so many lights in the soul of Miguel Mauricio. Chisels and gouges brought peace to him, always debating between his training and our traditions. Each curl sculpted in the wood erased the guilt felt over preferring this world. Saint James had fought and won the battle for Miguel Mauricio, and friars preferred his work and placed it right in the center of the main altarpiece, presiding over the altar.

The world we had known was gone, and Miguel Mauricio had preferred the College and what it involved and represented, while others still longed for what would never return. Varnish and inks covered Miguel Mauricio's heart with a layer, and now water was taking away the last vestiges of our world away by rinsing, cleaning, and purifying it all. My eyes wanted to see in the relief the allies that facilitated our defeat and yes, the brothers from Tlaxcala were there, depicted, dressed in the Spanish style, joining the Saint in battle, fighting alongside the foreigners. Miguel Mauricio had taken good care to cover the joints of the wood to grow the altarpiece in size. The initial surface would have been insufficient to unfold the magnitude of his pain and grief and I could almost picture him, filling the joints with plaster to make them unnoticed, to pretend they were one single plank. Such was the size of what reality had been.

Father Torquemada had finally obtained the jewel for his architectural masterpiece and consecrated the church in 1610, 3 tecpatl, a building he took pride of, since he had been the only architect to design and direct the works. Only after the altarpiece was assembled and set on the wall did Miguel Mauricio manage to see the dawn again, leaving his crossroads behind, having reconciled himself to the magnitude of what had happened. The church gates were closed with the flood and would only be re-opened on Christmas morning. Water had been all over, for months, and I had promised to myself I would leave the next day.

After the meager banquet, neighbors here would start moving away, taking their crosses and their belongings to dry land. Bells would announce Jesus was born, and the celebration of this year would be austere. Fires would burn in the atrium and the porcelain child, surrounded by a few expensive wax candles and scented incense, would ensure one more cycle in the calendar that we were now following.

The day before Miguel Mauricio had pretended to be busy, packing a sculpture that would be sent to the north, to the mineral of Zacatecas, so our only meeting would take place at the end of the morning mass. The crowd, coming from as far as twenty leagues away, as far as Real del Monte in Pachuca, was learning of the calamitous waters only when approaching the city. The sanctuary of Tepeyac had received them first, and friars and naturals knew their pilgrimages had a double purpose. Our Lady, Mother Tonanzin, was worshipped there, up in the hill, but they also came to Tlatelolco, to learn about divine things.

Nativity mass was the only day on which pine branches could be lighted inside the church. Men, separated from women, held them up, burning. Only those who had been educated here understood every word in Latin and meditated on the mystery of the message given in their hearts. Women held lit a few more candles in the back and in the glow of the weak light we witnessed the culmination of what we barely understood. Jesus was born.

The Spanish woman dressed in rags with the demeanor of a queen kept on smiling at Miguel Mauricio at the end of the corridor. She looked into my eyes briefly, rather searching for his eyes, his perfume, his light. She was a servant to a poor count, with a skin as white as the foam of the saline, like the pearls of a Virgin's cloak and she was carrying in her arms, triumphantly what I would never be able to give him.

The chorus broke in powerful voices of bliss and despair, claiming for their Saviour in the midst of the flood; the maiden had given birth to a child: "Hail Mary full of Grace, the Lord is with thee. Blessed are thou among women and blessed is the fruit of thy womb, Jesus. A child has been born to you and sovereignty will rest on your shoulders, forever."

• • •

Six hundred nautical miles separated Macau from the port of Cavite, that part of the coast in the form of a fishing hook, in the Bay of Bacoor, Province of Manila, in the Philippine Islands, named to honor His Majesty, Phillip II.

With such a good weather, the ship would see the protective wall surrounding the port in a few days. Mary Most Holy, Mother of All, was the Patron of the Manila Galleon and, safe from the harassment of the Dutch under her advocation, the ship was finally bringing the illustrious Spanish Captains, Juan Morales and José Nebra and Enciso, back from their mission. They would spend a few days in the city, giving themselves some small licenses, well deserved after fulfilling their sacred commission.

The iron wrought choir rood screen would be ready in a year, and the Cathedral of Mexico would receive the art of the east for its central nave in imitation of the Temple of Solomon.

They had unexpectedly added one more crew member on board, Huá Tuó, the healer, and in a few weeks, his services turned out to be essential. The passage of people from Dzin – or Chin, in Spanish – to the Americas was extremely restricted. But Chinese junks were seen all over this Spanish enclave, transporting goods through the seas of the south. Once in the Philippines, they even managed to sell them at the Parian, the market outside the walls of the fortresss that gave so much fame and fortune to Manila. Since Spain had taken control over the islands, they were outnumbered by locals in a proportion of thirty to one. That was no obstacle for Spain to completely rule over the enclave, where millions of pesos in silver were placed to pay for the greatly demanded exoticism of Chinese luxury.

In Cavite, ammunition, supplies, and victuals were stored to supply the fleet they called the Nao on its way to the New Spain court. Inhabitants here roused the distrust of Spaniards, they attributed bad manners and tricks to them and had labeled them as inconstant and full of lies and greed. In addition, they worshiped their own gods. Therefore, the record of the journeys of navigations, from and to the Viceroyalties of New Spain and Peru, tried to be meticulous and locals were forbidden to travel and settle there, with the exception of those sold in slavery, and their masters were totally in charge of getting them to those ports according to the rules.

Nebra estimated that they could continue to Acapulco with the Chinese healer and that the attention to him would be the usual, as so many of them were already in the port. With a good story, Huá Tuó would be allowed to enter New Spain and could even apply to practice his medicine there freely. The gratitude Nebra had for Hua Tuo, for saving his life and for following him blindly, even unintentionally, to these remote lands of the Crown, was great, but his righteousness would never buy the goodwill of a notary.

His military pride and his rank were considered sufficient to declare his status as a subject, under the orders of the Spanish Royal. His rank of captain granted Huá Tuó permission to freely carry sword and dagger, for the ornamentation and defense of his person. That would open doors for him everywhere. Nebra calculated his word in writing as Captain of the Militia would be enough to help Huá Tuó reach the heart of the Court when he so decided. Nobody doubted that the newly appointed knight could freely practice medicine there and that he would receive the corresponding honors when his time came.

A wave of heat greeted the Spaniards in the dirty wharves of Cavite. They boarded the carriage that would take them to Manila, traveling along its half-moon bay to reach the guesthouse attached to the Basilika Menore of Kalakhag, on the banks of the Passig River. They would wait for the departure of the Nao to leave this noisy city that offered the unimaginable: fresh food, stores, a hospital and schools of the Dominican, Augustinian and Franciscan orders. Outside walled Manila, the Captains would make some visits to maintain their business contacts and would spend every morning inspecting the stalls of the Parian de los Sangleyes, the famous market, looking for novelties they would later use as currency.

Huá Tuó went with them everywhere, admired. His thin surgeon's fingers could quickly distinguish porcelain wares made at the royal workshops from imitations. He fixed his attention on the details of a carved ivory tusk that reproduced a thousand tiny elephants or a benevolent matron, like the goddess he worshipped, along with what looked like her husband and son, with realistic details as tiny as the cord fibers that wove her cloak.

In each raid, the captains would throw on his shoulders a pair of mother-of-pearl chairs that would adorn the Captain's room or bundles of ethereal silk or a pink dalmatic so thin it would fit in a single fist, to cover the white shoulders of his wife in the morning. So, they filled their days of waiting until the Nao, loaded with tons of merchandise, sailed in on a festive atmosphere.

The sun was all over the ocean like gold leaflets and a silent Huá Tuó, in white linen, followed the last retinue of chests. Nebra had allowed him to gather as many surgical instruments as he wished in the market, and a box with divisions and dozens of jars guarded the powders of his macerated plants and roots. When all the cargo was loaded, "Our Lady of Remedy" sailed away. A powerful cannon shot broke like thunder on the bridge. A couple of more salvos would burst out in farewell, while the whole town left its sleepy routine to dismiss the fleet in a festive mood.

On board, Huá Tuó felt all his body weakened. He was placing the last piece of silk in a dark chest of maki-e lacquer, finished in gold dust, when the fabric suddenly floated before his eyes and, like it, his body lost its weight. He fell into a deep, empty unconsciousness until the shore disappeared completely. The fleet turned towards the horizon, and the doctor was still stunned, swaying on the mat of the tiny cabin he would share with the captains. Several times he wondered if this was the trip the porcelanist had agreed upon with his father the night before. He also wondered if he should continue to serve in that temple of unknown religion. Maybe this was the ship that would bring the relics of a young martyr, for whom they had been preparing a great reception.

But what was he doing on board a ship? Macau awaited the corpse of a young man like him, who had given his life for the Christian faith in the East and for him they had prepared a church and organized a luxurious procession. He feared to look out and discover the religious cortege of lacquered carriages, waiting for the martyr. He feared recognizing the two elders who spoke his language or the impatient Portuguese deacon of swollen toes, waiting by the shore, as if Huá Tuó was the one they expected, to whom they would make all the glories.

If his eyes were able to see the walls that hid the flooded rice fields, he would know everything, because that was his last clear memory: a huge staircase and incense scenting the temple of his goddess, dressed in blue as the sea, the indigo sky surrounding the wall of that fortress, on top of the mountain.

He got up and slowly climbed the three steps that separated the deck from the captains' lower cabin. There was nothing other than the open sea, nothing else around, not a line that could guide him, or a star to make a calculation. Confusion bathed his face in tears, and he only managed to bend on the railing, in sorrow.

"Nǐ hǎo!" said the boy who dragged huge and thick ropes.

"Nǐ hǎo," he replied, without even thinking.

The sailor struggled to stretch the sails, angry and upset because this would be his only task in the long journey. Three months still to come and he was already regretting the adventure of looking for the Septentrion for the first time, full of monsters and dangers. An absurd curvature, he said, would extend the trip north, to ride the dark Kuro Shio ocean current, leaving the risks of assault behind. The current flows northeastward, where it merges with the easterly drift of the ocean, the sailor said in his monologue and when reaching the Californias and Cape Mendocino to replenish the ship with fresh water, the fleet would continue coasting south the continent to the Port of Acapulco.

None of the destinations seemed familiar to Huá Tuó, who was increasingly confused, absorbed in the horizon and drying his tears with the back of his fine hand; his face turned towards the sails that kissed the clouds of seawater, on time to see the captains had finished their accounting work in the cellars and finally went to have some rest in their rooms. They noticed the surgeon's linen tunic from the other end of the deck and waved, joking in Castilian.

"Eh, barber, we are heading north now, right there, where your land is! Don't you want to jump and challenge the waves to swim all the way to meet your people? You can do what you like because... you're free!"

The young man turned around, recognizing the voices, but still not understanding. The sails replicated the whiteness of his clothes and, smiling, with the breeze on his face, he greeted them.

"Nǐ hǎo!"

An island that turned out to be a whale's back would not have surprised the captains just as much. The doctor was able to speak! And his smile illuminated everything around him, like a halo. They hugged each other and ironically, nobody was able to say a word.

Nebra poorly mastered Huá Tuó's language; he would never have been able to negotiate the making of the screen, but this moment of bliss did not require words at all.

Precisely up to the northwest the coasts of the Celestial Empire were, in parallel to their sail. Huá Tuó's place of birth was not visible from here, but he would carry it with him for the rest of his life. And to the east, the future was waiting for all of them.

The captains had to wait until they found help among the crew to undertake the long-awaited attack of questions. Was he a native of Fujian, officially a surgeon? Yes. A phlebotomist? Yes. A barber? Of course! He had an eagerness to cross the world, which had been facilitated by the hand of a porcelanist, whom he had cured in his father's house.

The Captain listened attentively to every detail of that fateful attack on Macau, the escape of the porcelanist's ships and the hiding in the church, of terror, death, and destruction. Huá Tuó did not yet understand the size of the sea they were crossing, nor about the distances still to come. Hardly could he imagine the kingdom of Spain the officers were describing. And yes, because the Spaniards had invested him, a dagger and a sword would be shining, hanging from his belt and along with the white tunic healers use, all that made him different from the rest.

The captains knew that in these lands, every inhabitant who prided himself on dominating his mind and body was skillful with the sword. In the well of silence, however, the hands of the surgeon had never forgotten any of his skills and the masterful demonstration he had given before departing had earned him the respect of those who witnessed it.

After hours of conversation, the reality of facing the unknown began to invade his heart. Fear was drowned in the night with the distillate of Philippine sugar cane that the captains had brought in quantity. The sugar plant had adapted magnificently to the climate of the seven thousand islands and Isla de Negros, one of the hundreds that made up the archipelago, would harvest enough to produce good low-price alcohols to accompany journeys.

The night ended with thanks to the heavens of the Celestial Empire for the existence of the doctor, his skills, and his recovered voice. Huá Tuó felt his throat scratched with the alcohol and the thousands of unsaid words, which had been waiting for months in his mind to come out.

The sapphire current of Kuro-Shio was announced by a trail of debris that began to form small floating islands as they traveled eastwards. Winds or storms might extend the trip a couple of weeks more, and on sighting the Californias, they would throw ballast, some cannons, the oldest and their fixtures, to travel lighter and recover the lost days. They would keep the bronze artillery because they would still have to face the possible attacks of gigantic monsters that threw powerful jets of water through their orifices or sea serpents with erect necks that everyone feared, but nobody had ever seen. Without that weight, the trip would improve until reaching the port of Acapulco.

When they spotted the port, the beards and hair of the entire crew had already passed through the barber's razor. He cut with precision, without spilling a single drop of blood, despite the swaying. The crew was made up of a hundred cabin boys and ninety-five sailors, Filipinos, Chinese, Spaniard from the kingdom of Castile and even blacks and Indians. With his services, Huá Tuó increased the weight of his gold coins satchel, and that gave him certainty before what he would face when they reached the mainland.

Clear and serene weather welcomed the ships in the Californias; neither monsters nor assaults had muddied their way. The supply of fresh water was replenished calmly, although they were alert at the sight of Indians, who in these regions were wild. So brute were they that they ate the fruit of the shells by hundreds, smoking them to open them up, throwing their precious content, smoked pearls into the water, blackened and stained by fire. An unexpected rain of arrows could kill them and fear proved to be more powerful than pearls. Precaution made them sail out of the stretch as soon as possible, and they headed south, promising not to stop until reaching the fort of San Diego, in Acapulco.

The construction that the Dutchman, Adrian Boot, was finishing, had proved to be very effective on repelling the last pirate raids, who also ravaged this part of the kingdom, although to a lesser extent than in the Gulf and the Caribbean Sea. Its five bastions, shaping a star, protected the most important port of all of America and the east. A perfect stone wall pentagon, surrounded by a pit, guarded in all directions. Outside the fort, the port was only a small hamlet of huts scattered around the humble parish and a small square. A dozen Spanish families controlled the unloading and transportation of goods with hundreds of slaves at their service.

En route to the dock, the crew began to worry. Only Huá Tuó, the healer, seemed to arrive there without an economic interest or contraband. The ships should render reports of the 2,500 pieces of cargo, valued at 315,000 pesos, registered in Cavite, back in Manila. But the more than two hundred crew members carried undeclared merchandise, and everyone feared their seizure. 208 half-drawers, 89 leather bags, 122 vessels and 40 bundles of clothes were confiscated and taken by black slaves to the Royal Warehouses, establishing an inquiry for fraud to the Royal Treasury.

Huá Tuó observed all the movements in detail and kept his reflections to himself. He had crossed half the world, and his young heart could still not find the months lost in silence back in Macau. Now he had to choose, and he felt lost. The Captain's sincere gratitude had made it clear that he was free.

As soon as the officers of the Royal Customs allowed the departure of the crew, a gleaming sea brought to him the poet's song that he had memorized in the source of his childhood.

"At last I can go through the ignored path, towards the light, towards the secret place, where hours sleep, and a sly air takes my sobs of joy away. I have finally arrived, free from the roads that held me back. Here I will contemplate the light of a brand-new day, free of silence, free of memories, burning in the sun, when it dawns."

Verses, visiting his soul, were the anchor he much needed now.

• • •

The sea of Holland, the rivers of Germania, the things of the flood, and the shipwreck. In each and every moment of History, water is an actor, its power, and majesty, omnipresent. Renowned architects had presented their projects to solve constant floods. The viceroy's cosmographer decided to take all the torrent from the central five lakes and lead them to the Panuco River, in a journey of five hundred kilometers, to then throw their majestic waters to the Gulf Sea. A crime on its own.

Ten thousand neighbors, all Indians, sighed, paying for tribute with the work of their hands for this titanic job they called Desagüe. Their labour was required to get rid of all the water incoming to the Valley. Spanish authorities had decided they had enough with the rivers and springs that flowed from the hills. Therefore, they would divert all the contents of the Cuautitlan River, which took its course to the Lake of México, and send them sixteen kilometers away. The river would now run along a straight path that would meet all the flow in a single open channel, towards Huehuetoca. An open pit would later go through a tunnel that opened into the heart of the mountains, a thirteen-kilometer long wound that would end at Nochistongo to finally reach the Tula River and then the Panuco, to empty at last into the Gulf of Mexico.

The work was still unfinished: the Cuautitlan had been diverted, but the mouth of the tunnel, of only three meters in diameter, had to be kept clean and unblocked, always using Indian hands and labor.

> In each and every moment of History, water is an actor, its power, and majesty, omnipresent.

The dream of channels and windmills the Netherlands engineer had offered was rejected and while for some, water was the Supreme God, worshipped by multitudes, here it was a plague, that penetrated and corrupted everything.

When I arrived, like a thunderbolt, that year of 1629, the cosmographer, alarmed by the violence of the storm, feared that the storm would bring water back to the central lakes, overflowing and destroying the unfinished works. In the name of Saint Matthew, that was exactly what happened. I destroyed all the mouths; I recovered all the channels, I exceeded all the projections.

Indians, once at peace with me, had to work without pay in the draining works along with tending their own crops, those of their masters, and the celebration of festivities, hence the slowness of the work. The cosmographer was prosecuted and imprisoned, guilty of negligence, but compassion moved the

Viceroy who granted him forgiveness. His calculations and directions were much needed.

In the past, when the works were started, everything had been a party. The cosmographer was respected, he presided over councils, his name was heard everywhere. He had cut the ribbons for the inauguration, while fifteen Indians carried the viceroy in a handcart. During the ceremony, they silenced their mouths when the first shovel sank in the heart of the soil. It was the most ambitious project of its time.

They would drain five lakes away to free this land and keep it dry forever. Every wound on the ground hurt Indians so bad while the works were offered for the honor and glory of our Lord. Thousands of cargo mules would tear the soil apart, reaching a depth of fifty meters. The cut would run through grasslands and plots, through mountains and valleys, until reaching the sea, a delirium of enormous proportions.

Friar Andres de San Miguel, of the Carmelite Order, carpenter and master of everything with the highest qualities of an architect in those times, raised his powerful voice whenever someone mentioned the calculations and the levels that were being considered to carry out the water works. He held in his bitter mouth a litany of curses, those he had learned so well in his days as a sailor. The project was absurdly expensive, and he had replied in writing that he would be present at the inauguration only and never again after the work was concluded.

> The cut would run through grasslands, mountains and valleys, until reaching the sea, a delirium of enormous proportions.

In 1607 he witnessed how the viceroy's fine fingers had sent a handful of straw into the channel, to prove that the current would easily flow to where they wanted. The friar he did not want to add one more single comment on the design of the plans. After all, the driving and ownership of the work had been snatched away from him. The friar well knew that the work went beyond the knowledge of the cosmographer and that I am fickle, violent if tempted

Happily, when they got rid of me, palaces and churches would be forever safe, they said during the ceremony. Only the Indians knew that as the deity I was for them I demanded adoration and they renewed their need to worship me, far away, up in the mountains.

Getting the cosmographer out of his printing press and his moon charts to become a hydraulic engineer had been a mistake; the friar was completely sure of that. A few mathematical operations had dazzled the Court's ignorance but Friar Andres, however, knew how careful the calculations of declinations and slopes must be. His precision had brought the water of Ameyalco back to the Holy Desert Convent through an aqueduct he designed to irrigate his beloved orchards of El Carmen, in Chimalistac. Water inspired him respect and reverence. He was originally a sailor from Medina Sidonia, a survivor of the shipwreck that destroyed the beautiful Santa Maria de la Merced, in Florida, and, thanking the heavens for a new opportunity, he had joined the Order.

He dedicated himself to designing works that would make the most of me, peacefully. His extensive treatises on vaults, mechanics, pumps, and aqueducts were unique and when he exhausted his interest in hydraulics, and his pride was full of the architecture and construction of three Convents, he dedicated himself to manufacturing stained glass windows, to gardening and research to write the best treaty on Mudejar coffered ceilings.

After a day in his carpentry workshop, he untied his sandals to wash his feet from the wood dust he was carving. The beautiful porcelain washbasin in his private room at the Carmelite Convent had running tap water, a luxury for those days, and the tiled walls were crowned by an angel with outstretched wings that occupied the entire vault of his rooms. The angel seemed to guess his thoughts. Rainwater would fill the system of wells and cisterns that fed the aqueduct, and the orchards would have a productive year. Would it be the same with the water works assigned to the cosmographer? Architecture had given him fame and his arrogance came from all the skills for which he was recognized. He had designed bridges over rivers, lavish churches, convents, and aqueducts, and he did not understand how benevolent water, which he made good use and advantage of, was now being fought as an enemy.

Here in El Carmen, on solid ground by the shore of the lake, water causeways transported wealthy sponsors in canoes who came to offer huge amounts to the friars, in exchange for masses and prayers. Their suffrages had paid for these gardens and orchards, which now surpassed the biblical vineyards of the Prophet Elijah, on Mount Karmel, where the order took its name from. Three thousand fruit trees offered beneficial rents to the Carmelites, and as far as the eye could see, bridges, canals, and ponds irrigated this paradise with life and the music of water, exuberancy leaving little space for the blacks and natives collecting the fruits.

This reverie of dry land seemed to be an ambition of the city only. The sound of rain through the window made friar Andres de San Miguel think that maybe he should postpone his coffered ceilings treaty, forget the inks, the varnishes, the polygons and the moldings to supervise the cosmographer with the permission of the viceroy and the order. Summer of 1629 had been prodigal but he was deeply worried about the measurements on the level of the lakes. If authorities had insisted, he would even had declined his vows in order to devote himself to the diligent study that a work like the drainage of the lakes deserved. But the Viceroy had ignored his first advances. The draft of his project was discarded by the Board of the Ecclesiastical and Secular Chapter and, dazzled by the solution offered by foreigners, they had preferred Heinrich Martin and even Boot, occassionaly, to lead the works.

Andres de San Miguel, hurt, exasperated, a human being, took the illest will against Henrich Martin, Enrico Martínez of the illustrated Germania.

The excavations, he knew well, demanded Indians be tied by the waist, hanging from beams crossed in the mighty channel to make its waterbed deeper or wider, at certain points. The current had already claimed the lives of some unfortunates.

For them, I was jade water, celestial water, which after a thousand measurements and traces was sent away through a tunnel, a marvelous wonder of construction tested on a given day of September, 1629.

They did not have any reserve with me.

I did not grant them any consideration.

PART III
THE JOY

CHAPTER 8
THE KWARA, THE TAGUS, AND ACALAN
1634

Meditation of Sekondi from the Kwara

I am made of water, my son; I am from the river. I am one of those who have come from the north, for four generations, leaving behind the towns and villages burned by the Yoruba, the fires that ended with our kingdom, in Sokoto. And I am from the River of Rivers, the one they called Oya, that we named Kwara and the Portuguese, Niger. I am from the waters of many names.

I am from Kaduna, where the Hausa, my people, found a new land, fleeing from the Yoruba, who have devastated everything, who have come to the villages at night, secretly awaiting the light of dawn, when women bring water from the river, walking upright, dignified. I am from there, from where we take our children by the hand on our way to the well, counting the trees, pointing to the monkeys or greeting those who come along the path of dust, telling our children,

"Do you see? Here comes Langule's son and Oba Oke's son. There she goes, the daughter of Alaafin and Sadaka. Say *Annu, yaya kake ba?* Say hello, how are you?, my son."

Around the well, we used to laugh, we used to tell stories and warmly greet those others coming, wrapped in our adire-eleko, large pieces of fabric dyed in indigo, as blue as the sea. While we talked, we ignored that there, in the bushes, the Yoruba lurked to hunt us, to take away our children, especially those who were becoming men, especially those who could be mothers soon.

No arrow hurt our hearts deeper than taking our children away. And the Yoruba took almost all of them.

I am from the river that listens to women running and screaming in despair, those who come back to the village yelling, pulling their hair and crying. The river hears how they go to the priest of Ifa and ask for the path they should take to look for their children.

I am from the place where men build huts by the river and leave them unfinished because they have been captured, as well, and they abandon the hunt of the animals they were following, to return to where everyone is gathered, to hear how it was and where they should go, to try to do something.

They consult the shape of the sage leaves with hope, asking what direction to take but receive no answer. They go out and look for the hermit, the outcast forced to live outside the village. They bring him food and gifts, and they ask him if he knows the way they took. They ask, scratching their eyes, shooing away their grief like flies, holding back their tears.

"Do you know where my son is? Do you know where my daughter is?"

But they return without clues. The priest cannot respond to their requests. The hermit does not know either. They get together and discuss if they should take their way to the road, go out to look for them, shout their names, take the grief of the whole village with them to catch some breath and transform it into a call that seeks and finds.

There is no shield for their pain. Fathers and mothers walk the dusty trails, the riverbank, they get into the jungle and ask the acacia tree. They even question the river, but the moon passes, one after the other, and sometimes they give up and then, again, their grief grows up even more. They never forget those who have left, those who have disappeared. They set up altars in their huts. A flower is a girl, and a spearhead is a boy that is gone.

The elders are brought for advice and comfort, the altars grow in fruit, water and flower offerings. Those who are gone leave a gap that will take so long to fill up again, so long to recover. But a child is the biggest loss, the one that hurts the village the most.

I am from that Hausa kingdom, my son, the one that has been attacked as the stealthy crocodile does. We have been captured by these enemies in nets, tied up like animals. Our captors seem to be permanently mad at us, and they have always waged war against us. They are angry, because they know of that splendor of Sokoto, of that glory of ours, of the Hausa kingdom of ours, of our glory they have been desiring with greed for a long time.

But there are others, the same color we are, black as the shadows, who come from far to seek us. We are not enemies with them but they come and they walk with other captives, they bring them by the necks, with a wooden shackle that cuts, that rubs, no food, not even sorghum soup they have. They walk for days, and in a queue, they can only bend down when they all do, when they are ordered to take some water from the puddles on the road.

They fill their rafts with them and go up the river. The mighty river. They try to find good omens in the shells and the ashes and ask them for a good journey. They get a bundle of osoro sticks and draw with them the path they will travel to show the captives where they are being taken. That is the road to the Portuguese enclave. Women and children serve them at night, and they use them. They are also good to have them pretend to be lost, when they get close to the villages. They train them to say:

"Do you know the way? I have my son with me, see? We are lost. We are hungry. Please, feed us, have mercy on us, take us to your people. We are tired."

That is the way for them to find out how many there are in the village, what dangers they might face, or to decide if it is better to move on and follow the road again. They move from north to south, and when they stop, they hear the song of the òdèrè bird there in the trees, and they make its sound, kah ha, kah ha, kah ha. Everyone laughs because they are in a good mood. But not the captives. They know they will make a good profit when they sell the captives; they will make a fortune because they carry maidens who will turn out to be productive and pregnant or strong and beautiful male servants.

And the irony is that they are just like us. They light the fire and bring water from the river, but they are indifferent to those who are tied up. Men cover the women with their bodies and fulfill their cravings. They no longer cut the grass to make mats. They do not like them at all. Now they get soft carpets in exchange for the captives, heavy carpets hard to carry, but more comfortable to sleep on. All this and more they exchange with the Portuguese. They get fire weapons to wage war to get more captives to get more fire weapons.

I am, my son, one of those everybody believes were claimed by the Spirit of the Waters, swallowed inside the walls of Elmina, prisoners that nobody sees ever again. We are not offerings, no, we are not, as there in the village they believe. We are not taken to Lawoyin, Onikoko or Awoyale or to other thousand spirits whose names must not be pronounced.

Instead, they fill ships with us to bring us to these lands, where we fight a thousand battles. Some of us defeat the dangers of the journey and the waterways or get free from the embrace of the violet sea. Others survive disease with the remedies of these lands: asclepia, izote, mocker or hemp. We survive, we prevail.

All these stories that I tell you, you understand, my son. You are used to my song as a child, you have listened to my voice in my language, and you understand it. You know that your mother has undertaken all challenges, and all of them have turned your mother into a warrior.

You were born here, and your color is not mine anymore, but you are also made of water and rivers. You carry our war inside, and my story, which is yours, and my language, which we speak in whispers. I know one day you will decide to hide that you know the language of the Hausa. You better stop speaking it, and you might try to forget all of our histories, because in these lands you are the son of Rosario, who was baptized with that name at the fortress, and who joined Pablo Paxbolon from Acalan Tixchel.

But it was Sekondi from Afri, my son, who brought you into the world. Sekondi, which means "the one who gets wisdom from experience". My name contains in its seven letters all this that I tell you today and nothing, or anyone can change.

The Spirit of the Waters lives inside me already, and no matter how dark the night is, I do not fear it because I have measured my strength with Him and I have triumphed. Peace is with me and no matter how hard the battle, I am here.

• • •

From a page of Captain Moisés Cohen Henríques' journal, 1629

More than the almighty stream of the Tagus that comes from the heart of the Kingdom, more than victory and fortune, celebrated to the sound of zithers, more than the keys to open long-forgotten doors, the strongest force that has driven me is the shape of thirty thousand ducats.

A hundred kilos of gold was the total cost of my loss; four hundred slaves were lost in the wreck because of the Spaniards and so my longing for fortune was fueled by revenge. It impelled my spirit and every new incursion in the high seas.

The waters of the Gulf of Mexico had witnessed the episode, the sinking of my beloved "Shield of Abraham," in domains of New Spain. The necessary, strategic escape I was forced to implement had hurt my pride, and it took years to recover the implacable faith and the credit of the investors. I swore there would never be another insult perpetrated on my property and retaliation burned in my veins.

Some time later, that same thirst of revenge united my destiny with that of a Dutch prisoner from Rotterdam the Spaniards had held captive for four years, Piet Pieterszoon Hein, Admiral and corsair of the Dutch Republic, who in the name of the United Provinces in the north had fought against the Habsburgs of Spain, seeking independence.

He had received the century, imprisoned in Havana for four years. Oh, the life of a sailor! As soon as he was exchanged for Spanish hostages, he returned to his lands, where he was appointed captain of the Dutch Company of the West Indies.

We met and got closer when we learned we shared a language. Portuguese and Spanish are related and he had got his Spanish at the dungeons of Havana. We both had a excuse to fight the Spaniards and when he found out about the detail of my sea charts, he knew he had got a treasure. As much as I valued them, I decided to join efforts to design a strategy together to avenge the fury that made both our teeth grind.

The Spanish Silver Fleet was moored in the Bay of Matanzas, in the Captaincy of Cuba, and a new "Shield of Abraham," with a license issued by the Dutch crown, joined Piet Pieterszoon Hein's splendid fleet, commanded by the best Dutch men of the sea.

Before the attack, the darkest of our humours joked about the meaning of the name of the bay; Matanzas means slaughter in Spanish and just as the drowned adventurers, surprised by aboriginals had seen their death, we would do the same with the sixteen Spanish ships we intercepted here. One galleon was taken after a surprise encounter during the night, and nine smaller merchants were talked into surrender. We ruthlessly attacked. We were superior in ability and number. The hand-to-hand combat was bloody, but brief, and the Spanish cowards must have seen in my eyes the glitter of hatred that made them surrender promptly.

The flames consumed every Spanish galleon, in the beauty of the blue bay, embers floating like a silk cloth. Our loot was fabulous! Twelve million florins in gold, silver, indigo, and cochineal filled our ships, while we spit the face of each wounded body and corpse, cursing their offspring in their own language so they would not miss it. We both mastered Spanish and this had been a massacre indeed.

I was the Jew from Lisbon, of ancestors expelled for their beliefs, who had lost a valuable cargo. He was a Protestant Dutchman who had lived an ongoing cruel war of independence fought for eighty years now, imprisoned in a Spanish pigsty. Spain governed our lands, and we hated it in the same proportion.

Together, we avenged the wreckage, my slaves out of Elmina and a fleeing fortune that still hurts my body. Four hundred negroes were nothing compared what we got here.

I knew the Spanish coast guard crew had returned to Veracruz after they saw the old "Shield of Abraham" sinking in the dark-ink water, years ago. They thanked the Christ of the Good Journey and had a loincloth embroidered in pearls as an offering for a clean attack and no human losses. One after one kissed the mantle of the Virgin of the Captives, but never in their prayers would they have imagined the blow we would inflict to their fleet in response.

We took the loot to Leyden, facing the Baltic Sea, and a crowd gathered at the docks and shipyards, eagerly awaiting. The lenders of the Hanseatic League doubled their investment, and our names were rife with glory. I could have finished that time with the raids, but the sea always calls back a sailor. So here I am again, sailing with the wind, distributing salted meat and beer among my people, looking for glory.

We have taken a strong turn to the south, sixty miles, fifteen leagues to the southwest, on the way to the Canaries. The Portuguese island of Madeira awaits us, with her blonde moon, while the god of Abraham and Jacob, who is inside our souls, guide our journey until we rejoice in the bright, shimmering sun again.

• • •

Written musings of Pablo Paxbolon from Acalan Tixchel

We have come from the waterways of Acalan Tixchel. I am the last of the merchants of a kingdom that built temples of doors that see the sun crossing the vanes of each hidden temple the jungle has swallowed. Its light illuminates each stelae that bears the names of all our people, those who did as we do now, going down the rivers to reach Nic-Anahuac, Nican Nahua, to trade.

We are emissaries without spears or shields. We achieve what is needed only with the power of our words. No war is needed. From those days, only our hair remains from our investiture, long and abundant as a stream, and that proves we belong to those who know how to row non-stop, to deliver goods and messages, taking advantage of the light of the moon.

A title in paper confirms my name, Pablo Paxbolon, the one who helped the conquerors and captured our people for their service, the one that gained control and favors in exchange for keeping peace in these lands, until the day some joined a hundred people the color of soot, fed up with abuse, to rise against him.

They assaulted his house, dragged him to the swamp and took his titles and documents away from him to throw them on the white road, before setting everything on fire. Like the sun that illuminates our arches and stelae, stars were aligned that night and a sublime hand, the color of coal, handed me the documents she had snatched from Don Pablo. Nobody who was not one of us, one of our people, could pass for him.

I was given the papers, and since then, I carry them with me, close to my chest, taking care of them like you do with a lily. Those documents gave me a new name, and for the kindness of those hands, my son, you are a Paxbolon too.

Nobody remembers that episode anymore. Gone with the breeze it is. But I always longed to see that dark face again, fading away with the night. And my wish was somehow fulfilled when I found my salvation, hidden like a treasure in the jungle, in the shape and the spirit of Rosario.

You are made of water, my son. You carry the longing to memorize all the waterways that can be navigated. The knowledge we brought from Tollan, the Place of Reeds, is your inheritance, the framework for your thoughts. Languages are yours, the Chontal, the Maya and the Nahua of our ancestors. All this you own to cross new rivers and lakes. It will be your duty to light the incense in gratitude and send the smoke of your prayers to heavens, where water resides.

We came to these lands but nothing was like we had figured out. When we arrived, we wandered and rowed from one island to the other, and they all were devastated, so we gave up. We had to return to the shores, to the road leading to Coyoacan and Mexicalzingo, looking for the protection of the highlands, the only dry land.

For months, we heard only the dogs in the city, howling and barking, day and night, while they stirred the garbage of its shores. They cried of hunger, like men, looking for their owners, who had emptied the city and left everything behind, palaces, houses, and workshops, to come here, to dry land.

Here, at Saint John the Baptist's church, we prayed loudly not to hear their howls. In a few months, they had gone wild, fierce as they were in their primitive state. Instinct gathered them in a pack and people said they were wandering around churches and residences, circling the temple of Santa Teresa La Antigua or surrounding the cathedral, which was barely walls and sacristy, dragging a big, fat rotten calf, trying to tear it to shreds of meat. They threw themselves into the water until they died, entangled in the scattered remains and rubble.

With the flood, we decided to follow the course of one of the main roads. There, we were safe. The great disease that had been unleashed was killing more than greyhounds, those Spanish dogs that conquistadors used to punish, attacking bound Indians like me. We managed to find a job at the Coyoacan weaving mill, manufacturing fabrics, while the level of water went down, until the happy day when the beam that covered the entrance to the road rose again to let people in and out the city.

The water of five years had given way, and Mexico rose again, as it always does after war or disaster. You will now have to follow your father's footsteps. You will travel through channels and ditches and may the Father of Light allow your trade to conquer the Queen of Anahuac, the great lady of Tenochtitlan, the beautiful Mexico City.

Then we will clasp our hands against our legs again, to the rhythm of the drum. We will cover roads with flowers and select honey for offerings so that fortune, my son, never abandons your path.

CHAPTER 9
THE NIGER AND THE GUADALQUIVIR
1634

Lucia of the Waters of the Niger

I am made of water. Three times, I am made of water. One, because amid my childhood memories, there is always a thirsty group that runs and screams in Hausa, hiding in the waters of our mighty river. Mothers submerge their toddlers in the stream, until they almost drown, to hide them from the captors; until they feel their heads explode, praying for the danger to pass.

I am also from the waters that flow into the Gulf, the rivers that feed the lakes of Atasta and Terminos, who witnessed how my life was almost taken in the wreckage. Distant words drowned in the ocean in exchange for new voices, pronounced by the plump lips of a strong black old man that initiated me into them.

And I am also, now, from this shore that irrigates the Magdalena River, the one that supplies the Hacienda del Apantle, in the Coyoacan village, the property owned by Don Luis de Dueñas, a town populated by people fleeing from the

Spanish city in disgrace and disaster. They all moved here to make their weaving mills prosper, their crops and their grazing cattle ranches succeed, running away from the flood.

Epidemics had taken a toll in the hacienda. On Easter, disease took the life of our Spanish housekeeper, and since then I have overseen the entire house, while Don Luis rejected two matrimonial alliances and purged with the scourge of discipline an unknown number of sins in the solitude of his rooms.

I am Lucia, the one who listens to the notes of the clavichord, in mahogany and ivory from the Philippines. The one who polishes its precious wood when the master is not playing or writing religious couplets. The one who learned to read and write in the atrium of Saint John the Baptist, stealing time from work, while the flood subsided.

I am the one who attended the lessons given to the Count's children at dusk, the master in penance. The one who hid a stolen book from his library, with a smiling angel on the lintel as accomplice, a book I had to hide if the master came to me one night or the other, when he did not feel like self-indulging in solitude.

I am the one who did not understand why he redoubled mortification and fasting, getting up at dawn, before the frenzy of setting the affairs of the hacienda in order. The one that amongst lessons, readings and work, looked for the treasured instant and the burn to see you again, Diego, waiting for your return.

I am the one that looks for the rubbing of your shirt at the end of Mass, the one who tries to walk next to you or follow you, behind the procession, pretending the same devotion the Indians displayed. The one that bends her forehead to call your name while the bells toll, while the sky burns bright at sunset, like fire in a branch of pine tree. The one without an occasion to see you; your face, indifferent; your eyes, elusive, always.

I am made of water when hope evaporates with each one of your rejections, the one that gets the courage to circumvent all the locks, the dust of the barn and the door of the cell where you sleep. I am the one who dares to write to you at night, tracing in letters how your memory moistens the buds of the rose bush and the fig tree flowers. I am the one that waits on her knees, like the angel, for your visit.

I am the one that closes the windows, so that the breeze does not take the petals of the vase away or the sheets of white paper, written with hallelujahs and hosannas that the master writes and sings.

I am the one that understood one afternoon, when the grit that dried his letters in ink dispersed, feeling her soul turning upside down, while she put the sheet music for his songs back in order again. The one that had to lean on the ivory and wood clavichord cover, painted with the din of a battle of ships in rough waters. I am the one that covered her mouth with her hands, undoing her heart in the foam breaking on the crest of a wave.

> You turn the day black, black for its darkest hours,
> May gloomy and obscure days you suffer,
> since so fond of black you are.
> May my sad writing, Lucia, tells you about misfortune.
> Never with more cause is water blurring my notes
> with black tears falling, made of black coal embers.

The master had written dozens of lines with his letters of curls and ornaments, and without being totally aware of what I had discovered, I went out of the living room, striding until everything was field and sky.

I do not want anybody else, Diego, to open my procession, to direct my ceremony and to take up my cross on shoulders, but you. Hollow, light and perfect it is as my heart is for you, Diego, officer of the Brotherhood of Blacks.

Turn your head and look at me, at least for a moment. Turn your bare back, glistening in oil, to me and sing your carol in my ear, to the sound of a gourd. Tilt the banner, when the procession you head cross the arch of the church since I do not even know what I am saying anymore.

My name was written on the music scores, and now I knew I must have noticed before, so distracted I was since you are the only one in me, Diego.

The master's fasting, his penance. And I am only a humble slave, and he is, yet he is not, my owner.

Look at me, Diego, stare at me because I feel I am darkened by the sun, like fields of ochre. Tell me, you whom I love, what should I do, since I soon might be forced to give up your love.

I will be like a reed of the islands, bending and kissing the water, to obey with my head whatever the destiny the master has for me. Look at me, cause of my joy, morning star, Diego.

• • •

Diego, from the Lake of Mexico

Is it that those words our mind configures may be completely locked in those lines that you draw, like grapevines? Is it true that the ink you carefully dry with gritty fingers can tell somebody about everything? I still do not believe it. But you spend your evenings, Lucia, given to what you call letters and from afar, I do not turn my eyes to see your eyes, nor do my hands dare to touch you.

Because you carry the writing with you, like the master, because you know how to read the account book, while these fingers of these clumsy and dry hands of mine, large and calloused, barely let me count the bundles of clothes the weaving mill produces, the weight of wheat or the packs of grass.

I do not dare to see you, Lucia, because you belong to the master. Because he owns your will, although you have not realized he does. Because we are both slaves and we must always know to whom we belong. What is the voice that commands, what are the orders that make us wake up, and attend while lowering our eyes.

I am the servant and laborer of invincible arms, who learned he should drown his hope one misty blue morning on my way back from the main road, when we all trusted the news on the conspiracy had finally set us free, slaves born here or brought from far lands.

I am Diego, the one who grew up in the workshop, enduring lashings and torture, chains and punishment. The one who dragged his sadness back that morning, through the deserted streets of the town, facing the avenues of water, hope crashing against the shore.

I am the child who chose to ignore the bad news that we would never be set free and drowned all future expectations in freshwater from the river. So much we wanted to hear that the plot had worked out and that we could seek revenge against the masters! But such longing vanished like gauze, floating on the waters.

All that we felt cannot be told with the strokes of your pen, with your writing, Lucia. Written words cannot tell what it feels like to be imprisoned in the basement of the wool cellar, tied to the foot of another slave, to prevent us from running away again, while months go by and winter comes and goes, and summer comes and goes.

Ink cannot keep the detail of the denouncement we made to the Royal Hearer, when brown Antón detailed the clandestine prison in the basement of the mill, the blows of the son with a wooden stick, much more cruel than the master. A sheet of paper cannot tell how his five black servants hanged us for hours from the rafters. No, they cannot.

You belong to this new master, and I am in debt forever to him because he accepted me and hired me, considered me and put me in charge of this land where I grew up. It is your perfume the reason of his flagellation, his generous alms pay for charity masses sung for his soul.

You belong to the master, and I cannot look at you, for I am his slave, the one who takes care of his belongings and his income. I must not look at you, I must not even hear the creaking of your skirt, because the master's music of ivory keys and golden strings that comes out of the window is for you only.

I will not look at you, do not insist, I beg you. Turn off this fire and go, my sachet of myrrh. Liturgy commands that in a feast of lights, the purity of crystal should not be stained by the slightest spot of black.

• • •

Hacienda del Apantle's Account Book, owned by Don Luis de Dueñas, Coyoacan, Mexico

Wad al-Kabir, the river of the great torrent, the only navigable one in Spain, is born in the Sierra Morena. On its way to the sea, it irrigates the fertile lands of Andalusia, to reach the marshy lowlands of that fishing village in Sanlucar, to then empty into the Gulf of Cadiz, in the Atlantic Ocean, like a cry from the heart.

The Guadalquivir has contemplated the great Roman walls for centuries and those who have bathed in its waters, when fortune is promised in distant lands as far as the New World, do not want more than to recreate the graveyards of the countryside there.

I chose Coyoacan, the village of the Marquis and Conquistador Cortes, and through a letter sanctioned by the Royal Audiencia of Mexico, I became the new owner of these lands.

It seems to me that no matter how much I have tried to convince them I dedicated this hacienda to the venerable Saint Benedict the African, natives insist on calling it "Del Apantle," since such is the name they give to their ancient aqueducts, as many as there are in these towns.

At one thousand steps, counted from the main door of the Saint John the Baptist church, there is a heap of stones that prove these are my properties, the length of a league to the south, in lands that cross the Magdalene River, and two leagues to the east. This river does not have the grandeur of the Guadalquivir of my childhood, but it is the beauty of the Lake of Mexico that compensates for its lack of lustre.

The hacienda has three hundred head of cattle, plots for maize and wheat, and it is supported with the work of the Indians living in the surroundings. Its management is carried out by the strong hand of a foreman born in this region, who takes care of my property as his own. I bought him from the previous owner, plus twelve pieces of slaves acclimated to these lands, brought from the Sultepec ore, who work on the harvests and wool.

The hacienda faces one side of the river banks and is two leagues distant from the main road. The yield in loads of wheat has been steadily growing up, although they are still insufficient for the demand of the markets of the city of Mexico now that the flood is gone. The Crown has promised to complete the works of drainage the flood interrupted, and because of the disaster, the sowing of olives and other plans I had were postponed.

The house is governed by a slave bought in a port of New Spain ... [a stain of ink makes the rest of the page illegible, and the next page has been torn]

[...] the frigate we boarded in Sanlucar, traveled on with permission from His Majesty. Seventeen trunks with household goods and a housekeeper from the Canary Islands were part of my belongings coming along. The old woman died two years later, here in the village of Coyoacan, a victim of humoral fevers.

Marina, my slave from Triana, was also a passenger, acquired in Seville while subject of servitude. She was twenty-five years old, of medium height and black, but of a lighter hue, with property deed duly signed and authorized by.. [a mold stain makes the rest of the page illegible].

• • •

Her name was Marina de Dueñas. Marina, of the sea and the waves of the Guadalquivir. We had left Spain and her past as a slave, stigma and impediment, to achieve our union in the Viceroyalty of New Spain, in Mexico. Taken by my hand, she had finally surrendered to the love that I confessed so many times, and we decided to come to the New World, to run away from the gossip and the condemnation of people, to start all over again: a Spaniard and a black slave, together, for interest or love.

While in the ship, full of settlers and church people, we had to stop the public display of our impulses, but we had hope that in these lands with more relaxed customs we could live a new life of our own. I bought her a slave to an old man who refused to tackle the violence of the boats of Triana to cross to Seville. The old man had attentively listened to my advice to go up to the lands of my childhood, where a safer way to cross could be found, the stream being calmer and gentler.

Her bare brown feet seemed to be floating on the sand while the old man watched the boats, holding her hand, fearing the flow. She was a slender maid, her neck with strings of sweat jewels and earrings of gold studded with silver, with bright eyes and a clear smile.

"Is it so impressive this gentleman I am demands some answers from you? May you please, at least, look at me while we have this conversation?" I said, jokingly.

Was it possible I felt like this just because so pleasing was the fragrance of her perfume?

The old man said that Marina would be put on sale at the next auction. That morning, she was dressed in a Bruges starched lace garment, and the bid reached a price that only I could match.

Since then, we were together, in the arms of sunsets, waiting for the moment to travel and make her the lady of my hacienda for her to be the mistress and I, her servant.

So much emotion had the New World brought that we forgot to keep track of the days. We approached the "Mary of the Incarnation" with a child in her womb, who would be born in these lands. As soon as I heard the news, I determined to do the seemingly impossible so that this son would always be transported in a golden covered litter and not even the smallest disdain would ever tarnish his heart.

On that transatlantic journey of months, everything changed in one night. The sea roared with waves like towers, the worst omen. In just a few hours, pain etched the corners of her mouth, her eyes opened wide and filled with the gray of death. The place our son had occupied was falling apart in red petals no compress could hold. On her knees, exhausted, our housekeeper announced no more gauze could contain her life.

We disposed of the body, praying in whispers and the Augustinian monk who solicitously blessed the shroud would never know the quality of woman we were throwing overboard. Her cemetery was the sea on the way to the New World.

My housekeeper urged me to search for a substitute for her body as soon as we landed, but during those days I bordered on madness.

The Church decreed that any maidservant may marry a free man or woman, but that they must be Christians and be married by a priest or a friar to enforce and make their marriage valid. Such was the commandment we both disobeyed and I knew we had paid for our weakness with Marina's life. My lame faith could not wait for the sacrament to be administered.

I cursed, I denied, I perjured. In a fit of distress, I came to lose my faith and to the blackest night and powers I pledged my soul if only I was allowed an instant of her perfume, her accent, and her soul to soothe mine.

Later, once in New Spain, it was the housekeeper who chose Lucia, a slave offered for sale by a man in the port. Suffering whistled in the string of discipline, which stings my back, seeking forgiveness for allowing me to waver, to be give in for the sins of the flesh.

Only Marina was like me. We came from the same river. My body sought consolation in vain.

On the roads and while in the kitchen, I watched black Lucia; I used her as masters do. She would never have her gifts and her voice. The housekeeper passed away from the epidemics caused by the flood and while having the black maid closer, slowly her hands became Marina's, her laughter echoed Marina's. Her determination to write the words her mouth spoke made her alien to my pain and there alone, in a house of wealth and loneliness, I broke my promise of abstinence. I, the master, visited her bedroom, yearning for the son we lost in the seas.

Thus, began the fast. So, the torture continued. Cursing, perjuring, and denying were leading me to the same type of death, again. A deed of purchase, the veredicts of church and society were upsetting it all.

I knew she would have to surrender by free will, like the river to the ocean, but she had set her eyes somewhere else and there is no commandment to resolve this.

Kiss me, for your love is better than wine; your name is perfume poured forth, a bundle of myrrh you are to me.

Comfort me, keep your left hand under my head, your right arm embracing me, until the day break, and the shadows flee away. Turn, my beloved, look at me! Turn away your eyes from him.

CHAPTER 10
THE TAGARETE AND THE RIVER OF SHRIMPS
1634

Alonso's letter, from the Tagarete stream

"Mariana, Mariana,

Out there, Indian dancers and musicians begin the celebration the friars have authorized. Here inside, a half-moon of silver glows on the wall of white, while I pray for the light that illuminates these lines that I must write to you. I know the sun will be filling your private chapel, there in Seville, and when you receive my letter, the rays will cover your beauty in gold.

Outside your house I know you hear, humble and narrow, the stream of the Tagarete that runs facing the city walls, on its way to the Guadalquivir. On my knees, with my prayers, full of repentance, I live again in my mind the hurried farewell scenes, all the unfulfilled promises I made, and a deep sorrow floods my soul. Five years are gone since that morning you waved a shy goodbye on the dock. Five, and after a deep examination, full of remorse I hold this quill to make my sincere plea to you, Mariana.

My lines are asking for the forgiveness of your parents, of your whole family, and most important, yours, forgiveness that only a sweet and patient heart like yours may have for those who have delayed the fulfillment of their duties for so long. I beg your mercy for the well-deserved reprimand you have wished for me, for the offenses that I have inflicted on you and those of yours. In the name of the suffering for Christ's sake, I appeal to the affection I keep for you and your memory.

This servant writing to you now, Mariana, is by no means the same person you wished farewell. Destiny wanted that the only letter of yours came into my hands only recently and, with it, all the memories, all the plans and the hopes came back to me at once.

The handwriting of the scribe and that signature of yours, trembling like a ripple on the water, unleashed all kind of regrets on me. Here in New Spain, I have been in the Augustinian Convent of Culhuacan for several years. The benevolent friars welcomed my stay, along with that of a faithful friend, and under the sacrament of confession, they have known how all my acts of the past still hurt me. One of the religious brothers, Friar Angel de Remesal, traveling from the city of Salamanca to these Indies, was the messenger who barely two weeks ago brought with him the only letter of yours that I have received.

What a joy it was to read you! And how many things have happened since you wrote it, but time and distance were nothing because your letter has made you present, next to me, Mariana, just like the first day.

Your missive, I must say, has been an event that rejoiced this community of friars and myself. A kind of a miracle, all friar brothers say, and as you will now see, friar Remesal has been an instrument of the Providence of God, Our Lord, so far.

Let me remind you that those who have crossed the immensity of the oceans may better understand the delay in the reception of all kind of correspondence. Edicts, laws and royal proclamations for these, His Indies, signed by His Majesty Philip IV, by the grace of God King of Spain, take just as long as the letter of the humblest servant to get here.

Private unclaimed mail for colonists who have not declared a fixed domicile is stored in the port of Veracruz, and only the Lord knows how inclement and miserable those weathers may be for paper kept in vaults. So many impediments the epistles suffer and how often they remain in the hands of the Post Office of the Indies, without reaching the roads. Only an act of God has decreed that your letter finds me, folded and closed with sealing wax, and my blurry name written as that of the addressee.

You may wonder how the fortuitous event occurred. Father Remesal, coming from the Spanish Salamanca hills by the Tormes River had to spend a few nights in the port of Veracruz. He was invited for dinner by the royal constable, and from him, he heard the most incredible stories of port and registration. Misplaced authorizations and passenger files to the Indies, lost luggage full of garments and memories, unloaded on the dock without owner to claim them, a property of noble officials having perished in the long journey. Orphans, entire families who passed away in the journey, victims of dysentery or typhus, had left their belongings on board, in the ships. Those happy encounters of promised women, meeting their fiancés for marriage that never happened, left luggage and documents all in the port.

Later that night, the friar and the constable talked about other travel collaterals: hundreds of letters stored in the cellars, no records to give a good account of the whereabouts of their recipients. The friar, who felt a great esteem and affection for me, well remembered my story. I am one of those many who have decided to heal body and soul, far away from the world, from its banalities and desires in the shelter of a convent.

That is how the good friar went to the port archives and found my name in a bundle, an envelope where Mariana, my lady, was displayed as the sender, illuminating the room with a divine ray.

The road from Veracruz to these lands became eternal for him. He knew that letter was addressed to Alonso García de Santamaria, type-founder, puncher and setter at the printing press established in this holy and venerable Convent he resided at. The same Alonso, who pledged his word to send for you that morning of salt and mist.

The Holy Virgin wanted that my voluntary seclusion made good use of its hours and I learned the trade of a printer and presser for the service of the gospel for the naturals here, while vain fortune attempts were left aside. God knows that behind these walls I never forgot the promise to send for you, and I should have done that as soon as I could.

Now, my humble hands want to dedicate this craft of my work, and from a special ream of paper, I have separated a few pages, to write this letter that begs for your clemency. I need you here. I need you to come.

Please grant me a positive answer and instruct me on how to get you the amount that will grant me the joy to see you again. Repairing promptly what my commitment was will be the lead that will govern my life and my effort, from now on.

If your love resolves this way, I will wait anxiously for the months of the trip and may my prayers accompany your navigation. The funds I may send will be sufficient to make a good, comfortable journey, which you will not have to fear. The future, I know it well, will be very different from what we planned with your father, but I trust happiness and faith will prevail, setting aside the search for honors.

Only the memory of your face will be my incentive, and I will be glad that upon receipt of this letter you respond as soon as possible for the arrangements to be made.

With a repentant and suppliant heart, I wish you well, praying the Lord to keep you under His favour.

Your slave and servant,
Alonso García de Santamaría.

• • •

A scene with Mariana from the Guadalquivir

The moat the Tagarete spring formed outside the city walls, near the old Jewish quarter, received on its shore of fine sand the slender white feet of Mariana de Salazar y Miranda.

A black woman, refreshing and rinsing her legs and neck under the Sevillian heat, quickly lowered her skirts for fear of offending the fine maiden who stepped down here to a place where only the crowds attend. Doña Mariana, indifferent to those who frolicked in the stream, observed the hurrying brook, which fell over little cascades in its haste, never looking once at the primroses that were glimmering all along its banks.

The watercourse was lost on the horizon. Her housekeeper sat on a stone, nervous about the daring of her mistress. What were they doing mixing with these low-quality people? What would they do if someone, God forbid, tried to approach them? She must have brought that handkerchief she used to moisten with orange blossoms perfume to soak the lace and rid the mistress of the stench.

The housekeeper prayed to heaven that the smell did not affect the child. The angel would be born when this heat of hell suffocates less. It would be a beautiful cherub and Friar Carrascal, the father, would come to the house every morning and devote his tender words and care to his mistress. Oh, the love and devotion he shows, kissing Doña Mariana's womb fervently. The housekeeper wanted to go back inside the walls that protected the city. Royal Sevilla had everything her lady needed. She wanted to buy a bouquet of aromatic violets for Doña Mariana at the oil gate, to get rid of the foul smell. She would lead her mistress up to the balcony where the child in her womb would rest safe and sound, rocking under the shade and dreaming of his noble future.

"Is this what we are here for, my lady?" she asked. "Just to make that letter reach the sea through these miserable waters? Is that what we have come for? Do you believe that this trickle of water from the stream will really take its content away for good? I could have done that! I have looked after you good enough and have listened to your trouble and despair. I have prepared good tisanes, have wiped your forehead in fever, holding you in my arms, ready to be at your service always! I could have done that for you, my lady!"

Those were sheets of white, glistening linen paper from that mill in New Spain, I know. Perfect, beautiful writing, but incomprehensible to the housekeeper.

The letter fell into the water and went away with all its shimmering reasonings and explanations to the curls of the Tagarete. Promises and explanations, pleas and appeals were diluted in the song of the creek stones.

While the words might never reach the great sea, they had finally closed the wound of a maiden who believed in a promise and waited in vain for it to be fulfilled.

Mariana spoke to her servant. "Come on, Soledad. Let's go now. White clouds will soon be gone."

• • •

Joy of Sebastián from the River of Shrimps

Tucu-tucutum, tucu-tucutum. The drums beat and rumble on the Day of the Exaltation of the Holy Cross. The distant percussions reach my ears, and my memory is now confused, entangled.

Is it this music that blows in the wind the one of my village? Is this the song women sing with their baskets full of fishery, in the Portuguese colony of the Rio dos Camarões, the waters of shrimps, or *cameroon*, as they pronounced, like those of the foreign ships say? Or is it that the past is no more and the sound of the cams, of our humble pulp and paper mill, is the only present that exists?

Despite the celebration out there, we keep on working, tireless. The book will be ready, and soon we will be done. The waters of the spring will stop when I lower the floodgate, splashing my face, revealing the place where I am for real. We started at dawn to solve the urgency of printing the book, but neither the master nor I am tired or fed up by this job we both love. It was here that we saved our lives, here in Culhuacan, under the consolation of the Augustinian friars, five years ago.

Tucu-tucutum, tucu-tucutum. The natives play their instruments out there, and the Friars have left hurriedly because they must watch the party and the frenzy of percussions can easily get out of control. They know that to maintain the order in these towns, they must grant some licenses from time to time. The Exaltation of the Cross is a big day, and the procession is accompanied by the only instrument allowed in this village. Solemn music replaces the scandal that was becoming last year when someone introduced conches and fire trumpets. Mulattos started a dance of turns, jumps, and leaps, inviting everybody to their frenzied debauchery.

By evening, the atrium will be illuminated with nine pounds of renewed wax and fireworks will light out Culhuacan's sky, drawing the attention of the Creator, who will turn His eyes to the faithful. I will then give thanks for His mercy, looking up and not down, as I do with the master, not down as I do with the friars, whom I serve.

I do not complain or regret it, for I have achieved here that the light of reading and writing, of types and ink to print books, light my understanding up, a slave of Christ, in whom I have found all the answers.

Tucu-tucutum, tucu-tucutum. The mill of Culhuacan manufactures paper to keep good account of sales, produce, alms, goods, and rents. In paper we print chronicles and epistles, sermons and books of prayers, without having to skimp on the cost of the sheets, as when they came from Europe. Mallets fall with rhythm, grinding the rags, reducing them to pulp and it is their cadence like that of the drum, like the beat of a heart.

Back in the village, the old chief Omohundro knew that it is with the drums that moods are fixed, that it is music what keeps a body balanced. Palms striking the tanned skin of the percussions was what was needed by those who dragged our people away, the Portuguese and the English. Entire villages had been taken away on foreign ships, never to return.

Chief used to say slavers must have had an unbalanced heart, without cadence or proportion.

Tucu-tucutum, tucu-tucutum. We distributed the pulp in the grids and leave them resting all night long, to drain the surplus water in the morning. Now that we have finished, master Alonso and I can join the church celebration. We will prove our devotion to Christ, made of cane paste, that the natives take on a litter with a damask canopy, full of flowers. Fruit at His bleeding feet will be distributed in the banquet that they have prepared to thank Mother Nature and not the cross as they pretend.

And while we eat, men separated from women, my hands await the moment to take your hand of beautiful fingers, hands that have sewn the satin of the heavenly silk sky for the Christ, blue as your skirts, blue and splendid as water around.

Paper can wait. We will smooth the dry canvases with the burnisher and will leave them ready to print the copies of the Catechism of Perseverance Friar Miguel Cantillana will take to the Convent of Cuitzeo, in the Province of San Nicolás de Tolentino de Michoacan.

Master Alonso's dreams of wealth and oil were burned in the lamps of the convent, and when we both became indispensable for the friars, I was asked to travel with Father Cantillana to look after him and protect him, for miles and leagues, until the road turned into a cobbled street that lead to a magnificent Augustinian convent, on the banks of a far-away lake.

In Michoacan, the frontispiece with Mary Magdalene carved in granite, presiding, holding her vessel of precious oil, welcomes visitors. It is oil, always the oil, like the one she used to anoint the bleeding face of Christ in His Passion. After the exhausting journey, Father Cantillana would spend a few days at the Seminary of Languages of St. John the Evangelist since it is through language how they sought to establish the City of God in those lands.

It was that first time, while we were securing our belongings on the saddles that a girl, a faithful and living replica of the face of the Magdalene, appeared before us, along with her mother.

Tucu-tucutum, tucu-tucutum.

"Take my child, my Lord," begged the old woman. "Take her to your service, because there is nothing left here, nothing of what we were."

A flame of compassion ignited in the heart of the friar, and after long insistence, his approval was shown when he told me that I needed to let her ride my mule.

Tucu-tucutum, tucu-tucutum.

A few months after, I asked for permission to marry the girl, my saint of the oil vessel, and together we received the blessing of Christ with a perfumed oil anointing, too.

All that ocean and the port, all the years serving the chores for the Captain and a hundred roads with Master Alonso were needed to find me in your hands, Elisa, your hands that embroider and sew the blue canopy for the Christ, overflowed with flowers.

Tucu-tucutum, tucu-tucutum.

Is that the drum that announces there will be a celebration? Yes, there will be a wedding by the Lake of Mexico, by the pier of Culhuacan!

The war of men will stop for that day and the river, full of shrimps, will sing Olodumare's blessing for the union. The priest of Ifá will write a poem for the bride, and the groom and Oshún will rejoice. Elisa and Sebastian will have their foreheads thrown to the ground and Saint Benedict the African will be merry and content, because Mary Magdalene, transfigured in Elisa, sent by the heavens, has come to give direction to this black man who left the river of shrimps one day, the land of the Fulani, against his will.

CHAPTER 11
THE FRESHWATER LAKE
1634

Eugenia from Iztacalco, in the Lake of Mexico

In the parish of Saint John, the Baptist on May the tenth of this year sixteen hundred thirty-four, the sacred sacrament of baptism is administered, imposing oil and chrism to Fernando, foundling infant, son whose parents are ignored, left in the courtyard of this Franciscan church and convent some days ago. It is his godfather in the sacrament, Bartolomé de Toledo, neighbor of this village, who contracts spiritual kinship and obligation to teach him the rudiments of our faith. It is his godmother Eugenia, Mexican, Major Mother of the Brotherhood of the Immaculate Conception, which serves for the relief, sustenance, and cure of diseases of the faithful, as she declares. The infant is seen, and this act is signed by Friar Jacinto de Rivera, Prior of this Franciscan Convent in the jurisdiction of Coyoacan."

Adulterers, creatures fathered by parents under prohibited relations or the nefarious product of incestuous affairs, children of public women or sacrilegious offspring of priests and religious, were thrown on the thresholds of churches and houses as newborns.

By their abandonment, their mothers' honor was saved. They knew there were not enough orphanages and foundling houses so they trusted the protection of the parishioners and the Holy Church. Those were the ways almost everywhere in this kingdom of New Spain.

Evicted by their parents, helpless, if they luckily survived the cold night or a feast of dogs and rats, these natural children, bastards, received the baptism two days after they were found, no matter what. They were often raised by neighbors or were sheltered as servants or apprentices in the guilds, without pay.

Some girls were endowed by the charity of a deceased prominent gentleman, who bequeathed to the church a certain amount to ensure the orphan entered a convent as a nun, on the condition that the recluse, in her days of endless prayer, would pray for the eternal rest of the benefactor's soul.

They were the fruit of the relationships forbidden by the Mother Church, and they carried that stigma for all the days of their lives.

The catastrophe that unleashed the Saint Matthew's Gale had produced such mortality and movement of people that the village grew in number of inhabitants and of abandoned children.

Stonemasons were the main branch of that family my husband, Miguel Mauricio, came from. We never untied the knot of our cloaks and dresses. He had had another life for a long time. Thus I came here, to this shore, leaving my islands of hunger and contagion.

Causeways had been closed for a long time, and fences tried to prevent the outbreaks of disease from touching dry land. The beam that blocked the passage of boats and canoes was still down, the sentry box abandoned. The fertile village continued to flourish, while I brooded my misadventure in a house at the heights of Coyoacan and the view of the entire beautiful valley gave way to understanding.

Friars and the goodness of our brotherhood had rescued my boat from sinking. We continued to pray and make offerings to our gods and managed to climb the stony hill to reach the House of the Mist, where the obsidian black mirror was buried, and where springs and rivers are born. We burned papers; we dared to take in precious vessels, offerings of flowers and soil from the bottom of the lake to calm those who presided here, the gods of water.

It was also bones of orphans that made up our offering. Little children, thrown away, that had been caught as prey by carnivores. We handled their remains carefully, secretly. We washed them and painted them delicate blue. This was an ancient tradition because we all knew what bones lock in; the soul, the spirit, what made you be who you are. Tiny polished bones we revered and adorned with necklaces, discs of wood, and a green stone inside the ruby that had been their mouth. These children were the symbol of birth, and we firmly believed our offerings reinforced with the prayers in the Dominican Convent.

Here, we had one brotherhood of Spaniards and one of Indians. The Mixtec brothers were here, too. They knew how to embroider and dye yarns and fabric, that is why the weaving mills had brought them here. They were so important they had a guild here, and their own chief was in charge of their tribute collection.

Only a few understood their language, and with the flood some of them ran away, hoping to return to their lands, far from the dangers of the growing city. The forced reconstruction and drainage works were also killing our people.

For those coming from the islands, we knew we had to make room down here. Coyoacan of the stonemasons had carved a jaguar mask to honor the gods and it was affixed on one of the rebuilt buildings, as a mark to never forget the level waters have reached. When the waters were gone and reconstruction continued, the palaces of counts and marquises used some of our precious stones, discs and snake jaws as propitiatory amulets embedded in their new foundations and walls.

With as much work as there was in the fields, at the end of my days I was left with the indispensable strength to drag my feet to the atrium and dedicate a few hours to decorating the altars and looking after the orchard and patios.

I spent five years rinsing my sorrow in the reflections of jade and crystal of the lake, but it was with the life of that little boy, an orphan, that I recovered a life of my own.

My beautiful criollito was made of silver, of snow and beeswax. He was my lamp from the East, wrapped in a blanket, who was left at the threshold of the atrium arches, to stay with me forever. His eyes lit my sky, and I covered his chest with kisses, washing his face of angel, every morning.

I found beside him a divine gift – forgiveness and forgetfulness. Both came to me like a fragrance to rinse my soul and make heaven on earth.

With the favor of the friars, soon his trembling hands will have learned the syllabary, and his strong fist will hold a quill, as mine have never been able to do. He will write the names of the baptized in the books, the alms of the brotherhood, and under my protection he will memorize the life of Christ and His Passion, while he learns the dates that I will teach so he knows the secrets of sowing and harvesting.

Time will pass placidly for him, the music of water accompanying his thoughts, and whether a prince or rower crossing to the islands, he will also be a glorious descendant of the nahuas and the culhuas, the founding fathers who know the secrets of black and red ink.

Their wisdom will be his, and his will be a coat of arms of clumps of leaves and flowers. He will go as high as the stars that line up. I will no longer seek more offerings to the steep rock and its gods since I have found consolation in him.

This will be my advice to him – to flee from the feast, to moderate and be austere, to revere the earth since from it he will get clothing and sustenance.

I will be his mother, Eugenia from Iztacalco and Zacatlamanco, a noble no more who rejoices in his heart, enriched before the sight of him, my fine flower, my creature, my son.

● ● ●

Miguel Mauricio's act of contrition, from Tlatelolco, by the little lagoon

Here, in Tlatelolco, the ditches were quagmires, and after Christmas the warehouse and the orchard were empty. The nights of vigil and prayer had not served at all and the great market now belonged to the water. The following year, more rain made everything worse, if possible.

The level was still as high as the height of two friars, and this had been the most important lesson we could have learned. We are as a drop of water in the ocean, at the mercy of nature. We left the workshops and the polychrome carvings, covered in resplendent gold. We left the cistern and its radiant painted walls and Saint James in the altarpiece of beaten gold leaves.

In that plank of wood, Saint James had fought all my battles. Unknowingly, my path to temperance began when wood was cut, right when the tree was short of sap, ready to become a smooth surface by the work of chisels, gouges, and adzes. I had to get rid of everything to form a new relief with my life. Without the resin of its veins, I had to seal each hole where a branch wanted to be born; I had to extract each knot and seal it with burns.

When we departed from Tlatelolco, the candles went out and only the church and its walls of stuccoed ashlars, the College of magnificent stone from our temples, were left. The aqueduct was broken and the streams from the northern springs did not come here anymore. At last I understood that everything was over, that new buildings needed our ancient rubble for a strong foundation to build anew and rise again.

The old word and the colloquies were no longer, and water had come to clean everything to begin again. We all had to flee from disaster without distinction –the friars, the natives, the residents of Tlatelolco and the black servants-. The small lagoon grew along with the lakes and I, Miguel Mauricio, quauhtlacuilo, master of the art of wood of the Imperial College of the Holy Cross, continued my pilgrimage on dry land, confident. I managed to safeguard the gift of life I was granted, a son who came to bless my existence when my heart was contrite, divided between what it was and what it was about to be.

Father Torquemada had chosen Saint James, after his nights of penance before consecrating Tlatelolco. Saint James was the knight of his battles, as well. He had real affection for me, and in addition to the information I was able to provide to complete his books, we talked at length about the great doubts our actions planted in his heart and his affliction to adequately explain our culture. He was convinced that God had chosen New Spain to be the head of His Church in the New World and that more learning and instruction was needed here than in Spain. After the episode in the courtyard with the lashed craftsman and his own penance, the Father devoted himself to completing his twenty-one scholarly books that explained our myths and traditions. He tried until his sudden death to reconcile his world with the new one that was being built, and fervently tried to include all that had to be learned from the north and the south.

Like him with fasting, a sackcloth, and a scourge, I also attempted to purge my faults. After the disaster, I heard nothing of the woman who was my wife and believing I was surely a widower, I asked for and was granted permission from the friars to meet a woman under the law again. Water took my past away and brought peace back to my soul, and I vowed to give my life to support with my art the hard work of Father Torquemada and the Order. My name was written on the palm of Thy right hand, my Lord, and my new union had been blessed, and for my son I knew that life always breaks through. I would continue my offspring and ride on wings of faith, like the apostle, proclaiming victory against old idols.

My son carries Spanish blood, like his mother. His accent is a music bell, and both are now all my richness. In wind and nothing, I had been wasting my strength when my right and my inheritance were inside myself.

When waters receded, I was already a new man. The roads returned to hold crowds of our people gathered to get rid of desolate rubble and destruction to start the reconstruction.

Only after the flood, we proclaimed our victory: the power to rebuild ourselves, to restore ourselves, my Lord.

CHAPTER 12
THE PACIFIC OCEAN
1634

Muleteers were driving the world on dry land. They went to the city of Mexico en route from the Pacific coast to deliver raw materials for mills to squeeze the pulp that would make the paper for these lands. Coconut shells, pineapple crowns, sugarcane bagasse and cacti waste. Cotton, yucca, and palm would become white canvases that would carry on their surfaces all the emotions that inspire humanity to write. Paper, in many places, had been escaping the control of the Ministry of Paper that was just being organized. Covenants, declarations of love, prayers, catechisms, and patents would be printed in New Spain, without paying the tax on paper, and such were the amounts and the risk to disseminate information of all kinds, everywhere, without control, that the Crown reinforced all royal laws to establish proper control a couple of years later. Everything was reorganizing.

Five years before, a caravan had taken Captains Morales and Nebra up the road from Acapulco. They had left grateful, and we said goodbye while I decided to stay in the port, hoping to recompose myself from all the latest events. Months had passed without deciding to start the trip. I was in no hurry to contemplate the mirror of water that surrounds the courts and the government of New Spain in its capital, Mexico.

There was plenty of work for me here. The captains would return a year later to collect their precious wrought iron choir rood screen. I might wait for them to be back, I told myself. They did not imagine that shortly after their departure, on their way to Mexico, water had stopped the works of their beloved Cathedral, sunk in the mud of the Great Flood for years. It would still be a long time for its beauty to eclipse faithful eyes.

My soul had to calm down, and it took me years to get there, while I witnessed how the Manila galleons fleet and its contents excited the spirits of people with each season; the brightness of Orient came every year on time, and the port of Acapulco lived for those brief months of merrymaking.

Each vessel brought people like me, slaves or adventurers enthralled by the legends woven around the kingdom of Spain that started here. With all the controls established by the Crown, some managed to overcome the sandbars and the mountains to hide in a small-town population, lost in the immensity of the kingdom. Some others were lost in the confusion of a revolt or joined the royal forces of the militia to fight the bandits who ravaged the port.

As slow as the flood was receding, others managed to get to Mexico City outskirts to work in one of the unlicensed barbershops. They called them "Chinos de Cortina", Chinese barbers working in their trade behind a curtain. They were healers and barbers that were continually denounced by those who were legally working. Only a few resolved to go further and reach Mexico City to present an examination before the Tribunal del Protomedicato, the royal authority which supervised the work of doctors, surgeons, apothecaries, and healers. That was what I was most afraid of; being subject to a test that only a few passes.

Some others saved some money to meet those of their own in the coconut plantations in Colima, seeking the protection of the remote Consulate of Chinese. People of all qualities from Asia were producing vessels of sweet coconut wine and selling them in Manzanillo to help sailors on the last part of their journey before coming to Acapulco. But I knew there was something out there for me. Fear resulted in time invested to finish learning the language while I struggled with my fear.

The delayed delivery and transportation of the choir rood screen was an opportunity to travel I passed on, and the screen departed on its way to the city. I had planned and later dismissed the idea of traveling alone.

It was on one hot afternoon that I followed the footsteps of an indigenous scribe performing an act in a corner of the square, where I was in my musings and meditations. He was a forger. He wrote and drew primordial titles and deeds, which he passed for ancient documents, for the equal benefit of Spaniards and Indians. Armed with his pen and his colors, his itinerant wit had flouted the regulations of public authorities. He had obtained some reams of paper and drew his own maps, with boundaries and borders and all the required detail to support notarial allegations on property and possessions.

The bells on top of the cathedral were tolling the proximity of the fleet, and the port was all crowds and confusion. What did I need to move on and get to the road? What was stopping me?

I told myself that this would be my last chance. The Indian with his grace transgressed all kinds of laws daily and I realized that I had to learn the art of going unnoticed. When the Indian left the port, I would ask him to show me the way and accompany him on his way to Taxco or Cuernavaca, in the Province of Silver. I even suggested he would receive a magnificent payment for confectioning a document that would complement that appointment Captain Nebra had granted in such good faith.

The Indian naturally distrusted my proposal. A Chinese intruder who called himself a knight, paying for a document, to join him like a shadow, for months? I would never know if he read in my eyes that his company would be the ultimate way to overcome my cowardice. I would accompany him in his wanderings, without complaint or encumbrance.

After several days following his routines in the square to the laugh of onlookers, he accepted my company when leaving the port. If stopped on the roads, my documents would ensure that we were left alone; he might even pretend to be my servant as a good as he was when it came to telling jokes, we would have better chances with the authorities.

We took the road, stopping for weeks in those places that could pay his prices, until after a few months we reached the mining town of Taxco. He was a master at closing a business transaction under the arches of any portal, while I watched in the distance the effect of his arts. At each stop he closed at least one transaction, demanding full payment and before leaving the towns at dawn, he would deliver fine jobs of which no one would doubt the authenticity.

He mixed up ancient stories that lent an air of truth to each statement, detailing glories and properties awarded for battles waged in the army or navy, fighting for the Kingdom. He knew the language of cadastral maps, genealogies, and titles that decided the rights over the destination of a community plot, a family or a town.

Riding with him had new surprises every day. Many times, we would have to run to escape the sheriff's musket, leaving behind a good writing that would support the distribution of a cattle ranch, based in his native language and Castilian; a confused memory of events he had composed. I had never felt more alive.

The maker of primordial titles traveled through villages, while I watched for hours the thousand ways of decorating the body in each region –traces of pigment on arms and legs, powdered faces or wigs, the ways to adjust the coat, as the Ba and the Yue do, and not like us, those of Fujian.

I cut their hair and beards, leaving them short or free, to the chest, using oil to make them shine or twisting the ends for a nice lock and curl. Carrying the tricorn hatched or not wearing anything, showing the skull without a hair or displaying the sacred tonsure. All were styles worn here.

I witnessed an immense variety of customs exhibited by the crowds, smiling in a display of black teeth destroyed by cavities and lack of hygiene, abscesses that I knew how to attend. I was gaining in confidence. In all our wanderings, my eyes often discovered gross imitations of porcelain wares from China. Only a few like myself knew the music of bells that silica has, coming as it does from the sacred mountain of Kao-Ling, north of Fujian, my port.

Selling fake crockery made by the locals, so overly blue, was the same scam that my Indian friend performed in each square. Dishes and pouring vessels so poor and defective that not even a blind man would dare to drink from them. I also saw, on the other hand, in the richest villas, real porcelain from the Celestial Empire, bronze jugs and swords, containers of glazed stoneware, ivory combs and silk cloths that I incorporated into my practice to scent them with eucalyptus of these lands, the final note of perfume after a nice shaving that always brought the benevolent smile with which my father in my memory closed his teachings.

Hua Tuó, from the province of Fujian, was learning about these lands with each step. My features would forever announce my origin. Converted by the Captain and the Indian into Rodrigo de la Cruz by the magic of a document, I continued to dominate with my sword, but never boasted about it. These fine hands were destined to more delicate works of all precision and surgery. Healing the body and restoring its balance was a divine task and my hands were the tool. That is what I had promised to my father.

To fulfill the mandate of heavens for me would be to obtain the permission of the Viceroy to establish a barbershop and to exercise as surgeon and phlebotomist in the noble New Spain, but inside of me, I would always be Huá Tuó, "the one who perceives the laments," like my ancestors from the kingdom of Dzin. For these people here, we were all Chinese, no matter if we came from the Philippines, Cambodia, Ceylon, China, India, Papua or Siam, places that the King or the Viceroy had never seen before.

Now I was decided to walk the roads to find my place in the Portal of Merchants or the vicinity of the convent of Saint Dominic, carrying from one side to the other my beautiful wooden chest of instruments.

After a few months, when we arrived at the Valley of Cuauhnahuac, the Indian and I parted ways. We had survived and I was stronger. I was ready. He would continue with his apocryphal writings, and I well understood how his work alleviated that orphan memory that his people had suffered since others had occupied their lands. False documents were the only way they could use to assert their rights. Thanks to the Indian, I had gathered the courage to approach the Court and have my knowledge examined to be allowed to practice medicine legally.

Now in Cuaunahuac, turned Cuernavaca as the language from Spain was doing with all Indian names the Franciscan cathedral was a mandatory stop when entering the city. Its interior walls, unraveling in colors, abounded in paintings of a multitude of men in shirts of Castile and tonsured friars struggling between boats and reeds, from top to bottom. This was a sacred place, a temple for both of us, to beg our gods for a good journey. After mass, we would go in different directions.

On my knees, with no other altar than my memory, I discovered with astonishment that those vessels painted on the walls had sailors who had my face and my features. We were the same! They carried a sword like mine and the clothes of my lands. In another scene, executioners with slanted eyes speared along the side of a row of prisoners, their sharp points piercing their shoulders. Some more, crucified, twenty-six of them, suffered with their limbs subject to crosses with iron rings. The paintings hinted that the European people who had previously rowed confidently had had a bad end. In the far east, the people from Spain had tried to convert men like me into Christian law. It was my own people the martyrs of these scenes, wall by wall, in greens, yellows and blues.

The sea bordered in cobalt and the story painted displayed men like me, who had suffered the same fate as the lute poet of our stories, with severed ears, exhibited in carts for the punishment of those who dared to even think of converting to Christianity. The mass ended, and my heart was tumbling. My people were there, crucified, nailed to that same cross that now was part of my name.

When I had walked through the entire nave of the church, I had to sit to gather my thoughts. We were only a few in these lands with my features and Rodrigo de la Cruz, who I am now, was free of such a fate but was right on his way to reach the Court to be examined. A piece of paper, discarded, had been drawn by the Indian with charcoal. It had my face on it. Rodrigo de la Cruz, immortalized in his strokes, would now have to forget his name and his beliefs, to confront the future but I must never dismiss my past.

Beloved Kwan Yin, owner and lady of the skies, your son Hua Tuó invokes the mercy of your lotus heart. Give me your compassion in this hour! Redeem my faults, soften my path and send your pure violet love that takes away sadness, insecurity, discouragement, and nostalgia. Transform, O Lady, all darkness into light, and give me your essence to purify my redeemed heart.

Here on my knees, in the exquisite Franciscan church of Our Lady of the Assumption, in the city of Cuernavaca, Rodrigo de la Cruz, your son, I beg to you.

EPILOGUE
1634-1636

Friar Andres de San Miguel looked through the window surrounded by his library of twelve thousand volumes. Outside, trees and bushes bloomed in the gardens of this paradise on earth he had designed for the Convent of Saint Angelo, his pride and tranquility. He had written about all the subjects that his curiosity had desired, and now he had before him one of his last challenges. Mature and intelligent, authoritarian and harsh, accustomed to challenge even his superiors, Friar Andres composed a mental list of the blunders that had caused the catastrophe of the great flood.

He reflected on that tunnel of the drainage channel which was never properly cemented. The calculations of its downward slopes had been wrong from the beginning, and the long grasses Indians used to reinforce the assembly of their croplands had come loose with the current, forming massive tangles that clogged everything. Channels and dikes were maintained with Indian labour, and some of them received a symbolic wage, but most of them were required to provide free work and service. The levees went slowly, piling all the debris of nature, and no edict had managed to clean them.

While he was lost in his thoughts, the gates of the convent opened to receive an old man, brought in on a litter by his black servants. He had come to negotiate with the friars what part of his income would go to the Carmelites Order at his death. Friar Andres smiled at the scene, certain that every work needs funds uninterruptedly to succeed and knowing there would always be souls at fault who would pay for the prayers and masses that would give relief and rest to their souls.

He returned to his thoughts. For weeks, he had been thinking about the details of the report he would render after supervising the Huehuetoca channel and the works at Nochistongo. He knew he had to strongly underline how the advice of the Indians and his precise mathematical calculations had been ignored. They had called him in emergencies, when the diverted Cuautitlan River demanded a double floodgate to control the waters or as when a ditch had to be made in San Gregorio.

Now that the waters were gone, he would try to deliver to the Prelate, his superior, the corrected report he had formulated during the worst part of the flood, the Relation of the Site and the State of Mexico City and the Remedy, which he had written in the midst of disaster. He hoped this time it would reach the hands of His Majesty, Philip IV, the King of Spain from the House of Habsburg. At last it would be understood that he should have been appointed for this titanical work, and not the foreign cosmographer, a simple mapmaker and not the expert the Court had wanted to believe.

The vision of turning the heart of New Spain a place of only dry land, forged by the residences and palaces owners, had preferred that mock of an architect, the scourge with which God had punished the city. The colonial officers were also responsible. They had rejected any proposal that considered a friendly coexistence with water. They only wanted to get rid of her and they had so much to learn about it! Indians had made vineyards where there was nothing before, just like him. They had invented chinampas, those plots of reeds and mud that turned water into firm, farmable land, and causeways.

A sailor himself, he had learned that water must be treated with reverence. That's why he took advantage of it, letting it free in fountains and aqueducts, like the Indians did, making a paradise on earth. They had to know it was not with their fine lace white gloves that they would learn about water. You had to wet your hands in its freshness, molding the mud and feeling it on your feet, digging ditches, to get to know its kindness.

That was what the Republic of Venice had done. They had sent their merchant vessels across the Adriatic using their canals and the Netherlands, too. Draining water was like turning their back on the work of God in this valley; their audacity had been punished with the flood.

The friar had written real treatises on engineering and hydraulics and had even invented a pump that was now used to expel waters from the underground mining labyrinths. He dipped his quill in the beautiful translucent porcelain inkwell, not knowing that his superiors were considering him, their most cherished architect, to build a bridge in Lerma and to carry out his last architectural work, the construction of the Convent of Salvatierra.

Three years would pass after the friar delivered his report that royal orders commanded him to be in charge of the water works. There was a new viceroy for these lands who proved his love for the territories –Lope Díez de Aux y Armendáriz was the first viceroy to be born on the American continent– and it was his most important commitment that the failures be resolved. The detail of how the cosmographer had fatally miscalculated, erring in depth and leveling, was key. Finally, the friar was appointed and his favors requested.

The gully that drained the water from the Cuautitlan River and the Zumpango Lake was draining two reservoirs that natives deemed sacred. Water reached the Tula River, flooding an extension of the mythical Tollan, the place of their origins. The Indians thought that this was sacrilege. While in charge, the friar would never know if the slowness of the works or the surreptitious collapse of a dam was sabotage by the Indians. The Crown had requested his help, and the Order had granted permission but only briefly, claiming he had other commitments, but his pride was finally glorified. Only by overseeing the works could the friar be freed from his human grudges.

Waterworks now knew of his corrected measurements, ten yards below the original level in some sections of the dikes and the gullies, as he always advised to both the ecclesiastical and secular councils. Draped with a hat that covered his white skin from the rigors of the Mexican highlands, the friar walked the entire length of the main channel, reporting to his superiors on the advance of each section.

He worked tirelessly, with a renewed enthusiasm. Under his supervision, New Spain was reconciled with water. Its regulated stream ran a smooth, orderly and clean course and the future generations just had to provide maintenance to his masterpiece.

A cobalt blue morning greeted him coming to test the strength of the temporary wooden bridge, soaked by the dew of the night. A breeze announced the new dry season and the works continued to widen the channel. A mulatto reached him to tell that fifty yards away, indigenous diggers had discovered a huge white bone they had rinsed with the water of the stream.

The bone gleamed in the sunlight and the slaves said it looked exactly the same like the one they worshiped in their village, where they bathed it in honey and flowers to appease the fury of the spirits that inhabited the heart of the earth. Native Indians claimed that this was the remains of a giant, the beasts of their stories that were once fed with resin and oak acorns and had once inhabited this land.

Their legends blamed the giants for earthquakes, and when they finally provoked the big destruction, they were all killed by the shaking land, their bones had been randomly scattered. They whispered that just as the giants had perished, some punishment would come for those who dared to challenge the natural course of water.

The friar remained silent in amazement. There was no answer in his sacred books for findings of this type, and he would worry about the bone later. He went back to his calculations and records and ordered the crew to hurry and continue, for they had to finish this stretch and later attend certain cuts in the ditch that were diverting the water to a crop plot and a mill. He was to travel to Lerma the following month and wanted to advance as much as possible in this, his most ambitious work.

The end of that century surprised New Spain, dressed in emeralds of water again. Works were still incomplete. The cycle would continue the same for two more centuries, defying cyclical floods in this land of clear lakes until early 1900s.

Neither vice regal decrees, the treatises of Vitruvius, the expertise of foreigners, or the hundreds of rations of corn, chili, and salt for the workers could defeat Nature, but they still insisted on getting rid of the lakes, as obstinate and stubborn they were, to continue inhabiting this land.

Encircled by waves, the Valley of Mexico continued to see water causeways and a thousand crystalline ditches rise and be broken for more two centuries.

Sweaty workers had to stop the works again. A beautiful tusk of ivory was gleaming again in the black soil. Exchanging glances, everybody agreed they would hide their finding from the friar. It was better to cut the tusk into pieces and distribute it.

For God's sake, no better talisman against water might be created when the treasures of the west and the east are in danger.

ENDNOTES

If you perceive the similarities that unite us, regardless of the color of your skin, through this story, I will feel rewarded. You crossed the bridge and here you are, with me.

Thanks to my training as a historian, in my Spanish classes I always try to include stories or passages of historical novels and I have fabulous anecdotes about it. At the Celebrating Languages conference, to which I was invited by the BC Association of Teachers of Modern Languages, I explained some reasons why the teaching of a language is greatly enriched when historical novels are used as a tool.

Historical fiction connects the student with a primary source an author has dramatized. Being it a real event, curiosity is stimulated since it presents characters with emotions and feelings that can be analyzed from different approaches. The student places himself in the past, tackles a complex situation, and develops his critical thinking by questioning the fact, provoking the analysis and emotionally connecting himself with those solutions that were found in the past, to extrapolate them to the present and transform it. The teacher enriches his curriculum with real events that occurred (or not) in a given time.

By using historical novels as a tool, several oral skills can be developed: elaborate lists of vocabulary, identify metaphors and idioms, conjugation of tenses, or words that are considered "more complex vocabulary", according to the level being taught. In the case of Spanish language, difficult concepts can be rescued to refine the mastery of the language, especially in the study of Advanced Spanish, reaffirming the lessons on gender and number, possessive pronouns, the use of the subjunctive, tacit subjects - you name it!

The 1629 Flood of Mexico was the most serious in the Colony and its solutions caused one of the most dramatic ecocides in history. The Valley of Mexico is a closed basin and its five lakes, at different levels, came together, depending on the strength of the rains and the emptying of the surrounding mountain rivers. The prehispanic albarradón was an enormous wall, sixteen kilometers long and eighteen meters wide, composed of two rows of wooden piles buried at the bottom of the lake, which was not very deep - approximately three and a half meters deep – filled with soil, debris, and stone. Its system of gates in each stretch regulated the levels of the waters, preventing floods. The rumble of the battle, the passage of the Spanish brigantines and the neglect to consider its importance as a regulator and distributor of lake water destroyed the albarradón during the process of Conquest.

This environmentally catastrophic event is seen after the reading of the text with a focus on responsibility concerning the decisions of the present, which irremediably affect the environment of the future.

Using that single example, teachers can assign activities to develop in group or individually, such as the preparation of a historical newspaper that gives account of the news (Extra! Extra! Mexico City is flooded'), a fictional interview to one of the characters or a letter that expresses the student's admiration or criticism regarding a particular decision. After all, the event happened, it was real; the novelist only portrayed it, dramatizing it.

The simulation of situations (What would have happened if ...?), or the change of narrator to re-tell a passage (omniscient narrator to the first person of singular) make the class enjoyable and even the analysis of the book, as a physical object, stimulates the student (Why did the author choose this cover? Why these characters? What authority does the writer have to speak about the topic? On what primary historical source was he based to fictionalize the event? Are there more sources that address the event?

All this supports learning and builds bridges of understanding. The individual is the one who writes history; his greatest discovery is the responsibility he must take on his actions.

Then, by connecting emotionally with facts and characters, the student develops his empathy, in a role-play game that identifies not only winners and losers but also those other vital, secondary characters that often affect history more than those who hold power and decisions.

My novel is based on a two-year investigation, but it covers the historical archives that I studied in 2008 and 2009. My only license has been the construction of the Cathedral of Mexico, which effectively received the rood screen for its choir, ordered in Macau and made in China, some years later.

However, no matter how exhaustive my research has been, none of us will know the full truth of the facts that I narrate, because the rendition of many more actors that remain anonymous is still needed.

That is the exciting part of my discipline. To patiently wait for more details to emerge, more stories, more findings that are still hidden somewhere. Honoring them has been part of this effort.

ABOUT THE AUTHOR

Rosa Elena Rojas was born in Mexico City. Canada has been her home for ten years.

A businesswoman since her arrival in Canada, she is a co-founder of Mexican Delight Gourmet, Inc., a corporation dedicated to the manufacture of corn and wheat tortillas and Mexican food.

She is a columnist in the newspaper *Sin Fronteras* and the magazine *Spanglish*, two very important Spanish publications that are distributed in British Columbia, Alberta and the north of Washington state in the United States. As a Spanish instructor, she taught an advanced Spanish conversation group at the Maple Ridge Public Library, B.C. She has volunteered in various non-governmental organizations that support the Latino community in Western Canada, such as the *Institute for Mexicans Abroad* and *Mexican Community in Vancouver*.

She completed her Master's Degree in History of Mexico with the research *The Brotherhood of Mulatos, Mestizos and Negros of the Holy Cross in Coyoacán, Mexico, XVII Century*, which she presented at the *LIII International Congress of Americanists*. She has published several peer reviewed articles in specialized magazines and open edition journals such as *Nuevo Mundo, Mundos Nuevos* (*New World, New Worlds*).

Rosa Elena currently works for School District 43, Coquitlam Continuing Education, in British Columbia.

Connect @ **rosaelenarojas.com**
facebook.com/rosaelenarojasauthor

FOR THE
WATERS ARE COME

IS PROUDLY SPONSORED BY

santarosa
MEXICAN DELIGHT GOURMET INC.

We know that immigrating means
bringing with you all the richness of your culture.

We proudly produce the best tortillas in British Columbia.

follow us
facebook.com/santarosabc

like us
facebook

visit us
121-1584 Broadway St.
Port Coquitlam B.C.
V3C 2M7
Canada

www.santarosabc.com | info@santarosabc.com | +1 778-285-9336

DERIVATION OF TITLE

In 1611, the first issue of the first edition of the Authorized Version of the English Bible, commissioned by King James I, was printed in London by Robert Barker, a member of a famed family of printers. On the other side of the globe, at the same time, one of the deadliest black slave uprisings was being clandestinely planned in New Spain (now Mexico). The facts of that uprising formed the basis for the events described in Chapter 1.

"For the Waters are Come" is a verse composed in seventeenth-century English as the translation of Psalm 69. Modern English considers this style of conjugation archaic, however, the text of the psalm provides a prescient connection to this book, whose title in Spanish is "Ser de Agua" (literally translated as 'being of water'). The author favored use of this verse, sung by King David to the tune of the lost song he called "The Lilies", to link it with Mexico's 1629 Great Flood: "Save me, O God; for the waters are come in unto my soul. I sink in deep mire, where there is no standing: I am come into deep waters, where the floods overflow me."

It is the author's hope that the reader feels the same connection to history as the psalmist to whom these verses are ascribed.

CPSIA information can be obtained
at www.ICGtesting.com
Printed in the USA
LVHW09s2055141018
593588LV00001B/2/P